WITCH-BLOOD

WITCH-BLOOD

STRANGER MAGICS,
BOOK THREE

ASH FITZSIMMONS

Print Edition ISBN: 978-1-949861-03-7

Cover design by BespokeBookCovers.com

www.ashfitzsimmons.com

CHAPTER 1

The stranger was glowing, and she was calling my name.

That alone shouldn't have been enough to concern me. I'd been in Faerie for just over a year by then, and I'd seen my share of its weirdness since leaving the mortal realm. But the last thing I remembered was crashing on Joey's couch in the barn, and though I was still on my back, his loft apartment seemed to have disappeared. I squinted and tried to make sense of my surroundings, but everything beyond the stranger standing over me was black, either formless or too obscured by her radiance for me to discern.

She was pretty, a petite blonde in a diaphanous pink dress that revealed more than a hint of what was hiding beneath it. As I was sixteen that October, that would have been enough to catch my attention, even if she hadn't been self-illuminating. After all, it wasn't every day—or any day, really—that I was awakened by an attractive stranger in see-through clothing.

I sat up on the black surface that had once been a sofa and tried to piece together my good luck. The woman wasn't one of my fae sisters, escaped from imprisonment, nor was she anyone I'd seen around my brother Coileán's palace. More importantly, I couldn't seem to find Joey in the darkness, and I couldn't hear Georgie's snores—odd, as the dragon's nighttime noises usually rumbled through the barn like a cranked-up subwoofer. This made the situation exponentially more concerning, as Coileán never allowed anyone to get close to me without being vetted first. My brother worried for my safety—not without cause, as letting a witch-blood run around unsupervised in Faerie is tantamount to introducing a miniature poodle to a pack of wolves and expecting everyone to play nicely. The unfortunate son of a faerie and a wizard, I had no magical ability to speak of, and so Coileán tended to leave someone nearby to keep tabs on me. Joey Bolin, a former seminarian without a shred of magical ability, might not have seemed like the natural choice for a babysitter, but he had three things going for him: he was quick with a sword, best buddies with a dragon, and dating my *other* sister, Helen, an extremely talented wizard and presumably the next grand magus of the Arcanum. If we got in over our heads, help was a phone call and a gate away. But Joey wasn't with me in the blackness that morning. Whatever the glowing stranger intended, she obviously wanted to get me alone.

For a split-second, I thought perhaps I was being visited by my mother's vengeful ghost. The last time Titania saw me, I was a newborn, and she was ordering my death. If she knew from beyond the grave that I'd had the audacity to return to Faerie—an untalented witch-blood, a *mongrel*, her genetic gift to me cancelled out by my wizard father's—she was sure to be at least peeved. But I've been told that I have Titania's eyes, and the stranger's were nothing like mine: hazel, fringed with thick, gold lashes, and far too old for her face.

By then, having spent a year in the realm, I'd grown somewhat accustomed to the odd look that faeries above a certain age share. A faerie of fifty or even a hundred might pass for a young mortal without using glamour, but get one much older than that, and his eyes stop syncing up with the rest of him. To the unwary, he might look indescribably interesting—there's something *different* about him that you just can't put your finger on—but anyone in the magical community recognizes that look as the one tell of a faerie's age. I saw it when comparing my brother and Joey side by side: at first glance, they could have been contemporaries, but Joey was all of twenty-six then, and Coileán's eyes betrayed him. The look was even more pronounced with Valerius, the captain of Coileán's guard and Joey's and my combat coach—twenty-something in most respects, but twenty-two hundred if you knew how to see it.

The stranger's eyes marked her as Val's senior by a significant margin, which in itself was a concern. The fact that she obviously knew who I was did nothing to make me feel any better about the midnight wake-up call—and in case it had slipped my mind, *she was glowing.*

I kicked my legs off the edge of where the couch had been and tried to sound like strange, glowing women were a fixture in my life, but all I managed was a weak, "Uh…hi?"

"Aiden," she said, softly and insistently, "you must get up now. Run."

"Huh?"

"Run, child." Her eyes bored into mine, and I noticed the tension in her face as my vision adjusted to her brightness. "I cannot help you now. *Run.*"

I tried to ask her what she was talking about, but she disappeared, and I felt rough hands on my shoulders, shaking me back and forth. Startled, I flailed and blinked…

…and the blackness was gone, replaced with the familiar contours of Joey's loft. The brass floor lamp had been switched on, and Val, who was shaking me awake, yanked my blanket off and pulled me to my feet. "Something's happened to Coileán," he said without preamble. "Oberon returned tonight, and he brought his court with him. I've got to get you out of here."

"Ober…*what?*" I mumbled, disoriented at being ripped from the dream.

But he was already shaking Joey awake, and I stared groggily around the room until Val gripped my arms and looked me in the eye. "My lord, the king is in danger. I can't protect you both. Go to Toula, stay safe, and I'll come for you when this is past. And don't let her come after me," he added, cutting his eyes to Joey.

I was still trying to put together why Val might be in the

loft in the middle of the night, but Joey was quicker on the draw. "What the hell happened?" he asked as he buckled on his sword—the steel one, not the bronze blade he used in practice.

Val shook his head. "I was off duty, I didn't see it, but Oberon's people are running wild in the palace. Something's happened, I don't know—"

"Want a hand?"

"Joey," he said, squeezing his shoulder, "you're a brave fool, but I'm not sending you up against Oberon, especially not *here*. Protect him," he continued, cocking his head at me. "Keep him safe until I send word."

Joey seemed poised to argue, but he acquiesced and nodded. "Fine, we'll do this your way, but I'm not leaving Georgie."

"As you like. Downstairs, then, and hurry." Carefully sidestepping Joey's armor collection, Val headed for the wooden staircase as the sound of shouting rose outside the windows.

By then, I'd woken enough to recognize that something was terribly wrong. Like Coileán, Oberon was a king of Faerie, albeit far older and somewhat more powerful—the only one of the original ruling Three left alive after my brother and Toula Pavli dispatched each other's mothers, Titania and Mab. But Oberon had grown bored of Faerie and forced his court to follow him to the mortal realm around 1700. He'd helped us a year ago when we sent a rescue party into the Gray Lands, the dangerous third realm, on a disastrous mission to retrieve Coileán's daughter, Moyna—who was also Oberon's granddaughter, though the old king didn't seem to care. That mission had ended with Nath taking control of the Gray Lands realm, Moyna and the remnants of Mab's leaderless court on the run in the mortal realm, and Coileán's girlfriend, Meggy, dead at his own hand. If Oberon was bothered by his youngest daughter's death, he didn't let on, and I hadn't seen so much as his shadow since then. The last I knew of him, he was running a bar in the Florida Keys and enjoying the sunshine while his people found ways to entertain themselves— which, unfortunately, seldom ended well for the mundanes around them.

That he'd returned unexpectedly was bad. That he'd brought his court along was worse. And as the pieces snapped together in my sleep-foggy mind, I could make out the catastrophic picture Val was painting. I looked wildly around the apartment, nearly expecting to see Oberon himself burst through the door. "What are we going to—"

"Take this," Joey interrupted, tossing me his barn jacket, then half-pushed me out of the loft. I barely had time to grab my tennis shoes before he had pulled on his motorcycle boots and the brown oilcloth duster he favored for riding, grabbed a bag, and was heading toward the enormous black dragon blinking blearily below us. "Rise and shine, sweetie," he said, slipping into the sing-song tone he used only around Georgie. "We've got to go."

Go where? she thought, looking at Val and me for a clue.

I'd been in Faerie long enough that the dragon's telepathy didn't faze me, even at ungodly hours. For Joey, it was by then second nature—after all, he'd raised her from a hatchling.

"Going to go see Toula," he said, and climbed onto the base of her long neck as she started to uncurl. For once, he didn't bother with a saddle and harness, his usual safety precaution against falling from an unfortunate height. "Val, whenever you're ready."

Val flicked his fingers, and a massive gate materialized in the barn—but then, anything big enough to accommodate a dragon half as long as a football field had to be massive. Peering through the hole in the fabric of the world, I could see nothing but dark pastures, but a blast of cold air reminded me quickly enough of the season. Joey reached down to give me a hand, and I scrambled up behind him as Georgie stretched her legs and twisted her van-sized head back and forth.

"Be safe," Val reiterated, then gave Georgie's neck a last pat. "I'll send word as soon as I can."

"Probably won't do any good to ask you to come with us, will it?" Joey replied.

He shook his head and raised his voice above the growing hubbub outside the barn. "My place is here. Go now."

With that, he stepped aside, and Georgie lumbered through the gate. I looked back as the hole closed and caught a last glimpse of Val, who distractedly smoothed his close-cropped brown hair as the noise crescendoed around the barn. His tanned face wore an expression I'd never seen on him and couldn't quite place until I recognized the fear in his dark eyes. I started to call to him, but the gate snapped shut, and then we were alone—Joey, the dragon, and me, ripped from our warm beds only to find ourselves stranded in a cow pasture in rural Montana.

For me, a homecoming of the worst kind.

Even in the darkness, I could see the reduced background magic of the mortal realm, swirling colors that seemed muted after Faerie's abundant supply of the stuff. Not that it really mattered to me—I could neither enchant not cast, only nudge inactive magic around—but still, it was a reminder that I was back in a place I'd hoped to avoid for, oh, the rest of time.

Smells wrong, Georgie thought as she flattened the frosted weeds, but she perked almost instantly and turned her head toward the sound of lowing cattle. *What is—*

"Not ours," Joey insisted, then sighed and began to dig in his bag. "What do you want to bet he didn't let Toula know we were coming?" he muttered.

I looked around us until I spotted the familiar lights of the decoy trailer park hiding the Arcanum's headquarters, the repurposed missile silo where I'd grown up. My stomach knotted at the sight, and my nose and arms tingled with the memory of fractures. "So what do we do?" I asked.

Joey pulled a phone from his bag—not the little flip

phones Coileán had made for us, but the cheap burner model he reserved for conversations with my sister—and tapped it to life. "Do you have Toula's number handy?"

"No…"

"Didn't think so. Hang on." He dialed a preset and waited, and I was sliding my arms into my borrowed jacket when I heard him say, "Hey, gorgeous. Something's going down in Faerie, and I'm sitting outside the silo right now with Aid and Georg…yeah, yeah, he's fine, we're fine. Calm down, it's okay, I'm sorry. Anyway, it's kind of chilly, and I don't have Toula's number, so would you please give her a call and let her know we're out here? Or the grand magus?…No, hon, it's all right, you don't need to come home…"

I tuned out the still-uncomfortable reminder that my friend was deeply involved with my big sister and tried to come to terms with our situation: something had happened to my brother, I didn't know how to help him, and I was sitting atop a giant dragon outside the heart of the greatest magical organization in the mortal realm—a place filled with folks who, on a good day, were apathetic about whether a particular faerie lived or died. I hadn't seen the silo—or my parents—in over a year, but something told me that not much had changed in my absence.

Georgie snorted as Joey put his phone away. *I'm hungry.*

"I know, girl," he said, fishing an elastic from his bag and pulling his blond snarls into a rough ponytail.

They smell good…

"They're not ours," he repeated, earning another snort from the dragon. "And they don't re-grow in this realm, so we can't just take them. Bear with me, Georgie, I'm going to figure something out." He sighed again, a white puff in the cold night, then turned around to face me. "Helen says she loves you, don't do anything stupid, and call her as soon as Toula gets us settled."

"Got it, boss," I said, then stopped and replayed my words in my head. Joey spoke Fae as well as I did—Coileán had seen to that—and as it was the only language Georgie understood, my conversations around the two of them were usually in Fae with a heavy sprinkling of English. I'd been immersed in the language for the last year, but slipping into it in the silo would be seen as odd, at the very least. I'd have to be mindful of that, I mused, conscious that I was focusing on minutiae to avoid processing the overwhelming larger problem.

Before I could sink too far into my thoughts, another gate opened outside the trailer park, and Toula—the Arcanum's witch-blooded yet freakishly talented envoy to Faerie, not to mention Val's little sister—came running through behind a floating orb that illuminated the pasture ahead. Her ratty, untied bathrobe flapped behind her, exposing flannel pants, a tank top, and fluffy white slippers that, on closer inspection, resolved into rabbits with mouths full of pointed teeth. "Are you okay?" she yelled as she sprinted through the weeds. "What the hell is going on?"

Joey and I slid off Georgie as she approached. "We're fine," he called back. "And I don't know. Val didn't have any details."

She came to a panting stop and looked at the three of us in the orb's light. "Where is he?"

"Back there."

"*Why?*"

"Because he's trying to help Colin with whatever just happened. Oberon's involved, but that's all I've got, really."

"Damn it," she muttered, absently running one hand through her spiky hair. For half siblings born two millennia apart, Val and Toula had more than their share of common tics. "So you left him to go up alone against friggin' *Oberon*? Is that it?" she demanded, her blue eyes flashing.

Joey kept his voice low even as Toula's rose. "He wouldn't come, and he told me to look after Aiden. What was I supposed to do?"

She paused, considered us again, then huffed her frustration. "What you did, I guess. I'll get dressed—"

"Val said to stay here," he cut in, shaking his head. "It's not safe."

"I wasn't anticipating a picnic in the park," she retorted.

"And we don't even know what's happened, so how about giving it a few days, huh?"

Toula wrapped her robe around her and glared at Joey. "Val could be dead in a few days."

"He's a big boy. Yeah?"

She stared out at the moonlit mountains with thin-lipped disapproval, but I could that see she was wavering. "He's going to be okay, Toula," I said. "He knows the realm as well as anyone, and he said he'd be in touch. And this might all blow over…"

Toula and Joey gave me twin looks of disbelief, but she rolled her eyes and tied her robe sash. "I'll give him until morning," she muttered, then pursed her lips and pointed to Georgie. "We've got a problem," she said, switching to Fae.

The dragon looked around, saw nothing distressing, then realized the problem was her. *I haven't eaten any!* she protested. *Ask them, I haven't touched the flock!*

"Herd, sweetie," said Joey, reaching up to rub her nose. "A bunch of cows is a herd."

Herd, flock, whatever, I haven't touched it.

"And thank you, because I don't want to explain one more thing to Greg tonight," Toula said, hugging herself against the cold. "But that's not what I meant—there's no room for you underground."

That's all right, she replied, sinking to her belly and curling her tail around her. *It's not so bad out here.*

"Negative. There's nowhere to hide you topside."

For an overgrown lizard, Georgie had become remarkably adept at facial mimicry, and her brow ridge rose in emphasis of her bemused thoughts. *Hide from what? Are the cows dangerous? You don't seem concerned about them…*

"I'm not," said Toula, moving closer to Georgie's snout. "There aren't any dragons in this realm, honey. If someone saw you, they might try to hurt you. Understand?"

So…I go home?

"Not if all hell's breaking loose in Faerie," said Toula, frowning at the trailer park. "I could shrink you temporarily, get you through the doors, but the Council's going to have a cow if they find out we've got a dragon down there."

Georgie cut her eyes to the herd but kept the question to herself. Idioms didn't always work in direct translation.

Toula thought for a moment, stomping her damp slippers to keep warm, then paused and considered Georgie with an odd expression on her face. "This will feel weird," she told the dragon, "but it shouldn't hurt, and it'll let us keep you safe. Can you trust me?"

Suddenly uncertain, Georgie turned her head to Joey, who nodded reassurance and stepped clear. "I'm right here, sweetie," he soothed. "Nothing bad's going to happen."

"Just keep your fingers crossed for me, okay?" Toula quietly replied.

Before either Joey or Georgie had time to reconsider, a streamer of blue light flew from Toula's fingertips—active magic, bright against the muted colors of the background. It expanded like a bubble, surrounded Georgie in a split-second, and flared so strongly that even Joey, who couldn't detect magic if his life depended on it, squinted as the energy release echoed on the mundane side of the visible spectrum.

When I opened my eyes and blinked away the after-image, Georgie had vanished. In her place, lying stunned on her stomach in the crushed weeds, was a pale girl with long black hair—and, awkwardly enough, not a stitch of clothing.

The girl sucked in a breath, raised her head in confusion, then caught sight of her hand and telepathically screamed.

"Holy *shit*," Joey muttered as he yanked off his coat, then ran to her and threw it over her as she curled in on herself. "It's okay, honey, it's okay, I'm right here," he said, talking over the scream echoing in our heads. "You're safe, it's okay—"

NOT OKAY! NOT OKAY!

"Come here, I've got you." With that, he wrapped the edges of his coat underneath her and scooped her into his arms as if she weighed nothing. "It's over, Georgie, just breathe, I'm not going to let anyone hurt you," he murmured, holding the bundle against his chest as she hyperventilated. "It's over, just calm down."

As he tried to pacify her, Toula came up beside him and snapped her fingers next to his shoulder. "Georgie. Hey, Georgie, look at me."

The girl's head popped free of the coat, and she turned her wet face to Toula's.

"It's temporary," Toula insisted. "We've got to hide you, and this is the best way to do it. This is not the end of the world."

What did you do to me? she demanded in a mental shout—loud, but better than the screaming had been.

"Transformation spell," said Toula, keeping her voice low and no-nonsense. "Glamour wasn't going to cut it, not with the physical constraints below. You're still you, just…compressed."

Georgie held up her hand and glared at Toula. *Compressed? This isn't compressed! This is…is…*

"A temporary human form."

Where are my claws? she shouted, then clumsily patted her face. *My teeth…my nose…everything's wrong, it's all squishy, and…and I think it's leaking…*

"You cried a little," said Joey as he shifted her on his hip. "It's nothing to worry about. Happens to the best of us."

She looked around, torn between panic and anger, and finally focused on him. *You're too big,* she thought plaintively. *You're not supposed to be this big.*

"Just let me be the big one for a change, all right?" he said, studying her expression. "We're a team, Georgie—it's my turn to take care of you."

But she shook her head, and her eyes welled once again. *I don't like this, nothing's right, put me back the way I was.* She paused, realized she was crying once more, then slapped the tears away. *Please, Joey, you've got to make her change me back. Please…*

Her first sob escaped, and Georgie buried her head against his shoulder as she wept. Joey turned to Toula, who crossed her arms and looked embarrassed. "She'll adjust before long, I bet," she said. "And it's only until we figure something better out…oh, come on, honey," she begged, smoothing Georgie's hair, "please don't cry. I'm sorry, I really am, but I don't know what else to do."

I stood outside their little huddle, momentarily forgotten and coming to terms with the notion that the massive dragon I'd just ridden had been reduced to a child of about ten.

"How long is this going to last?" Joey asked.

Toula looked up from her ineffective attempts at comfort and shrugged. "Assuming a constant magical field, either until someone breaks it or she crosses back into Faerie. A gate would take care of it pretty quickly. I mean," she hastily added, "that's my best guess. I've never worked a transformation this involved, and, uh"—she paused to look at Georgie's streaming eyes—"it appears to be incomplete."

"What do you—*oh*," said Joey as Toula moved her orb closer to Georgie's face. "Can you fix that?"

"Maybe, but I'm not doing anything else to her right now." Catching my confusion, she explained, "Her eyes are still red. Can't exactly pass her off as albino," she mused, "not with hair that dark, but maybe no one will notice."

Georgie's tears began to slow as Joey rubbed her back. After a moment, they dwindled to pathetic sniffles, and I chanced joining the others. "She, uh…why is she so young?" I asked.

"The spell considers relative age," said Toula.

"Physical growth is fast for dragons, but she's still a kid," Joey added as Georgie started to hiccup. "Here, hon," he told her, hoisting her head over his shoulder, "take slow breaths, they'll stop—"

His instructions ended in another hiccup and a jet of fire that narrowly missed his ear and scorched a patch of dead grass. "Shit!" Toula yelped, then magically smothered the blaze while Joey and Georgie looked on in shock. "I told you it was incomplete," she muttered when the fire died away. "Godzilla's back around dark magic—we're going to have to be careful."

Joey and Georgie stared at each other in silence until she hiccupped again, taking pains to keep her mouth closed. A little plume of smoke drifted from her nostrils, and her lip started to shake.

"Does it hurt?" he asked, pulling her head back against his shoulder.

She closed her eyes and let him rock her. *No, but it makes me hungry. The fire…it's burning inside again, and I have to feed it…*

Carefully, he shifted her weight and pressed one hand against her abdomen. "She's warm to the touch," he told us, sounding dazed. "Like she swallowed a space heater. Remember how hungry she got in the Gray Lands?"

As if on cue, Georgie's stomach growled. *Can I have a cow now?*

"I'll see about getting you a few burgers," said Toula, raising her light as the grand magus approached through the field. "Once we're inside. And, uh…how about letting me do the talking, guys?"

Grand Magus Harrison was an institution. His predecessor, Grand Magus Callahan, had been old-blood Arcanum, a wizard of wizards stretching back a thousand years. I never met Callahan—he had a heart attack in 1969, almost thirty years before I came around—but his official portrait looked much like what the average mundane would expect from a top wizard: long white hair tied loosely behind him, a longer white beard falling over his ceremonial velvet robe, half-moon glasses at the end of a crooked nose, and piercing blue eyes beneath bushy brows that seem to follow the viewer around the room. In other words, Callahan looked like he came straight from central casting.

But because he died without a named heir, the next year in Arcanum politics was little more than a drawn-out Council meeting to discuss and dismiss potential candidates. A number of names were put forth—not a few of them belonging to magi of the Inner Council—but the eventual winner was the dark horse, a thirty-five-year-old Tennessean without a drop of old Arcanum blood in him. There were plenty of raised eyebrows when he took the helm. Greg Harrison was young, the first wizard in his family, and—the real scandal to certain wizards—black, but he was unequaled in terms of talent, respected by those who'd worked with him, and a Harvard man who'd gone to school on scholarship. He might keep his hair short and eschew the beard and robe, but Harrison was undoubtedly grand magus material.

As I'd been raised with a healthy respect for (and maybe a touch of fear of) the grand magus, I found it disconcerting to be standing outside with him in the middle of the night, trying to give him a coherent reason for our presence in the Arcanum's pasture while ignoring his bathrobe and old Reeboks. Once Toula ceded the floor, I stumbled, I shivered, and I tried to keep his attention off the sniveling bundle in Joey's arms with all of the grace and suaveness of any scared, disoriented teenager. To his credit, the grand magus heard us out, but then he folded his arms and said, "We're not going to get anything accomplished tonight. I suppose y'all had better come in out of the cold, and we'll see what's to be done in the morning."

By then, however, I'd woken and processed enough to protest. "Coileán could be *dead* by morning. And Val—"

"Mr. Carver," he replied, quietly cutting me off, "I know this is upsetting, but I'm not about to invade Faerie, *especially* not at this time of night. Let's not be foolish, hmm?"

Toula's hand clamped on my shoulder, silencing my rebuttal before I could get myself in trouble. "We'll deal with this after breakfast," she murmured, squeezing me for good measure. "Come on, it's freezing out here."

She remained at my side for the walk back into the trailer park—despite his age and arthritis, the grand magus apparently saw nothing to be gained by using a gate as a shortcut—and I felt her take my hand as we passed the first decoy trailer in the circle. I couldn't put a name on my jumble of emotions at that moment, but fear and dread were among them, and the sick feeling in my gut was only partially out of concern for my brother. Toula had seen firsthand why I'd been willing to put the silo behind me. Out of habit, I glanced to the left and right as we passed the trailers, checking the usual hiding spots for my old classmates—Russell Mulligan, Milo Brown, Morgan Kramer, Dan Solomon, Leo Rossi, and Terrance Anders, sons and grandsons of Council magi who'd made "Whack a Dud" their longtime favorite game. Though I hoped they'd been sent to reform school while I'd been away, I doubted they'd ever get more than a slap on the wrist and a stern talking-to, with *their* connections. No one on the Council had seemed to give a damn about my health, in any case, and I'd been a walking poster child for CPS intervention.

But my tormenters were either gone or asleep, and we entered the silo without molestation, earning only curious looks from the pair of night watchmen as the grand magus waved us inside. When we'd descended a level to the guest rooms, the grand magus pointed down the hallway and said, "Toula, I believe number five is ready. Would you please get Mr. Bolin and his, uh…friend…situated?" he asked, taking a careful look at the face peeping out from Joey's coat. Toula nodded and led them away, and he escorted me to the room across the hall. "I think," he said, unlocking the door with a touch, "that any family reunions should be saved for daylight. Don't you?"

As I was by turns strung-out and weary that night, the last thing I wanted at that moment was a reunion with my parents. "No rush," I muttered, brushing past him toward the neat bed. "They don't need to know I'm back."

"Well…actually, they do." He closed the door behind him and stood in the entryway as I dropped my jacket onto a floral-print easy chair. "The official line is that they shipped you off to boarding school last year. If we don't want to raise any eyebrows—"

"Home on fall break?"

"Maybe. Let me deal with it in a few hours." He started to leave, but then he hesitated, looking suddenly uncomfortable. "And in the meantime, I'm going to have to ask you not to wander from this floor."

I sat on the edge of the bed and tried to read the unspoken in his expression. "No unattended faerie lords. Got it," I replied, kicking off my shoes.

"Beyond that. As you might imagine, your, uh…your *friends* are still living here," he said, emphasizing the euphemism with a raised eyebrow. "Absence may make the heart grow fonder, but I'd rather not test that hypothesis on top of everything else." The grand magus paused, then added, "I hope you won't be offended if I don't address you properly, but—"

I waved it off. "Keep the peace, let Dad save face, I get it."

"Did Coileán ever tell you what Titania did to him?"

"He did. Never knew about my aunt. That…explains a lot."

The grand magus nodded slowly. "You're a smart kid, Mr. Carver. Always have been. So I'm not going to stand here and lie to you that he loves you and wants you back."

"I kind of figured that out."

"Yeah. Wish things were different."

"Yeah," I mumbled.

"Well." He cleared his throat and rubbed the hole in the elbow of his bathrobe. "With all of that in mind, I believe it goes without saying that no one is to know what's happened until we sort something out."

"*I* don't even know what's happened. Val said he'll send

word, but—"

"But you're in the dark for now," he finished, and sighed. "I suppose I've dealt with worse. Get some sleep, son, and we'll talk about it over breakfast."

He let himself out, but almost immediately rapped and opened the door again. "One last thing," he said quietly. "Just checking, but the girl with you…"

"Georgie," I offered.

He gave me a knowing look, then cocked his head toward the room across the hall. "I seem to remember hearing something about Mr. Bolin raising a dragon by that name. Strange world, isn't it?"

"Yes, sir."

"Mm. And I'm not suggesting there's anything odd about the little lady, but should you need it, there's a fire extinguisher down the hall to your left." The grand magus pushed his glasses down his nose. "Don't y'all burn down my silo, now."

With that, the door latched, and I was alone. I stretched out on top of the comforter and stared at the off-white ceiling, not bothering to turn off the lamps.

Sleep wasn't coming, and it was going to be a long night.

CHAPTER 2

If I'd never seen the inside of the silo again, it would have been too soon. There weren't enough rose-colored glasses in the universe to give me the warm fuzzies about my childhood in that hellhole. If someone had deigned to teach me about magic and the workings of the three realms, then I might have looked upon the experience as at least useful, but the night classes my peers took were barred to me, the unfortunate dud. What little I learned of magic came to me piecemeal, often due to my own investigation—but then, as the Arcanum saw it, there was no sense in wasting their time and mine with a proper education when I'd never be a wizard.

In general, magical talent is inherited like height or hair color or shoe size: if you look at a pair of wizards, you can make a decent guess as to how their children will turn out. That said, there are freaks on both ends of the spectrum, gifted wizards like my sister who wow the world from day one, and an underclass of witches and duds who quietly go away. I'm sure it's tough to be a witch, able to do a little with magic but never strong enough to pass muster, but for someone growing up in an Arcanum installation, being a dud is hell. There's no known cause for the condition, and to my dismay, I learned there was no cure. Every so often, for no good reason, wizard parents will simply have a child who can't cast the most basic of spells. And while a few witches may linger on the fringes of the Arcanum, maybe through marriage or out of pity, there's just no place in a magical organization for a person who can't use magic at all. As soon as they're old enough, duds go out on their own, and most never look back. Of course, if most duds have classmates like mine, then I understand the impulse to put as much ground between themselves and the silo as possible.

There's no official test for a dud, and the Arcanum hesitates to make any formal classification until age twenty, when it considers a wizard to have come of age. Though rare, late bloomers happen—one of the Council magi when I was growing up was thought to be a dud until he was ten, when he fell off his bike, broke his leg, and blasted a hole through a nearby tree in response to the pain. But anyone who knew me knew I was a hopeless case—which, combined with Helen's fame as the heir apparent to the grand magus, made me a target. Kids whose mothers and fathers and grandparents were on the Council suddenly found an upstart in their midst in my sister, and because kids are fundamentally assholes, they took it out on me. Their parents were fundamentally assholes, too, which is why I was excluded from classes in magic, even the classes that didn't require proficiency with a wand. But I had a computer and a better handle on technical infrastructure than most of the Arcanum luddites combined, and so I tried to educate myself.

For any success I had in that regard, the Arcanum can blame my father. Dad worked in the Archives, cataloguing newly acquired works, preserving older books and scrolls, and providing research assistance to the Council when asked. As he had led the push for digitization, he also oversaw that massive project and its team of junior archivists. But while Dad and his people taught themselves about scanning and database construction, they didn't bother so much with security. Consequently, by the time I was twelve, I'd figured out how to work my way into the system—it was too easy to be called hacking—and help myself to some heavy reading. The Arcanum may not have seen any point in educating a dud in the ways of magic, but I decided that there was no reason why I couldn't at least learn the history. If there's one thing at which the Arcanum excels, it's documenting its own past, and I found dozens of books to read, covering topics as broad as the Great War and as specific as the day-to-day jottings of individual grand magi.

Eventually, as I was tracking down a lead to a promising-sounding scroll in a footnote, I stumbled upon the Arcanum's files about the courts. They weren't protected— not from me, at least, since I'd worked out a few common passwords—but I paused before I sneaked a peek. My parents had seldom mentioned anything concerning Faerie, and when they did, it was brief and followed with a warning to keep my nose out of such matters. I gathered that faeries were dangerous and never to be trusted, but no one around had ever volunteered specifics. After a moment's hesitation, however, the temptation proved too strong, and so I dove in.

Over the next few years, as I spent more and more time locked in the safety of my room, I returned to those files and tried to fit the puzzle pieces together. In broad strokes, I knew this to be true: there was a world beyond the borders of ours from which magic came, and that world was ruled— or had been ruled, there were some disagreement in the records about that—by two queens and a king, each with a court of followers. Nothing good came from any of them, and the Arcanum had successfully eliminated hundreds of faeries over the centuries. For the more notorious survivors, the Archives kept copious notes: approximate age, court affiliation, past alliances, known aliases, assumed kills, any pictures. Reviewing the files felt a little like flipping through mafia rosters, and I sketched family trees as I dug through them, trying to determine how one faerie was connected to another. Without fail, though, I found myself returning to the big three: Mab, location unknown; Oberon, last seen in Florida; and Titania, who held Faerie by herself. I didn't suppose I'd ever need the information I was reading, but if the Arcanum was going to throw me out eventually, I wanted to know what was lurking out there before they cut me off.

I kept up my nighttime reading until the ninth grade, when I could poke around during the daylight hours as well, thanks to my sudden switch to homeschooling. Hel had graduated and moved across the country to start at Vanderbilt, leaving me on my own—and at the mercy of the kids she had helped keep at bay.

I don't like to think about that year. Let's just say that I can describe in incredible detail what it feels like to break a bone. I know what my skin smells like when it's on fire. I'm also familiar with the exquisite pain that comes with battered internal organs—injuries that Mom treated in-house, despite the Arcanum's protocol about major trauma, so that we wouldn't raise a stink. If CPS had made silo visits, I'd have been in foster care in another city, but it's hard to have government oversight of a facility that no one without a magical connection knows exists. It was the ruptured kidney in October that convinced Mom that perhaps homeschooling was the right choice for me. I cleaned out my locker and piled a stack of textbooks on my desk, and that was that. My parents weren't going to make me study— they certainly weren't teaching me—but I had no friends in the silo, and I didn't dare to roam the halls on my own. And so I dug in, passed the requisite tests, and seldom saw daylight.

By the summer, I'd graduated high school, and I was stuck. My parents weren't sending me off to college at fifteen, especially not to my first choice, MIT, but Mom had broached the idea of taking online courses. Though I looked through the offerings, I found it hard to see the point. I'd surfaced a grand total of four times since leaving school, and what I wanted more than a new academic challenge was to see daylight without an escort. Still, I was out of options, and I was bored enough to return to the restricted faerie files…and to my surprise, there had been changes.

Titania and Mab were confirmed dead, as was one of Oberon's sons, a longtime nuisance known as the Puck. The status of Mab's court was still unknown, but the file for Titania's said that one of her sons, Coileán, had inherited the throne.

I remembered seeing his name—in truth, I'd looked up the pronunciation—and I pulled up his file for a refresher. Age unknown, alias Colin Leffee—and, oddly enough for a faerie, alias Ironhand. His last residence was a little town in Virginia, and he dealt in rare books. I skimmed down the page, then paused at a bolded, underlined heading: *Fifty-seven confirmed kills. Do not engage.*

The list of his victims was long and stretched across two continents. I started with the most recent and read backward, but I closed the file once I reached the tenth, simultaneously grateful that I'd never be called upon to fight a faerie and worried that something like *him* was out there, unchecked.

The grand magus called the next afternoon.

Dad had gone to work, and Mom, who had a great talent for healing spells, was putting in a few hours at the infirmary before reorganizing our family library, a project she or Dad undertook every few months when the paperback situation got out of control. I was having lunch when the house phone rang, and my first thought was that Hel was calling home to explain a bookstore purchase—it was September, and her sophomore course load was heavy. But when I lifted the receiver and answered through a mouthful of peanut butter, the voice I heard on the other end wasn't my sister's, but the slightly gravelly voice of the grand magus. I almost choked, and he waited while I coughed my windpipe clear before telling me—and in retrospect, he was strangely calm about it—"Mr. Carver, I need to speak with you in private. Could you be in my office in half an hour?"

I was still wearing nothing more than my boxers, but I squeaked out something in the affirmative and ran off to dress with a racing heart. My palms began to sweat as I pawed through my closet for a clean and mostly unwrinkled shirt. I remember thinking Mom was going to kill me if I didn't at least put on a tie, but in my panic, I couldn't seem to find one. Then again, as I was sure the grand magus had discovered my Archives snooping and was about to kill me himself, I wasn't overly concerned about my wardrobe choices.

Twenty-nine minutes after hanging up, I had thrown on a black golf shirt—it had a collar, I reasoned, and that was close enough—and a pair of khakis, run brushes over my teeth and through my hair, and skidded to a panting stop outside the grand magus's door. Steeling myself for the blow to come, I rapped and waited, hoping he was feeling merciful.

The door cracked open a moment later, and there he was—craggy-faced, white-haired, and looking down at me through his glasses with a grim sort of smile. "Good afternoon, Mr. Carver," he said, opening the door wider. "I thought that had to be you running in the hall. Come in, son, come in."

I slipped in after him and tried not to stare at his spacious office, easily twice the size of my parents' apartment. He showed me to the pair of green leather couches, and my eyes wandered to the abstract paintings on the white walls and the well-stocked polished oak bar in the back of the room, which practically sparkled in the fluorescents. I don't know what I was expecting to find, maybe something a little heavier on stone and candles, but the grand magus's space seemed warm and thoroughly modern. I tried to imagine Hel taking private lessons in there—my sister, the prodigy, had specially trained with the grand magus for years—and came away slightly disappointed at the lack of wizardly ambiance.

The grand magus lowered himself to the couch opposite

mine and folded his gnarled hands in his lap. "We need to talk."

I willed myself not to give my guilt away with a nod. "We do?"

"We do," he said, then slumped against the cushions and peered back at me. "I understand you got your diploma. Congratulations, young man, that's most impressive."

"Thank you, sir," I mumbled, waiting for the blow.

But the grand magus stayed his hand. "I know you haven't had it easy of late. Between Helen and your mother, I'm pretty sure I've heard about every scratch and bruise you've ever gotten. And believe me," he added with a wry smirk, "I know it ain't always easy being the different one."

At that, I fought the urge to argue with the grand magus that being an African-American wizard in Montana couldn't compare to being a dud, but I had sense enough to keep my opinion to myself. "Yes, sir."

He nodded and watched me, and I tried not to squirm under his gaze. After a long moment, he sighed and shrugged. "There's something you need to know, and I'm trying to figure out the best way to break the news to you," he said, rubbing his chin, "but there's no easy way to do this. Mr. Carver…"

I tensed, anticipating the announcement that I needed to find a new place to live.

"Mr. Carver," the grand magus said slowly, "you're not a dud."

"I…huh?" I said, finding that my prepared apology for the hacking no longer fit the conversation.

"You're not a dud," he repeated.

"Grand Magus…sir…" I said hesitantly, "I, uh…I don't mean to be rude, but I'm *pretty* sure I'm a dud."

He shook his head. "Not in the slightest."

Despite my earlier trepidation, my hopes started to rise—perhaps someone had finally figured out how to fix me. "But…but I've never been able to do anything with magic!" I protested. "I've tried, but…what am I doing wrong? I couldn't even get a dragonscale wand to work!"

Without a word, he pulled off his glasses and polished them clean with his shirt, and I got the sinking feeling that he was stalling. When the lenses were smudge-free, he slipped them on and looked at me once more. "You're not a dud," he said yet again, but softly. "You're a witch-blood, Mr. Carver. It's high time you knew the truth."

He could just as easily have slammed a sledgehammer into my stomach. "What?"

"Witch-blood." The grand magus's mouth tightened, and he seemed to force himself to go on. "Your father," he began, but hesitated. "The details aren't for me to tell. Suffice it to say that your mother isn't your biological mother. You were, uh…well, you were a surprise."

I stared at him in disbelief. "My…mother?"

"I'm just grateful that Rachel's a blonde," he replied, almost talking to himself. "With Howard and Helen as dark as they are, at least you were plausibly Rachel's. But…" He took a deep breath and exhaled slowly. "Now that your, uh…*biological*…mother is dead, it's safe to tell you the truth."

The grand magus watched me in silence, and I realized that he was waiting for me to force his hand. Fighting a surge of nausea, I heard myself mumble, "Who's my mother?"

He nodded—whether in resignation or approval, I didn't know. "Her name was Titania."

"*What?*"

He sat there impassively as I started to hyperventilate. "You know something about the courts, do you?" he asked, then frowned, rose, and sat beside me. "Okay, son, put your head between your knees," he said, pressing on the back of my neck. "Take a deep breath…atta boy, let it out. Feeling woozy?"

"Feeling sick," I mumbled, clutching my ankles.

The cushion shifted beside me, and a few breaths later, the grand magus's squat office trashcan landed by my leg.

"Wouldn't be the first time that thing's seen action," he said, patting my shoulder, then sat opposite me again and waited while I pulled myself together and tried not to be ill.

Mom, the one parent who actually took care of me, wasn't my mother. Dad had cheated on her with…

No.

No.

I was a dud, damn it, but I was Arcanum through and through. I wasn't fae, I couldn't be…

The grand magus cleared his throat. "If you're thinking badly of your father right now, don't," he said. "I can't explain it, but…don't blame him." He paused, watching me struggle, then murmured, "Titania left you up top when you were a day or two old, and we figured out who you belong to. The Council and I just thought you'd be safer if we kept the truth quiet for a while."

I lifted my head from my knees to find him watching me with concern. "So what now?" I muttered. "Truth comes out, what difference does it make? Whether I'm a dud or a witch-blood, I'm still stuck in my room."

He hesitated, then replied, "Well…yes and no."

"Sir?"

"As I said, Titania's out of the picture." The grand magus folded his arms and looked off into the corner of the room. "I know Coileán. The old boy's going to want to know about you."

"Me?" I yelped.

He nodded. "And he's probably going to be pissed, but there's nothing I can do about that now. Oh, not pissed at *you*," he clarified, catching my expression. "He'll give me grief about keeping him in the dark, but he'll get over it. He's not stupid."

My heart started hammering as I thought over what I'd read. "Coileán…you mean—"

"Your older brother," he said. "*Lord* Coileán, if you want to be polite about it, which is usually a wise move. We may not have a great history with the courts, but I've always found that it's safest to avoid unnecessarily antagonizing faeries. He's half, incidentally."

"Half…"

"Fae. Which is lucky for us, as the full-blooded ones are impossible bastards. Coileán's reasonable enough," he continued as I eased upright. "Stubborn when you poke him the wrong way, but at least he's open to negotiation. Did they mention any of this to you in class? I know they go over the big Three, but…"

I shook my head. "They don't let me take classes. Dud, remember?"

"Oh…yes, of course. Sorry," he mumbled with a grimace. "Doesn't matter right now. What I'd like to do is get him down here and make the introductions, then test to be sure your dad was right about who you came from."

At that moment, I wasn't sure what was more concerning, the fact that the grand magus wanted to invite a faerie into the silo or the fact that I might be kin to one. As I tried to process the last five minutes, he returned to his desk, punched a code on the intercom, and waited until a female voice I didn't know answered. "Hi, Toula. Need to see you for a sec."

When he cut the connection, I was staring at him, aghast. "Was that—"

"Ms. Pavli is a help to me," he interrupted, returning to the couch. "And she's also a witch-blood, so bear that in mind."

The grand magus seemed unfazed as a streak of white light appeared beside the door, then widened into a rip in the fabric of existence. A gate, I realized as I gawked—that was a *gate*, the sort of higher-level magic I'd read about but had yet to see…and the woman who stepped through, sporting spiky black hair, a tank top, and purple sweatpants, had to be Apollonios Pavli's daughter. I knew her by reputation—or, to be fair, I knew about her father, executed before I was born for the murder of forty-three wizards in Chicago. To my surprise, Toula looked more like a twenty-something on a lazy Saturday morning than the face of evil incarnate.

"Hiya," she said to the grand magus as she closed the gate behind her. "What's going on?"

He gestured to me but kept his eyes on Toula. "Have you met Aiden Carver?"

"No, can't say that I have," she replied with a squint. "Carver…any relation to—"

"Helen's brother," he confirmed. "Half brother, I should say. Tell me, does he remind you of anyone?"

Toula peered at me in silence for a few seconds, then pursed her lips and glanced at the grand magus. "Honestly? Maybe it's just me, but I think that kid looks kind of like Titania. What was I supposed to say?"

I cringed, and Toula's blue eyes darted back and forth between the grand magus and me as she realized the truth. "Oh…oh, *shit*, Greg, you don't mean—"

"That's the hypothesis we've been working with for the last fifteen years."

She whistled low and rubbed her bare arm. "Does Colin know?"

"I was about to tell him."

"Good," she snapped, "because if you don't, I will." She looked at me again, then slid beside me on the couch, moved the grand magus's trashcan out of the way, and took my hand. "Hey, bud, are you okay?" she murmured, giving my face a closer inspection. "Did Greg just tell you, too?" I nodded, and she aimed an exasperated sigh at him. "Dude, I'm sorry, I know it's a shocker," she continued as she squeezed my hand. "He sprung it on me last March, and I'm still working through everything. You grow up Arcanum, and then one day, you find out that your missing mother is, you know, *Mab*. Surprise!" She released me and slid back on the cushion, putting a little breathing space between us. "Look, the test is easy, and we'll get this settled. If Greg's right about you…I mean, it could be a lot worse. Colin's all right, as faerie lords go. Can you, uh…can you do anything with magic?"

"Nope," I muttered.

"Don't worry about it." She stood and turned to the grand magus, then asked, "Official business? Want me to look presentable?"

He gave her a long glance over the top of his glasses. "If you could shoot for professional, that would be a welcome change."

"Gramps doesn't care," she replied with a shrug, but an instant later, her sweats had changed into a black suit and high heels. "Better?"

The grand magus waved her on, then stood and motioned for me to join him as Toula opened another gate. "I may need to do a little prep work," he told me quietly. "Why don't you wait in the hall?"

The silo's walls were thin, and so I heard the muffled voices when Toula returned. Hers was easy to pick out, and I knew the grand magus's well enough. The third sounded younger than his and moderately pitched, a smooth baritone, and as far as I could tell, unaccented. Then again, I couldn't make out what was being said, so all I was left with was snippets of unintelligible sound and my churning stomach. An hour before, I'd been making a sandwich and thinking of starting a new robotics project from the scraps in my bedroom—and now I was eavesdropping outside the grand magus's office while he spoke with his assistant, the witch-blood daughter of Apollonios Pavli, and the faerie king who might or might not be my brother. It was enough to make me want to slink off and hide in the janitor's closet.

My mind whirled. If I really was—I forced myself to think it—*witch-blooded fae*, then my complete magical ineptness made perfect sense. I hadn't read much about mongrels, but I'd heard that they seldom had any ability to speak of. That didn't explain everything I'd just witnessed Toula do, however, but I put her aside for the moment. The bottom line was that if the grand magus was right, I was half fae. But I *couldn't* be fae, my family was full of wizards all the way back...

If I was fae, I mused, no wonder Dad was so distant.

And what would Hel say?

Before I could give it much thought, the door opened again, and the grand magus cocked his finger. "Mr. Carver? You can come in now, son."

I took a long breath, straightened my shirt, and, feeling like I was heading for the gallows, slunk back into his office.

Toula was sitting on the far couch, facing the door. Beside her sat a man in a gray dress shirt and blue jeans. He seemed about Toula's age, as far as I could tell—certainly no older than thirty—and I studied his face, trying to find something familiar there as his eyes widened. Certainly not his hair, which was wavy and dark brown, and barely skimmed his collar. I'd been towheaded like Mom my whole life. His brows were darker than mine, too, and arched above striking green eyes—old eyes, I realized, eyes that didn't fit the rest of him. With a little flutter of dread, however, I thought I saw something similar in our noses and chins, but it was hard to be sure, as he was staring at me like he was seeing a ghost.

"What—" he began.

"Lord Coileán," the grand magus replied, "allow me to present Aiden Carver."

His jaw dropped, and I stared at him, suddenly sure of two things: there was a faerie in the silo, and he was my brother.

Toula confirmed it a few minutes later, and she and the grand magus left Coileán and me alone to get acquainted. We both drank—Coileán, it seemed, had few reservations about giving alcohol to minors—and I caught myself sneaking glances at him, looking for hints of myself. He had a few inches on me and, I guessed, probably better muscles—not a bodybuilder, but someone familiar with the concept of free weights. While he was relatively pasty, I could tell that, unlike me, he'd at least seen daylight in the last five months. His accent was a puzzle in that he seemed to have none—for all I could tell, he could have grown up in the Midwest, and whatever time he'd spent in Virginia had done nothing to change that.

I knew I should be cautious—even the little I'd learned had stressed that faeries were, on their best day, dangerous. But Coileán listened as I told him about my family and my bullies, and he echoed Toula's sentiments about my situation. He gave me space even as he stressed that he wasn't going to hurt me. And then he made the offer that changed the course of my life: *Want to live with me?*

The rational, logical, prudent side of me pushed for no, but all I could see was a way out of my bedroom and a chance—even a slim chance—that I could learn to do magic. Maybe I wouldn't be a full-fledged wizard, and I didn't hold out any hope of being Hel's equal, but if I went with him to Faerie, then maybe someday, I wouldn't be a dud anymore.

I still couldn't quite get my mind around the idea that I was a high lord, but I decided to deal with that later and ran out of the office to pack my things…and straight into the guys who'd delighted in making my life a living hell.

If anything, my prolonged hiding had only made them more bloodthirsty. Morgan and Leo pinned me to the wall, and Milo, who had the hardest fist among them, broke my nose with one blow. Russell, their leader, stood back and gave orders for a minute before jumping in to take his turn, and his other lieutenants, Terrance and Dan, sat on my legs for a while to make me an easier target. By the time they'd tired and resorted to kicking me, I'd managed to curl up enough to protect my face, but one of my arms was long gone, my legs ached, and I could only hope that my insides weren't bleeding again.

And then, somewhere in the haze, I heard a door open,

followed shortly by a series of thuds. The next hands to land on me were Toula's, and as she tried to find out if I still had my major parts, I looked up to see the guys pinned against the walls, hanging a few feet off the ground. Coileán had his fingers around Russell's throat, and the expression on his face was terrible—rage, barely restrained.

He was terrorizing magi's sons—within sight of the grand magus—just because they'd attacked me.

I wanted to laugh when Russell wet himself, but my chest hurt too much.

Once he let them go, Coileán turned on the grand magus. I tried to diffuse the situation—the guys had just beaten me, after all, not come after me with wands—but Coileán looked like he was ready to skin a wizard or two by the time Toula got me to my feet. Maybe I should have been scared, and maybe the pain was clouding my judgment, but all I could think then was that I had a brother willing to beat the crap out of *magi's* sons on my behalf, never mind what else he was or what he had done.

That did it. Mom cried, but I packed my stuff and followed Coileán back to Faerie.

The next year was a roller coaster. In the beginning, I had five other brothers and sisters in the realm—and then I had four, imprisoned for their part in the plot that had led to Coileán attacking his daughter and accidentally killing his girlfriend, Meggy. In the months following her death, he retreated even from me, spending more time alone in his office while he mourned. Still, I seldom wanted for company. Joey was social by nature, and he didn't seem to mind having me hanging around with him and Georgie when he wasn't canoodling with Hel. Val had started giving Joey rather painful lessons in swordplay and self-defense around the time that I moved in, and once he learned that the extent of my knowledge on the subject was figuring out which part of a sword was the business end, he took me on as well. I made Joey look like a master by comparison, but Val was patient, and he seemed to intuit just how hard to push. By the time that Coileán started seeking companionship again that spring, I was almost competent—not talented, and nowhere near ready to spar in earnest, but able to at least hit Val once every two or three rounds.

As he'd spent millennia in the realm, Val was always willing to answer my questions about the place, but Coileán took it upon himself to start patching the larger holes in my education. The massive palace library—a misnomer, really, given that a good part of its holdings could have filled a decent-sized art museum—was put at my disposal, but more importantly, Coileán started taking me with him, showing me what he did all day and why. Toula was a fantastic tutor for magical theory and Val for swordplay, but my brother wanted me to know the ins and outs of Faerie—and I got the sense that he wanted to know me.

At least Coileán had been in the mortal realm long enough for us to have some common ground. I couldn't exactly meet him in the middle—I was almost eight hundred years his junior, and most of my life to that point had been spent in a bunker, taking computers apart to see how their guts fit together. He'd traveled, worked, fought, run, found time for flings…and, he admitted one night, he'd tried more than a few mind-altering substances, and he would be happy to give me the highlights if I swore never to undertake the same experimentation. In general, though, he gave me anything I wanted, as if he were trying to make up for the previous fifteen years. When he had a break, he'd escort me—and sometimes Joey—on day trips out of the realm, showing off his favorite spots. I saw more museums and galleries in three months than I'd seen in my whole life, and I gorged myself in some of the most amazing restaurants in the world. Coileán wasn't embarrassed to buy guidebooks and take recommendations, and slowly, as we contemplated monuments and ate far too many desserts, we started to become…well, brothers.

I began to get him. I saw the loneliness deep inside his shell, buried under all his raw feelings about Meggy and Moyna. The flashes of self-loathing. The moments of mixed despair and relief when another report arrived without news of Moyna's whereabouts. The anger at the inevitable whenever he parted from the few mundanes whom he considered friends, his quiet rage against death—a future they'd accepted as the natural pattern of life. I tried to put myself in his position: he'd lived long enough that nearly everyone he'd ever cared for had died, leaving him with a court that tolerated him, another court that resented him, and a small circle of friends with modest life expectancies. And then there I was—young, unsure, talentless, and hopelessly mortal, but still somehow the closest thing to family he had.

Coileán actually *liked* me, but more astounding to me was my realization that he desperately wanted me to like him, too.

And I did. Fifty-seven dead wizards or not, he treated me like I was more than an inconvenient also-ran, more than the dud hiding in Hel's long shadow. My sister loved me—I never doubted that—but my brother tried to understand me, even if he had no idea what I spent my free time building, or why. Eventually, he sat down and let me give him the short course in computing basics, though he fretted the whole time that he would make my machine explode. We agreed that my work area was an enchantment-free zone for safety purposes, and he sat beside me through a long afternoon to see what he'd been missing. I didn't go into programming—I didn't want to scare him off—and as for my pet robotics projects, I kept them safely out of his way. My room contained the single greatest concentration of iron in the realm, and I'd seen him stiffen and twitch whenever he got too close to my scrap reserves. But despite the land mines around us, Coileán stuck it out. It obviously bothered him when he didn't know what I was talking about, and he paid attention when I went through the terminology. As for me, I didn't care if he confused a CD drive for a pop-out cup holder—he was trying, which was all that mattered.

Outside the safety of my room—I mean, in all honesty, no faerie was going in there if he could help it—Coileán was more like Hel when it came to me than either of them cared to admit. Sure, I had free run of the palace and its gardens, but if I went elsewhere, I went with an escort. Joey could be trusted to keep me safe with Georgie, and Coileán knew that Val wouldn't let anything happen to me, but he also knew too well what some members of his court—hell, of our family—were capable of, and he sheltered me accordingly.

He *cared*.

And now…well, I was back in the silo, the epicenter of my miserable childhood, praying to anyone who might be listening that my brother was still alive.

CHAPTER 3

Without a set schedule in Faerie, and faced with the phenomenon of days that lengthened and shortened at random, I gave up on my alarm clock shortly after arriving in that realm. But I had a pair of windows in my room that faced the sunrise, and so I let my circadian rhythms do what they wanted and woke when the light was right, usually sometime around ten. It felt great, and aside from Coileán's occasional ribbing about sleeping my life away, I had no complaints.

Down in the silo, however, finding myself without windows for the first time in months was jarring. An electric clock squatted on the bedside table, and the green numbers had changed every time I rolled over to check, but I had no real sense of time and was too wired to sleep. I tossed and turned until six, and then I gave up, called it a night, and knocked on Joey's door.

He looked haggard when he stuck his head through the crack. "You, too, huh?" he muttered, opening the door wider. "Come in, but don't try to take Georgie's food."

My nose twitched at the unmistakable aroma of sausage patties, and I followed it past the bathroom to one of the rumpled beds, where Georgie was sprawled on her stomach, shoveling meat into her grease-streaked mouth. Someone had coaxed her into an oversized T-shirt and leggings—Toula, I assumed—and haphazardly tied her hair back from her face, but that was as far as the humanizing process had gone. Georgie's red eyes glanced up from the platter of sausage as I rounded the corner into the bedroom, then quickly fell back to the bounty before her.

"Early breakfast?" I asked, plopping into one of the pair of chairs by the untouched table. Joey's boots and gear lay on the floor between the beds, and his blankets looked as disheveled as mine.

It's not working, she replied as she bit a patty in half.

"What's not working?"

Not enough. Too slow. These are useless, she thought, pausing to flash her teeth at me. *They don't rip well, and then you have to chew everything to mush.*

"We've already been through the Heimlich twice tonight," Joey added as he collapsed onto the other chair. "One of the minor inconveniences of the human body is the inability to swallow pounds of meat at a time."

I forgot, she protested, giving him a disapproving stare. *You don't have to tease me.*

"I'm sorry, sweetie," he mumbled, "I'm not teasing you, I'm just—"

Exhausted. I know. Though only exhibiting the dexterity of a particularly gifted infant, she managed to close her fist around another piece of sausage and bring it to her mouth. *But this is really hard, and it's not filling me up.*

"Keep at it, we'll figure something out," he told her, then turned his baggy eyes to me. "Toula's been bringing up leftovers from the kitchen for the last three hours, but it's not putting a dent in her appetite. Maybe her stomach didn't shrink all the way, or maybe it's the fire, but Georgie can't eat fast enough."

If you'd just give me a cow—

"Same problem," he said. "It'd take you hours to get through a cow. Anyway, I don't know what your system can handle right now, so it's safer if we stick to cooked meat."

She swallowed and sighed, then cut her eyes to the door when it slammed open. *Got it?*

"Got it," said my sister, striding into the room with a bulk-sized jar of protein powder in her arms. "Sorry, had to wait for my neighbor to get back from the gym." Spotting me, she tossed me the jar and pointed to the bathroom. "Sport bottle's in there, read the package directions, start with one serving, and we'll see how she handles it. And you were supposed to call me, remember?"

"Little distracted," I replied, heading off to mix the drink. "I thought you were staying in Nashville."

"Yeah, that was a big 'nope.' Give him just a minute, Georgie, and we'll try a shake, okay?"

Catching a glimpse of my greasy blond squirrel's nest and baggy eyes in the bathroom mirror, I decided that I looked only marginally better than Joey that morning. I made up a batch of the concoction, which smelled like chemicals and claimed to be chocolate, and offered the bottle to our former lizard. "Probably best if you hold your nose and drink it," I said, waiting for her to take it from me.

Georgie frowned as she considered the mechanics of the situation, and she let Joey pull her up into a sitting position against the wall. "Here," he said, taking the bottle from me and holding the straw to her lips. "Put that in your mouth and suck on it."

Suck…

He mimed a fish face. "You pull the liquid up the straw. It's faster to drink it this way.

Hesitantly, she bit down on the straw and waited. *It's not working.*

"Look in here," said Joey, tapping his forehead. "See how I do it. I know your mouth feels weird right now, but believe me, this works."

Georgie stared at him for a long moment, then closed her lips around the straw, screwed up her face, and managed to pull a sip of shake into her mouth—which she then promptly spat onto the comforter. *That's disgusting!* she complained as she reached for the sausage platter. *You actually eat that?*

Joey took a test sip and made a face. "Okay, this isn't going to win any awards, but it's not *that* gross."

It tastes awful.

"It's chocolate—"

"Which the poor thing doesn't eat," Hel interrupted, smacking her forehead. "Don't worry," she told Georgie, "they make an unflavored version. I'll buy some once the health food store opens, and we'll blend it with something you like."

Her eyes lit up. *Sheep?*

"No sheep, but I could puree some hamburger and mix it in. And unless something's changed of late, Thursday is butchering day—I might be able to get blood from the kitchen. Would you like that?" Georgie nodded with her cheeks puffed full of meat, and Hel patted her leg before turning to me. "Hey, Aid. You didn't sleep, either?"

"Still waiting for Val to get in touch."

Hel looked around the room, saw that it was just the four of us, and murmured, "Are you sure Val's not involved in this somehow? I mean, he got you guys up in the middle of the night and threw you out without a real explanation…"

She let the thought hang, but I shook my head. "Something else was trying to warn me when he came to get us," I said, reclaiming my chair. Joey's brow furrowed, and I hastily explained, "I was having this dream. I mean, I thought it was a dream. There was this woman, and she was telling me to run…" His face remained blank, and I mumbled, "Just me, huh?"

"Yeah, but I wouldn't write it off yet. And I know Val," he added, looking reproachfully at my sister. "He was *scared*. I haven't seen him like that since the Gray Lands."

She grimaced as she always did at the mention of our brief invasion of that realm. Hel had migraines for a month from the strain of holding a gate open from Faerie against a wall of dark magic, and Joey said she had nightmares as well. I hadn't mentioned to him that he, too, sometimes relived that excursion in his sleep, loudly and with much thrashing at the blankets—but if he didn't know, Hel was bound to tell him eventually at one of their weekend sleepovers. Personally, having been responsible for pumping magic over the border that day, I remembered little but excruciating pain.

"I'm not saying he's up to anything, I'm just putting the idea on the table," said Hel. "Since we don't have much to go on—"

"He wouldn't do that."

"It's only a consideration," she soothed, motioning Joey down. "We have to consider all possibilities, and right now—"

"Why, because he's fae?"

She sighed and closed her eyes, a technique I'd seen her employ when trying to keep her temper in check around me. "Did I ever say that?"

"You're thinking—"

No, she's not. Georgie kept chewing as Hel and Joey turned to face her. *And you're not thinking normally,* she added, thrusting half a sausage patty at Joey. *It's all weird and jittery in there.*

"You need sleep," Hel coaxed, cupping his stubbled cheeks in her palms. "Let me help you, babe."

He pointed at me and shook his head. "Someone has to—"

"I'm more than capable of looking after my brother," she interrupted, then pulled at his wrist until he surrendered and let her lead him to his bed. "Just for a few hours," she said as he stretched out and settled in, then placed her hand over his eyes, muttered under her breath, and sent a stream of magic like purple light to envelop his head.

When the show stopped, Joey was unconscious and breathing easily, and Hel cracked her neck as she turned from the bed and stepped over his sword. "Okay, here's how this is going to work," she told me, glancing at her watch. "It's seven-fifteen at my place. Store opens at eight. I'm going to get the powder and come straight back. Don't leave Georgie unattended, all right?"

I'm fine.

"You can't walk," Hel countered. "No one leaves her

alone. Got it?"

I gave her a thumbs-up, and Hel surprised me with a tight hug. "I'm so sorry," she muttered. "We're going to get to the bottom of this, but you've got to bear with us. Do what the grand magus says."

She pulled away, but I stopped her as she opened a gate back to Nashville. "Hel...do Mom and Dad know I'm—"

"I haven't seen them," she replied, then stepped through without answering my question.

When the gate closed behind her, I slumped in my chair and watched Georgie doggedly chomp through her platter. She focused on the food for a few minutes, then looked up and found me staring into space in her general direction. *Your mind doesn't feel right, either.*

"I know."

Sleep. I won't do anything stupid.

I considered the dwindling stacks of sausage and shook my head. "You're going to need more of that before long."

I need more than just this, she replied as she ate. *I could eat about, oh, six to ten sheep right now. And this is like, "Here, you want a sheep? Have an ear."* She scowled as she chewed, miserable in her hunger.

"Are you all right, girl?"

Of course I'm not all right. I'm famished, the fire's back—it's not as easy to control as you might think, she added, glancing at a scorched spot on the carpet, *and in case you're now blind as well as exhausted, I'm stuck in this ridiculous form.*

"Ridiculous?"

Ridiculous. Back limbs are too long, teeth are flat, and I seem to be missing my wings.

The force of her glower was muted somewhat by the fact that it was coming from a preteen girl in a pink T-shirt, but her red eyes gave Georgie's expression a touch of its usual understated menace. "It's just for a little while—"

You say that, but you're not the one in a body you can barely control. And everything's so particular with you people, she griped. *I mean, what's the point of this?* She tugged at the neck of her shirt, leaving greasy fingerprint stains around the collar. *It's not cold in this room, so why bother with clothing?*

I floundered for an answer, then settled on, "It's just the way things are done. Humans cover certain, uh…things…up."

But I'm not human, she protested. *And there's no part of me that you haven't seen before.*

"It's…you know, it's…like…" I paused, felt a flush creeping up my neck, but managed, "Girls your age can't just walk around naked. Boys can't, either," I hurried to add before she found a new hook. "It's, uh…I mean, it's different with babies, but—"

Why?

The flush reached my face in record time. "There are *bits* that you're not supposed to show other people, Georgie."

She frowned, puzzling this out, and I felt her probing my thoughts for the explanation I didn't want to give her. *Reproductive parts?* she asked incredulously. *What's the problem? I'm not interested—I'm not going to give anyone the wrong idea. Also, yuck,* she thought with a grimace. *Look, Aiden, I don't mean any offense, but you're not at all interesting as mates. Too small, for one thing…*

Maybe it was the stress or the lack of sleep, but I couldn't help being a little miffed. "We're not *that* bad."

I didn't say you were bad—we're simply incompatible. How would that even work? she mused, staring into space as she grabbed another patty. *That's not…* She paused, seemingly disturbed, then slowly cut her eyes back to me. *You—not you you, but humans, faeries, whatever—you're not interested in us, are you?*

I chose my words carefully. "Very, very few, and I don't think they really consider the physics."

Good. And for the rest, ew. She resumed eating, apparently still hungry even if a little disgusted. *I mean, I knew Joey wasn't, but he's never told me much about human mating.*

It was entirely too early to be having a frank conversation about sex with a dragon in the guise of a fifth grader—actually, there would never be a right time for that conversation—but Georgie was either unfazed by or unaware of my discomfort with the topic. Or, I reasoned as she licked her fingers clean, she knew darn well that I wanted to crawl into a hole and was enjoying herself at my expense.

Since Joey's sleeping, could you answer something for me?

"Uh…maybe," I muttered as my cheeks burned.

It's kind of personal, and I don't want to upset him…

Her thoughts took on the odd cast reserved exclusively for matters concerning Joey. Georgie liked almost everyone, and she'd learned to give as well as she got—she'd dubbed Toula "Spiky" after one too many teasing jabs—but her relationship with Joey was of a different character altogether. It was no secret that she loved him, but that love didn't fall into the neat categories of human affection. She'd do almost anything he asked of her, and she'd defend him as needed, but he was also something of a parental figure to her—though, I was relieved to see, not a potential love interest.

"This is between us," I told her, dreading the question.

Georgie seemed relieved at the promise of secrecy. *Well,* she thought as she grabbed the last three pieces of sausage, *I was wondering why Helen hasn't had a clutch yet.*

"A…clutch?"

Yes. She nodded and popped a whole patty into her mouth. *They've been mating, but I haven't heard about a clutch. Is she hiding it somewhere? Or is something…wrong?* She paused mid-mastication and peered at me. *You look confused. Am I not being clear?*

"No…no, that's, uh…that's very clear. Too clear." I rubbed my temples as if I could get *that* image out of my head. "There are…ways…to avoid getting pregnant," I mumbled, wishing Toula would appear and save me. "And, um…I don't think Helen, uh…"

She doesn't want a clutch?

"Probably not."

Does Joey know?

"He's…" I found the carpet fascinating. "He's…I think he's on board with it."

Oh. Georgie finished her breakfast, but her brows knit as she considered this new twist. *So…if they don't want a clutch, then why are they mating?*

A knock at the door saved me from death by embarrassment. "All right, who needs bacon?" Toula called as she let herself into the room. "Oh—hey, Aiden, how long have you been up?" she asked, then stopped in her tracks and gave me a second look. "Are you feeling okay?"

"Never better," I muttered, rising from my chair before Georgie could corner me again. "Hel made Joey sleep, and she'll be back a little after seven. I…I'm just going to get a shower now," I said, and slinked out of the room.

When the grand magus's assistant arrived to fetch us, I was clean, if still in my pajamas, Joey was dead to the world, and Georgie was slurping down a grayish-pink slurry like there was no tomorrow. The poor guy looked around the room, took it all in, and shoved his hands in his pockets. "I was asked to bring you downstairs for breakfast with the grand magus," he began, "but if you're not ready—"

"Those two aren't going anywhere," said Hel as she popped out of the bathroom, blender in hand. "I'm keeping Joey under until he can think straight, and the girl's staying with us."

The assistant glanced from the blender and its bobbing chunks of hamburger to the bottle in Georgie's hands, looked at Hel like she might have lost it, and turned to me. "Mr. Carver, if you'd like to dress—"

I spread my hands and shrugged. "Didn't exactly have time to pack."

"I'll handle this," Toula cut in, and a clean pair of khakis and a sweater appeared on the table between us. "Go make yourself presentable," she ordered, shooing me toward the bathroom, and Hel stepped out to give me a moment's privacy. Shortly thereafter, I heard Toula tell the runner, "It's been a long night, and I'm not putting on real pants if there's not an emergency. Greg's seen worse."

"The grand magus—"

"Knows me," she interrupted, then pounded on the bathroom door. "Get a move on, bub, I'm hungry. You want socks?"

I opened the door and pushed my damp hair from my eyes—without Mom around to nag, haircuts had been on the back burner for months. "Thanks, but I'm fine. Canteen?" I asked the assistant.

"No," he replied, standing back as Toula swept into the hallway, bunny slippers and all. "He's dining in his office today. Hurry, now, don't keep him waiting."

She turned and gave him a withering look. "I will personally reheat his oatmeal if it comes to that, but I'm not taking orders from a third-rate bureaucrat this early in the goddamned morning. Got it, sunshine?"

"Ma'am," he mumbled, and speed-walked toward the elevator.

I didn't want breakfast—my stomach was knotting more tightly with every hour that passed without word from Val—nor did I care to step through the grand magus's office door again. The last time I had been in there had been to return to Faerie, right after my father told me, in the most colorful of terms, exactly how dead I was to him. They'd changed the locks in the two days I'd been away, giving Coileán's palace a test run, and so I got to stand at the door to my parents' apartment and listen as Dad shouted at me through the wall and Mom quietly cried. He'd called me a blood traitor and a useless sack of shit; he'd sworn and lamented that I hadn't been left topside for the wolves. By the time he progressed to comments about my newly discovered bastardy, I gave up and walked away, followed by his muffled harangue until I hit the stairwell and put another door between us.

At the time, I didn't understand the source of Dad's anger. True, I'd walked out of the silo for Faerie, of all places—which, in the average wizard's mind, was worse than abandoning the States for Moscow at the height of the Cold War—but that fact alone didn't explain his vitriol. After all, I'd come from *somewhere*, and the aural testing had proved my maternity. No wizard was a fan of the fae, granted, but my father had apparently had a fling with Titania herself. The grand magus had offered me no details about my conception, saying only that it was Dad's story to tell, but as I left the silo for the last time, I raged inside at my father's audacity—he'd cheated on Mom, and yet *I* was the bastard?

Once Hel started visiting the palace, I nurtured some small hope of hearing from our parents again, but no message ever arrived. My sister had nothing to tell me—she was a sophomore with a full course load and a new boyfriend, and she seldom went home—but Christmas passed and summer came, and still there was nothing but silence from the silo. Eventually, I mentioned this in passing to Coileán, who, after some consideration, took me aside and told me the full truth. My father's sister, Ella, had been kidnapped and taken as a changeling—a faerie's plaything—and Dad, a young wizard of no particular ability, ran into Faerie to find her. By the time he arrived, she was dead. Rather than kill him for the insult of showing up in her throne room uninvited, Titania decided to have a little fun with him. Dad's saving grace may well have been that he was handsome in his prime. Titania overpowered him and used him until she was satisfied, then threw him out with his sister's body as a parting gift—and nine months later, Val left me in the cold outside the silo, saved from my mother only to be foisted onto my unwilling father.

I'd seen the paintings and sculptures of herself that Titania had commissioned through the centuries—by then, all tucked away in the palace library—and so I knew what she'd looked like. More importantly, I saw it in the mirror every morning. Dark-haired and green-eyed, Coileán favored his father, but our mother was a brown-eyed blonde, and I was her spitting image.

I don't know why Dad decided to raise me. Coileán said that Mom had a strong hand in the decision—they'd wanted another kid, and I needed a place to go—but I can't imagine living for all those years with a reminder of the worst day of your life. I'm sure the grand magus wouldn't have faulted him if Dad had wanted nothing to do with me from the start. But he *had* raised me, and there we were with sixteen years of water under the bridge, and not a peep from him.

Dad had always favored Hel, but I'd chalked that up to her being the firstborn, his little girl, and a magical prodigy, the pride and joy of the family. And then there was me, the dud, the brown dwarf orbiting my sister's bright star. Sure, my report cards were always glowing—and aside from permanent honor roll status, I got paid for tech support in middle school—but nothing I did warranted more than a nod from Dad, no matter how hard I tried to please him. Growing up, I'd thought it was just because of my ineptitude with all things magical, but now his apathy made sense, as did his anger.

Surely, I thought, he felt something at least vaguely paternal toward me. I'd never given him trouble—surely he understood that I hadn't gone to Faerie to spite him. I'd been a virtual prisoner of my bedroom when I left home, and there was a chance—a small chance, Coileán cautioned, but a chance nonetheless—that something in the other realm would rub off on me. Maybe, just maybe, I'd be able to manage a wand someday. I hadn't turned my back on the Arcanum—I was trying to save my sanity and find whatever talent might be buried within me.

But as he made clear when he told me through the front door that he wished I'd died at birth, Dad saw things differently.

As I followed the assistant and Toula down the carpeted

hallway toward the grand magus's office that morning, I wondered whether my parents knew that I was back, and if so, whether they cared.

The assistant paused outside the heavy wooden door, then gave a perfunctory triple knock and cracked it open. "Sir? I brought, uh…two of them."

"Show them in," I heard the grand magus say. Toula touched my shoulder, a brief tap of reassurance, and led the way as the assistant held the door open.

The office was as I'd remembered it: the windowless, more functional twin of my brother's. Coileán had appropriated the basic elements of the grand magus's décor, but had worked them into a stone-walled room with plush Oriental rugs and a vaulted ceiling covered in a twinkling mosaic of the night sky. He opted for natural light when available, candelabra when not, and a lone brass standing lamp for evening reading—and in the last few months, he'd thrown in a fireplace for kicks. The grand magus's pair of green leather couches I recognized as among Coileán's thefts, as well as the full bar. Unsurprisingly, my brother had opted not to copy Magus Harrison's bridal portrait, which hung beside her husband's desk.

The grand magus had taken a seat on the couch facing the door, but he wasn't alone. I saw two people sitting on the couch opposite him, steadfastly not turning to look as we entered, and my palms begin to sweat. A brown-haired man and a blonde woman—I knew my parents, even from behind.

"Sir," the assistant began, "Ms. Carver has incapacitated the young man, and she insisted that the girl remain with them…"

While he tried to explain himself, Toula leaned toward my ear and whispered in Fae, "I'm right here. Breathe."

I nodded, watching the grand magus dismiss our escort, and wished my mouth hadn't suddenly gone dry. Chiding myself to be calm wasn't working—I could tell myself all day long that Coileán wouldn't have been afraid of my parents, but the fact remained that they were *my* parents, and they still hadn't looked at me.

Once the assistant had seen himself out, the grand magus stood and gestured to the bagels and fruit spread across the long coffee table. "Hungry? Thirsty? And here, have a seat," he said, stepping to the side and freeing a pair of cushions for us.

Toula took the spot beside him and popped a grape in her mouth, and I slid onto the end of the couch without a word. Dad stared at a spot above the grand magus's head, but I caught Mom's eyes flick toward me for a second—an acknowledgement of my existence, however brief.

A steaming cappuccino appeared in Toula's hands, and she raised the cup toward the other couch in a snide salute. "Rachel, Howard, so nice to see you again. We really should get together more often, you know." Dad looked at her blackly, and she smirked. "Oh good, you're awake. Hope you don't mind, but I can't abide crappy coffee. Here, Aiden," she said as another cup appeared in her free hand. "I picked up this technique in Rome last summer."

I took it from her and drank, if for no other reason than to give my hands something to do besides clench in my lap, and was pleasantly surprised. Then again, Toula and Val had made several trips around Italy by then, and her repertoire of coffee-based beverages had grown. Her palate was also more sensitive than Coileán's, making her reproductions nearly indistinguishable from their models. She wasn't shy about sharing her favorites, either, and when she thought I'd been alone in my room too long, she'd woo me out with pizza from her favorite hole in the wall or a curry she'd discovered in D.C. Toula gave Coileán hell, but she'd practically adopted me, for which my stomach was more than grateful.

My father continued to look anywhere but at me, and the grand magus cleared his throat. "Children, maybe we could all try not to provoke each other, hmm?" he said, cocking an eyebrow at Toula. She continued to sip her coffee as if she hadn't heard him, and he sighed softly. "Guess it was too much to ask for this not to be awkward. Aiden," he continued, shifting on the couch to see around Toula, "now that you're back with us, your parents have some thoughts about your education."

"Back?" I echoed. "No, I...this was just Val's idea, as soon as he sends word—"

"He hasn't yet," Toula interrupted, staring at my dad. "Which tells me that he was right to get you guys out of there."

"Fine," I retorted, "and we're out. So what do we do about him and Coileán?"

The grand magus stalled while he refilled his cup from a silver carafe. "Aiden," he said slowly, stirring in cream, "everything I've heard from you and Mr. Bolin suggests a coup. What would you like us to do about that?"

"We can't just *leave* them!"

"We don't have a choice." Putting his cup on the table, he clasped his hands over his knee and watched me sputter. "You want me to pit the Arcanum against the single most powerful faerie in existence, in *that* realm, on behalf of your brother?"

"And mine," Toula muttered under her breath.

"Son," he continued, "that would be suicide. I'm sorry, but if Coileán's not strong enough to take care of himself, there's nothing I can do to help him, and I'm not going to sacrifice my people to make the attempt. You've got to understand what we're up against."

I stared at him in shocked silence for a moment, then managed, "I've got to do *something*."

"And I don't mean to be cruel, but what exactly can you do? Unless you've discovered magic in the last year—"

"I'm in." Toula drank once more, and her half-empty cup vanished. "Pretty sure Joey wouldn't mind lending a hand. Georgie will help if we can get her fed."

"The dragon?" the grand magus asked, and my parents' eyes widened. "Leftovers aren't doing the trick?"

"Carver's working on it," she replied, seemingly unfazed that the grand magus had figured out Georgie's identity, and I wondered what she and the grand magus had discussed during the night. "Whatever I did didn't change her appetite, and her internal combustion is back online. She's starving."

"I'll see what else can be done," he muttered, frowning at his abandoned coffee. "But what does that make, Toula—you, two mundanes, and a juvenile dragon? Come on, you're smarter than that."

She sat back and crossed her arms. "I bet Carver would chip in."

"Over my dead body," Dad snapped.

He looked poised to spring across the food and tackle her, but Toula didn't flinch. "She's twenty, isn't she? I don't think you get a vote."

"And I'm also putting my foot down," said the grand magus before Dad could explode. "Assuming that Helen were foolish enough to go along with this, which she isn't."

"You're sure about that?"

The grand magus eyed Toula guardedly. "I'm quite sure that she understands the futility of going against one of the Three. She told me that Coileán impressed that upon her in, shall we say, memorable fashion."

"Sure, sure, but you know as well as I do that if *he* goes," she replied, tossing her head toward me, "she's not going to be far behind."

"Which is why he's not going anywhere," the grand magus said as Dad purpled. "Now, Aiden, your parents and I discussed this…*unpleasantness*…early this morning. I think it would be in your best interest to remain within the silo for the time being. Let me explain," he insisted, cutting me off before I could protest. "I'm not sending an unarmed teenager out to fend for himself if there's a chance that Oberon's coming after him. You'll stay here, and the Arcanum will pay for some online courses for you. No sense in making you twiddle your thumbs, right?"

"I…I mean…" I stuttered, looking at my parents for an

explanation, but Mom's lips were tight, and Dad just glared.

"You'll have your own apartment," the grand magus continued. "Mr. Bolin may stay with you until he figures out his next move…and I suppose there's the matter of the dragon to consider. Well, we certainly have units large enough for three. You'll be comfortable."

Dad continued to glower, and Mom finally broke her silence. "We had thought a program back east might be…you know, easier," she murmured, "but this is safest for now."

"Just as long as you don't have to see him, right?" Toula interjected. "I mean, let's not stop a good thing, Voss. It's not like you've checked in on him lately."

Mom looked at the carpet and flushed, but Dad had reached his breaking point. "Who the hell do you think you are?" he yelled, going to his feet. "You are *nothing*! You're lower than nothing, Pavli! How dare you even *speak*—"

"That's enough, Howard." Toula and Dad turned to the grand magus, who remained seated but managed to convey his displeasure through sheer ocular force. "I know you've had your differences, but Toula works for me. Sit down."

Slowly, not taking his eyes off her, Dad lowered himself to the couch once more.

"And Toula," the grand magus continued, rubbing his forehead, "you know that's unwarranted. How about a little sensitivity?"

"If you'll excuse me," she replied, "I don't think we're seeing eye to eye on what's warranted here. I've gotten to know your son," she said, ignoring Dad to focus on Mom. "He's a good kid, Rachel. Brilliant. Whatever else you did, you did *something* right."

Mom risked a quick glance up from the floor but dropped her eyes again almost immediately. I'd never seen her so cowed—but then again, I had no idea what had happened in my absence.

"Now, he's not going to say anything about it," Toula pressed on, nodding toward me, "but how do you think it feels to be cut off from the only family you've ever known? I mean, sure, his sister's been coming around"—Dad's teeth clenched at that—"and his brother would do just about anything for him, but you're his damn *mother*. Let Howard have his tantrum—you adopted that kid, you raised him, and he's sitting here right now, Rachel, he is *right here*, and I don't have to tell you that he's scared to death. The least you can do is look him in the eye!"

And to her credit, she did. Mom raised her head and looked at me as Dad stormed from the room, then whispered, "I'm sorry," before following him out.

The heavy door echoed as it slammed, and Toula let out a long breath. "Fucking hell, Aiden," she muttered. "I tried."

I patted her arm, then looked around her at the grand magus. "Appreciate the offer, sir, but I won't be here long. I'm going to find out what happened, and I'm going to get Coileán back, even if you're not going to help me."

"That wasn't an offer," he replied, peering at me over his glasses. "You're not leaving the silo."

"Excuse me?"

His gaze didn't waver. "Toula's right—if you jump into the fire, Helen will try to pull you out. I'm not going to risk losing our next grand magus because you're too young to think things through. So here's how this works, Mr. Carver: you either play ball by my rules, or I'll put you to sleep until this blows over. And if you think I can't deliver on that," he added, giving Toula a long, meaningful look, "then just try me."

Her face screwed up in surprise. "Greg—"

"Don't you 'Greg' me, missy. If the old boy can't take care of himself, it's not my job to rescue him." He shook his head and picked up his cup from beside the largely untouched breakfast spread. "And I won't have it said that I got our people killed on behalf of a damn faerie. Is that understood?"

Toula's muscles tightened, but outwardly, she kept her

cool. "So...what I'm hearing is that, assuming you're right and there's been a coup, you're happy dealing with Oberon?"

"If it comes to that—"

"Have you ever *met* Oberon?" she interrupted. "Because I have. He's an asshole on a good day, *Greg*. Now, you and Colin have your differences, I get that, but just think about what you're saying."

"I am," he replied, wincing as he pushed himself off the couch. "And I know this isn't easy for either of you to hear, but I've got to think about the greater good. If that sounds harsh, I'm sorry." He tugged at his cardigan with his free hand and waited while we stood. "I'll have an apartment set up for you in the next day or two," he told me, "and until I discuss this with the Council, I'll have to ask you to keep a low profile. Toula, do you think the dragon will eat offal? There should be some fresh in a few hours."

She looked at him, slowly blinking, then nodded. "Yeah. Couldn't hurt to try. Come on, Aid."

CHAPTER 4

Joey was many things, but he was no coward, and our sudden incarceration grated on him. The apartment we were assigned was nice enough—a little smaller than my parents' and furnished like a better Holiday Inn—and one of the grand magus's younger assistants had hooked up a television for us, but we couldn't escape the fact that we were stuck in a glorified windowless cell. Joey's phone was useless: it couldn't get a cell signal three stories underground, and the silo had yet to invest in Wi-Fi. More tellingly, despite the grand magus's instruction that I was to begin online courses, the computer brought in on the second day of our captivity was a clunky desktop model roughly as old as I was, slow and lacking a modem. If the dearth of outside communication hadn't been enough to impress on us the true nature of our situation, the guards stationed on our hall made it crystal clear.

As Georgie sprawled on the couch, drinking gallons of beef smoothies and staring at the TV, Joey paced and thought aloud, scheming of ways we might break out. With one sword and one shapeshifted dragon in our arsenal, however, the ideas weren't exactly forthcoming. If he were quick and lucky, he might be able to disable the security forces, though pitting two wizards against one guy with a pointy stick left the odds in the house's favor. Assuming we could get by them and make it to the surface, we were in the middle of nowhere, miles from a real town, and the Arcanum's vehicles were magically protected against theft. We'd have to hoof it out of there, but how far could we get on foot before the Arcanum dragged us back? I wasn't going to set any land-speed records, and even if Joey had been a sprinter, there was still Georgie to consider. She'd taken her first wobbly steps before the grand magus ordered Helen back to Nashville, but Joey still piggybacked her to and from the canteen, the in-house dining option for wizards who didn't cook. Not only was Georgie unsteady on her feet, but she was also growing more lethargic by the day. Despite the enormous quantities she was eating, she couldn't satiate her appetite, and we kept finding her asleep on the couch with her straw still in her mouth.

To our dismay, we discovered on our second morning in the silo that we couldn't look to Toula for help. She'd slipped a scrawled note under our door, saying only that the grand magus had a problem elsewhere that needed her attention. *Who knows?* she'd concluded. *Maybe he'll come around if his little fires are put out.* That was it—no forwarding address, no phone number, and no way to reach her. With Hel and Toula out of the silo, Joey and I were on our own, and we were outgunned.

By our fourth day underground, Joey was climbing the walls. "It's *Sunday*," he griped over breakfast while our escort was busy flirting with one of the cooks on the other side of the canteen. "The least they can do is let me out for Mass."

"Security risk," I muttered into my pancakes. "And good luck finding a Catholic church around here. Nothing but Pentecostals for miles."

He sighed and stabbed his eggs. "Heathens. Georgie, honey, try to eat."

She sat between us, listlessly pushing her sausage links around her plate with two fingers. *My mouth hurts.*

"Did you bite your tongue?"

No. It hurts here, she thought, and ran her hands down the sides of her lower jaw. *And I broke a tooth.*

"On *what?* Open up, let me see," he coaxed, and Georgie's tongue prodded the offender. Joey reached inside and wiggled it around. "It's not broken, just loose."

How do I fix it?

"You don't. It'll come out on its own, and a bigger version will grow in." Seeing Georgie's confusion, he explained, "You do this all the time, you just don't notice. I've found your teeth everywhere around the barn."

But that doesn't feel like this, she protested. *And I've only got one set right now…*

In her true form, Georgie had teeth like an overgrown shark: perfect for ripping, slightly curved to the rear to hold prey, and abundant. She had three series growing at any one time, fit together in her jaws like razor-sharp nesting dolls. When a tooth wore down or fell out, the one behind it moved into place in a matter of hours. The new wrinkle of a loose baby molar was just one more annoyance with her current body, and she rested her chin on the table and snorted her displeasure.

"She's been eating constantly since Thursday morning," I told Joey. "Her jaw's got to be sore from overuse."

"Yeah," he said, rubbing Georgie's back. "But good luck getting a doctor to look at her around—"

"*Dudley!*"

I jerked up to scan the room for the source of the shout and spotted Russell by the juice table. "Shit," I muttered, sinking low in my chair, "aw, *shit*, what else is going to go wrong?"

By then, Russell was striding across the canteen toward our table—unaccompanied, at least, but that was a small comfort. My former chief tormenter had grown his dark hair out into a short, sloppy ponytail, but otherwise, he was as I remembered: a little taller than me, a fair bit thicker, with deep-set brown eyes fringed by girlishly long lashes. Russell pulled his wand out of the back of his waistband as he approached and smiled. "Look who's back! The Dudster! Did they kick you out of your nerd school already, Dudley? Came back to see your old friends?"

The neighboring diners turned at the commotion, and

Joey went to his feet. "Help you with something, kid?" he asked as his fingers closed around his greasy table knife.

Russell glanced at him, then smirked at me. "Found yourself a boyfriend, huh? Someone to wipe your bottom for you since your babysitter ain't here?"

I saw the wand in his hand, but I managed to recover my spine. "The grand magus asked me to stick around for a few days," I told him. "Joey here is assisting me. So unless you'd like to drag the grand magus into this, I suggest you beat it and let us eat."

He leaned over the table, no longer smiling. "And who's going to make me, Dudley? You?"

Is he bothering you?

I looked at Georgie, who couldn't follow the conversation, but gave no sign that I'd heard her. Turning back to Russell, I said, "I've done nothing to you, and the grand magus isn't going to like it if I'm all cut up."

"Who said anything about cuts?"

"Or broken," I continued. "So do us all a favor and go away."

He ignored me. "Heard your dad threw you out. Sent you off to school so he wouldn't have to look at the dud. I don't like looking at you, either," he murmured, leaning closer. "I don't like your face, Dudley. And you know what happens to people I don't like?"

Russell never saw it coming. While he was focused on me, Joey vaulted onto the table, dull knife in hand, and caught Russell's neck in the crook of his arm as he slid off the other side. "Drop the stick!" he bellowed, holding the knife in the hollow below Russell's right ear. "*Drop it*, you little son of a bitch!"

Joey had a solid chokehold on him, but Russell's wand hand had a mind of its own. Before I could shout a warning, he raised his wand, pointed it behind him...

...and began shrieking as both wand and hand burst into flame.

Joey pushed him away and turned to find Georgie

standing beside me with her skinny arms folded. A puff of smoke escaped her nostrils, and she smiled as Russell plunged his hand into a pitcher of ice water and wailed.

"That…is some precision breath control," said Joey.

I didn't want to hit you, or I would have just gone for the head. Stupid wizards. She plopped back into her plastic chair and sighed at her plate. *I'm still hungry. Can I put the rest of this in a shake?*

As Russell was led to the infirmary, our escort hustled us back to our apartment and locked the door from the outside. "So," said Joey as the footsteps in the hall receded, "on a scale of hand slap to execution, how much trouble do you suppose we're in?"

"He's a magus's son," I muttered, joining Georgie on the couch. "Magus Mulligan's a bastard, but that family's been on the Council for generations."

"Uh-huh. And the fact that your buddy started it?"

"Irrelevant. Not like the grand magus has lifted a finger in the past—why start now?"

Can I have a smoothie?

"Sure, hon," said Joey, heading for the little kitchen. "And if they decide not to kill us," he called around the corner, "we're going to need more protein powder soon." He started assembling the blender, then paused and said, "No, you did nothing wrong. I appreciate it, really."

I read worry on Georgie's face and realized I wasn't part of a conversation. "Russell would have hurt Joey," I told her. "You did the right thing."

But you're scared now.

I patted her back and shrugged. "Nothing new around here. Hey, want to watch TV?"

While Joey finished blending and I played with the remote, Georgie leaned against my shoulder and drew her legs onto the cushion. Sunday morning programming was lousy, even with cable, and I had just begun flipping through the movie channels when she perked up and pointed at the black and white picture. *What's that?*

"That?" I said, checking the on-screen guide to be sure. "*Godzilla.*"

Oh. She frowned in thought at the rampage for a moment, then remarked, *Doesn't look very realistic.*

"Old movie, bad special effects."

She snorted. *And why is she wrecking that town?*

"It's a he, not a she, and he's upset about something to do with nuclear bombs, I think."

No, I'm pretty sure she's female.

Georgie looked up at me and grinned, but I decided not to argue—I was expecting an angry mob of magi to come barging through the door at any moment, and we still had yet to hear from Val, which boded nothing good. But we were trapped, and so, lacking a better idea, I watched movies with Georgie for the rest of the morning and tried not to think about my impending doom, while Joey wandered in and out of the den, alternately making shakes and brooding.

Just after noon, someone rapped at the front door, and Joey, with a quick glance at me, cracked it open. "Ye—oh. Hello," he said, stepping back to reveal the grand magus on the threshold. "If you came for lunch, I can offer you a choice of Pringles or a kidney."

"Thank you, Mr. Bolin, but I've eaten," he replied. "Actually, I was wondering whether your, uh…little friend might like a steak dinner."

"Probably," he said, sounding puzzled, and re-asked the question in Fae. Georgie's eyes lit up, and he nodded at the grand magus. "She's interested. What's the catch?"

"None. You may have noticed the herd topside—I think we can spare one." He stepped back and beckoned to Georgie, and Joey hoisted her onto his back when she struggled to find her footing. "Still a little shaky, I take it?" the grand magus asked.

"Just a little. Aiden, hand me that," Joey told me, nodding to his sword belt on the kitchen table.

The grand magus's mouth twitched. "Don't trust me, do you?"

"I like to be prepared," he replied, awkwardly fastening it while Georgie clung to his neck. "If you've heard about this morning, you might understand why I'm on edge."

"Of course. You'll want your coats, too—it's breezy up there."

I fetched them and propped up Georgie while Joey dressed, and then the grand magus led us past the guards and toward the surface. The fact that he was taking us without a security detail was momentarily reassuring, but then I remembered that he didn't *need* one.

The Arcanum had divided its pastureland into four sections, two at use at any given time and two left to re-grow. Grass could be coaxed up fairly quickly with the right spells, but the neighbors asked fewer difficult questions if the fields were left fallow, and so the cattle were rotated to keep queries to a minimum. Then again, as far as the locals knew, the herd was owned by an old man who lived in a modest farmhouse near the run-down trailer park, a crusty coot who kept to himself and posted trespassing warnings all around his land. Magus Fredericks was indeed a crusty coot, but his house, like the trailer park, was just another surface decoy.

The grass had long since gone to straw that October, but as we hiked to the far pasture, we passed clumps of cows gathered around mysteriously green patches, quietly gorging themselves and ignoring us. Georgie eyed them hungrily, and the grand magus noticed the direction of her stare. "Soon enough," he told her, but Georgie looked at him blankly, and he held up a hand to stop Joey's progress. "My Fae has always been iffy," he said, rubbing his palms together, then pressed his fingertips to Georgie's temples and whispered, "*Logos.*"

She yelped and twisted to get out of his grasp, but the grand magus was strong for an old man and held on until her whimpers subsided. "There, now," he said, stepping back a pace as Joey's hand inched toward his sword, "that wasn't so bad, was it?"

Georgie frowned and held her head. *That hurt!*

"It's over," he replied, "and that process can be a little painful. I'm sorry, but I figured you'd prefer to understand the local language, since you're going to be in this realm for a while—"

It didn't hurt when Coileán did it, she rebutted.

The grand magus spread his hands. "And that's enchantment versus spellcraft for you, my dear. Sometimes one is a better tool than the other. Any headache?"

She pulled her hands away, waited, then shook her head.

"Good. Now, then," he continued, glancing around at the pasture, "there's one other thing I need to do."

In an instant, Joey had put a sword length—and a sword—between him and the grand magus, and Georgie watched from her perch with wide eyes. "She was *defending* me," he said, his voice low and clipped. "That little shit was armed, and she was defending me. He started it, not Georgie."

The grand magus looked at the weapon pointed at his gut, then raised his eyes to Joey's and held his stare. "You mistake me, Mr. Bolin. And you think ill of me, but I suppose I can't blame you for that. Haven't given you much cause to think otherwise, to tell you the truth." He nudged the point of the sword away from him with two fingers but kept his distance. "Toula is excellent at what she does, but there are a few tricks she has yet to learn. That transformation, for example," he said, pointing to Georgie. "Solid enough, but she didn't take all of the variables into account. If you leave her as she is, that dragon's not going to see Thanksgiving. Can't get enough food down her to keep up with her metabolism—she's starving to death. But I think you figured this out already, yeah?"

Joey hesitated, then slowly sheathed his sword. "You can fix her?"

Change me back?

"Yes to you," he replied, pointing to Joey, "and a technical yes to you, too, but it would be a bad idea," he said to Georgie, who deflated at the news. "But what I can do is slow your systems a bit, put your insides more on par with your outsides."

Is this going to hurt?

"Maybe," he admitted, "but it beats starvation, right?"

Joey lowered Georgie until her feet found the ground, then let her lean against him while the grand magus rested his hands on her shoulders. I watched the pale yellow magic swirl around her, interacting with the spell already in place, and she squeezed her eyes shut and cried out before falling to her knees. Joey was on her in a flash, but the grand magus stepped back, seemingly satisfied. "Now," he said, dusting off his hands, "how about a heifer?"

A few minutes, a short walk, a killing spell, and several judicious sword cuts later, Georgie was up to her elbows in a cow, by turns ripping handfuls free and burying her face in its side. Her shirt was ruined, and she looked like an extra from a slasher movie, but I could hear her contented thoughts as she smacked and snorted over the corpse.

"Well, now," said the grand magus, who had staked out a spot sufficiently clear of the spatter zone, "that's something you don't see every day."

"Don't forget to breathe!" Joey called, also standing well out of range of the flying gore. "It's not going anywhere, Georgie—take your time!"

She dug in and yanked, then pulled the cow's heart out and sank her teeth into it with relish. A look of bliss crossed her face, and I fought my stomach's urge to go be sick in the corner. I'd watched Georgie eat hundreds of meals, but she hadn't been quite so cute the last time she disemboweled her food. When she'd worked a chunk out of the heart, she held it at arm's length, cocked her head in consideration, then blew a thin, focused jet of flame at the meat until it blackened. Satisfied with her work, she bit through the charred layer with all the relish of a Girl Scout on s'mores night.

As Georgie moved on to breaking ribs, the grand magus wiped his face with a handkerchief and turned away from the carnage. "I'm sorry it took so long to get y'all out here," he said to Joey and me. "Council didn't want to give her a whole cow, but I said she was wasting away without fresh meat."

"So they caved?" I asked, surprised.

"No. They think I brought her out here to eliminate her." Seeing our expressions shift, he folded his arms and said, "Come on, gentlemen, how long did you think anyone was going to be happy keeping a dragon down there? *Especially* after this morning. Russell said you did it, by the way," he added, glancing at me, "but that notion didn't take too long to debunk. Grace Mulligan is adamant that Georgie not be allowed back."

Joey had already gripped his hilt. "And you're telling us this because—"

"Because I'm trying to make you understand what I've been up against," he said. "And why it's taken me so long to get you the hell out of there. Now, is there anything you left underground that you absolutely cannot live without?"

We stared at him, neither of us fully comprehending what he was saying, and Georgie belched another stream of flame at her lunch.

The grand magus moved close to us, lowered his voice to a bare murmur, and said, "It's taken a few days to get the arrangements in place, and I kept you in the dark for your own safety. You're going to Virginia. Toula and Helen are meeting you there. It'll be up to you to figure out what's happened in Faerie—and I'm sorry, I can't help you—but at least you'll be free to move about."

"You're...I'm sorry, *what?*" Joey asked in disbelief.

"The Council has a stick up its ass and its head in the

sand," said the grand magus. "They're adamant that we not get mixed up in court affairs. This is none of our business, as far as they see it. But as *I* see it, if something's happened to Coileán, then the only power left in Faerie is Oberon—and I do *not* want to live in a world in which his power's unchecked. Old boy gets bored, and we're toast." He looked into our eyes in turn, then nodded. "So here's what's going to happen. In a few minutes, a gate will appear from nowhere, and you three will make a run for it while I'm distracted. Toula will take the fall for now. You can't trust a Pavli, you know."

I raised my voice slightly to be heard over the sounds of Georgie's rooting. "And there's some reason why you couldn't have told us this plan, like, four days ago?"

"Security, Mr. Carver." He paused as Georgie began systematically burning the hair off the cow, then said, "There are certain highly complex spells protecting my office—security measures, all overseen by a select group of wizards trusted by the Council. And, I fear, loyal to the Council. I'm not entirely convinced, but I think my office may be bugged. No need to take that risk when—"

A rip in reality opened beside us, and I recognized the alley behind Coileán's old building in Rigby...which had been Meggy's building until their daughter ran off to the Gray Lands, and Meggy came back a corpse.

The grand magus smiled tautly as the hole widened. "Right on time. Georgie, dear, I'm afraid you'll have to leave the rest of that here."

She looked up and saw the gate, then patted her bloated stomach, leaving bloody handprints on her shirt. *I'm set.*

"Oh, sweet *Jesus*," Toula muttered from the other side, covering her mouth as she stared at Georgie. "Carver!" she called over her shoulder. "Incoming! Someone's going to need a bath, *stat!*"

Joey helped Georgie to her feet, then gave the grand magus a quick nod and carried her through the gate. I looked from the ruined cow to the old man, and I saw the weariness in his eyes. "Grand Magus—"

"Go," he interrupted, patting my shoulder. "Do what you need to do."

I had one foot in Virginia when he said, "And Lord Aiden?"

Turning back, I found him watching grimly beside the cow. "Yes, sir?"

"Be careful, son," he said, and shooed me on.

Hel apologized to Georgie, but there was no way, short of another spell, to avoid the garden hose. She ensorcelled it to spray warm water, but October was October, even in Virginia, and Georgie was shivering by the end of her shower. The runoff ran red to the gutter behind Coileán's building—now Stuart Purcell's building, I reminded myself, still half-expecting to see the familiar book racks in the shop instead of Stuart's displays of dried sage and candles and healing wind chimes. Rigby's self-professed white wizard was as magically gifted as a plastic wand from the discount bin, but my brother had come to have a grudging almost-fondness for the weirdo. "Wizard Stu" was mundane, misguided, and possibly a touch deranged—having seen true magic, he was on a fool's quest to teach himself how to wield it—but he firmly believed that civilians should be protected from eldritch horrors and that it was his solemn duty to step into the breach. Thus, when Toula had shown up on his doorstep and explained the situation, Stuart was more than willing to let us crash on his couch.

He was less than enthusiastic at the sight of Georgie in all her gory splendor—I think he came close to passing out, to be honest—but he warmed to her once she was hosed down. For the first time in days, Georgie seemed content, full and clean and dry, and she curled up on a pile of polyester ceremonial robes and fell asleep as Stuart's terrified cats watched from beneath a draped table. Mrs. Cooper, Stuart's great-aunt and Coileán's matronly former neighbor, had wandered across the street from her shop with tea and cookies, and Joey and I took over the tea nook with Toula and Hel to catch each other up.

We'd just covered Georgie's performance that morning when someone rang the after-hours doorbell, and Stuart jumped up to unlock the front door. "Expecting company?" Joey asked, reaching for his sword.

Hel waved him back into his chair and stood when the door swung open. "Over here!" she called, waving to the trio of newcomers. "Tea's on, and I will *cut* you if you hog the oatmeal raisins again, Vivi."

I recognized two of them—Vivian Stowe and her fiancé, Hal Perryman, the Fringe's rising star and the coach of Rigby High's doomed football team, respectively. Though the product of half-fae parents, Vivi, the lone unfortunate among her siblings, had turned out mortal—her thick-framed glasses and steel wristwatch were proof enough of *that*—but she made up for her magical shortcomings with technical expertise. Hal was as mundane as they come, but the elders Stowes had apparently decided that he was good enough for their little girl, and the Fringe had offered him what amounted to junior membership. As a support organization for those with even the barest smidgeon of magical ability, the Fringe wasn't overly picky about its recruits.

"Can it, Hermione," Vivi called back to my sister. "I lick it, it's mine. Deal with it."

"Whatever happened to sharing, huh?"

"Sharing," said the stranger with Vivi and Hal, a black-haired, youthful-looking man in a tweed blazer and tailored jeans, "goes out the window when you're in a pack of thirteen."

"You should have seen the pumpkin pie last year," Hal muttered. "Horrible, I tell you."

The man elbowed him in the side, and Hal shoved him back good-naturedly. "Mr. Purcell, good to see you again," the stranger continued, nodding at Stuart, "and

Mrs. Cooper—radiant as ever, how do you do it?"

"And *you*, sir, are a shameless, lying flirt," she replied, swatting him on the arm, but her smile lines broke through her shellac of foundation.

Vivi rolled her eyes and cocked her thumb toward him. "Folks, my idiot brother. Idiot brother, you figure it out."

"Rufus Stowe," he said, casting a glance at our table. "And let me guess: that one's the wizard, the one with the spiked hair is Toula, the guy with the damn *broadsword* must be Joey, so that makes you...Lord Aiden, is it?" he asked me.

"Only if you're feeling fancy," I replied.

He grinned at that. "Good. I was rather concerned that a high lord with an Arcanum pedigree would be an insufferable ass, but maybe you'll prove me wrong."

"And maybe you'll tell us what you're doing here," Joey interjected as he stood. "Correct me if I'm mistaken, Vivi, but I thought your family's allegiance was to Oberon."

"Well, *technically*," said Rufus, "but 'allegiance' is such a strong word." He helped himself to Mrs. Cooper's cookie tray and leaned against a wall of dreamcatchers. "Vivi gave me the skinny. I want to help you."

"And what's in it for you?"

"Preservation, I suppose," he replied, sounding surprised at the enquiry. "Check if you doubt me," he added, tapping his head. "I'm not leading you into an ambush, if that's what you thought." A second later, he jerked, almost dropped his cookie, and stared at Toula open-mouthed. "You checked?" he said, sounding hurt. "You actually *checked!*"

"I'm not an idiot, sweetcheeks," she replied, wrapping her hands around her teacup. "And he's legit. Stand down, Percival."

Joey gave Rufus a long look, then released his grip on his sword and sat. "For the record, it's an arming sword, not a broadsword. Different hilt."

"I'm not a medievalist," Rufus protested, "so why don't

we settle for 'anachronistically employed pointy thing'?"

"It does the trick." Joey smirked, then tapped the tabletop. "If you're in, then you'd better pull up a chair."

He looked around at Stuart's offerings—mismatched patio furniture of painted steel—then produced a wooden chair from the ether, flipped it backward, and bellied up to the table. "So, what do you know about current events?"

"Little and less," said Hel. "You're the one with the in with Oberon, you tell us."

Rufus sighed and steepled his fingers in front of his face. "That's the problem—I *don't* have an in with him." Hel's brow furrowed, and as Vivi and Hal squeezed in, he explained, "I've never met the man. Our parents have done an excellent job avoiding the rest of the court. They may still have some allegiance to Oberon, but as far as I'm concerned…well, I didn't vote for him." He paused when the doorbell rang again, then raised a finger in greeting as Stuart admitted Rick Matherson, a Fringe coordinator and one of Rigby's resident bartenders. "That's the last of us?"

"Yep. We're not calling the priest in yet," said Rick, who squinted in the noon light as if he'd just rolled out of bed. Then again, considering his profession, he probably had.

Rufus looked around at the assembled and shook his head. "I realize that a plucky band of underdogs is the American way, but we're going to need more than pluck. Do you have any—"

"Wait, *wait*," Hel interrupted, holding up her hand to silence him. "You're telling me you've got no court affiliation?"

"On paper? Sure, I do. In reality, though…" Rufus shrugged and poured a cup of tea. "Look—Helen Carver, yes?"

"Yeah…"

"Ms. Carver, I'll be blunt: I've never been to Faerie, I have no desire to relocate there, and the thought of Oberon getting a wild hair and deciding to conquer this realm terrifies me. Whatever's left of Mab's court is in shambles, and last I heard, Nath was dealing with her own problems at home. If Coileán's out of commission, who's to stop Oberon? I mean, say he does decide to invade—what are we supposed to do, call out the Green Berets? I'm not trying to be flippant, but Kevlar's no defense to magic."

"*We?*" she asked.

"Yes, *we*," he retorted. "I was born in this country, I work here, I pay taxes—and if we're going to be picky about it, I've lived here quite a bit longer than you have." He added milk to his cup and swirled it, eschewing the dainty silver teaspoons Mrs. Cooper had provided. "Honestly, I'd rather keep the current system in place, imperfect as it is, because I know what the alternative looks like."

"And I thought you said you'd never been to Faerie."

His eyes darted to his sister's. "Our parents are native. We've heard plenty."

"Mom and Dad haven't been back since 1423," Vivi added.

"For various reasons," said Rufus, "but that's immaterial at the moment. The bottom line is that I'm willing to assist you, the *Fringe* has said it's willing to help, and, uh…"—he glanced at the would-be wizard in the corner—"Mr. Purcell has volunteered the use of his store."

"And any further assistance required," said Stuart.

"Generous," Rufus muttered. "So—one certified wizard, six functional mundanes, two of us who might pass for fae if you squint hard enough, and…Mr. Purcell. Is that the long and short of it?"

Joey pointed to Georgie and her makeshift bed. "One dragon."

"One *ensorcelled* dragon," Toula quickly clarified, looking at Stuart, "who is not going to suddenly shapeshift and destroy your shop."

Mrs. Cooper clucked her tongue, then pulled a robe from beneath Georgie and covered her up. "Poor little thing's tuckered out," she said. "Do you think she's going to be hungry when she wakes? Growing children have big appetites…"

"Oh, probably," Joey sighed, rubbing his forehead.

"I've got some chicken salad in the fridge, if you think she'll eat it."

"Worth a shot," he replied, looking up to smile at her, then noticed movement below the display table near Georgie and paused. "Hey, Stuart? Why don't you do us all a favor and hide your cats for now, okay?"

As it turned out, Georgie did eat chicken salad—about two quarts of it, in fact—and then, declaring herself stuffed, she curled up on her pile of robes again and fell asleep. Joey seemed relieved to see her satiated, but it was a grim sort of satisfaction, tempered by the general frustration of his company.

The afternoon lengthened, Rick brought over half his top shelf to smooth over frayed nerves, and Vivi made a run for Chinese takeout as night fell, but even food and alcohol did little to improve the mood. We were stuck at square one, and no one could decide on the next step.

Barging into the palace was easily excluded as a viable solution. "I don't know what experience the rest of you have with Oberon," said Toula, "but I don't want to cross him without a significant advantage in our corner. Marching in and demanding answers looks a lot like suicide to me."

"Assuming he's even there," Joey muttered. "He could be back in Florida now, for all we know."

"If Oberon's not there, then where the hell is Val?" she countered. "He wouldn't leave us hanging like this if he were able to get word out."

Though we were dealing with hypotheticals, that Oberon had established more than a foothold in Faerie seemed like a given by that point, and Toula's mood only darkened as the hours passed.

The second idea was received marginally better than the first: open a gate somewhere in the backwoods of Faerie and stay low until we knew the situation. "I've been out in the country," said Joey. "Made rough maps of a good deal of it. I don't have my notes on me, but if I gave you landmarks, would that be enough to make a gate in the right place?"

"Conceivable," said Rufus, tapping his plate with his chopsticks, "but how far out do you suppose we'd have to go?"

"And you're forgetting the realm," I mumbled, then cringed when the others turned to me. I'd never liked being the center of attention—probably because it often ended in pain when I was growing up—and I sank a little in my chair as they waited.

Rufus put his utensils down and gave me a once-over from across the table. "Speak up," he said as my shoulders hunched. "No one's going to bite you, kid. Hell, you've got more inside information than at least half of us here," he added, and Rick and Vivi nodded at the next table over. "Now, what does the realm have to do with anything?"

I took a deep breath to center myself, then said, "It's sentient. Coileán says it's like an alarm system—it tells him when someone crosses over who's not supposed to be there."

His forehead wrinkled in surprise. "Such as?"

"Wizards. Anyone from Mab's court. He says it's not fond of some mortals…I think it's okay with anyone from his or Oberon's court, but it's picky about outsiders."

"Colin says it does *not* like me," Toula confirmed. "Or her," she said, cocking her head at Hel.

Rufus resumed his attack on the tepid chow mein. "What I'm hearing, then, is that if we decide to go over, the two of you are out."

"If you want the element of surprise, yeah." She grabbed the rice carton and a spoon. "And to be safe, I wouldn't send anyone who hasn't spent considerable time there already. Don't give the realm anything new to consider."

"So…" said Joey, "that would leave Aid, Georgie, and

me."

"And that's a big, fat, *no*," Hel snapped as she speared a shrimp.

"Helen—"

"*No.*"

"Helen," he tried again, "let's be reasonable about this—"

"Reasonable?" she echoed, dropping her fork. "In what universe is it reasonable to send two unarmed mundanes into Faerie alone?"

"We wouldn't be unarmed—"

"Excuse me, two mundanes with a sword between them. Not even a magical sword—a good, old-fashioned, piece of metal. Oh, and let's not forget Georgie!" she cried in mock amazement. "Why, Faerie is just *lousy* with dragons. I'm sure no one will think twice if you go flying around—"

"That's not what I'm suggesting!"

"Then what? How is that possibly going to end with anything but a couple of corpses?"

As the two of them glared at each other and reddened, Mrs. Cooper stepped between them and spread her hands. "You know, y'all don't have to decide this right now. No one's going anywhere tonight, so let's not fight, okay?"

When her attempted placation proved ineffective, Rick rose from his threadbare armchair by the robe pile and pointed to the staircase. "Carver. Bolin. Upstairs, both of you," he ordered. "We're going to have a little chat."

They started to sputter, caught the looks the rest of the room was giving them, then grudgingly marched after Rick. When the door slammed, Georgie whimpered in her sleep, and Vivi took Rick's vacated chair to scratch the dragon's head until she calmed.

While the others took advantage of the silence to put down a few more bites, all ignoring the muffled voices rising in the apartment above us, I pushed my plate back and cleared my throat. "There's, uh…maybe one thing we could try." Toula's eyebrow arched in query as she chewed, and I said, "Grivam. I think he owes Coileán a favor or something."

"The merrow king?" asked Rufus. "You want to drag *him* into this?"

"There's an ocean gate into Faerie," I said, racking my brain for details I'd nearly forgotten. "It's how the merrow go back and forth. If they've been over lately, they might know something."

"Or they might be convinced to find out," said Toula, putting the rice aside. "I mean, Grivam drives a hard bargain, but if you're right and Coileán has one on him…"

Rufus pushed his plate away. "Where's the gate? And minor detail, but does anyone know how to find Grivam?"

"I can probably call him," she replied, "but as for *where* the gate is…"

"You don't know?"

"Oh, I know, but you're not going to like it." She looked around the room and lowered her voice. "Who wants to find out whether Oberon left anyone behind in the Keys?"

CHAPTER 5

For the second time in under a week, I woke in the middle of the night when someone shook me back to consciousness. But instead of Val, as I'd hoped in the second between sleeping and waking, I found my sister standing over me when I opened my eyes. "Wha—"

"Get up, we've got company," was all she said before running down to the store.

I pushed myself off the air mattress Rufus had created for the occasion, blinked in the dim light of the apartment's den, and listened to the voices rising from the ground floor. Hel had left the door open, and I scrambled downstairs to see what the fuss was about.

"What's going on?" I asked, spotting Toula and Rufus standing by the shaded windows. "Who's there?"

Before either could explain, an amplified voice from outside the building echoed through the door: "*Fotoula Pavli! This is your second warning! Come out with your hands exposed and surrender the prisoners!*"

"Apparently," Toula muttered, "I'm under arrest."

"For *what?*"

"The charges were a little muffled, but I'm in trouble with the Arcanum for liberating the three of you." She mumbled at the wall, and a dim green web appeared around the room, ringing it like a layer of paint. "He left them in place, but they're on standby," she said to Rufus, then squinted at the nearest patch of glowing magic. "And if I'm reading this correctly...yeah, this is more for camouflage than defense."

"Can you tweak it?" he asked.

She looked up in annoyance. "It's one big enchantment! You want me to work with *that?*"

"*Fotoula Pavli!*"

Rufus tapped the wall and made a face. "Got a better idea? Unless you can re-ward this in the next, say, sixty seconds…"

She growled low in her throat, but she planted her palms on the door and closed her eyes. "Feed it. I'll try to patch the wiring, but I don't have time to rebuild this and power it up."

"Roger that." He took his place beside her and touched the wards, and a brighter green spread from his fingertips as the enchantment came back online. "How long—"

"Longer if you keep talking."

While they were engaged, I sneaked a peek past the closest drawn shade and found a dozen men and women on the sidewalk, all dressed in black jumpsuits. They sported dark helmets as well, obscuring their identities behind smoked polymer visors, and black combat boots. I didn't need to see their outstretched wands and the active shields around them to identify them as Arcanum, but I noted something troubling about their uniforms. Arcanum security always wore a patch, a star of four crossed wands, marking them as authorized to use force. These wizards had no such markings, and they continued to bellow for Toula to come out.

A light flicked on in the building behind them—Mrs. Cooper, I realized, seeing her silhouette appear at the curtains. She'd gone home to bed around midnight, as had Rick, Vivi, and Hal, leaving Stuart to host Joey, Georgie, Toula, Rufus, Hel, and me overnight. We were supposed to finalize plans for Florida in the morning, once everyone had a few hours of sleep and Hel and Joey stopped sulking at each other, but this was, putting it mildly, an unexpected wrinkle.

The wards blazed, and Rufus said, "It's on. How

long—"

"Just another min—"

A concentrated blast from the wizards outside blew the front door off its hinges and threw Toula halfway across the store. "Shield!" Hel yelled, stepping into Toula's position, and Rufus knelt beside her with a wide shield glowing orange as she turned her attention to the unfinished patch. "Damn it, what were you *doing*?" Hel asked.

"Workaround," Toula mumbled, picking herself off the floor and patting the back of her head. "Can't cast the change directly. Got to cast the enchantment into changing."

"Oh…controlled damming, got it. Shit, this is going to take forever—"

"Li's Trident. Replicate…"

"*Oh*, gotcha…" Her hands danced over the wards as she continued the adjustments. "Joey, is she bleeding?"

He bent over Toula and parted her hair. "Not that I can tell—"

His examination was cut short by a second blast, most of which bounced off Rufus's shield and ricocheted to shatter a lamppost. "Goddamn it," Hel snapped, "who authorized lethal force?"

Toula pushed Joey aside and, with minimal weaving, returned to the door. "Those are assassins. That's the only kind of force they use."

"*What*?"

"Assassins," said Toula, redoubling her work on the wards as Rufus began to sweat. "That ain't security, sweetheart."

Hel began to sputter and stepped back from the door. "But…but to get authorization for an assassination—"

"—would take an act of the Council," Toula finished. "Greg said I was the fall guy for this, didn't he? Maybe we should have expected repercussions."

"Assassins over a jailbreak?"

The look Toula flashed her was almost pitying. "The

Council gets a chance to be rid of me, and you don't think they'll take it? And...*there*." She moved away from the wards, pursed her lips, then nodded. "Right, that should hold for a bit, but we need to evacuate."

"And get the Fringe folk out of here," said Joey, joining the other three by the door. "That means you, Stuart."

Our host began to protest, but Toula cut him off with a curt, "*No*. Go pack a bag, you're getting out of town until they stop looking for us here, and...oh, shit," she muttered as the door to Tea for Two opened, "what is she doing?"

From the shop across the street stepped Mrs. Cooper, wrapped in a fluffy pink bathrobe and sporting a head full of pin curlers. "Excuse me!" she called as she marched into the street. "Just what do you hoodlums think you're doing? It's three in the morning, and I'll have you know we have *noise* ordinances in this town!"

"Get inside!" Toula shouted out the hole where our door had been. "Eunice, *get back inside!*"

But Mrs. Cooper, who had once fought off faeries with a steel teakettle, ignored her. As the helmeted wizards turned to assess the newcomer, she reached into her robe pocket and extracted a small pistol, which she raised and cocked. "Don't make me call the police, now," she said calmly. "Get out of here."

"Mrs. Cooper," Joey tried, "they're armed, go—"

She looked past the helmets, straight into our building. "Get out of here," she repeated, her voice clear and steady, and I realized she wasn't talking to the wizards between us.

Toula turned around and ripped open a gate into Mrs. Cooper's tearoom. "What are you doing?" Rufus demanded. "With the defensive wards active—"

"Stay here, keep them safe," she ordered. "If I can't get back through my own wardwork, I deserve what's coming to me. Just try to distract them while I grab—"

The rest of that thought ended in a scream—high, strong, but brief—and a thud. I whipped back to the window and spotted a pink lump in the road behind the black suits: Mrs. Cooper, sprawled on the asphalt at the wrong end of a wand.

Stuart, who had witnessed the whole thing from the staircase, gasped and ran for the door. "Auntie Eunice!" he cried. "No, Auntie Eu—"

Joey grabbed him around the waist before he could bolt from the building and wrestled him to the floor. "You go out there, you're dead," he said, unable to hide the tremor in his voice. He sat on Stuart to pin him until he stopped thrashing. "I'm sorry, God, I'm so sorry," Joey continued as he held Stuart down, "but you can't help her."

The wizards outside, who had certainly noticed our wards by then, continued repeating their demands as if they'd never been interrupted. Toula closed the gate she'd just made, and I cut my eyes to Hel, who stared at the squad in slack-jawed horror. "That..." she whispered, "they can't do..."

"Want to bet?" Toula muttered.

Hel wheeled on her and jabbed her finger toward the street. "They just killed her! Little old lady! Holy...I don't even, I...what did..."

Toula grabbed Hel by the shoulders and squeezed until my sister stopped babbling. "Here's what's going to happen," she said quietly. "We've got to run, Carver. Taking that squad out first probably won't stop the Arcanum, but it might buy us a little time. And as I find that I'm suddenly in the mood for blood, I'm going to kill as many of those sons of bitches as I can. Rufus, you in?"

He'd paled, but he rolled up his sleeves and nodded.

"Now," she continued, staring into Hel's wide eyes, "you don't have to go out there if you think you can't hack it. I understand. If you think you can, though, I wouldn't mind making this duet a trio."

"Helen, wait a minute," Joey began, but she shook her head and looked back at Toula.

"They just killed a barely-armed mundane," she muttered. "I can't stand for that."

"You're in, then?"

"I'm going to be the grand magus," she snapped, pushing Toula off her. "Of course I'm in. And Joey…"

Having released Stuart, he stood a few feet away, watching her with tight shoulders. "Are you sure about this?" he murmured.

Hel stormed across the distance between them, grabbed his face, and pulled him into a long kiss. "Not at all," she said when they broke apart. "So if something happens to me, you'd better damn well take care of my baby brother."

It was Joey who pulled her close that time, and she lingered in his embrace until Rufus said, "Ms. Carver, will you be joining us sometime this century?"

She kissed him once more, quickly, then headed for the door. "Shields ready?"

"Yep," said Toula.

Rufus eyed Hel curiously. "Do you, uh…do you want a wand or something?"

My sister looked at him with disdain. "I'm sorry, but what part of 'grand magus' was unclear?"

"*Wait.*"

Toula groaned in exasperation and turned back from the vanguard. "No, Stuart, you're not going out there, end of discussion. Play wizard later."

"I'm not pla—oh, forget that," he said, and pointed to the armchair in the corner of the store and the worried occupant curled up on its seat. "She's the dragon I saw in Faerie?"

More or less, Georgie replied.

Stuart jumped at the mental intrusion, but recovered almost immediately. "Can you breathe fire?"

She nodded. *Here, yes. I can't do it in Faerie, but here, the magic's different—*

"Then for crying out loud," he exclaimed, throwing his skinny arms in the air as he turned back to the three at the door, "why not use the sentient flamethrower before you run out there and get shot?"

"Okay, first," Joey snapped, getting in Stuart's face and putting his extra five inches to good use as his hackles rose, "Georgie is *not* a 'sentient flamethrower,' got it? That's my partner, that's my friend, and she can barely get around right now, so why don't you back off before we lose anyone else?"

It's getting easier...

"Don't help him."

"Actually," I mumbled, "he's got a point." Joey flipped on me with dagger eyes, but I stood my ground. "Not out the front—across the street. Those three take the main line, Georgie sneaks up from the rear. If she's up to it?" I added, looking at her.

Georgie nodded emphatically. *If I could lean on someone, just in case...*

"If you're going, I'm taking you," said Joey, scooping her out of the chair. "Toula, gate."

Hel opened her mouth, but she held her peace and muttered under her breath as Toula ripped the universe open again. "If you go out there," Toula warned him, ignoring Hel's distress, "you're going to be beyond the wards, and there isn't going to be much I can do from here to help you if you get in trouble."

"Just take care of Helen," he said, then shifted Georgie onto his hip, patted his sword for reassurance, and stepped through the tiny wormhole.

The fatal flaw in the Arcanum's assassin squad was that there had been a dearth of targets in recent years. Official policy was to avoid faeries unless confrontation was absolutely critical, which left few opportunities to practice clean kills. Sure, the wizards out front were magically talented and coordinated, but they didn't have a full handle on our situation, and so Rufus, at least, was a nasty surprise for them to face.

They didn't have to look at him long, however, because

the far nastier surprise was the little girl in Joey's arms who paused in the doorway of Tea for Two, took a deep breath, and incinerated half the force. As the rest of the wizards stumbled around to see why their fellows were screaming and flailing, Toula, Hel, and Rufus took the opportunity to rush out from the store and attack them from the rear. In the chaos, the squad didn't last long.

When the last fell and was smoldering in the street, Stuart and I emerged to check for survivors and hurried to Mrs. Cooper's side. But try as we did, we couldn't find a pulse, and even Stuart gave up after a few minutes, stepped to the sidewalk, and sobbed. With some hesitation, Georgie wobbled over to him and patted his back. *I'm really sorry I set her head on fire*, she thought. *That was an accident.*

Hel and Joey stood together, their arms around each other for mutual support, and stared at the carnage. Toula was busily pulling the helmets off the dead to ascertain their identities, and I looked to Rufus, who lurked on the edge of our group with an odd expression on his face. "Good shooting," I told him. "Two torso shots in two seconds—wish I had aim like that."

He nodded, smiled weakly, then turned around and vomited in the gutter.

While Rufus lost the last of his dinner, Toula came over and produced a glass of water from memory. "First kill?" she murmured, holding it out to him.

"Yeah," he croaked, taking the glass with a shaky hand. "What gave it away?"

The ghost of a smile crossed her face, and she waited while his stomach calmed. "Aiden's right, that was some nice shooting. Hunt much?"

"No, skeet. About forty years ago." He straightened, rinsed out his mouth, and spat into the storm drain. "So, you're going to make me feel better and tell me your first time was like this, too?"

"Nah. I knocked off Titania, and then my mother showed up, and it all went to hell. No puking, just a lifetime of angst to work through." She looked around at the corpses in the street, then closed her eyes and spread her hands. In an instant, the dead had vanished, and Toula stopped Stuart before he could cry out. "No bodies means fewer questions," she murmured, "and there was nothing we could have done for her. Magic can't always do miracles."

He rubbed his eyes dry and sniffed, but his chin continued to tremble. "In the Circle, there's talk of dark—"

"Stuart, please, not now," she said wearily. "We've got to hurry."

He gave up and let Toula lead him back into his building. I started to follow, but I reconsidered and ran up into Mrs. Cooper's apartment first to turn off her lights.

It was the least I could do.

By the time I got back through the wards, Toula had gathered everyone in the store and assumed command. "We can't know which of us they're tracking," she told Hel, who stood by with her arms crossed. "My blood's on file, yours certainly is…I bet they've got a sample on Aiden, too, and if not, all it would take to find both of you would be a finger prick from Daddy. But they've got finite personnel, so we may as well make them split and stretch. Come on, Carver," she murmured, "you know I'm right."

Hel considered this in tight-lipped silence for a moment, then muttered, "Doesn't mean I have to like it."

"Who said anything about liking it? This is about evasive maneuvers, not vacation planning." She looked around the room, considered our numbers, then pointed to Rufus. "We need someone with talent on the Florida excursion. Up for it?"

"Sure," he replied, frowning, "but what about—"

"*He* has to go along," she explained, nodding to me, "and my job right now is to stay the hell away from him."

"Wait," I said, pushing toward her through the display tables, "what am I doing? Where're you going?"

Toula sighed and ran her hands through her mussed spikes. "We're trying to get a meeting with Grivam, right? Well, you don't just ask a king for a chat unless you're decently connected. Our best shot might be if the request came from you."

"Me?" I mumbled, feeling queasy.

"High lord trumps Greg's gofer," she replied with a smirk. "So you're going. Rufus, you're the muscle, and you're going to have to send the message down."

"I don't even know where we're heading," he protested.

"Which is why Percival's going with you," she continued, pointing to Joey. "And to be safe, let's throw in Thunder Lizard."

Georgie, who was leaning on a table of paperback grimoires for balance, rolled her eyes and thought, *I do have a name, you know.*

"But you're such fun when you're peeved," Toula replied, then turned her attention to the remainder. "We need to get Vivi, Rick, and Hal up and packed. Stuart, you're going with them. Carver..." She considered my sister for a few seconds, then said, "You know the Arcanum hubs as well as I do. Keep the mundies under the radar until we can rendezvous. I'm going on the run, but I'll be in touch."

"A suggestion," said Rufus, seeing Hel's unease. "My parents' home. They've all been guests before."

"Maybe so," said Joey, "but since, you know, we're trying to sneak up on *Oberon*..."

He shook his head and held up two fingers. "First, I don't think that's going to be nearly as great a problem as you anticipate. Second, if I tell them there's an Arcanum hit squad after Vivi, they'll do whatever it takes and tell the old bastard to screw himself."

"Protective much?" Toula muttered.

"Of the baby, their only daughter, the *mortal?*" he countered. "Why would that surprise you?"

While Toula woke the others and delivered the bad news, Rufus stepped behind the counter and borrowed

Stuart's landline to make the arrangements. One brief call later, he returned and flashed a quick thumbs-up. "They're all expected. How soon?"

"Rick's on the way," Toula replied, then pointed to the gate floating to her left. "Hel just went through to help Vivi pack. Coach is having to make up a family emergency and put calls in before they leave town." She watched as Stuart lugged an overstuffed black Samsonite down the stairs, then asked him, "Cats?"

"Remarkably...resourceful," he muttered, punctuating his words with the thumping suitcase. "They have...a cat flap."

"Just remind me to deactivate the wards, then," she replied. "And hey, Stuart?" He dragged his case to the floor and turned to her, and she murmured, "I'm really sorry, man. She was...*quality*."

"Thanks." He glanced at the floor for a moment, then added, "Don't suppose they make them like that anymore, do they? We had our differences, but Auntie Eunice..." He sniffed and angrily swiped at his face. "There's no body. She deserves a funeral at least, she would have wanted that Reverend Martin guy to do it..." His voice trailed off, and as he hugged himself, he seemed to lose about twenty years.

Rufus stood in awkward silence as Stuart fought back a fresh bout of tears, then asked, "Would you have a good-sized piece of wood, by chance?"

"I...well, I've got a little out back," he replied, puzzled, "but it's just firewood, and it's still wet after the rain Saturday morning..."

"Never mind, I can make that, too." Rufus closed his eyes and gestured, and a fat log appeared in the middle of the store. "Please don't be offended," he said, then spread his hands over the log. As the enchantment took effect, the wood morphed into Mrs. Cooper's form and features, down to an off-white nightgown and a mask of cold cream. "Glamour," he explained before Stuart could object. "Unless someone puts samples under a microscope, it should pass embalming without much notice."

Stuart hesitated, then touched the figure's bare hand. "Still a little warm," he declared, surprised, and pressed harder against the fake flesh. "And it feels right…"

"Best I can do." Rufus waited while Stuart completed his examination, then said, "If we put her in her bed and lock up, the person who finds her will think she passed in her sleep. No fingers pointed at you, no unsolved homicides. Acceptable?" Stuart nodded, and Rufus levitated the body from the floor. "Toula, would you get the gate?"

She opened a fresh one and watched them as they set about arranging the decoy in Mrs. Cooper's bed. For the first time since I'd met her, Toula looked her age. Granted, this was only about a ten-year difference, but she seemed drawn, as if the bluster had finally gone out of her. "You all right?" I asked.

"Ha." She turned away from the gate, frowned at a flurry of motion on the floor, then plucked one of Stuart's cats out of its latest hiding place and rubbed its ears. "Honestly? I'm about as far from all right as I've been in a while," she said, running her fingers down the rumbling cat's neck. "Eunice Cooper was one of the good ones. She was always kind to me, and that…" Toula paused and swallowed. "That's rare, you know?" She shifted the cat to her shoulder and stroked its back, and when she resumed, her voice was lower and harder. "Greg never said anything about an assassin squad. Either he's lost control of the Council or he's a sick bastard, and I don't like those choices. So no, Aiden, I'm not all right. But I'll make do."

Rufus and Stuart stepped back through the gate, and the cat, suddenly terrified, hissed and jumped from Toula's arms. "Sorry about that," said Rufus, rubbing the back of his neck as the cat scrambled for cover. "Did I interrupt something?"

"Faeries," she muttered, closing the gate with a flick of her fingers.

"Oh, look who's talking," he retorted, and followed her

toward the staircase.

"What do you mean? Animals love me."

"Only because you're confusing."

Stuart and I watched them go, and when the apartment door slammed, he quietly said, "They're scared to death, aren't they?"

"Looks like it," I replied, and spotted Georgie picking her way around the tables. "Need something?" I asked her.

No. She caught herself just before tripping into a ceremonial drum, then steadied her steps, walked up to Stuart, and threw her arms around his waist.

He stiffened, surprised to find himself in an ambush, then bent and hugged her back. "Thank you," he mumbled into her hair.

I really am sorry about setting her on fire.

Stuart patted her shoulders and sighed. "Just don't eat my cats."

It was only four in the morning when the last of the stragglers showed up with a suitcase, but there was no sense in waiting for dawn. "Be careful," Rufus told Vivi, stooping to kiss her cheek before she passed through the gate to their parents' place. I could tell she'd been crying—her face was still splotchy and bore telltale mascara tracks—but for the moment, she was holding it together. "Did you pack a coat?" he asked her.

"*Rufe.*" She pushed her smudged glasses down her nose and met his dark eyes. "Don't worry about me, okay? And don't do anything stupid out there."

She hugged him, grabbed her bag, and passed through the gate to join Rick, Hal, and the elder Stowes, and Rufus gave his parents a little wave as he beckoned my sister forward. "Helen, you're up," he said, but she lingered for one last kiss from Joey.

"If you get yourself killed out there," Hel whispered, "I will never forgive you. Got it?" Joey squeezed her and let her slip free, and she looked up at me. "Same for you, Aid. Don't be a hero. Come back alive. Understood?"

"I don't have to kiss you, too, do I?"

She punched me in the stomach and attacked me with a too-tight hug when my defenses were down. "Call when you can," she said when she released me. "When it's safe, when you've got a phone—"

"We'll call," Joey assured her, and he watched her go until Rufus closed the gate behind her. "So," he muttered, looking at the few of us remaining, "time to hit the road?"

"Get on your way—I'll lock up. And here," Toula offered, then opened another gate onto the parking lot of a seafoam-green stucco motel with a giant pelican on the roof. "I remember seeing this place when we drove through Miami," she explained. "It's maybe three hours to East Rock Key from there. Get a room, get a car, whatever you need. And speaking of which, did anyone think to bring a wallet?"

Joey nodded and shouldered his bag. "Take care of yourself, Glinda."

"Shut up," she said, flashing a weak grin, and watched with Stuart's jittery cats as we trundled off into the cool predawn.

CHAPTER 6

As the odds of finding an open car rental place before sunup were slim, we decided to check into the motel for a few hours, if for nothing more than a place to sit. Leaving the rest of us and his sword in the parking lot, Joey headed inside to book a pair of rooms. Rufus had offered to pay, but Joey turned him down and flashed a debit card, explaining, "I've been making trips out of Faerie. Boss wanted me to be prepared."

Joey neglected to mention that most of these trips had been to Nashville, but from the look Rufus gave me as Joey trudged toward the sliding glass doors, the subtext was clear. I gave him a half-smile in return—it was the most I could manage that night—and Rufus leaned against a palm tree and sighed. "You may have noticed the young man trailing after my sister like an oversized kitten," he said, tucking his hands behind his head. "Just stay out of it, Aiden. Believe me, unless someone's getting hurt, it's the best thing you can do."

I didn't know how he was comfortable standing there with his shirt sleeves still rolled to the elbows. The night was chilly, and along with my coat, I was glad to have Georgie leaning against me. Her balance had vastly improved in the last day or two—she probably could have toddled around on her own—but with the fire burning inside her, she was the functional equivalent of an electric blanket, and I didn't mind holding her steady.

When I said nothing, Rufus considered me more closely. "If you're not in the mood for conversation, tell me. Then again, I don't know about you, but I'd talk about the tax code with an IRS agent if it meant I didn't have to think about what I just saw."

He had a point—I kept seeing Mrs. Cooper's crumpled body behind my eyes, and the last thing I wanted to do was cry in front of the others. "It's not that I'm against them dating," I replied, forcing the raw image from my mind, "it's just...*weird*. I mean, he's my friend, and that's great, and she's my sister, and that's great, but putting them together..."

He chuckled softly. "She's still the obnoxious big sister who bossed you around and took all the good toys, isn't she? It's clear that she still thinks of you as the weakling to be protected."

That rankled me, but I tried not to let on. "Hel's always looked out for me. It's not *weakness*—it's a matter of being stuck with a pack of armed sadists and no access to guns."

"I didn't say you were weak. I said *she* still thinks of you as weak." He gave me a careful once-over and closed his eyes. "Personally, I think you'll surprise her one day when you find your footing, but that's going to depend on you, kid."

"And what's that supposed to mean?" I snapped as sorrow and fear morphed into anger.

One eye cracked open, and the corner of his mouth twitched. "Vivi tells me you're bright. You haven't said much, but I know you've been listening. Someday," he said, watching the lobby, "you're going to stop believing that opening your mouth always invites a beating, and when that day comes, I bet you'll be amazing. But it's not going to come until you convince yourself that you're more than just a weakling to be protected." He pointed to the lobby doors. "That kid's not much older than you are. Doesn't have a shred of magical ability, does he?"

"No..."

"And that hasn't stopped him, has it?" Rufus watched me try to formulate a response to that, then said, "I don't know everything that happened to you in that damn silo, but I've heard bits and pieces. Aiden..." He struggled for a moment. "Look, this is going to sound incredibly hypocritical, but you don't need magic. Don't get me wrong," he hastened to add, "it's great, and I'm glad I don't have to do without it, but I'm the exception. Stop and consider how many *billions* of people there are in this realm who don't even know it exists, who go on without it and do amazing things. Look at literature, look at art—or if you want something more concrete, look at NASA. You think magic put a man on the moon?"

I shrugged. "It could."

"Maybe, maybe not. The natural gates open onto the surface of this world, right? Do we have any idea how far magic radiates? I mean," he said, folding his arms, "in theory, you could open a gate from Faerie directly onto the moon, but I doubt it's ever been attempted. And if something went wrong with the enchantment, poof, you're very, *very* dead." He caught my look of incredulity and began to flush. "I've given this some thought, all right? I lived through the sixties. But all I'm saying is that a lack of magical talent doesn't make you weak. *Mundane* is such a poor term for it—there's nothing mundane about you, or about him," he said, jutting his chin toward the hotel, "or about my sister, or her fiancé, or that poor lady..." Rufus paused and stared into the night in silence. "I've known plenty of mundanes," he said after a long moment. "They've been passing through my classroom for the last sixty years, and let me tell you, some of them are among the most extraordinary people I've ever met." My brow creased, and he grinned at my bemusement. "American history, University of Southern Alaska. Joined up after I got my PhD and stuck around until they slapped *emeritus* on my office nameplate and told me I could teach whatever the hell I wanted."

"*You?*"

"Why not? What was I supposed to do, sit around in my

parents' basement for the next thousand years? I get out, I write, I go to conferences in Cleveland—and I don't think you're too young to appreciate the scenic beauty of a town overpopulated by coeds." He smiled wistfully at the deserted parking lot. "So listen to someone who's had more experience with so-called mundanes than those Arcanum idiots ever will. You're not weak, Aiden—you just don't know your strength yet. And here he comes…*yes*, plastic keycards," he said with relief, hoisting his duffel as Joey flashed a pair of paper envelopes. "I take it you don't have the metal sensitivity, right?"

"Lucked out," I replied, wrapping my arm around Georgie to lead her inside. She had almost dozed off standing up, and she shuffled slowly around the few cars in our path.

"Then you can't fully appreciate the wonder that is modern hotel keys," said Rufus. "Or any keys, for that matter. We went to keycards about ten years ago across campus—it was such a joy to not have to paint my office keys with liquid plastic. Now," he said, glancing at Georgie, "let's just hope this is the sort of establishment that doesn't think twice about two grown men, a teenage boy, and a sleeping girl checking in at four a.m."

Fortunately for us, by the time we made it into the lobby, the desk clerk had already retreated to the back room and the taped wrestling match Joey had interrupted, leaving no witnesses but the security camera as Joey carried Georgie in and Rufus and I took up the rear. The place stank of ammonia, and the overhead fluorescents buzzed and sputtered, but no one complained. Aesthetics didn't matter at that hour.

Our rooms were a few doors off the lobby, and though the walls were thin, any neighbors we had appeared to still be asleep. Joey and Georgie took the first room—no one wanted to have to explain where he was if she woke in a panic and couldn't find him—leaving Rufus and me with a bed apiece and basic cable.

With the door locked and latched behind us and the air conditioner chugging in spite of the chill outside, I found myself at that odd intersection between exhausted enough to drop where I stood and too wired to close my eyes. I stretched out on the old palm tree–patterned bedspread and tried to sleep, but my mind kept replaying the last two hours, a pernicious highlight reel that alternated between Mrs. Cooper and the mob of dead wizards. Frustrated and still riding the adrenaline surge that had carried me through the night, I sat up and stared at the bluish twilight out our window until Rufus stirred behind me and asked, "You drink coffee, kid?"

"Today? Sure." I turned and found him lying on his back, gazing at the Greenland-shaped water stain on the ceiling. "I think I saw a coffeemaker in the bathroom, if you want me—"

His finger twitched toward the cheap dresser, and a pair of steaming mugs appeared. "That was an offer, not a request. And if you're wise, you won't use those things," he added. "You never know what else they've made besides coffee."

"Oh?"

He grimaced. "A few years back, half the department went to Denver and got snowed in for three days. We had a grocery store down the street, and most of us made do with cereal and microwave dinners, you know, as one does, but a couple of my TAs got creative with the coffee pots. 'Poached Salmon à la Ramada,' they called it."

"That's disgusting."

"No, what was disgusting was the fact that the fish had overtones of artificial orange—someone had cleaned the carafes with furniture polish. Or so I was told," he hastily added. "I wasn't about to get near that mess. And then the little geniuses tried it again with the *department* coffee pot, and there was a near riot…well, long story short, the TAs bought us an apology Keurig, and they lived to graduate."

"Noted." I helped myself and returned to my bed, and Rufus sat up and waved his coffee across the room. "Feeling lazy, are we?" I asked.

"This could be a long day. I may as well make the best of it," he replied before drinking deeply. "Magic does have its little perks."

"You must have freaked out when Faerie sealed off. Having to actually get out of bed to get your food…"

He put the coffee aside and whistled. "That was *terrifying*, and I thank my lucky stars our spring break is early. By the end of that week, I couldn't hold a glamour together to save my life. Holed up in my apartment with Netflix and a mystery flu until the magic came back." He shook his head at the memory and reached for his mug again.

"You seriously couldn't get by without glamour?"

Rufus chuckled and drank. "I did mention the 'emeritus' part of my title, yes? I've been operating under my real identity all along—had to put together a face to match, see?"

As I watched, his dark hair thinned and whitened, his face wrinkled into crevasses and developed a crop of dark splotches, and the hands wrapped around his mug grew gaunt and bony, the skin translucent over raised blue veins. "I won't be able to keep this identity much longer, I'm afraid," he said in a voice suddenly raspy and weak with age, "but I hate to let it go. Starting over is going to be such a pain." Instantly, he was young again as the glamour dropped, and he sipped his coffee while I goggled. "Come, now," he said with a smirk, "surely you've seen that trick before."

"Well, yeah," I replied, "but not to that extent…"

"I suppose no one really wants to look ninety-one," he mused. "It's not an easy act to keep up—appearance and voice are simple, but you've got to remember to move slowly and at least pretend you're brittle. On the plus side, I can ignore half of what's said at department meetings and chalk it up to poor hearing," he added. "I'm missing one of the damn things today, in fact. Can't say I'm altogether sorry to be in Miami again, though I wish it were under better circumstances."

I drank, burned my tongue, and forced the hot coffee down. "What if he won't talk to us?"

"Grivam?" Rufus leaned back against the headboard and sighed. "We'll think of a Plan B, then. I'm still trying to figure out how to get a message to him in the first place."

"When Coileán did it, he just put his hand over the water, and a beam of light came out of his palm or something." I blew on my drink and shrugged. "Look, if you want specifics, I'm the wrong guy to ask."

"No, that's...that's actually helpful," he said, frowning at the ceiling. "Assuming Joey knows where we're going and where to find a boat, I can *probably* do something along those lines. It's either that or stick my head underwater and try yelling."

"And what if Oberon's still there?" I asked, ignoring his attempt at levity. "Or what if he left a skeleton crew or something?"

Rufus waited for a moment as I stewed, then said, "Cross your bridges as you come to them. As for this one..." He thought briefly, drumming his fingers on his mug. "Well, I suppose the safest thing to do would be to leave the three of you a few miles back up the road and scout out the island alone. If he does have people waiting, I won't set off any alarms. Might even be able to get information that way without bothering with the merrow," he added, perking up. "See? Crisis averted."

I drank in silence, keeping one eye on the glow in the east, then looked back to find Rufus watching me. "We have to get over there," I muttered.

"As soon as we can rent a car."

"Not the island—Faerie." He said nothing, and I glared at the slow-rising sun. "Coileán's in trouble. I can't help him from here."

"And you can't help him by running in blindly, either,"

he pointed out. "Thirteen dead already, son—I'd rather not add to that tally, if it's all the same to you."

"But I've got to do *something*," I protested.

"You are, and you will," he said in a voice that brooked no argument. "And for now, drink up."

As I learned that day, Joey could function surprisingly well on limited sleep if given sufficient caffeine and a plate of waffles enchanted out of the ether. By nine, we were on the road south in a rented Toyota, Joey at the wheel, Rufus riding shotgun (and sporting a pair of gloves, just in case), and Georgie and me napping against the car doors. I felt bad about conking out on Joey, but without so much as a learner's permit, I was useless. In any case, Rufus seemed to intuitively know just how much conversation to make to keep the driver conscious.

The morning—or what little I saw of it—was gorgeous, partly cloudy and rising out of the mid-seventies, a welcome change from the last few days in Montana and Virginia. Traffic on Route 1 was light heading out of Miami, and I woke periodically to glimpses of the sea as we wove through the northern Keys. Admittedly, I missed most of the scenery, and I didn't snap back to full alertness until Joey pulled the car to a stop in the parking lot of a little strip mall in Key West. I realized that the sun was high and warm, and then my stomach suggested that lunch might be an excellent option.

"Oh good, you're alive," said Joey as he turned in his seat. "Here's the drill: the three of us are going to get something to eat," he explained, pointing to Georgie and me, "and Rufus is going to backtrack and have a look at East Rock. Does that work for everyone?"

I nodded, and Georgie blinked blearily beside me. "How're we meeting up again?"

Joey flashed what appeared to be a black iPhone. "Rufus'll call us when he's heading back. Also," he said, glancing at Rufus, "you should know that I'm keeping this. Boss may have untold power, but the best he can do is a *flip* phone."

"See, this is why TAs are useful—they make me stay current," he replied, carefully unlatching his seatbelt. "And yes, do what you like with it. My number is programmed in already. Do you have an address for Oberon's bar, by chance?" he asked as he pulled his own phone out of his blazer.

As they talked logistics, I helped Georgie out and held her upright until she found her footing again. *Where...* she began, squinting at the cars around us, then thought, *I smell meat.*

I looked behind me and found a burger joint in her sights. "Wait just a minute, okay?" I said, wondering how long Rufus's breakfast platter of ham would hold her.

Georgie scowled but made no complaint. A moment later, I caught her with her eyes closed and her face turned skyward, basking in the afternoon sun. "Feels good?" I asked.

Very.

I thought of all the times I'd caught her stretched out beside the barn with the same expression on her face and smiled to myself.

By the time I'd guided her out of the way of the parking lot flow, Rufus had taken the wheel and was pulling onto the street. Joey stood beside the vacated space with his hands in the pockets of his jeans, watching our rental car disappear. "My sword's in the trunk," he said quietly.

"That's probably a good thing," I replied, "considering we're, you know, in *public.*"

"Yeah, but I don't leave that with just anyone," he said, then gave me a long look. "We don't know him well, and we're trusting him with a lot."

My guts knotted as the lunchtime traffic passed around us. "Has he said someth—"

"No, no," Joey said, cutting off the question before I

could ask it, "but I'd feel a lot better if our bases were covered."

"So would I, but in light of the circumstances…"

A car pulled up in front of us and flashed its headlights, and we stepped away from the empty parking space. "Nothing to be done for it now, I guess," said Joey as he steered Georgie toward the smell of burgers. "At least we can check in with Helen, right? Stop her from coming after me in my sleep."

I followed them toward the restaurant, skirting an errant balled-up paper sack. "Okay, I know she's persistent, but she's not *vicious*."

"Maybe not, but I make it a point these days to piss off as few magically inclined folks as I can. Safety first."

With Georgie happily devouring half a dozen hamburger patties, Joey pulled out his new phone and called my sister. "We're alive, we're in Florida," he said as soon as she picked up. "No one panic. How're things up there?"

I timed the ensuing silence. Joey listened for a solid five minutes, adding occasional monosyllabic responses to prove that he was still on the line, then told Hel he loved her and put the phone away. "How bad?" I asked, pushing the remnants of my fries to Georgie.

He made a face and picked at his cold burger. "Well, let's see. Toula's been in three time zones since we parted, and there's a squad one step behind."

"She can't…disable it?"

"Oh, no, that's not the problem—she says she's killed four assassins this morning. The reinforcements just keep coming. There's a death warrant out for her."

"*What?*"

"Keep your voice down," he muttered, glancing at the neighboring tables, but the other diners seemed too engrossed in their meals to pay us any attention. "Vivi and her buddies have been busy moles, apparently. The Fringe hacked into the Arcanum's network, and Vivi's been helping herself to their communiqués all morning."

"Considering that half the tech crew in the silo can't be trusted to program a VCR, I'm not surprised," I replied, "but a *death* warrant? What the hell, man?"

"I know." He closed his eyes and rubbed his forehead. "There's a warrant out for Helen, too, and for the three of us," he said quietly. "Arcanum's had a crew outside the Stowes' place for the last few hours, but no one's breaking that standoff—five wizards out in the cold, freezing their asses off, against at least two well-seasoned faeries and Helen? If those idiots got through the door, they'd be toast."

"Yeah," I muttered. "So they're tracking Toula and Hel...what about us?"

"Vivi says they got a twenty on us about an hour ago, but the current order is to hold back."

"Did she say why?"

Joey smirked and bit into his burger. "Ever seen a wizard in the Keys? This is Oberon's turf. They don't know if he's still lurking, and they don't want to find out the hard way."

"So," I said, raising my voice a notch as Georgie noisily sucked the burger juice from her fingers, "if he doesn't finish us off, they'll get us when we're on the road?"

"Bingo, bud." He took another bite and grimaced. "Food's about the last thing I want after that news, but I guess I'd better keep my strength up. You, too," he added, pushing my half-eaten fries back toward me. "Go on, Georgie's had enough grease without those."

I don't do vegetables, Aiden, she added, snarling her nose.

I added more ketchup and watched Georgie mop up her last crumbs. "The grand magus takes covering his tracks to a whole new level, doesn't he?"

"Forgot to mention that," Joey said between bites. "Looks like Harrison's on house arrest, or whatever you people call it." He looked up from his lunch, found me gawking with a fry halfway to my open mouth, and shrugged. "Yeah, Helen didn't sound too pleased. Council had a no-confidence vote after we ran—guess they saw through his cover story. All of these warrants and hit squads are their doing."

"*Shit*," I whispered.

"Exactly. He's not going to be able to help us, so let's hope Rufus isn't feeling too back-stabby today." Joey picked up his soda cup, rattled the ice inside, and rose. "Need a refill. Georgie, honey, that's mine," he said, giving her a warning look as her hand crept toward the last of his burger, then walked off while I tried to make sense of the rapidly unraveling world.

We couldn't sit in the restaurant indefinitely—not when we had no idea what was waiting for Rufus or when he might be back—so we took a short walk across the island toward a public beach. Georgie, at least, was full and decently rested, and she was happy to flop down in the warm sand and nap while Joey and I sat beside her and fretted. I offered to keep watch if Joey wanted to sleep—the shadows under his eyes seemed to darken as the caffeine wore off—but he turned me down. There was a hotel just down the street, and we discussed our contingency plan: get a room overnight, find a car in the morning, and decide whether we could risk leaving the island with targets on our backs.

But shortly before three, Joey's phone rang, and he answered it on speaker. "What's up?" he asked as I scooted closer to the outstretched phone.

Rufus's voice, though somewhat distorted with static, sounded almost happy. "There's no one here," he reported. "Not a soul. The island's deserted."

"You're sure?" Joey asked.

"Positive. There's a few trespassing warnings posted, but other than that, it's empty."

"What about the bar? Did you check the outbuildings? And the houses—"

"I'd have checked them if they existed. But I mean it—the place is empty. Sand, trees, sea oats and scrub, and a wide patch where the road ends. I'm standing where this bar of yours should be," he continued, "and there's not even a cigarette butt. It's *gone*."

"You don't think there's, like, a glamour on it or something?"

"Joey," Rufus sighed, "give me a scintilla of credit. I'd know a large-scale enchantment if I ran into one."

"Sorry," he muttered.

"And where are you? Still eating?"

"We're on the beach," I chimed in. "Straight across the island. Are you heading back? And by the way, the Fringe says the Arcanum's going to have a hit squad on us as soon as we're far enough north. Just putting that out there."

He grunted. "Delightful. Get back to the strip mall—I'll open a gate by the Dumpsters, yes? Call me when you get there."

The conversation ended, and Joey stood and shook the sand off his clothing. "Moment of truth?" he murmured.

"Looks like it."

He bent to nudge Georgie awake. "Then let's get this over with. I guess there are worse places to die than Florida."

Half an hour later, hidden in the shadows beside the world's most odiferous trash bin, we stepped back as a gate appeared and Rufus walked through with a clothes-wrapped bundle in his arms. "Looking a little pink, there," he said, frowning at Georgie's blossoming sunburn. "And here," he continued, passing the bundle to Joey. "I'm sure you feel naked by now."

Joey pulled the shirts back to reveal the hilt of his sword. "What—"

"Saw it in the trunk. Sorry about the laundry, but I'm not touching that without better gloves." He pulled his pair from his pocket and showed us the holes burned through the fingers. "Need to buy new ones. The ones I enchant whole-cloth don't stand up to repeated exposure."

I noticed that he'd wrapped band-aids around his right fingertips. "You're burned?"

"Not too badly," he told me. "I've had far worse. But anyway," he said, turning back to Joey, "I thought that would make you feel better. I mean, if the Arcanum drops in, at least you might stab one of the bastards before you go."

He passed Rufus back the clothing and quickly belted his sword on with a low, "Thanks, man."

"Not a problem," said Rufus, ignoring Joey's discomfiture. "Shall we?"

The three of us followed him back through the gate onto a lonely stretch of white beach. Once the rift closed, the only sounds beside our footsteps were seagulls, the gently rolling waves, and the rustle of the palm leaves overhead and the long grass up the dunes. Joey stopped in his tracks and turned in a circle, scowling at the empty horizon. "Okay," he said slowly, "the bar was *there*"—he pointed to an empty patch of dirt at the end of the road—"and the houses started back that way…"

If I hadn't previously seen the island developed, I might have thought Joey was delusional—there were no footprints but ours, no car but our rental, and no indication that East Rock Key had ever been more than a nature preserve. Even the road was partly covered with a thin layer of the ubiquitous fine white sand, which appeared to be unchecked in its re-conquest of the place.

"So," said Rufus, carefully sliding his injured hand into his pocket as he surveyed the island, "seeing as we have a bit of privacy, what do you say we go fishing for mermaids?"

Procuring a boat was a minute's work for Rufus, who rubbed his chin, squinted at the sand, and imagined a sturdy wooden rowboat into being. "Backup propulsion," he explained as he levitated it down to the water. "In case something happens to me, I'm sure you'd rather not drift out into the Atlantic."

We climbed aboard, and as Rufus skimmed us over the waves, Joey directed the craft around the island to a sheltered spot and called a halt. The sun was beginning to dip, and for the moment, we were the only boat traffic in the vicinity. "This is the place?" Rufus asked.

"As far as I remember," Joey replied. "But even if we get a message down, there's no way to know how long he'll be in coming up. Hard to hurry Grivam."

"Well, then," said Rufus, stretching his injured hand over the light chop, "I do a mean Chex Mix, if I do say so myself. Here goes nothing."

I watched as a bolt of light shot through the green water and disappeared. Rufus retracted his hand, blotted it dry on his trousers, and shrugged as he produced a plastic bottle. "And that's that, I suppose. Who needs sunscreen?"

After a little convincing, Georgie allowed Joey to rub the lotion onto her reddening face and arms—*Tell me again why this is preferable to scales*, she thought, wincing as her fine coating of sand turned to sandpaper on her tender skin— and Rufus, as promised, did his part to keep us fed and hydrated between drifting us back toward the meeting spot. As the sun set, he produced a few glow sticks—no metal parts, unlike flashlights—and Joey called up cartoons on his phone to keep Georgie entertained. I sat back on the last bench and watched the stars pop out of the indigo sky, regretting that I couldn't turn off the bright haze from Key West on the horizon. Light pollution was seldom a problem in Faerie, but sometimes I missed Montana's predictable stars—or at least, what little I'd seen of them.

Joey finally allowed himself to doze after a dinner of sandwiches, and Georgie slid into the bottom of the boat beside him with the phone, her new favorite toy. I'd begun to think that a catnap might not be a bad idea when something large splashed beside us, the boat rocked, and a pair of hands gripped the side. Georgie sat up in a panic, but Rufus called a fireball into being on his palm, revealing the merrow king's webbed gray hands and hairless, cetacean head off to port. "Who would summon me?" he asked in Fae, looking about the boat before one of his black eyes settled on me. "Ah, young Aiden," he said, flashing too many teeth in the merrow approximation of a smile. "Now, isn't this surprising."

"Lord Grivam," I said, wishing my voice would hurry up and finish dropping, "I'm sorry to trouble you, but I've come to ask a favor."

"Indeed?" He gave the others a second look and paused on Joey, who had woken and sat up in the commotion. "Ah, yes, I remember you," he said, favoring Joey with another of his predatory grins, then cocked his head at me and waited.

I took the hint. "My companions," I said, trying not to stutter. "These are Rufus and Georgie."

Grivam nodded to each but focused on Rufus, who still held his flame aloft. "I was wondering who sent the message," he said, "in light of present company." With that, he turned back to me and hooked his elbows over the side of the boat. "So, young Aiden, you wish to bargain?"

I exhaled to calm my nerves. "No, my lord. I want you to honor your bargain with my brother."

His inner eyelids blinked slowly once, twice, as he held my stare and I held my breath. "I do have an arrangement with Coileán," he finally replied, "but we never made the benefit transferrable."

"And I seem to recall Coileán giving you shelter without question and destroying the monster that was hunting you," I retorted. "The latter of which was above and beyond the terms of your agreement. You owe him, my lord, and you know it."

He blinked again and briefly flashed his teeth. "Big words, young Aiden."

had set up a decent fire and Joey had contained it, Rufus had created a billowing pavilion of the type seen on brochures for Caribbean resort spas. The walls and canopy, little more than thin gauze to keep out the flies and admit the breeze, stretched around four plush beds and over a teak floor. Candles hung in lanterns around the tent and squatted under glass globes on low tables between the beds, casting a warm light around the room. A quartet of wooden chairs ringed the makeshift fire pit and the whole spitted pig that was coming to a crispy finish. Even more bizarrely, Rufus had erected a bathroom in a wooden outbuilding a few feet beyond the tent, complete with a hot and cold shower and sauna.

You can try to dissect and understand magic, or you can roll with it. I chose the latter, collapsed into a chair with a huge helping of roast pork, and watched for meteors until late in the night.

I had hoped that Grivam would return in the morning, but the sun rose with no sign of him. Rufus made breakfast, Georgie wrapped herself in white sheets against the sun, and Joey and I paced the beach, waiting for a familiar gray tail to break the surface. Noon passed quickly—as did Joey's leftover pork barbeque sandwiches—and by dusk, even Georgie had emerged to search the sea. Rufus took a good look at her burns, set up a small enchantment to speed her healing, handed her a tube of aloe, and sent her back to bed.

By Wednesday, we'd moved beyond restless. Joey and Rufus went so far as to spend the morning snorkeling, and when even that failed to raise a blip from the deep, Joey announced that he was going back to Key West for provisions. I thought he was just looking for a reason to get off the island, but he quickly set me straight: "If we've got down time, I'm building a nail gun," he explained. "Served me well in the past, and that's one thing Rufus can't make for me."

He left at lunchtime, promising Georgie he wouldn't be gone long, and returned mid-afternoon with two fully laden plastic bags, one from a hardware store and the other from a sporting goods shop. The first went onto a table Rufus made for the occasion, far in one corner of the pavilion, where his odds of being hit by stray iron were slimmest. The second was dumped onto my bed, and Joey divided the contents between the two of us. "Boot knife," he said, passing me a slim blade in a black leather holster. "Bowie knife. Multi-tool. Here's a belt to hold everything on…"

I tried the belt and shifted under the unfamiliar gear strapped at my hips. "What, you couldn't get another sword?" I teased.

He looked around the tent, then plucked a full bronze blade from off his bed. "I asked Rufus to make this while I was gone. Softer than mine, but it's something," he said, passing me the hilt. "That's about the size of your practice sword, right?"

I tested the weight and balance, then nodded. "Not as useful as iron."

"There's not exactly a blacksmith in Key West," he replied with a snort. "You're going to have to use a two-blade technique—slash with the bronze, stab with the Bowie at close range."

Neither of us discussed the obvious as we divvied our gear. No word from Grivam in two days could only mean bad news from Faerie—and bad news could only mean that someone would have to go over.

I just hoped my sister didn't get wind of it before we were on the other side. Oberon was one thing, but I did *not* want to see Hel angry.

CHAPTER 7

Wednesday night came and passed without greater incident than an amateur fireworks show from a neighboring island. While Joey kept testing his gun and returning to the table for tweaks, Rufus and I sat outside, playing chess by firelight and trying to field Georgie's questions about the game. Having taken a walk down the island at sunset, I'd realized why we had no curious boaters coming ashore: Rufus had thrown a massive sort of glamour over our spit of sand, disguising the tent, the outbuilding, and even our fire pit as scrub and shadows. Once outside, I could see the contours of the enchantment, fine pink lines stretched in an iridescent bubble over our makeshift compound.

I've wondered from time to time what the world must be like for those who can't see magic. Trying to explain what I see around me is sort of like trying to explain color to the colorblind—non-sensitives just don't have the framework to understand what I'm saying. For instance, what does it mean to a colorblind person if I say a chair is green? What is *green* to someone without a conception of color? That quality of the chair simply can't be perceived, no matter how many adjectives you throw at it.

Telling a true mundane about the way I view the world is much the same. I look around and see the neat workings of spells, the chaotic jumbles of enchantment, and bursts and streaks of wild, untapped magic in its vibrant spectrum—which includes colors that don't have standard names in any language. I see the ways magic is shaping my environment. My understanding is that mundanes see none of this—magic is undetectable to the vast majority, which boggles my mind. The closest I've ever come to knowing how mundanes go through life was that brief period in which Faerie was closed off—it was incredibly weird, like watching the world fade to black and white. Imagine growing up in Oz and suddenly finding yourself in Kansas, wondering where the hell all the Technicolor went.

In any case, the folks who passed by our island had to have been mundanes, as Rufus's enormous, yet surprisingly neat, enchantment and our resort-quality digs drew no attention. His camouflage was almost too good, in fact, as our messenger nearly missed us when she came ashore Thursday morning.

Shortly after dawn, as we were demolishing another of Rufus's buffet breakfasts—I don't know about the others, but indolence in a tropical paradise gave me an appetite—a willowy young woman walked out of the surf like a naked, bedraggled Venus. She padded a few feet up the beach, looked around with a little scowl, then leaned to the side and wrung out her long black hair.

Catching sight of her, Joey jumped out of his chair, goggling like he was seeing a ghost, then ran down to the shore to intercept her. "Ilunna!" he called, waving to get her attention. "Ilunna, over here!"

The naked woman—Ilunna, I gathered—straightened and looked around in confusion until Joey ran through the barrier of the enchantment. She stumbled back in shock—seeing someone appear from thin air might reasonably make you do that—and he caught her before she tripped. "Hello, again," he said in Fae as he steadied her. "Been a while—"

Having regained her balance, Ilunna grabbed Joey's face and went in for a passionate kiss. As Joey flailed, Rufus chuckled in the chair beside me, and Georgie frowned at the scene. *Are they going to mate?* she asked us, turning for an explanation.

"Judging by that reunion, I'm guessing they already have," said Rufus. "I mean, I'd heard that the merrow were…uh…*physical*…"

"I'm guessing that's the legendary Merrow Chick," I offered. "And yeah."

Rufus laughed again as we watched Joey extricate himself from the damp embrace. "Ilunna," Joey gasped, "it's nice to see you, too, but I've got a girlfriend, I can't—"

"Can't what?" she replied, bemused. "And you learned to speak properly! Silly boy, when did that happen?"

"Can't…*that*." He looked back up the beach and frantically beckoned for us to join them, and Ilunna beamed as we appeared from behind the invisible wall. "Uh…Ilunna, this is Rufus, Aiden, Georgie…"

If Joey had been planning on proper introductions, Ilunna saw no need for the formality. Rufus stood closest to her, and so he was the second of us to get a kiss—and the first, I couldn't help noticing, to return the gesture with any skill. Both were slightly flushed as they separated, and without further warning, Ilunna's open mouth was pressed against mine. Being sixteen and less than inexperienced, I was too startled to attempt any of the techniques I'd only read about, and if Ilunna was expecting to find something with her gently probing tongue, she came away only with a hint of the bacon I'd just eaten. Still, she smiled when she released me, and I gazed after her in a reverie as she approached Georgie.

But Georgie was having none of it. *Forget it*, she thought, holding her hands in front of her face. *Ew. No.*

Ilunna paused, thrown in her rhythm, and cocked her head. "Have I offended?"

"Not at all," said Rufus, who had somehow managed to hook his arm around her waist while I was distracted. "The little one is actually a dragon. Now…Ilunna, was it?" he asked, leading her up the beach. "May I offer you some refreshments?"

As they wandered toward the barrier and disappeared, Joey stepped close to me and murmured, "All right there?"

"Uh…"

He patted my back. "First real kiss?"

"Uh-huh."

"With tongue, no less."

"Yeah," I mumbled, still tasting the salt of her lips on mine.

"She's too old for you," he said quietly. "About Helen's age." I gave him a sharp look, and he held up his hands in placation. "I'm just telling you, that's all. And keep in mind that this isn't her default mode," he added, lowering his voice to a nearly inaudible level. "Merrow, remember?"

I stared at him steadily, saying nothing, and Joey finally rolled his eyes. "Okay, I'm not going to lie and say it was unpleasant, but once you know what merrow really look like...more teeth, less, uh...*that*..."

Rufus stepped back through the bubble, interrupting Joey's clumsy attempt at imparting the wisdom of experience. "We're waiting, kids. Is something wrong?" he asked, then caught sight of my expression and grinned. "Oh, Aiden," he said, shaking his head, "no. She's not just out of your league—she's not playing the same *sport*."

Coileán had told me about the free-loving tendencies of the merrow, but I had never seen someone so comfortable in her own skin as Ilunna was on the beach. She lounged in a wooden Adirondack with her legs crossed, swinging one foot to an unheard rhythm, and sipped from the oversized goblet Rufus had given her. The glass's contents were strongly pink, its wide rim crusted with sugar and adorned with a hibiscus blossom, and I wondered just how many college bars he'd had to frequent to come up with that concoction.

The scene looked like a spring break fantasy come to life, complete with an overly affectionate coed, but Ilunna quickly revealed the brains behind the window dressing.

"Father said you needed a spy," she told me, grinning as she brushed her salt-stiffened hair from her face. "So I presented myself to the king. A goodwill ambassador, you understand."

I could readily imagine how much goodwill Ilunna would generate by walking into a room. "Did you see my brother?"

She shook her head and sipped her drink. "No, I did not. Father told me where I would find him—the path from the shore to the old queen's palace is clear enough, if long," she added, absently rubbing her foot. "He wasn't there. The old king was."

The lovely, warm memory of Ilunna's lips faded, and I felt sick all over again. "How, uh…I mean, what did you…"

Ilunna waited for a moment while I fumbled for the words, then put her drink aside and clasped her hands in her lap. "I don't know the courts on sight," she explained softly, "and I can't relate the names of all those I saw. You'll forgive me for saying this, but the lot of you look very much alike."

I let it slide. "But you saw Oberon? Did you speak to him?"

"Of course. He was gracious—his people showed me about the upper world and gave me comfortable quarters. *Confusing*, but comfortable," she muttered. "I dined at his table for two days, but he seemed uninterested in physical pleasures," she added with a little frown. "Please be honest—is this form unpleasant to you? If something is amiss, I'd rather know."

I could only gawk, but Joey jumped in to fill the silence. "You're gorgeous," he said, "and if Oberon wasn't, um…*receptive*, then he's probably got something on his mind."

She beamed at him, momentarily making me forget my troubles. "Oh, good. Mother says upper-worlders are odd about joining, so I didn't know if his reaction was normal."

Joey glanced at me, then at Rufus, and asked her, "His reaction to…what?"

"Well," said Ilunna with nonchalance, "I've found that

people are usually more willing to talk after joining, so I tried to join with him after our first meal. He excused himself, and I thought perhaps I had caused offense."

Beside me, Joey muttered in English, "Do *not* say anything."

"If he chose not to join with you," said Rufus, sliding into the breach, "then he's a blind fool. But you say he's living in Titania's palace?"

"Yes, exactly," she replied. "I saw nothing of Coileán— I never even heard his name. The mood was…festive, I suppose. So I learned what I could, and here I am." She spread her hands, retrieved her drink, and tucked the floral garnish behind her ear.

"How about the security situation?" asked Joey. "Were there many guards?"

She nodded. "Everywhere. I was never alone with Oberon." Looking around the fire pit at the four of us, she said, "Truly, I don't know what's become of Coileán, but I *can* tell you that Oberon is in Faerie."

"Any sign of Valerius?" I asked, but Ilunna only shrugged.

"I was never introduced to anyone of that name, so I'm afraid I have nothing to offer you. And that's all I can do— Father has forbidden me to go back there," she continued apologetically. "Court conflicts are dangerous things, you understand."

"Yes, and thank you. Believe me," I muttered, "you've done more than the Arcanum would."

"So my father's debt is repaid?" I nodded, and her shoulders relaxed. "Good. I had hoped not to disappoint." She glanced around again, and her dark eyes settled on Georgie. "Forgive me if this is rude, but did I hear you were a *dragon*?"

Georgie snorted and bit into a cold strip of bacon. *Why, need something roasted?*

Ilunna seemed unfazed by the telepathy—but then again, I had no real idea of how the merrow communicated when they were underwater. "No, I just didn't realize you could shapeshift."

We can't.

"Ensorcelled," Joey explained.

"*Ah.* That can't be an easy transition. I mean," she continued, seeing Georgie's face work, "mine is difficult enough—balancing on these silly things takes practice." She raised her foot and wiggled her sandy toes.

Georgie's crimson eyes widened. *YES. And this,* she thought, tugging at her hair with her bacon-free hand. *What's the purpose? It doesn't warm, and it's one more thing to be washed. And all the bathing...* She shook her head and sighed. *And the clothing. I just don't understand.*

Ilunna frowned in confusion. "Why wear it if it bothers you? I don't see the point, either."

At that, Georgie leaned forward and jabbed her finger at Joey. *You see? Do you hear that?* she thought excitedly.

"I did," he replied, rubbing his face, "and I'm telling you that walking around in the buff isn't subtle."

The merrow shrugged. "Subtle or not, it works for me."

I can't be sure, but I think I heard Rufus whisper, "Thank you."

As Ilunna was pleased to see Joey again, she was thrown when he explained that getting physically reacquainted was out of the question. "It's not that I don't like you," he hurriedly explained in the face of her befuddlement, "and last time was...uh...great, but I have a girlfriend now." This garnered only a blank look, and he added, "Who is a wizard. And who would be very upset if I cheated on her."

"It's an upper-world thing," Rufus explained, slipping into their twosome at just the opportune moment. "Alas, the boy is spoken for. If you just wanted a little amusement, however..."

Ilunna gave him a once-over, cocked her head, and grinned, and I watched as the two of them disappeared into the pavilion together.

When the curtain dropped behind them, Joey perched on the arm of my chair and muttered, "Unbelievable."

"He *is* single," I said.

"And she's, like, twenty."

I shrugged. "Faeries, man."

"You're telling me." He paused, considered my expression, and punched me in the shoulder. "Dude, *no*, you weren't going to get any of that action. I don't care if she volunteered."

"Look," I protested, "just because *you're* attached—"

"I promised Helen I'd take care of you. That means no merrow until you're legal. Deal with it."

"Killjoy."

"The term you're looking for is 'responsible adult,'" he replied, and downed the remainder of Ilunna's pink concoction while we watched the sea and waited for the party to end without us.

To his credit, Rufus only stared wistfully at Ilunna's disappearing wake for ten minutes or so before getting his head back in the game. "All right," he said once the other three of us could reenter the bedroom, "what's our next move? Coileán's MIA, we have no data on Valerius, and it sounds like Oberon's made himself at home. Plan? Want to head up to Alaska and coordinate? We can't stay here forever," he added. "The Arcanum's going to wise up eventually and realize the danger is past."

Joey met my eyes and nodded, and I looked back at Rufus. "We're going over. Today, if possible."

"*Today?*" He grimaced and sank onto his bed. "You did hear Ilunna say the place was guarded, yes?"

"Which is why we need you to let us into the backcountry," I said. "Let's get some camping gear together and try to sneak in."

"Aiden," he said, rubbing his closed eyes, "you know

that's not safe—"

"Nothing is safe! There isn't a safe option! What do you want me to do," I asked, "wait around and hope the Arcanum doesn't get me? Hole up in your parents' guest room? Wait for Toula to surface? Hope Coileán spontaneously appears and figures this out?"

"I'm just saying that it isn't safe. I never said I wouldn't help you…though it would just be the two of you, you know."

"Understood."

No, not understood. Georgie sat up and shook her head. *I'm going with them.*

Joey dodged her glances for a moment, then sighed and murmured, "Sweetie, you can't. Aiden and I can stay low, but…I mean, we can't hide you. You're huge."

She looked at him incredulously. *How much smaller do you want me to be?*

"The problem," Rufus explained, "is that the spell on you now will break as soon as you enter Faerie, and neither of those two can redo it."

Georgie stared at us, shocked and momentarily confounded, and her eyes began to well. *I'm not leaving you, Joey,* she insisted.

He stood and crossed to her bed, then sat beside her and pulled her against his chest. "It's just for a little while," he soothed. "I'm going to keep you safe. You'll go with Rufus, and he'll take you to Helen…right?" he asked, glancing over the top of her head.

"Exactly," said Rufus. "You'll stay with my parents. Mother does a lovely whole roast chicken—"

But her sniffles had turned into full sobs by then, and Joey rocked her while she cried. I could feel the fear in her unguarded thoughts, ringing in my head like the buzz of a muted television in the next room, but I had no comfort to give her. As Georgie cried, Rufus and I rose and left her with Joey on the off-chance that he'd know what to say.

Once outside the tent, Rufus shoved his hands in his

pockets and contemplated the tranquil sea. "It might be safest if you used a permanent gate," he murmured. "If the realm's keeping an eye on things, you might get through under its radar if I don't punch extra holes in the world."

I shaded my eyes against the late-morning sun. "You know where to find one?"

"Actually, yes. There's just one *tiny* problem."

"Which is?"

Rufus slowly exhaled. "The gate's in Glastonbury."

I grew up in the Arcanum's heart, but the middle of nowhere, Montana, hadn't always been the center of the magical world. The organization was born from a prolonged series of hostile takeovers, and for most of its existence, its headquarters moved around Europe among a set of castles owned by the oldest and most prestigious of wizard families. Sure, it wasn't an egalitarian system, but it worked well until the nineteenth century, when enough wizards looked around, saw the direction the rest of the world was heading, and decided that leadership should be based at least nominally on merit. The first new-blood grand magus set up a system of installations, each overseen by a magus and his subordinates, where wizards could congregate and their children could be educated in spellcraft. Those installation heads were ultimately responsible to the grand magus and his local magi, the Inner Council, who governed from a castle in Glastonbury for a hundred years until World War I convinced the Arcanum to consider relocation once again.

In the mid-1960s, the grand magus saw the potential in the giant missile silos being built across the American West, assembled a team to hex one in Montana, and managed to buy the property for a song. When he moved in, he announced that the silo would henceforth be known as "Arcanum 1," and much of the rest of the American and Canadian wizard community followed him underground. The other installations were now officially designated

Arcanum 2 through 7. Some were fairly unpopular—not many wizards wanted to live in Mongolia—but Arcanum 2, the magically camouflaged castle hidden to the southwest of the Glastonbury Tor, was always a bustling community.

I'd never been to Glastonbury. Hel had, however—the grand magus saw to it that she went on a slew of field trips—and she'd come home with stories about the place. Disguised as a patch of trees and a field, and protected by wards that subtly discouraged trespassing, the castle was everything a wizard could want: properly atmospheric, spacious, and, wonder of wonders, above ground. True, living next to a bunch of hippies on a perpetual quest for the Holy Grail could be somewhat grating, but as a kid, I would have given my right arm for a study-abroad program at Arc 2.

Then again, with the Arcanum's hit squads after me, the thought of an English vacation no longer seemed quite so exciting.

Waiting for sundown in Florida would put us in Glastonbury in the middle of the night, the safest time to go sneaking around. Still, the thought of popping over blind didn't sit well with us, and not only because I couldn't say exactly where Arcanum 2 was located. I couldn't just call Hel and ask for pointers—she'd have thrown a fit had she known what Joey and I intended to do—but Rufus had a backup source who knew how to keep a secret, even if she wasn't gung-ho for our plan.

"You're idiots, you know that?" said Vivi, her voice made tinny by Rufus's speakerphone. "This is grade-A idiocy. Hey, want me to call ahead? Make reservations at the castle for you? Have an escort waiting?"

"If you could arrange a limo, that would be superb," said Rufus, rolling his eyes, "but I suppose I could make a sedan work. In the alternative, how about asking your little friends on the ground what we should anticipate?"

"Call them my 'little friends' again, and so help me, I'll shove a railroad spike up your ass."

"Love you."

"Jerk," she muttered fondly over the sound of tapping. "All right…I've got a couple of folks online. Let me make some calls, and I'll get back with you. And you're still idiots."

"Ta," said Rufus, and she was gone.

While waiting for Vivi to call, we took stock of our gear. Joey and I had weapons, at least—he'd honed his sword and completed his nail gun, and I'd finally found pockets and belts for the small blades he'd given me—but we weren't prepared for an expedition. With a little work, Rufus soon had us kitted out with sturdy camping backpacks, sleeping bags, fuel, and even cooking implements. "Aluminum," he said apologetically. "Light, but not as strong. I'd give you steel, but—"

"I'm not asking for a miracle," Joey interrupted as he fit the little pot and plate into his bag, then paused and frowned. "Which I say as you make several thousand bucks' worth of gear appear out of thin air. *Damn*." He looked up from his packing. "When did my standards get so warped?"

Rufus smirked. "How long have you been living in Faerie, again?"

"Probably too long, all things considered. Well," he said, shrugging, "if this is normal, I'm not going to fight it."

"That's the spirit, lad. And how do you like your jerky, bland or insanely hot? I've never been good at splitting the baby with that one."

By mid-afternoon, our packs were stuffed with the necessities—we wanted to travel light, but with no set timeline for our excursion, we over-prepared. The greatest concern was food; foraging was an option, but there are few prey species native to Faerie, and there was no telling if we'd encounter anything edible that had wandered over from the mortal realm. Rufus did the best he could, filling our packs with dried meat and fruit and homemade MREs, but even that seemed paltry for a trip any longer than a week.

There was still no word from Vivi, and so I returned to

the beach for a little last rest in the waning sunlight while Georgie again tried to talk Joey into letting her come along. I'd just settled into one of the Adirondacks when Rufus approached and handed me a glass bottle. "Take the edge off."

I lifted it close and smelled beer. "This is the real deal?"

"Of course. I don't do that Natty crap," he replied, pulling up a chair beside me. "I don't care how long you live—life's too damned short for terrible beer." He sat back, swigged from an identical bottle, closed his eyes, and sighed. "Enjoy this while it lasts, too. October isn't exactly peak season in the old country. You'll want that coat tonight if we're going to skulk around the Tor."

"The old country? Thought you were American," I teased. The beer wasn't bad—Coileán had been breaking me in with low-alcohol brews, and aside from a slightly stronger burn, I couldn't tell the difference from Rufus's concoction.

"I am. My parents aren't." He drank again, deeply, then twisted the bottle into the white sand at his feet. "Brit on both sides. Well, *English*—there wasn't a unified Britain back then." He looked over, saw me watching him, and turned back to the sea. "Born around the start of the fifteenth century, both of them. Mother's the elder by a few years, but they're close. Changeling brats, you know."

Rufus didn't have to spell it out. The Arcanum had taught me little in the way of practical magic, but my limited lessons had included a litany of the evils faeries had wrought upon the world. Stealing helpless humans, imprisoning them for decades, and turning them out to die when they tired of them was at least in the top ten fae atrocities.

Unable to read his expression, I tried to proceed with caution. "When Oberon left…"

"Oh, they were gone long before he moved away," he replied. "Half fae don't always have the best time of it over there, and they decided to get out. Took their parents with them," he continued, staring at the dusky horizon.

"Mother's father was from Yorkshire, Father's mother was from Nottinghamshire. They actually considered themselves married." He glanced at me again, saw my raised eyebrow, and smirked. "Apparently, they got together around the time that their children were developing feelings for each other. No shared blood, no scandal."

"Still."

"It was what it was," he replied with a shrug. "Anyway, my parents decided to leave, and they offered to take their changeling parents with them. Father said he thought the four of them might set up house together for a time, at least while everyone was acclimating."

"Didn't happen?" I ventured.

"Not in the slightest. Everything was great until they got over—they started in York, as I recall—and then my grandparents told my parents to leave and never come back. You know, I'm sure they weren't thrilled to find themselves suddenly twenty-odd years older, and I suppose being abducted and held against their will turned them *slightly* against all things fae, but their own children…"

He let the thought hang, and I nodded to my beer. "Your grandparents and my dad would probably get along well."

"If they weren't five hundred years dead," he agreed, retrieving his beer. The fine crust of sand around the lower third of the bottle sprinkled onto his khakis as he drank, and he absently brushed his lap clean. "Well, I assume—my parents never saw them again. They roamed, had a son, settled down, had another few sons, moved when the time came, had more sons…tried their luck in the States in 1839, kept moving north and west, kept having sons. The last three of us were born in this country. And Vivi, naturally," he added, drinking again. "A few of the older boys went back to England, but we talk occasionally. Don't always have much to say, you know."

"You're not close?" I asked between swigs.

"Depends. The kids, Harry and Vivi—sure. And my youngest older brother, Leonard, was living at home when

I came around, so we're friendly enough. He's a painter, our Leo. But, say, *Ned?* That's my eldest brother, Ned," he explained, catching my confusion. "He was five hundred sixty-four last April. Grew up during the War of the Roses. I mean, he's a good chap, but we don't have much in common, you understand." He paused for a drink. "What's the spread with you and yours?"

"My siblings? Four and a half years with Hel...seven hundred ninety-seven with Coileán."

He grinned. "Did the math, did you?"

"An approximation. *He's* not even sure of his birth date. Tacks on another year when January rolls around and says it's close enough."

"Sounds like my parents." Rufus closed his eyes again and let the breeze tousle his hair as I drank in silence. After a moment, he murmured, "I was the youngest of our bunch for forty-three years. They'll stop treating you like a child eventually, but it'll take some time."

I finished my beer and sighed. "Hel still treats me like I need a babysitter. Any idea when that's going to stop?"

"Aiden," he chuckled, turning my empty bottle back into nothingness, "my mother still chides me if she catches me going out the door without carrying a coat, just in case. Some things never change." He twitched as his pocket began to vibrate, then rose enough to pull his phone out and put the call on speakerphone. "Is that you, favorite sister?"

Vivi snorted. "I'd better be your favorite sister. And I've got news for you."

"Took you long enough," he replied, dropping me a wink.

"What part of 'news' did you not hear?" she snapped.

Rufus's expression clouded. "Is everyone—"

"We're safe, and Toula's come over. Someone down south recalled the assassin teams."

"Oh?"

"Yeah. I've got a folder of Arcanum communiqués right here. There was talk of suspected faerie movement near the silo until this afternoon, and then the lines went quiet."

He stood and picked up the phone. "You're joking."

"Not in the least. I've got a buddy in Moscow who's trying to patch us into the silo's security cameras, but it's taking time. Bastards do have a few protocols in place, as it turns out," she muttered. "Anyway, the long and short of it is that something's going down in Montana, and I don't have a ton of intel at the moment. All we've got is that the other Arcs are on standby."

"Meaning?"

"Meaning that if you numbskulls want to go climb the Tor tonight, you might be able to slip in and out without a squad on your heels. Got it?"

"Got it." He hesitated for a moment, then said, "Vivian, listen to me. Whatever's going on at the silo—"

"I'm not stupid."

"I'll be there soon," he said, and hung up. When he turned back to me, his eyes were worried, and he pointed to the pavilion. "Load up. If you're going, you're going now."

CHAPTER 8

"It's strange, you know."

I glanced around at our pack as we trudged across a field toward the night-black hill ahead. Three guys, two loaded down and ready for a stint in the wilderness, and a sniffling girl hugging her arms against the chill, sneaking into a park long past sundown—nothing out of the ordinary, really. Then again, it was nearly eleven on a cold Thursday night in Glastonbury, and not many of the locals seemed to fancy a hike. "What's strange?" I asked Rufus.

"The To—oh, *shit*," he muttered, pulling his shoe from a pile of partly-hardened droppings. He permitted himself a tiny flame in his cupped hand, which he kept well shielded from view, and held it just long enough to assess the damage and will his tread clean. "Why don't people clean up after their pets?" he quietly griped as we pushed on. "And I was saying that the Tor is strange. You've got a natural gate, a *stable* natural gate, sitting on top of a substantial iron deposit. Ever seen the Chalice Well? It runs red. Ferrous oxide all through it."

"You've done the tourist thing around here, huh?" Joey whispered, plodding along a step behind him.

Rufus grunted. "Interdisciplinary conference in Bristol back in the nineties. One of my brothers was staying in Bath at the time, and he offered to show me the sights before I went home. So we passed through Glastonbury, and he dared me to try the water."

"And you *did?*"

"He said it would just tingle. Brothers can be real

assholes, you know that?"

"Only child," Joey replied.

"Must be nice on occasion." He paused and pointed to a paved footpath, barely made visible by the waning moon. "Straight up, then. Stay low, stay quiet, and if we have to separate, meet at the top as soon as you're able."

I took the rear, following Georgie to ensure that she didn't get left behind. The path was smooth enough, and our good luck held—I didn't see another soul on the hill. My eyes adjusted as I puffed along, gradually revealing to me more than just the clouds of my breath: dormant grasses lining the trail, a red chip bag tossed by the way, the undulations of the Tor's terraces as we crossed them. After a few minutes of silent hiking, I looked back over my shoulder at the lights of the town below, hearing little besides our footsteps and the distant hum of passing cars.

Joey was the first to break the monotony. "Looked this place up while we were packing," he said when we called a quick halt for a breather. "Legend says there's a fairy king living in the hill."

"It would surprise me if Oberon *didn't* know about this place," Rufus replied. "And the gate's hidden—enough time, enough convolution, and sure, the story makes sense."

"Legend also says King Arthur's buried around here," he said, and pulled out his phone. "I can show you the page—"

"Oh, I'm sure he's around here somewhere," said Rufus with a dismissive wave. "Maybe he's on the Tor itself, I don't know. There are bound to be skeletons in any direction if you dig deep enough."

I couldn't quite make out Joey's expression, but he sounded incredulous when he spoke. "You're saying there's really an Arthur?"

"Fifth- or sixth-century chieftain with great PR, as I heard it. Get a guy with martial prowess, give him a companion who's half fae and up for a little adventure, add a band of swords, and let it stew for a few centuries. Of course, it's all tenth-hand by now, so take that for what it's worth." Rufus shrugged and stuffed his hands in his pockets to warm them.

"But the Grail legend—"

"Later addition. The Grail makes a nice quest story, but the Arthurian canon is nothing but a patchwork of tales strung together and assigned to a cast of characters. Read the *Morte*, did you?"

"Unfortunately," Joey muttered. "You get stuck with a name like Percival…"

"Ouch. Family name?"

"Family of Ren Faire aficionados. And who cares if there's nothing Arthurian about a Ren Faire? It's all horses and swords and m'ladies and giant drumsticks, so Mom and Dad got to let their freak flags fly when it came time to name me." He paused to look at the quiet night around us. "So of course, now that I'm grown and don't actually have to spend weeks at a time playing at Merrie Olde England, I'm questing around England with a sword strapped on. Figures."

"They cursed you," Rufus concurred.

The wind gusted on the hill, and Georgie slid closer to me. I hugged her as well as I could, wishing we'd been able to convince her to wear something more substantial than a T-shirt, and she shivered against me even as her midsection burned. Noticing our awkward embrace, Rufus flicked a finger, and Georgie found herself wrapped in a heavy black parka. "Told you," he murmured, then nodded to the tower at the summit. "Shall we?"

We trooped the rest of the way up in silence, even Georgie, whose faint psychic wheedling at Joey I'd overheard for the last couple of hours. When we crested the Tor, I took a moment to survey the formless panorama below, a black landscape dotted with clusters of lights beneath a partly-shrouded swath of stars. I could pick distant Arc 2 out of the shadows by the spellwork encasing it, a monstrously large, flickering silver bubble that put

Rufus's beach work to shame. It shone in the night, a lighthouse glowing in the middle of a dark sea, made all the more prominent by the lack of visible light. "There's the castle," I said, tapping Joey's shoulder and pointing, but he could only squint and shrug.

What castle? asked Georgie, joining us at the edge of the path.

"Arcanum 2," I replied, making room for her between us. "See the silver?"

No...

"Dragons smell magic," Joey explained. "She's as blind as I am."

Rufus, who had come closer while we took in the view, offered a quiet snort. "Gaudy, if you ask me. That's like Vegas popping out of the desert." He turned and gestured toward the stone tower rising from the top of the hill. "Gate's in there. Come on, let's get this over with."

I followed him toward the ruined church, a black monolith against the sky. There was little left of it, only a buttressed tower with empty arched doorways, roofless and open to the elements, and I looked around in vain for a hint of a gate. As if sensing my thoughts, Rufus pointed downward, and I noticed a faint trace of magic glowing in the floor. "It's beneath us?" I whispered as Joey and Georgie wandered in.

"Exactly. As I've heard it told, the architect of the church was an Arcanum plant—they built over the gate to keep idiots from wandering through. It's never been totally accessible," he continued, squatting over the stones, "but putting a monastery over it was one way to keep it under wraps." Rufus spread his hands, frowned, and looked back up at us. "I'm sorry, but this feels like such a cliché thing to do. Open the mountain, send the hapless heroes into Faerie..."

"Who're you calling hapless, bub?" said Joey, smiling weakly as Rufus's palms began to glow. "Come on, we've all got places to be."

His eyes were uncertain in the faint light. "You're sure about this?"

"No, but I'm not seeing a better idea right now, are you?"

"Well, no," Rufus admitted, "but it's...you know, I've become somewhat fond of you two over the last few days, and—"

"Open the pod bay doors, HAL."

He chuckled in spite of himself. "All right, Sir Percival. But you must realize that once you're through, you're stuck. I'll have to put the floor back together, and unless you're packing a chisel in there..."

"We'll manage," I said, trying to sound more confident than I felt. "Right, Joey?"

He nodded. "We'd better."

Rufus opened his mouth again, but whatever he had planned died unspoken. Shaking his head, he turned his attention to the task at hand, and Joey and I stepped back as the floor rose in chunks. The outline of the gate glowed purple in the earth, but in the light of Rufus's illumination, I could see water rippling on the other side—a trans-dimensional lake at the top of the Tor. "How deep does this go?" I muttered, nudging the surface of the water with my toe.

"No idea," said Rufus, who held the floor aloft like a Tetris board come to life. "I've never been across. You *can* swim, yes?"

"Reasonably well," said Joey, reaching into a pocket of his pack. His hand emerged a moment later with one of Rufus's homemade green glow sticks, which he cracked and shook to life. "Well," he said, looking around our little circle, "I guess this is it. Rufus, you, uh...take care of yourself, okay? And Helen. And—"

Georgie threw her arms around him and squeezed, and Joey hugged her tightly before he pulled away. "I'm coming back," he told her, stooping to her eye level. "I promise you, sweetie, I'm coming back."

Can you keep that promise? she asked as her red eyes welled.

"Going to do my best." He hugged her again, then nodded to Rufus and stepped to the gate's edge. "Come on, Aiden, let's do this."

"Wait." Rufus wiggled a finger beside our backpacks, then stepped aside to join Georgie out of the splash zone. "Waterproofing. I figured it couldn't hurt." He cleared his throat and waved us on, and Joey plunged feet-first into the dark water.

I gave them one last look and felt my throat clench. "Tell Hel I love her, okay?" I said, and jumped before my doubts could get the best of me.

I sank like a stone.

Swimming lessons had never been a priority in the silo, possibly due to the fact that we were living in the middle of a pasture and hadn't installed a pool. I suffered through the swimming unit in first grade—our gym teacher had almost drowned in a lake as a boy, and he strove to impress upon us that water was a foe to be conquered, not our friend—but I wasn't going to win any awards for style. I could dog-paddle with the best of them and execute a convincing dead man's float, but anything beyond that turned into an uncoordinated mess of flailing arms and legs and quick breaths that occasionally led to choking on inhaled water. In other words, I could save myself well enough to pass gym, but it wasn't pretty.

But this wasn't the overly chlorinated concrete pool with its faded lane lines and reliable heater. This water was icy and black, shocking in its coldness, and I almost gasped before I remembered that I couldn't breathe the stuff around me. Sputtering, chest burning, I continued to sink, weighted by my gear and my clothing. I looked about frantically for the surface, but the water was ink in all directions, and I panicked, sure I was going to drown.

Just then, I spotted a green light high above me, waving

back and forth like a beacon, and my tennis shoes hit soft mud. Calling upon whatever strength I had, I pushed myself off the bottom and struggled for the light, hoping I'd reach the surface before my air gave out. But the light remained stubbornly small, and the thrust that had propelled me toward it began to slow with the drag of the water. I floundered, grabbing for anything solid, but felt only water and weeds around me. Kicking and clawing, I fought the need to breathe and closed my eyes, willing myself higher even as I knew I didn't have the strength…

…and something grabbed my wrist and yanked.

The night wind on my wet face was the single best sensation I've ever felt, and I sucked in a huge gulp of air before falling into a violent fit of coughing. I choked myself trying to expel the water from my lungs, and by the time I could breathe again—painfully, but at least I was breathing—I realized that the hand on my wrist had become an arm around my chest, towing me to shore. I gave in and floated, too exhausted to fight. A moment later, the back of my head hit something firm, and the arm hauled me onto the grass.

"Still with me?" Joey panted.

I lay there on top of my sodden backpack, shaking with cold and adrenaline, but nodded and croaked, "Thanks, man."

"Worst gate *ever.*" He shucked off his bag and rose, holding his glow stick like a flashlight as he turned in a slow circle. "Does any of this look familiar to you?"

Reluctantly, I unstrapped my bag and squelched to my feet. We were standing on the bank of a large pond, which lay in a little clearing surrounded by thick woods. If there was a path through the trees, I couldn't see it. The moonlight we'd enjoyed in Glastonbury was gone, the unpredictable stars were next to useless, and the raw magic drifting around me was as helpful as an after-image. "Nope," I muttered.

But as I continued to scan our surroundings, something

seemed to pull me in one direction, and I stopped to give the scenery a second glance. There was nothing different about the woods on the other side of the pond, nothing to set them off from the ring of trees around us, but *still...*

"I think we go that way," I said.

"Yeah?" Joey peered through the darkness, but quickly shrugged and stuck his light back in his pocket. "We'll see about it in the morning. First things first—we've got to get dry."

At least Rufus's waterproofing enchantment held. Mercifully, the insides of our bags were untouched, even after our submersion, and we were able to towel off and find a change of clothes before striking off in search of kindling. Within half an hour, we'd gotten a respectable fire going. Our tents were of the pop-up variety—Rufus really had done his best—and following Joey's lead, I draped my wet things on top to let them drip overnight. There was nothing to be done for my shoes but keep them close to the fire and hope for the best, and his duster was going to be damp for days, but at least we were warmer.

Neither of us could give an approximation of the time more precise than "somewhere between dusk and dawn," but my stomach, still stuck in Florida, insisted that we were past due for dinner. Joey decided to risk the pond water—"I've yet to get sick off anything in Faerie," he explained as he set it to boil—and before long, we had passable stew from a couple of rehydrated pouches. We ate in silence, listening to the crackling and snapping of unseen things moving in the trees, then washed up and turned in.

Zipped into my tent, wrapped in a surprisingly soft bag, I willed sleep to come even as I dreaded the morning.

I don't know how long I slept, but my back was stiff and the sun was filtering low through the forest when I poked my head out to see how bad the situation was in the light of day. The fire had almost burned itself out in the night, and Joey crouched beside the remains, stirring the gray ashes with a stick until the embers began to flare. "Going to get more wood," he said, his voice a creaking bass with the hour. "Start the coffee, okay?"

Wearing my sleeping bag like a cape, I dug the necessary tools out of my backpack and started measuring out coffee grounds. When I headed to the pond for water, the grass was cold and damp against my bare feet, and the pond had become crystalline blue, a softly-tinted window onto the weeds rising out of the muck deep below. It wasn't so much a pond as a small lake, I mused, tracing the path of a darting fish below the placid surface, but if it had a name, I was in the dark about it.

Something larger moved among the weeds, and I squatted on the shore for a better look. I wish I hadn't: the light wasn't strong yet, but it clearly showed the inhuman thing that swam out and looked up at me. I caught my breath and tried to back away, forgetting my position, and fell over my heels in my hurry to escape. Joey caught me crab-walking away from the lake at top speed when he returned with an armful of dead branches, and he dropped them and ran to my side. "What's wrong?" he yelled.

I paused in my escape and looked up at him, panting with the shock. "Something's in there."

"In where?"

"Lake," I managed, pointing at my track through the dewy grass. "In there."

He drew his sword and strode to the bank, then gazed into the water as I picked myself up and tried to regain a semblance of my shattered dignity. "Kind of looks like an old woman?" he called.

"Uh-huh."

"Green? Long hair?"

"Yeah, that's it," I mumbled, brushing the grass and dirt off my palms.

He grunted and sheathed his blade. "Well, hope you didn't want a bath, but as long as we stay out of the water, she shouldn't bother us." He picked up the pot I'd dropped, filled it, and headed for the fire. "Got the coffee together?"

Blushing in shame at my freak-out, I passed him the grounds and started tending the fire. "You've seen that before?"

"Yup." He fitted the pot into its tripod and stood to crack his spine. "Ran into a couple the last time I was out in the bush. Library had a book with some notes on them, too—really," he said, giving me a good look, "it's not coming to get you. Chill, Aid."

"But what—"

"Ever heard of Jenny Greenteeth?"

"Well, yeah, but that's just a folktale…" I shut up as Joey's head swiveled back and forth. "*Seriously?*"

"Why are you surprised?" He gave the coffee a stir and sniffed appreciatively. "One of them must have slipped across at some point, so presto, cultural memory. Anyway, the person who wrote the notes on them just called them 'green ladies.' Wasn't too detailed, but he made it pretty clear that they stay submerged." He ducked into his tent and returned with a mug, then stood by the fire impatiently until the coffee boiled. "Of course," he continued as he poured his breakfast, "they *are* carnivorous, so we'll just keep—"

A splash interrupted Joey's reassurances, followed quickly by a second as a pair of green hands clawed at the bank. The creature's head followed an instant later—humanoid, but with overlarge eyes, frilled gills below the ears, and skin the color of a ripened lime. Its mouth opened too widely, revealing sharp brown teeth, as it began to pull itself from the water.

"Goddamn it," Joey muttered, putting his mug down, "that's *it*. If we survive this, I'm updating the field guide."

"There's a field guide?" I asked, scrambling for my tent.

"There damn well will be!" Before I had time to grab my sword, Joey's was flashing, and the thing half out of the lake shrieked on contact. He only slapped it with the flat—he hadn't cut it—but the red stripes bubbling off the green lady's back made it plain that the things were native to the realm.

"*Git!*" he bellowed, aiming a kick at the creature's forehead, and the screeching thing slipped back into the water as quickly as it had appeared. Joey stood on the shore as it sunk into the deeps, then wiped his blade on the grass, leaving a streak of black residue behind it. "Got a towel handy?" he asked with remarkable nonchalance. "I don't like putting this up wet."

I passed him my drying towel from the night before and watched him clean his weapon. "So...want to take that coffee to go?"

Joey looked out over the placid lake, sniffed, and nodded. "Yeah, that might be for the best. We pack in shifts."

Twenty minutes or so later, we'd thrown on our damp clothes and stuffed our gear into our backpacks. Given the fact that I was able to zip my bag, in light of my subpar packing skills, I was beginning to suspect that Rufus's creations operated along the same lines as a good old-fashioned Bag of Holding. While I tightened my shoulder straps, Joey doused the fire with his coffee pot. He tried to be subtle about it, but I caught him giving the lake a long, hard look before he scooped out more water.

When the site was clear, I turned in place until I felt the same tug I'd noticed the night before from the opposite side of the lake. "That way?" I suggested, gesturing to the trees, but Joey shook his head.

"Mountains," he said, pointing in the other direction. "If I can get a little height, I might be able to figure out where we are."

My gut protested, but Joey was the one with the wilderness experience in Faerie, even if much of that experience had been from the air. And so I followed him into the woods behind our dead campfire, trying to gauge our direction from the rising sun. As far as I could tell, the mountains lay ahead to the northeast, but our path meandered as necessary. There was no trail, and so we sidestepped felled trees, circled a series of tiny green lakes, and wove around suspiciously marshy ground. The day warmed with the rising sun, and though my coat and shoes nearly dried, I felt myself sweating under my clothes and the heavy pack.

Around noon—or what passed for noon that particular day, given the variable day lengths in Faerie—we stopped in a sapling-dotted clearing for lunch. The place seemed safe enough, quiet but for a pair of competing birds that had claimed trees on opposite sides, and Joey and I sat on our bags to break into the jerky. "Forest fire?" he guessed, examining the area. "Lightning struck a tree, it burned its neighbors, and the hole's closing up?"

I began to agree with him, but I'd seen storms—even rain—so infrequently in Faerie as to make the scenario unlikely. I was puzzling this over when a truck-sized patch of grass to our right shifted upward ever so slightly, and something that looked suspiciously like an overgrown tarantula leg slipped out.

As I watched, frozen with my jerky halfway to my mouth, another little hillock to the left of the first started to twitch.

"Trapdoor," I muttered.

Joey, chewing contemplatively, glanced my way and said, "Huh?" around a mouthful of meat.

"Don't move."

"What—"

"Don't. *Move*."

His breath caught as he noticed what I was staring at, and he whispered, "Silk. See it?"

Once I was looking for it, I did. Crisscrossing the meadow were trip lines of nearly invisible silk, each disappearing into the grass—and presumably, into the burrow of a spider. "Two ahead of me," I whispered back.

Joey slowly turned to look over his shoulder. "Three behind us. I see legs."

"We run?"

"May have to hack our way through," he replied, followed by an exasperated huff. "Why did it have to be giant spiders?"

I carefully eased myself off my bag and back to my feet, then checked for the bronze sword at my hip. "You're arachnophobic?"

"Not particularly," he said, moving in slow synchronicity with me. "But there's always a fucking giant spider. Every story, every quest—giant spider. I was *really* hoping to avoid them."

"You said it yourself," I muttered as I slid my pack on. "If it's in every story, there's got to be a reason for the cultural memory, right?"

The nearest spider poked another three legs and its head out, and Joey grabbed his bag. "You know, we can talk about shared folklore later, okay? Ready?"

The spider to my right struck first, and I was suddenly grateful for every bruise Val had given me over the last year. I caught it between the eyes—well, between *two* of the eyes—on the point of my sword, and it fought back with a rasping hiss. Its fellow retreated, but the trio behind us took the opportunity to move in—and met Joey's two-handed defense, the sword in his right hand and the nail gun in his left, plucked from its homemade holster. He sliced through one spider and shot the second's head full of metal as my target shuddered in its death throes. Joey pulled his sword loose and turned, only to find the third spider rearing up on its back four legs like a mutant horse. Before it could slam its fangs into him, I yelled and threw myself against its side, toppling it with the surprise blow. Joey's sword flicked, and the spider never had a chance to right itself.

We stood together in the clearing, panting, and studied

the motionless trapdoors around us. With a grimace, Joey wiped the ichor on his sword against the hairy side of his first kill, grunted at the streaked blade, and nodded to the mountains. "Still hungry?"

I looked around at the four corpses and shook my head.

We rested in shifts that night, one of us keeping the fire high while the other caught a few hours of uneasy sleep. "At least we're learning," Joey told me over another dinner of rehydrated stew. I wasn't hungry, but Joey's spoon scraped the bottom of his dish over and over again, cleaning up every morsel, while I picked at my own serving. "I've never seen anything on giant spiders in the library, so maybe they're a recent addition," he continued between bites. "They're not iron-sensitive—maybe they came over from the Gray Lands."

"The merrow aren't iron-sensitive, either," I reminded him as I stirred potatoes and carrots around.

"True," he said, and mulled this over for a moment. "But then again, neither are dragons. And since there's nothing on them—"

"Can we not talk about this right now, please?" I mumbled, casting glances at the forest around us. We hadn't dared to try our luck with a third clearing, and the space between the trees barely left room for a single tent and the fire.

Sensing the direction of my thoughts, Joey nodded and resumed his attack on his food. "Sure, Aid. Hey, if you're not going to eat, why don't you take the first rest? I'll stand guard until midnight," he offered, tapping his watch. "Or, you know, something close to midnight."

I handed him my plate and headed for the tent, where I passed out with my shoes still on. When Joey woke me, I could tell it was later than midnight—a faint lightening of the eastern sky promised relief—but I took his post, tended the fire, and made myself coffee to pass the time. I didn't have to wait alone long. The sun was barely above the horizon when Joey reappeared, puffy-eyed but conscious, and I passed him the coffee without a word.

The ground began to rise as we hiked toward the foothills, and I let my mind wander. We'd left Florida on a Thursday. That meant the day before had been Friday, and today was Saturday…

I realized this nightmare had only begun ten days ago. It felt like half a lifetime.

We reached the base of the nearest mountain around sunset, where we called a halt. There was nothing to be gained by making the ascent in the dark—we hadn't brought proper climbing gear, and even if we had, I didn't know what I was doing on the end of a rope. Joey had fallen into exhausted silence after lunch, and once my tent was up and the fire steady, I shoved him toward the sleeping bag. He collapsed without protest, and I sat alone beneath the mockingly unhelpful sky, praying for a boring watch.

I grabbed a few hours of sleep on the flip side of midnight, then roused myself enough to follow Joey up the hill in the red glow of dawn. The going was easier than I'd feared, more grassy slopes than boulder-studded ravines, and Joey's eagerness to get our bearings seemed to propel him onward ever faster. Around midmorning, he scrambled to the top, gave me a hand up the last rocky face, and looked out over the panorama.

To the east, south, and west, the world spread below us in a carpet of uninterrupted green, a verdant forest seemingly without end. The northern view was blocked by more mountains, gray peaks rising to a bare, saw-toothed skyline. "So…how far do you think we can see?" I asked, straining my eyes for a glimpse of the familiar.

"Maybe ten miles. Maybe a hundred. Depends on the curvature of the realm, and I don't think anyone's ever measured it."

Joey's voice sounded dull, and I found him staring out at the forest, absently rubbing his blond beard. "And?"

"And," he muttered, "I don't recognize a damn thing." He looked at me and slowly shook his head. "Aid, I don't have the faintest idea where we are."

CHAPTER 9

In times of crisis, we fall back on what we know. I sat on the windy mountaintop, shivering every time a cloud crossed the sun, while Joey went off alone. It was Sunday, after all, and he'd missed at least one week of Mass already, so I told myself I was letting him be while he prayed. In truth, the look on Joey's face scared me, an expression like panic hiding just below the cracking façade of calm, and he clutched his silver crucifix and rocked back and forth as he mouthed the silent words. Maybe it was cowardice on my part, but I left him alone, hoping he would recover quickly.

But the day warmed to noon, and still Joey sat alone with his thoughts and his God, gazing out at the wilderness like he was staring into the abyss. There was no place to make a fire, and so I helped myself to the jerky and a bottle of water, drinking it slowly to make it last. And then, when the shadows changed direction and Joey showed no sign of joining me, I gathered up my courage and approached him. "Want to think about camp?" I murmured, keeping back a few paces. Joey appeared coiled, poised to leap, and I didn't want him going off the rock or onto me.

He looked up slowly, as if piecing together who I might be and why I was making noise at him, then seemed to remember what had happened. "We're screwed," he muttered. "Camp here or anywhere, we're screwed."

I ventured closer to his perch. "We're not screwed. We just need to find something familiar, that's all."

"What was I thinking?" he mumbled, turning away from me. "I can't do this. It's impossible, it's suicide…"

I let him ramble to himself for a moment, then stepped beside him and said, "*Joey.*" He glanced back at me, dazed and on the verge of a breakdown, and, with a prayer to anyone feeling merciful, I wound up and slapped him hard across the face.

The blow knocked Joey's head to the side, and he grabbed my arm even as his other hand covered his struck cheek. "What the *hell*—"

"Snap out of it," I interrupted as his eyes focused. "We're screwed if we stay up here and starve. If that's what you want to do, fine, but I'm getting off this damn rock, and I'm going to find Coileán. If you want to come along, great."

My hand was losing blood from his grip on my wrist, but at least Joey had risen from his introspective funk. "Hit me again," he said quietly, "and you'll go off this rock headfirst. Understood?"

"Going to sit here all night?"

"*Understood?*"

We locked eyes for a long moment, and then I nodded and broke out of his grasp. "Get up," I said, heading for my backpack. "We're going to find civilization. If we hurry, we can make the valley before nightfall."

"And which way are we going, pray tell?" he asked—but at least he was standing, I noticed as I glanced over my shoulder. "You got a GPS unit you forgot to mention or something?"

I shrugged my bag on and pointed toward the southwest. "We go that way."

"We *came* from that way," said Joey, kicking a rock down the path we'd used that morning.

"Yeah, and as I said on Friday, that's the way we need to go."

"Why?"

"I don't know!" I yelled, and my voice echoed around the hills. "Something's pulling me that way, and that's all I've got, all right? So we can stay here like idiots and think about it until the food runs out, or we can trust that just *maybe* my gut's right about this." I buckled my chest strap into place and glared at him. "Got a better idea?"

"No," he said softly, watching my anger fizzle. "No, I…I don't. No."

He sounded defeated, and his cheek glowed from the impact. "Joey," I said, grabbing his slumped shoulders, "come on, you've got to stick with me. I can't do this alone, man. You're the only one of us who's remotely competent."

That earned a small smile, but he sighed. "We're lost in the middle of Faerie with a few days' food and water, no compass, and no map, and now you're telling me the way out of this mess is back by the giant spiders."

"We'll walk around the goddamned spiders. Come on."

"I mean…you know, I really don't want to get us killed, and we don't even have a way out of here—"

"Joey—"

"—and I'm *scared*, okay? I'm scared. We're alone, and I am so fucking scared right now."

The silence hung between us for a moment, and then I said, "I'm scared, too, Joey. But we can't stay here."

I released him. With a slow nod, he wandered over to his abandoned bag and shouldered it, then led the way down.

We camped at the foot of the mountain that evening, using the same clearing we'd found the night before. Joey remained quiet and contemplative, and I set about building the fire and making dinner while he sat on his sleeping bag and ran his thumb over his crucifix. After coaxing a few bites down him, I told him I'd take the watch and sent him to bed.

Sunrise found me stirring the ashes of our dying fire, willing the coffee to boil, and I cut my eyes to the tent at the sound of a zipper. A few seconds later, Joey emerged, disheveled but dressed, and sat next to me on his upturned backpack. "Hey," he grunted.

"Morning."

He took my stick from me and attacked the fire. "About yesterday."

"Yeah?"

"You still think we head southwest?"

I considered the weird tug in my head, then nodded. "Yeah."

"Good." I looked up from the coffee, frowning, but Joey had eyes only for his work. "Got that feeling, too. Wanted to make sure I wasn't imagining things." A smoldering log caught, and he nudged it until it bloomed into flame. "So what's pulling us that way?"

"What do you think?"

"You're asking *me*?" He paused and considered the question, then swirled the coffee in its pot. "I guess, if I had to say...I think it's the realm."

"I think so, too," I said quietly.

He rose for a moment and returned with our mugs. "You think the realm's on our side, then?" he asked as he poured.

I shrugged and blew on my liquid breakfast. "I don't know that the realm *takes* sides, Joey."

"Maybe it should," he muttered, and drank, grimacing at the bitter taste. "Is your intuition giving you any idea of the distance we have to go? Mine is suspiciously silent about that."

I cupped my hands around my warm mug as if I could absorb the much-needed caffeine through osmosis alone. "Mine, too. Maybe it's trying not to depress us. If we were really seeing a hundred miles up there..."

I left that thought unfinished, and Joey sighed. "Let's hope for more than ten. The palace could be just over the horizon, you know. And hey," he added, perking slightly, "if we hit the coast, we can follow the sea down. Maybe even make a boat."

"Can *you* make a boat?"

"Well, no," he admitted, "but this is Faerie. I'm not giving up on miracles."

I thought we had done a fair bit of walking in the previous three days.

Looking back, I laugh at my naiveté.

My tennis shoes had been nicely broken in prior to our extended hike. Toula made them for me the summer before after seeing the toes of my old pair flap, and in the four months since, they'd been through their share of mud and rock and grass and had worn down to that happy, comfortable place between "fresh out of the box" and "beyond all hope of salvage." Since popping back into Faerie, I'd managed to dodge blisters, but my feet and legs were beginning to complain, especially after our mountain expedition. By the time we backtracked to the lake gate, however, my feet chafed with every step, and my old pair of socks had sprung small holes. The new pair Rufus had given me was holding up, but I knew I had to rotate my socks if I wanted to avoid further podiatric unpleasantness.

If I was in discomfort, Joey was in hell. At least I had sneakers—his footwear of choice on fleeing Faerie had been his motorcycle boots, which, while great for riding, were less comfortable on a long march. He didn't complain much, but his socks were stiff and stained, and I'm sure he was as grateful as I was that Rufus had thought to throw padded bandages in with our gear.

Our coats stayed on during those first days in the woods, even when the temperature climbed. Though our backpack straps were padded, they still rubbed against our shoulders, and the coats offered some small measure of protection. Within a few days, though, everything began to stink, and the coats came off for short spells, if for no other reason than to give our shirts a chance to breathe.

We spoke little at first, other than to check that our weird internal tugs were still in agreement and that we hadn't veered too far from the most direct path. Neither of us was sleeping much or well—partly due to our condition, partly due to fear for the ones left in the mortal realm—and as we began to more stringently ration our food, we didn't have the energy for extra conversation. Water, at least, was abundant, even if it meant risking a trip to an inhabited pond, and neither of us came down with cholera, despite our lack of filtration. But to our mutual sorrow, the coffee ran out on our tenth day in the wilderness, making mornings and the uncomfortable process of dressing our wounds all the more unpleasant.

If we were spared some of the usual hardships of the great outdoors, like mosquitoes and poison ivy, we made up for it with the larger fauna. It wasn't just the spiders, which seemed to have infested every decent clearing. Several species from the mortal realm had crossed over and made their homes in the forest, and Joey and I saw our share of mice, rats, and foxes within the first week. The night after we lost our coffee, we ended up camping in a tree after hearing an ominous howling around us. Daybreak revealed five sleek wolves prowling at the base of our tree, watching us and panting with excitement. Joey dispatched two with his nail gun, and the other three fled in terror. Only when we reached the ground again did we realize that the wolves were oversized, a couple of feet longer than we were tall and sporting two-inch canine teeth. It was impossible to say whether the wolves had crossed from the other realm and flourished or whether they had started from more nightmarish stock out of the Gray Lands, but in the end, the promise of fresh meat pushed aside any questions about its origin. Joey and I butchered one of the wolves and roasted what we could over that evening's fire, giving ourselves a day off the trail in the process. The meat was beefy and gamey, a little off-putting, but we shoved the leftovers into our bags for the next day's meals. Still, without any real way to preserve our kills, we were forced to leave much of the two carcasses behind.

The next evening, we made camp beside a shallow stream and took the opportunity to rinse ourselves and our gear. While our clothes dried by the fire, we turned the leftover meat into a mediocre stew, then leaned back against a pair of trees and tried to tally up the distance we'd covered. The going had been uneven, and with breaks for meals and medical purposes, Joey estimated we'd done perhaps fifteen miles a day. That put us only one hundred twenty miles from the gate, give or take—and neither the palace nor the sea was anywhere in sight. My gut told me we were still headed in the right direction, but the fact that we'd yet to come across a familiar landmark was discouraging.

After we were full and the dishes were clean, Joey gave me the first rest. I relieved him in the small hours of the morning, and he reported nothing out of the ordinary—the wolves, at least, seemed to be avoiding us for the time being. I stuck a strip of jerky into a mug of hot water, both to soften the former and flavor the latter, and sat down on a pile of decaying leaves to wait for the dawn. The night, like all the ones preceding it, was pleasant, clear and just cool enough to warrant a coat, and I peeked through the canopy at the few visible patches of stars to pass the time. When that got too boring, I found a twig, cleared a spot of dirt near the fire, and tried to draw myself a Sudoku game. If I put together a workable board, erased enough numbers, and looked away for an hour or so, I reasoned, I could come back and actually do the puzzle before morning.

The sky was beginning to lighten, and I'd just remembered where the nines were supposed to go, when I heard a snuffling in the trees ahead. Grabbing an extra stick of firewood, I made a quick torch from the campfire, then stepped away from comforting glow to find what was lurking. There was nothing behind the first five trees, nor the second...but *something* was behind the deadfall straight ahead, something large and noisy, and the sounds I was hearing were awfully familiar. Deciding not to face the unknown by myself, I quickly backtracked and ducked into the tent to shake Joey awake. "Something's close," I whispered, holding the smoking torch away from his sleeping bag. "And eating. I heard bones snap."

He swore under his breath, but he rose and shoved his

swollen feet back into his boots. With another torch in his left hand and his sword in his right, Joey followed me back to the deadfall and the sounds of crunching. He listened for a moment, then beckoned me around to the right of the pile of downed trees...

...and straight toward the tail of a green dragonet.

"Shit," I whispered, jumping back with him behind our shelter before the twitching tail could find us. I hadn't gotten a great look at the beast—the light was still too faint, even with torches—but I guessed it was at least a solid thirty feet long. A young dragon, sure, but not a hatchling by any means. "What do we do?" I asked Joey. "Pack and sneak out?"

"Dude," he muttered, leaning around the pile to give the dragonet a further inspection, "I don't know."

"You're the friggin' dragon whisperer!" I protested.

"*One* dragon, and we bonded! That's not a transferrable skill," he hissed, and stepped back behind our shelter. "Okay, best thing we can do is pack and run..."

Joey's voice died as the sound of the dragon's eating suddenly silenced. We held our breath, each of us straining to be as quiet as possible, but then, ever so softly, a voice echoed through our heads: *Hello, food.*

Run, Joey mouthed, and pushed me toward our camp.

I was panting beside the campfire before I realized he hadn't followed me, and I wheeled around to reverse course, ready to help him. Before I could make it halfway back to Joey, however, I heard an echoing screech...and then, a long moment later, Joey came walking out of the trees without his torch, holding his sword at his side. His T-shirt was splashed with blood, as were his face and arms.

"What..." I began, but he shook his head and crouched by the stream to wash his blade.

"Georgie is never to hear of this," he said, his voice low and shaking. "She is *never to know.* Swear to me, Aiden, that none of this leaves this place."

"I swear," I mumbled, disturbed to see him so unsteady.

Joey wiped his sword dry against his jeans and turned to me. "I mean it. This isn't Ilunna all over again—no jokes, no hints, *nothing*. God is my maker, if you ever—"

"I said I swear, Joey."

He considered this, then nodded wearily and sheathed his blade. "Let's get out of here," he muttered, and in one quick motion, he ripped off his bloody shirt and tossed it onto the fire.

Though the dragon seemed to have been traveling alone, the incident killed even the little conversation Joey and I had managed to make. Over the next week, we communicated largely in grunts and hand signals, peppered with profanity every time something predatory crossed our path. At least Joey had bought a few boxes of nails—he was quick with his gun and improving with practice, and the combination of improvised ammunition and a steady sword arm brought down another wolf, a couple of coyote-looking things, and a small bear. But we butchered his kills in silence, ate, and took turns sleeping, moving through the endless trees as if reliving one long, awful day.

The monotony was worse than the physical pain, which dulled to a low, constant ache. There was nothing around us but woods—an occasional rivulet or pond, maybe a little rise or fall in the terrain for variety—but the forest was ancient and untouched, and it stretched forever in all directions. Sometimes, we could make a straight path through the trees, following the tug that strengthened as we closed on its source; other times, we lost hours whacking our way through thick brush and thorns. We'd camp when the light grew too dim, wherever we were, build a fire for protection against the unseen, and wait for sunrise to do it all again. When Joey slept, I tried to find the sky beyond the canopy above us, but often, I had to content myself with watching the raw magic swirl around me, the colorful lights I could poke and prod but never actually use.

I can't stress enough how much we stank. Everything—our clothes, our bags, our tents, our skin—carried overtones of wood smoke from the campfires. Adding to that bouquet was the wet mustiness of gear left too long on damp ground, the sharp notes of meat *just* this side of spoiled, the metallic hints of other creatures' blood on our clothes, and the omnipresent, acrid fug of two guys who'd been hiking for days without a proper shower or washing machine. I'd never been able to cultivate facial hair—a quirk of my fae blood, I'd learned—but Joey's short bristles had matured into an impressive full beard, which sometimes caught bits of food or dried juice from our undercooked dinners. He tried to keep it clean, but Joey had seldom sported more than a few days' growth before, and his unchecked beard—which, like everything else, was soon greasy and smoky—was just another factor to annoy him.

I kept reminding myself that at least no one was suffering from a gastrointestinal ailment, but something in me insisted that this, too, was only a matter of time.

And in my all-too-brief hours of sleep, my mind went back through the gate. We'd been gone for days—what had happened to Hel and Toula and Rufus and the others in our absence? The last thing I'd heard about was a disturbance outside the silo. Had Oberon mobilized and moved on the Arcanum? Had he broken through their defenses? Was the grand magus dead? Were my parents? My subconscious conjured up dreams of burning pastures under a red, smoke-choked sky, an infinite horde of faceless faeries running through the corridors of the silo, and the corpses, all of them, accusing me with their sightless eyes. I'd failed them. The useless dud, the tainted witch-blood, the worthless traitor—I'd failed them all.

I tried, I insisted in those nightmares. *Don't you see that I tried?*

The last corpse I'd stumble over before waking in a cold sweat was always my father's. The others were silent, but even in death, his lips continued to form the words that rang in my head: *Not my son. Not my son.*

On waking from those dreams, I finally admitted to myself what I'd denied all along: I'd never really been Dad's son, and I never would be.

Curled up in the dark, waiting for sleep to return or Joey to rouse me, I thought back over all the signs I'd either missed or ignored, all the little moments that should have proven to me from the start that he would never want me. As I looked through scene after scene of his absence or apathy, I cycled back to my first memory, one I ineffectively tried to keep buried.

In that memory, I was three years old and change, and my parents had company over for drinks one evening— Mr. and Mrs. Fisher, whose daughter, Liana, was in my sister's class. Hel and Liana had retreated to Hel's room to play with the boxful of dolls stashed under the bed, but I remained underfoot in the den, pushing a plastic locomotive around the carpet. If it was past my bedtime, no one seemed to notice; the adults were busy with each other and their glasses, and I was busy rubbing my bare knees raw as I sent my train to explore the wonders to be found under the coffee table and the spare chairs. I don't know why I loved that train so much—it was yellow and red and rounded, very un-trainlike, but having never seen a real train, this didn't bother me then. I also had no true concept of what trains sounded like, so mine made *vroom* noises as I gleefully slammed it into the furniture legs.

I was barely listening to the grown-ups, though I kept one ear perked in case someone should mention cookies. My mother had made a tray of break-and-bake chocolate chip cookies with dinner, and having had one, I was hopeful there might be more and so stayed close to the action. The smell of melted chocolate lingered in the den, even though dessert had long since been packed away, and I imagined that my train was delivering cookies somewhere very important, probably to someone like me.

As I crawled near the couch again, absorbed in my train, Mr. Fisher reached down and pulled it out of my hand. "Let's have a look at this," he said, and I sat back on my heels, distressed to see my toy in the stranger's lap. "Oh," said Mr. Fisher, using the sort of slow and exaggerated tone reserved for idiots and the very young, "isn't this nice!" He looked down at me then and, with all seriousness, added, "I think I'll keep it."

I wasn't supposed to throw tantrums—Mom and Dad had made that abundantly clear, and I remember fearing a smack across the backside—but the thought of losing my train was pushing me to the breaking point. "That's mine!" I protested, climbing to my feet to snatch the train back from the giant. "Give it back, that's mine!"

Mr. Fisher just smiled and pulled a stick from behind him. A wand, I realized—it looked much like my parents' wands, dark brown and smooth, tapering to a point, not to be touched—and he must have hidden it under his polo and shoved it in his waistband. Before I could reclaim my toy, he flicked the wand in the air and whispered a word, and my train was floating two feet above my head, bobbing out of my reach on a thin streamer of red light. "If you want it," he said, grinning in challenge, "take it."

In desperation, I looked to my parents for help, but my mother was sitting tight-lipped on the far end of the couch, and my father just sat back in his recliner and watched me in silence. As I began to panic, I tried jumping for the train, then climbed onto the coffee table and took a flying leap for it, but the toy always seemed to bob just out of my grasp. Panting, frustrated, and on the brink of tears, I stood in the middle of the den and watched it dance above me, waiting for one of the grown-ups to explain the rules of this new game. But after a moment, when no one offered to help, I couldn't hold it any longer: I burst into angry sobs, sure that my train was never coming back.

And then, over my weeping, I heard my mother tell

Mr. Fisher, "Stop it, Chris, give it back to him."

I wiped my eyes and nose in time to see the train drop to the carpet, and I dove to the floor to scoop it into my arms. When I looked at the couch, Mr. Fisher was frowning—not angry, I knew that face, but upset. "It's good for them to practice—"

Dad cut him off, his words low and clipped: "Boy's a dud."

The Fishers jerked in synchronization, and Mrs. Fisher leaned around her husband to stare at my father. "Now, Howard, you can't be sure of that, he's just a little thing. Liana was a slow starter."

"He's a dud," he repeated, glaring at me as I swatted the last of my tears away. "Doesn't have it in him."

Mr. Fisher looked at me for a long moment, then turned back to my father as he absently rolled his wand between his palms. "You know, sometimes it takes a little extra provocation to make them spark. Add some gas to the fire, know what I mean?" Dad's eyes narrowed, and Mr. Fisher explained, "If you push him far enough, he'll figure out how to push back."

"And I'm telling you he's a dud," said Dad.

"With a sister like Helen? Doubt it." He frowned at me, then readied his wand. "Come on, let me try—I bet I can get him started."

I saw Mom shoot a worried glance at Dad, but he shrugged and folded his arms. "You'll see," he muttered, and waved Mr. Fisher on.

The wand twitched, Mr. Fisher's lips moved, and suddenly, the red light was all around me, pressing against me like a blanket of knives. I screamed and fell, my precious train forgotten, as I tried stop the stabbing pain that enveloped me. As I curled up on the floor, I wailed for my mother and scrunched my eyes closed as if darkness would make the agony end...

...and then, as quickly as it had come, it stopped, and I heard my sister's voice above me: "You leave him alone!"

I uncurled and tried to sit up, but I was shaking too hard to make it off the floor.

Hel stood between Mr. Fisher and me with her arm out and palm raised, blocking the red stream from his wand with a purple stream of her own. I couldn't see her face, but she had braced herself as if she were pushing against a wall. "That's not *nice!*" she shouted at the couch, employing the same cadence our mother had used on us countless times. "We don't *hurt* people!"

Mr. Fisher's wand dropped, and Hel bent to pull me from the floor. "Come on, Aid," she coaxed, shielding me against her favorite turquoise overalls as she led me from the room. "Come on, we're going to play in here."

I didn't make it far. As we shuffled down the hall, my stomach roiled in warning, and suddenly, I lost my dinner all over the carpet and my shoes. I cried anew, scared and hurting from the acid burning my throat, and registered a fresh wave of shame when my bladder gave way. Hel called for our mother, and within seconds, Mom had carried me into the bathroom and was pressing a cold washcloth against my face. "It's all right, sweetheart," she murmured, "let's get you to bed."

The memory fades there. I don't know what eventually became of my little train, and I've never asked how much trouble Hel got into for chastising an adult. If Mr. Fisher ever apologized for putting me through excruciating pain, I've long since forgotten it. You don't take many memories out of early childhood, which, at least in my case, is a mercy.

But I do remember that my father walked past the bathroom while I was hiccupping away my sobs. He moved purposefully down the hall toward his bedroom, sidestepping the mess I'd left, and he didn't look at me as he passed the open door.

And so I lay there in the dark tent, tasting bile once again, unsure if it was worse to remember or to dream.

Two days after the bear steaks ran out, I killed a deer with Joey's nail gun, earning a pleased nod from my companion when he woke to fresh venison.

Maybe the influx of recognizable food had a restorative effect on Joey, or maybe he was just settling into a rhythm, but slowly, his mood began to improve. He wasn't enjoying our trip by any means—neither of us was—but after a long three weeks in the bush, the forest had started to thin, and the stronger sunlight seemed to do us both some good. Over breakfast that morning, Joey showed me the notebook he'd been keeping of our trek, including his preliminary maps. "All approximations," he said as I flipped through his pen sketches of the lakes and streams we'd passed, "but if I could get Georgie up and get an aerial perspective, I might be able to make more sense of it."

He was finally planning ahead again, I noted, but didn't comment on it. There was no sense in jinxing us.

The next day, Joey nudged me awake from another bad dream and silently beckoned for me to follow him outside the tent. Fearing the worst, I reached for my sword, but Joey shook his head and urged me to hurry with hand signs. When I scrambled out through the flap into the dawn, I looked through the trees to a little brook we'd missed in the darkness, and my breath caught in my throat.

"How about that?" Joey whispered, grinning beside me.

I considered the white stallion on the far side of the water, who had bent for a drink. He was beautifully formed, tall and muscular, unmarred but for a little dappling of gray on his flank. More striking, however, was the long horn he sported, a spiraling white spear with a wicked point.

"Unicorn," I whispered back, at a loss for more helpful commentary.

Joey nodded. "Gorgeous, isn't he? That boy's got to be at least seventeen, eighteen hands. Hard to tell from here, but...*wow*."

"Going to take a closer look?"

"Not a good idea. See the horn on that thing?"

I cut my eyes to him and smirked. "Come on, man, I thought you were good with horses. Not even going to try?"

"First, that's not a horse," he replied, waving dismissively at the unicorn. "Second, if I remember my folklore correctly, he'd never let me get close." It was Joey's turn to smirk. "Takes a virgin to tame a unicorn. Be my guest, bud."

"You don't know if that's actually true," I protested.

"What, that you're a virgin?"

I glared at him, then looked back at the stream in time to see the unicorn raise its head. It spotted us and stared for a moment, then nickered, tossed its mane, and trotted off into the shadows.

"Well," said Joey as it disappeared, "there goes your chance to prove me wrong, stud."

My face flushed, and when Joey looked at me again, he saw my embarrassment and started to laugh. I tensed, trying to find a way to defend myself, then gave up and punched him in the stomach. Joey bent with the blow, gasped, and laughed all the harder—genuine laughter, the kind that turned his face as red as mine and squeezed tears from his eyes. He collapsed to his knees and kept laughing, and as I watched him, I felt the laughter well up within me, too. We still didn't know where we were or what had befallen the people we cared about, but we laughed. And we sat there together in the weeds, howling at nothing and everything, until the anxious birds around us cried out and flew for their lives.

CHAPTER 10

Joey was in relatively good spirits over dinner and offered to take the first watch, so I found myself sitting alone outside the tent as the world shifted to the bluish-black of impending dawn. Truth be told, I preferred the second watch—I'd acclimated somewhat to our abbreviated sleep schedule, and so rising in the wee hours of the morning was becoming an excuse to get a jump on breakfast. Granted, it wasn't *thrilling* to sit in the cold for a few hours by myself, but it beat returning to the dreams that had plagued me throughout our expedition.

At least I had something to do that morning besides sit and listen to unidentified noises in the forest. We hadn't collected enough wood the night before, and the fire was burning low. I'd seen a couple of downed trees near our campsite, however, and so I cracked on a glow stick and laced it onto a lanyard to go gather another armful of branches before Joey woke.

It wasn't hard to backtrack to the spot I remembered— my eyes had adjusted to the low light already, and the glow stick, while not powerful, was enough to keep me from walking into trees. A short hike later, I found the deadfall and threw the lanyard around my neck to free my hands. I picked up a few long sticks, kicked a rotten chunk out of the nearest tree, and was contemplating hacking a larger piece out with my sword when an owl screeched overhead.

Assuming the bird was just another inter-realm wanderer, I glanced up to see where it was heading, but then I noticed something yellow and luminescent gripped in its feet. The bird began to circle me—whatever it was holding was jerking in its grip—and with another cry, it released its prey and took refuge on a low-hanging branch. The glowing thing plummeted into the middle of the deadfall, and I dropped my bundle of sticks to take a closer look. I couldn't tell whether the owl had been carrying something that glowed with magic or in the mundane spectrum. Maybe it was due to my chronic lack of sleep, or perhaps to the simple fact that I was alone in the woods and bored, but my curiosity got the better of me.

Before I could climb over the tree in my way, however, the owl decided to press its luck. I saw it rise and flap toward me…and then I saw it dive *for* me, talons extended.

It wanted my glow stick, I realized too late, just before the bird grabbed a clump of my shirt in each foot. I yelled and tried to beat it off with one hand—my other arm had gone up to shield my face—but the owl held fast until the lanyard broke. With its prize secure, the owl left me as quickly as it had come, flying off with its useless trinket dangling behind it like a fading beacon.

I caught my breath, checked myself for injuries, and looked around until I spotted the glowing thing in the pile once again. Now equal parts irked and curious, I scrambled over a rotting trunk and peered down into the nest of dead branches where the owl's intended meal had landed.

It was definitely glowing, I noted, not reflecting active magic, and I had to squint to make out details. Something moved in the center of the radiance, and, without thinking, I reached down to pick it up.

The thing below me shrieked incomprehensibly as my hand loomed, and I bent closer, not quite believing what was coming into focus. "That's…*impossible*," I whispered to myself, and then I yanked my hand back, yelping in surprise at the sudden pain in my finger. Sticking it in my mouth, I tasted blood—and I finally accepted that my eyes weren't playing tricks on me.

The creature in the deadfall was tiny, maybe six inches

long if he stretched. And it was definitely male—he was humanoid in appearance and naked but for a sword belt and a brown loincloth. His eyes were too big, though, like an anime character come to life, and they glared up at me through the golden haze surrounding him. His left hand clutched a long, sharpened thorn like a sword, which he waved at me as a warning. But the real kicker—the thing that made me question whether this was all just a weird dream—was the two pairs of delicate wings that sprouted from his shoulder blades. The ones on the left looked much like those of a monarch butterfly, orange and black with white speckles around the edges. As for the ones on the right, I couldn't say; he had fallen hard, and his wings had crumpled beneath him.

A fairy. I was being threatened by an honest-to-God *fairy*.

He squeaked again and scowled, accenting the sounds with jabs from his makeshift sword, and I understood that he was speaking—I couldn't make sense of it, but he clearly wasn't stupid. "Hey, there," I said in Fae, backing off a step with my empty hands raised, "you're all right. I'm not going to hurt you."

The little thing lowered his sword and watched me uncertainly, waiting for the blow.

"Help?" I asked, cocking my head.

He frowned—I supposed my language was as foreign to him as his was to me—and tried to stand, but he cried out when the branches beneath him shifted and sent him tumbling.

I stepped closer and knelt beside the trap in which he'd landed. "Help," I murmured, showing him my empty hand, then slowly lowered it into the nest of branches and waited.

He considered this development with great suspicion, then tried again to stand. Something was wrong with his right leg, though, and the effort failed with another squeak of pain. He sat back on the branches, clutching his calf, and watched me with a mixture of fear and defiance.

I lifted my hand out of the nest and looked around for a moment—the glow had cost me some of my night vision—before finding a suitable twig. Snapping it free, I carefully lowered it into the nest and held it in front of him like a handrail. He studied my offering, realized my intention, then gingerly pulled himself upright, leaning on his good leg. I managed to get my palm under him before he lost his balance again, and he tumbled back into my hand, no heavier than a young bird.

Before he could have second thoughts, I raised him from the deadfall and stood, and he clutched my thumb to steady himself as we rose together. When I was sure he wasn't going to fall off, I lifted him closer to my face for a better look and confirmed what I'd suspected: his right wings were wrecked, and his right leg was oddly bent and swollen in a familiar way. I knew all too well what a fractured bone looked like. His big eyes were less defiant now, and his thin chest rose and fell as he fought his visible fear. "Help," I said again, ruffling his disheveled blond ponytail with my breath, and, keeping my other hand beneath my outstretched palm just in case, I carried him back to camp.

By the time Joey woke and started gawking at the newcomer, I'd begun first aid. The firelight had revealed scratches and bruises I'd missed earlier—he hadn't gone willingly with the owl, that much was apparent—and I'd convinced him to try a numbing gel by demonstrating it on the stab wound he'd given me. I offered him water as well, using my plate to make a shallow enough surface, and ripped the pad off a bandage to give him something to work with. That still left the problem of his broken limbs, though. I didn't have the faintest idea of what to do with his wings, but legs were old hat.

"Is that…did you *splint* that?" Joey asked, pointing to the creature's immobilized leg.

"Basic field dressing," I said with a shrug.

Rufus, ever helpful, had stuck a pack of toothpicks in with our cooking gear. I'd broken one in half, filed down the ends, and given the pieces to my patient with another bit of padding. Fortunately for us both, he knew what to do, and the thin fiber that had held his hair back unwound into a long enough rope to secure the splint. I'd let him set the bone—my fingers were too large, I suspected—and he cried out as he did the deed, but at least his injury was stabilized.

Joey watched as the creature cupped his hands in the water in my plate and drank a few long gulps. "Correct me if I'm wrong," he said, "but I'm pretty sure Colin said *that* doesn't exist."

"Do *you* think he's ever spent a lot of time poking around out here?" I replied.

"Well, no, but…come on, the wings!" he protested. "It's got little butterfly wings!"

"*He's* got little butterfly wings."

"Okay, he, then. They're still…" Joey gestured at the creature, then threw up his hands in frustration. "What the hell is he?"

"Beats me," I said, "but he's hurt. We can't just leave him, man."

I'd deposited him on my semi-clean towel, and the softness and the fire's heat were having an effect on him. He was struggling to stay awake, but he must have been exhausted after the night, and as Joey and I watched, he carefully rolled onto his good side and closed his eyes. Joey stared at him until he was asleep, then returned to the tent without a word. A moment later, he came back with a tissue and carefully covered the little guy. "Rest day it is, then," he said, and sighed. "Who wants jerky?"

Our guest woke mid-morning, sat up in alarm, then cried out when he was reminded of his injuries. He looked down at the tissue covering him, then up at us in query. Joey grabbed his own arms and mimed a shivering fit, and the creature's head bobbed in comprehension. Easing himself into a sitting position, he looked around at the remains of our campsite, then at the trees, and pointed his arm toward the deadfall, babbling in his unknown tongue.

"Well," I muttered, "that's pretty clear. Side trip?"

"Do we have any idea how far?" Joey asked as the creature looked back and forth at the two of us, searching for signs of understanding.

"Nope. But he can't hobble around—if we leave him here, he's probably a goner."

"I know," he said, pushing himself to his feet with a grunt, "I was just hoping you could give me some good news."

I motioned for my patient to stay still, then shouldered my backpack and knelt beside him. "Help?" I said, extending my hand, and offered him a finger for support. Draping the tissue around his neck, he clutched my finger, then rose and limped onto my open palm. Once settled, he wrapped the tissue around himself as well as he could—the wings made this somewhat tricky—and again pointed toward the woods.

"Impatient, isn't he?" said Joey as he stuffed my towel back into my sack and drenched the fire. "Can you make any sense of him?"

"Not a word," I replied, holding him out like a living, glowing compass, and with the creature navigating, we set off into the unknown.

I'll say that there are more pleasant ways to hike than with one hand outstretched at all times. We had to take a break that morning when my arm cramped up, and another when my passenger suddenly felt the call of nature. He crawled to the edge of my hand and took care of business over the side, and I looked away, partly to give him a little privacy, but mostly because I had no idea how to cope with the situation. There are moments in life that don't come with instruction manuals, and I seemed to be stumbling into them all that year.

By nightfall, my arm was an aching mess, but the creature continued to point us through thickets of weeds until Joey pushed aside a curtain of leafy vines and revealed a wide clearing. We froze up on instinct—clearings had been nothing but trouble to that point—but then I spotted the flashes of color darting in and out of the grass and trees. My passenger squeaked and pointed more emphatically toward a massive tree on the far side of the little meadow, and, trusting that he would have given me some signal if there were spiders to worry about, I obliged.

We weren't halfway across before we were surrounded by more of the creatures, a buzzing, chirping rainbow that flew around us like a swarm of oversized gnats. Our guide said something to them, and the cloud parted, flanking us like an escort but allowing us passage. I cut my eyes to Joey, who shook his head and tramped onward without stopping to give too much thought to our state of affairs.

The tree toward which we were directed was ancient, a mammoth specimen that would have taken half a dozen men to encircle. As we approached, a few of the creatures landed outside a hole in the trunk—not a natural cavity, as I had first assumed, but a delicately carved entryway into the living tree. I stepped up to the hole, mindful of the eyes on me, then carefully brought my passenger level with the floor. Immediately, four of his similarly dressed fellows appeared and hoisted him to his feet, then hustled him off down the tunnel into the trunk.

Unburdened and suddenly at a loss, I stepped back and showed the others my empty hands. "We'll just be going," I said, hoping the meaning was clear enough as I continued to backpedal, and I turned to join Joey. "So," I told him, "I'm thinking that camping here might not be the best idea—"

"*Stranger!*"

The voice was high and warped, like the cry of a child

who'd been sucking far too much helium, but I pinpointed it to a blue-glowing creature back at the hole. After seeing that the remaining guards weren't about to attack me, I returned to the tree and looked her in the eye, trying not to think about her almost total lack of clothing. "Me?"

She seemed relieved to hear me answer in Fae. "Queen talk you," she replied. "You wait." I nodded, and she disappeared back down the tunnel.

"What's all this?" Joey asked as he stepped closer.

"I'm not quite sure," I murmured, considering the number of sharpened thorns that had appeared around us in the last seconds, "but I think we're about to have an audience."

"With *whom*?"

I started to shrug, but I froze as a tiny woman draped in a green toga stepped out of the tree and stared at us. She was larger than my patient had been—maybe eight inches high—and her wings were delicate confections of violet, blue, and black. She glowed with a soft purple light, and her black hair, which fell to her waist, was crowned with a tiny circlet of what appeared to be baby's breath.

I looked at Joey, then back at the newcomer, and hoped I wasn't about to screw up. "Your Majesty, I presume?"

She smiled and daintily dipped her chin. "Well," she said in perfect Fae, "isn't this a surprise."

We made camp in the clearing that night at the queen's insistence. Lailu, as she introduced herself, had questions, and the night was already too dark for us to find a new campsite. Once Joey and I had built a fire and pitched our tents, she flew out of the tree with a handful of guards, settled on top of my backpack, and clasped her miniscule hands. "Tell me why a pair of daig are crossing the forest," she said, raising her voice over the crackling fire. "What business have you here?"

I lay on my stomach atop my sleeping bag beside her and

propped my head in my hands, the better to understand what she was saying. Her Fae was virtually unaccented, but she was a fast talker, and her voice's pitch made the words seem almost foreign. "Daig, ma'am?"

She waved her hand at Joey and me. "You. Daig. The giants who shape the world."

"Oh…uh…" I looked to Joey for help, but he only made a face and shrugged. "Joey and me, we're not daig, ma'am. We, uh, look like them, but…no world-shaping powers here."

Her head tilted in bemusement. "Daigul? Perhaps the Lady was mistaken, then."

"What lady?"

"The *Lady*," she repeated with great emphasis. "She warned me you would come. Kuni was injured, and two daig would bring him home. She told me this last night when he did not return to us."

"I'm really sorry," I said, scooting closer to her in case the problem was my hearing, "but I don't know what lady you're talking about. You're the first person we've had a conversation with in weeks." That earned another puzzled head tilt, and I tried, "Many days. How many, Joey, twenty-two?"

"Twenty-three," he muttered.

Lailu considered this, then seemed to come to a decision and nodded. "She has not made herself known. I see. But she knows you."

"But who—"

She spread her arms. "The land. The Lady is the land. And she…" Lailu paused, choosing her words. "She is concerned for you. Tell me," she said, picking her way down my backpack to stand in the grass, "has something happened? We do not concern ourselves with daig matters, but the Lady's visit left me troubled."

Joey cleared his throat. "Oberon's done something to…to the other king," he said, quickly cutting his eyes to me. "We're trying to learn what happened."

The little queen examined each of us carefully. "You have Titania's look about you," she said to me after a long moment. "The Lady had told me she was dead. This new king…blood to you, is he not?"

"He is," I admitted—and the gears clicked. "Ma'am, this Lady of yours…fair hair, brownish-green eyes, a little shorter than me? Kind of tiny all over?" I added, realizing as I said it how absurd that detail must be to our hostess.

Joey stared at me curiously, but Lailu smiled. "So she *has* revealed herself," she said. "I cannot speak to her relative size, I'm afraid—you're all enormous," she said dismissively, "but when she appears, that sounds much like her form."

My brow furrowed. "When she appears?"

She nodded. "The Lady often speaks *here*," she explained, touching two fingers to her smooth forehead. "Warns me."

I sat up and turned to Joey. "The realm. The voice in Coileán's head. She's talking about Faerie…"

"How do you know—"

"Because I've seen her!" I cried, slapping the ground. "She tried to warn me the night we ran. I dreamed about her, and she told me to get out." I ran my hands through my hair and shook my head. "You know what this means? Friggin' Faerie *has* been on our side all this time. If we'd opened a gate instead of going the lake route…"

His dark eyes widened as his jaw dropped. "The last three weeks—"

"All that walking—"

"Giant *fucking* spiders—"

The queen waited while we talked over each other, airing our every grievance with the realm's idea of the great outdoors. When we finally lapsed into stupefied silence, she said, "The Lady told me you would be weary when you arrived. You are safe here for the night. Take your rest—you're guarded." She pointed skyward, indicating the lights that flickered through the trees ringing us, then began to pace through the grass on bare feet. "Two daigul walk the woods for days and days, and the Lady watches over them—she cannot be pleased with Oberon if she has not warned him of your coming."

"You're sure she hasn't?" Joey muttered. "I mean, do you have any idea how far she's let us walk of late?"

Lailu's lips curled into a smirk. "If she had, you would be dead. She protects us, too," she continued, folding her arms. "When the daig fought amongst themselves, the Lady led us here to safety. I have protected my people since. The daig do not know where we are…and the piq do not intervene in daig affairs." She offered a brief shrug. "Not that there's much we could do, you understand. We are like daigul, only…not quite so big."

"You can't enchant?" he asked.

She shook her head. "No. As I said, like daigul."

Fearing the worst, I hesitated before asking my next question. "How far *are* we from…uh…the daig? Titania's palace?"

The queen mulled this over. "Several days' journey, but not days and days. Maybe three. Maybe five. Not more."

I realized I had been holding my breath as Joey let out a long exhalation beside me. "That way?" I asked, pointing in the direction of the ever-present tug.

"Precisely." She stepped back and nodded to her retinue, who took wing and retreated to the tree. "Stay here tonight," she said again when we were alone. "Go your way in safety. Your presence in the land will remain our secret, I promise you." She hesitated, then murmured, "You have put me in your debt. The favor you did me was unasked, but that does not negate the good. Kuni is my brother's son, and I feared him lost. Ask of me what you will, now or later, and if I can even the scales, I will."

"Oh," I rushed, "you don't have to—"

"I insist. Your name, daigul?"

Joey nodded me on, and I whispered, "Aiden. The old queen's son."

Lailu smiled. "A daigul, prince among the daig, asleep in my garden. I never cease to find wonders. Rest easy," she said, and flew off into the shadows.

Our food supplies were running low—the fresh meat had run out once again, leaving us with the last of the jerky to carry us through until we found something to kill—but Joey had noticed a few blackberry bushes on the edges of the circle, and no one stopped us as we helped ourselves. Given their size, I figured it would be pointless to ask the piq for a meal. Still, even hungry, I slept like the dead. For the first time in weeks, both of us got a full night's sleep. We woke just after sunrise to find the fire little more than ashes, but flashes of light in the foliage reminded us that we could afford to lower our guard. After eating quickly so as not to waste the day, we packed and started onward. I caught Joey looking over his shoulder as we hiked into the trees, and I guessed what he was thinking: in case of danger, we knew at least one relatively safe place to hide.

Once the clearing was out of view, Joey leaned close and said, "Piq. Pixies."

"Yep."

"Those were *pixies*."

"Looks like it." A thought occurred to me then, and I groaned. "You know we're going to have to tell Stuart, right? He'd be all over this."

Joey snorted and pushed aside a low limb. "They seemed decent enough. Why would you want to unleash Stuart on them?"

"Point taken. But we're telling Coileán, yeah?"

"Oh, hell, yes," he muttered. "Soon as we find him. 'Hey, boss. Just spent weeks in the woods tracking you down, and just so you know, there are friggin' pixies out there. If you're going to keep calling yourself a faerie, you might want to check out the adorable competition.'"

I laughed to myself. "Those *wings*, man. He's going to be

so pissed."

Joey came to a halt and grabbed my shoulder. "Okay, for everything we've been through together, you've got to promise me that you won't tell him unless I'm there. I've got to see the look on his face."

"Deal," I said, grinning, "if you'll do the same for me."

We walked on, skirting a weed-choked pond, and Joey fell in behind me when the path narrowed. "Listen, Aid…"

"Yeah?"

He hesitated. "Look, I don't want to jinx us or anything, but…assuming we make it back in one piece—"

I reached out and rapped my knuckles on the nearest tree. "Continue."

"Superstitious much?"

"It can't hurt," I said, stepping to the side as the trail widened again. "What's up?"

Joey shifted his backpack and kept his gaze pointed ahead. "If we make it out of here…Helen and I…"

I waited for a moment while he sought the words, then said, "You're going to ask her."

The little I could see of his face under the beard and grime began to flush. "So what do you think she'd say?" he mumbled.

"*I'm* not the one dating her."

"Come on, bud, be honest with me. Snowball's chance?"

There was something small and scared in his eyes, and I pushed my discomfort with the topic aside. "At least," I allowed. "But if I were you, I'd bathe first. Maybe shave. At least tame the chin beast."

Joey's shoulders relaxed, and he rubbed his beard, then found something foreign trapped within it and tossed the debris to the side. "Don't be jealous of this gloriousness."

"You look like you've got a still hidden back in the woods, man."

"It just needs a trim."

"Yeah, with a weed whacker."

He shoved me toward a tree, and I laughed. Maybe, I

thought, the inevitable wouldn't be so bad after all.

The land had been undulating for the past few days, which Joey took as a good sign. We'd both been to the mountains north of the palace—perhaps, Joey mused, we were passing through the edge of its foothills. The terrain had slowed us somewhat, but we called an early halt that day after only a few miles of trekking when we crested a ridge and came across a flock of wild sheep in the valley below. Though they slid away when we stepped from the trees, the sheep didn't bolt, and we spotted several lambs among them. The herd stuck together in a tight, white clump, making the most of the little meadow, and Joey arched an eyebrow as we quietly dropped our packs.

It was too good an opportunity to pass up. I've never been a fan of mutton, but with our supplies as low as they were, I wasn't about to turn my nose up at a windfall of fresh meat. We butchered an ewe and two lambs in the valley, then dragged the carcasses back up the ridge, where we made camp and started cooking. As night fell, we stuffed ourselves, and Joey took the first rest while I looked out over the valley, relishing the sight of an uninterrupted swath of starlight.

The terrain leveled again the next day, then started a gentle descent. We made good time, snacking on leftovers whenever we stopped, and passed another quiet night in the woods. On our third day out from the piq settlement, the descent was sharper than before, and the vegetation on the forest floor thinned. We supplemented the last of the mutton with wild berries when we made camp that evening, but I couldn't sit still at the fire—the tug in my mind was strong and insistent, and I wanted to push on, darkness be damned. Joey stressed what a stupid idea that would be, but I could tell he was uneasy as well, and he offered to help when I announced that I was going to climb a tree and see the land. Having grown up underground, I knew roughly jack about climbing trees, but I managed to make an undignified ascent and peeked out from the leafy canopy.

And there it was. The towers glowed in the last of the sunlight, and the windows began to illuminate from within, one at a time, like stars coming out. The barn seemed dark, as did the gardens and the long oak grove, but if I strained, I could hear a faint melody on the breeze. As I watched, a few figures appeared from the palace and began lighting torches around the gardens, and I ducked back within the concealing branches, struck with the irrational fear that they could spot me from that distance.

Joey was waiting when I dropped out of the tree. "And?"

"Got to put out the fire," I said, reaching for my canteen. "We made it."

CHAPTER 11

We didn't wait for dawn.

The night was still black when we packed up our gear and camouflaged it with leaf litter. I wore my sword; Joey carried his blade at one hip and his nail gun at the other, and he pulled his duster on over the top to hide the bulges on his body. Moving as quietly as we could, we made our way through the woods until we reached the narrow stream separating the wilderness from the end of Coileán's expansive lands, then paused to inspect the terrain.

As far as I could tell, Oberon hadn't redecorated the parkland. I recognized the grounds, even by starlight, and saw no indication that he had redone the gardens. More importantly, I saw no sign of guards, at least not on our side of the palace. Almost all of Coileán's court lived to the south of him, down through the low hills and along the coast. There was nothing of consequence along the northern border to defend against—after all, no one lived in the woods. Seeing nothing to give us trouble, Joey and I waded through the cold stream and ducked into the ancient orchard on the far side, taking shelter among the fruit trees as the sun began to rise.

And that was when we heard a woman singing.

Joey's eyes widened, and he jabbed his finger at the apple tree beside me. I nodded and jumped up into the branches—an easier climb than my last, given the gnarled trunk—and Joey took the one to my left. There we sat, holding our breath as the stray bits of stone in the dirt below us flashed pink in the dawn, and listened as the singing intensified.

The singer was female, that much was clear, but she seemed to be either making the tune up as she went or forgetting her place every few bars and trying again in a different key. I began to sweat, even in the cool morning, but I willed myself to be still as the voice crescendoed—and then, through the leaves, I spotted Astrid.

One of the perks of Coileán's position was having a staff to make life easier for him. In particular, he had put out a call for kitchen aides. Sure, he could will a feast into existence with a snap of his fingers, but it wouldn't necessarily be a *great* feast. Astrid and the others who kept the table set were culinary masters, either by luck or through experience. Most of them, like my brother's guards, were half fae and had spent at least a few years in the mortal realm. I didn't have résumés on all of them, but I'd lurked around the kitchen long enough for Astrid to tell me about the decades she spent in Paris and Rome and New York, moving from café to restaurant for the sheer pleasure of cooking. That fact alone showed her passion for the practice—it took a rare faerie to willingly work in a room whose primary decorative element was stainless steel. She also had a soft spot for doing things the hard way, which explained the basket over her arm.

I waited a moment longer to be sure I'd identified her correctly, but the strengthening light made me certain. Astrid's hair, so blonde it was almost silver, shone in the sunlight that filtered through the peach trees across the aisle, but the clincher was her apron: full-length, bleached white, and covered with laden pockets. I couldn't see Joey, but as she stopped below his tree to pick an apple, I decided to test my luck and leapt.

Astrid whirled about and gasped when I landed at her feet, then dropped her basket in shock. I held up my empty hands, ready to plead with her for silence, but her face broke into a wide grin, and she threw her arms around me. "My lord!" she whispered into my hair. "Where have you *been*?

We thought you dead, and…" She pulled back and wrinkled her nose. "Moon and stars, child, when did you last bathe?"

Before I could begin to answer, Joey landed behind her and thrust the point of his sword toward the base of her neck. "Astrid, I don't want to hurt you," he said quietly, "but if you give me any reason to imagine that you might be thinking of doing something—"

She'd stiffened in the presence of so much steel, but she released me and lifted her hands in surrender when she heard his voice. "Joey? Is that you?"

"Yeah."

Astrid sighed, her face washed with relief. "Put the sword away, you silly boy. I haven't been so excited to see anyone since I met Julia Child." She turned to look at him over her shoulder, and he sheepishly lowered the blade. "Oh, gracious," she muttered, "you're a mess, too, aren't you? What crawled onto your chin and died?"

"Want to tell us what the hell's going on?" he countered.

"Gladly," she replied, stepping clear of his sword. "But might we go somewhere a little less open first? And for my sake, at least, might I tidy up the two of you?"

After a month on the run, I could have done with a nice, long soak and a deep-tissue massage, but getting magically willed clean was a better use of our limited time. If we were going to be stealthy, it wouldn't do to announce our presence via stench. Astrid took care of the basics as soon as we'd retreated behind a thick holly hedge, but she fretted when Joey insisted that the beard stay. "Why not just put a flashing sign over your head, then?" she protested. "*Mortal right here, take your best shot.*"

He rolled his eyes. "The court knows me already—"

"Oberon's doesn't, and they're all over the palace. Looking the part might buy you a moment."

Joey didn't like it—I think the unkempt moonshiner look was beginning to grow on him—but he knew Astrid was right, and the beard vanished.

When we were no longer so offensive to basic notions of hygiene, she scanned the area again for signs of motion, then pulled us close and dropped her voice to a whisper. "He came in the middle of the night," she began, continuing to glance over our shoulders as she spoke. "With his court. Not all of them, but a fair number. They swarmed the palace, overwhelmed the guards…" She grimaced at the memory. "The king was asleep. They caught him unawares."

My guts felt like she'd thrown them in a vise. "Is he—"

"He lives," she said, saving me the question. "But he's trapped. Oberon put some sort of enchantment on him—he's in an unbreakable sleep."

"Stasis," I said. "There's a spell for that, too."

"I don't know the workings," she replied. "But whatever he did, it's strong enough to bind your brother."

Joey frowned in confusion. "Colin's got the same power Oberon has. I thought the realm gave them both a little something extra."

"That's my understanding," said Astrid, "but consider Oberon's age—Lord Coileán is powerful, but against *him*?" She sighed and briskly shook her head. "They're close, I suppose, but the difference, plus the surprise…"

"And I'm sure our loving siblings didn't complain," I muttered.

Astrid's face tightened, and she hesitated before replying. "My lord…I don't want to distress you more, but your siblings…"

"Joined Oberon?"

"Are dead," she said quietly.

I stared at her for a moment, not quite comprehending what she was saying, and Astrid wrung her hands. "He killed them the first night. They were trapped in the cells—they didn't have a chance. When no one could find you, we feared the worst."

I leaned against the hedge, letting that sink in, and mumbled, "All of them?"

"All but the king. And some of their children," she added. "Some of their line have fled the realm, some went into hiding, but the ones who remained—"

"*Why?*"

She offered a little shrug. "If you overthrow a ruler, you're wise to take out any potential contenders to the throne who could avenge him."

I rubbed my face, fighting the pounding in my head. "So that leaves Moyna and me. Unless he's killed her, too."

"Oh," Astrid muttered, "*she's* very much alive." My head shot up, and I saw that her lips had become a thin, white line. "Word trickles down," she said bitterly. "The girl joined forces with her grandfather. More than that, I can't say."

But Joey's eyes widened as he turned to me. "When Vivi called, the faerie activity outside the Arcanum…"

"You think?" I said.

"I don't know, man, but if they thought the Arcanum was sheltering us…"

He let that hang, and my stomach knotted at the implications. "And what about you?" I asked, turning back to Astrid. "You swore allegiance or something?"

She looked pained. "We were given a choice: swear fealty or be locked away until he decided what to do with us. I thought I might be of more use to the king on the outside. I've been hoping someone would come," she continued, looking at us both, "though…well…"

"Well what?" asked Joey.

Astrid seemed almost embarrassed. "I'd rather hoped it would be Toula. Or, um…you know…"

"Someone with talent," I finished, and she nodded. "Last I heard, Toula was tied up with the Arcanum situation. Unless the Arcanum has killed her by now—let's just say we left a mess back there," I explained, hoping Astrid wouldn't push for details. "But since our rescue team is only Joey and me, will you help us?"

She clasped my hand and dipped in a slight curtsy.

"However I can, my lord. What's your plan?"

"You say there's some sort of enchantment binding Colin?" said Joey. "First thing we need to do is break it."

Her face clouded. "Would that I could, but I'm not that strong. I doubt all the staff together would be able—"

"Exactly. So we'll go about this indirectly," he said. "What's the easiest foolproof way to break a spell or enchantment?" We looked at him blankly, and he smirked. "Drag the affected person into Faerie. The barrier takes care of it. We just need to get him out, then pull him back through."

"Well," said Astrid, "in *theory*..."

"Do you know where he's being kept?" he asked. "Can you, like, gate us in there?'

"Yes and no," she muttered. "He's been left in a room on the ground floor of the palace, but it's open. I think the old bastard is using him as decoration, to be frank." She folded her arms and glared into space. "The room is warded. You can walk in, but you can't open a gate into it or from inside it—Misha tried that, and the guards got him. They aren't stationed there at all times, but they make regular sweeps of the halls. And I'm sure there would be an alarm if the king were to be taken from the room." Astrid looked at Joey and shook her head. "So no, gates are useless."

"Not necessarily," I said. "What if you got us to him, let Joey and me handle dragging him out of the room, and set up a gate down the hall? Oberon hasn't warded the entire palace, has he?"

"Not to my knowledge..." She mulled this over, then nodded. "Yes. If we were quick about it and quite lucky...I could get you in between rounds. That would give you a few minutes to grab him, but you would have to be fast, and I don't know how close I'd be able to stay."

Joey looked at me, and we silently reached a decision. "Sounds like our best shot," I said. "Unless Val is hiding around here and wouldn't mind adding a little muscle."

"Valerius?" she scoffed, then turned and spat in the

grass. "He sits at Oberon's right hand. I wouldn't look to *him* for help."

"*What?*" Joey cried. "That's...that can't be right, he's Colin's friend—"

"He got us out of here in the first place," I said, frowning at Astrid. "If he were working with Oberon..."

"Perhaps he had a change of heart once he saw the new regime," she muttered. "I don't know his mind. But he keeps company with Oberon and his ilk, and I've not seen him on the guard rounds in weeks. Dresses like a proper lord now." She sniffed her displeasure. "Everyone knows he's one of Mab's. I don't mean any disrespect to the king, but he was a fool to trust Valerius."

The news came as a sucker punch, but I pushed it aside. "Fine. We'll deal with him later. How do we get into the castle?"

Astrid looked around again for safety, then murmured, "Will you trust me?"

"Not like we have much of a choice," said Joey, but I saw the hurt in his eyes over Val's betrayal. "What do we do?"

She stepped back a pace and smiled tightly. "This won't be painful."

I saw the magic flash around her, and then a bluish cloud enveloped me. Too surprised to cry out, I closed my eyes in preemptive defense...

...and when I opened them again, I was staring at Astrid's boots. My eyes were at the level of her toes, yet I was standing.

I looked around until I saw Joey some distance away, half-hidden in the lush grass. Before I could run to him, something scooped me off the ground and into the air—a hand, I realized, seeing its twin descend toward Joey. At the end of the breathless ascent, I found myself looking up at Astrid's face from the hollow of her palm. "Temporary, I promise," she whispered. Her plosives were gusts of wind in my hair, and I held on as she lowered me into the darkness of her apron pocket. Her other hand shook Joey off beside me a few seconds later, leaving us trapped in the warm darkness of her clothing. Without another word, Astrid began to walk—but where she was taking us, I couldn't tell. At least Kuni had been able to see from his seat in my palm. Astrid's idea of transportation left much to be desired.

"You know," Joey muttered as he made himself secure in the corner of the pocket, "this plan might have a few holes we should have considered ahead of time."

I'm not going to say that the day I spent being bumped around in Astrid's pocket was the strangest of my life, but no matter what happens to me in the future, it'll probably remain in the top five.

Unless you're riding in a pocket, you don't think about how much your clothing moves when you walk, especially something like an apron, which shifts with every step. The particular pocket in which we'd landed hit Astrid at mid-thigh, making our ride feel kind of like a hammock from hell. Adding to the general misery were the fact that Joey and I couldn't really talk—we didn't want to draw attention to Astrid with mysterious squeaking—and the disorienting task of trying to figure out where we were in the palace by smell and sound alone. The latter was easier to work around, since Astrid spent most of her time in the kitchen. Mercifully, she stopped by the counter at one point to peel and core the fruit she'd picked that morning. Every so often, her hand would slip into her pocket and drop a few crumbs for us—a bite of apple, a sliver of ham, a crust of bread— and so Joey and I passed the time by gorging ourselves. In retrospect, this might not have been the brightest idea we'd ever had, since a swaying apron and a full stomach don't exactly mix, but we held it together and even managed to doze in shifts.

For her part, Astrid went about her day as if nothing

were out of the ordinary. She spoke little but did so politely, making herself as inconspicuous as possible. I heard unfamiliar voices laughing a few times—Oberon's people almost certainly—but Astrid said nothing to them, and they paid her no attention.

As the hours passed, Astrid moved back and forth between the kitchen and the dining rooms until the night grew late and she finished her work. Joey and I bumped along as she walked upstairs to her quarters, and then, after a large jostle, the movement stopped. He started crawling over to me in the dark, but before we could speculate together, Astrid's eyes appeared at the top of our pouch. "I'm going to bed," she whispered. "You're on a hook on the back of my door for the moment. We'll wait for the palace to quiet before we do this, so try to get some sleep."

At a loss for a better idea, Joey and I divvied up the last of the food and stretched out, making ourselves as comfortable as we could. I know I dozed off, because when I opened my eyes again, it was still pitch-black, but we were moving once more. Joey reached out and squeezed my arm, offering reassurance in the darkness, and I fumbled until I made contact with his shoulder. It would be all right, I repeated to myself. All we had to do was drag Coileán out of bed and through a gate. Piece of cake. We didn't even have our backpacks to slow us down.

After a time, there came a heavy click, our movement stopped, and the only sound I could hear was Astrid's breathing. Something descended into the pocket, and I realized it was a crooked finger when the short nail brushed against me. I climbed aboard and held on, and following a long rush of wind and a plunge like a roller coaster, I found myself on the carpet. The finger retreated, but it returned a moment later with Joey—and with another flash of enchantment, we shot back to our proper sizes. As we checked ourselves over for missing pieces, Astrid lit a tiny flame in her hand, silently showing us where we were: a seldom-used sitting room tucked far in the eastern wing of the palace. "He's down the corridor and around the corner, the third closed door," she whispered, and extinguished her fire. "The guards will pass shortly. Once they've gone, you'll have no more than ten minutes to retrieve him. Are you sure about this?"

"No," said Joey, "but I think we're long past that." He patted Astrid's shoulder and slipped to the door, then pressed his ear to the crack. "Footsteps in the far hall," he muttered as I joined him. "On stone. Give them a second to get by us."

We waited in silence for a minute that stretched into a month, and then Joey slowly depressed the brass door handle and eased into the hallway. I followed him with my heart hammering in my throat, straining for any sign that the guards had decided to vary their rounds for the fun of it, but the wing remained dark and quiet, and we reached the door without being discovered. Joey softly exhaled as he worked at the handle, and with a little *snick* that seemed to echo all around us, we were in.

Joey closed the door to cover our tracks, but I had eyes only for the four-poster bed in the center of the room. A tall taper had been lit on a stone pillar at each corner of the bed, clearly revealing the identity of the immobile man laid out on top of the blankets. I hurried to his side and looked him over, checking for damage, but Coileán seemed uninjured—at least from what little I could see of him that wasn't covered by his T-shirt and sweatpants. He really had been taken unawares, I thought—unprepared, barefoot, and still wearing his makeshift pajamas.

"Coileán," I whispered, bending to his ear, "it's me. Joey's here, too. If you can hear me, we're going to get you out of here, okay?"

He remained still, but I noticed his eyes darting back and forth as if he were dreaming. He frowned in his sleep, and a little wrinkle had formed between his dark brows. Whatever was going through his mind couldn't have been pleasant. I tried patting his face to wake him, but he remained insensate, locked in the stillness of sleep.

Joining me, Joey watched my useless efforts for a moment, then muttered, "If you think we can wake him, there's one other thing we could try." I arched my eyebrow in query, and he reached under his shirt for his silver crucifix. "Pain might rouse him."

I didn't like it, but I stepped back while Joey lifted his necklace off over his head and wrapped the chain around his fist. "Sorry, boss," he whispered, then slowly lowered the tip of the cross toward Coileán's exposed hand.

As I watched, Coileán's eyes picked up speed, his wrinkle deepened, and his breathing, which had been slow and regular, sped up into shallow gasps. "Stop," I said, catching Joey's wrist. "He knows what's going on, he just can't do anything about it. See?"

Joey pulled his hand back, and Coileán's face relaxed a degree. "Shit," he whispered, and slipped his necklace back on. "Okay, we're going to have to do this the hard way. I can probably get him in a fireman's hoist, but to be safe, let's each take a side. Help me swing his legs around."

I began to do as he asked, but before I could take two steps, the world went black and formless, and I was falling.

I tensed, expecting a hard landing, but whatever I hit was soft and formed itself to my body—honestly, it felt kind of like room-temperature Jell-O. With the initial shock past, I managed to get my knees under me and stood, and found that the soft ground had suddenly firmed. Then again, there was no ground to speak of, nothing but darkness in all directions, and I was on the verge of panic when I heard a familiar voice behind me say, "We haven't much time, Aiden."

I spun around, and there she was: the glowing stranger from my dream, now wearing a long blue gown with lacy sleeves, her luminescence the only light around. She stepped close to me, then caught my chin between her finger and thumb and tilted my face down toward hers. "Poor child," she said softly, reaching up to pat my cheek. "I know you've struggled of late, but I had to see if you were strong enough."

I stuttered in spite of myself. "You...wait, you're..."

"I answer to many names," she said with a grin, "but yes, you're correct. You've come to rescue Coileán?" I nodded frantically, and she clasped her hands as her face grew serious. "You'll never get him out of this room alive. You haven't moved, by the way," she added, seeing my expression. "I mean, you're on the floor now, but this place...well, it's outside of normal time and space, really. We need to talk."

"But we've got someone waiting, all we have to do is carry him—"

"Straight through the wards around the door," she interrupted, "which will kill all three of you. And Oberon, too, though I could be mistaken about that. It would *weaken* him, surely, but you'd have no guarantee of taking him with you. I assume you'd rather live to see the dawn, yes?"

I frowned down at her. "Astrid didn't say anything about that."

"Because she doesn't know. She's still very much a child." Faerie folded her thin arms and watched me try to work around this new wrinkle. "You cannot take him out that way," she said as I began to pace. "Or out the window. He'll have to break the enchantments himself—the one holding him, and the one on the room. For him to do that, someone will need to distract Oberon."

"What do you mean?"

Her smile returned, but with an edge. "A bind like the one Oberon has made isn't a static thing. Oh, the boy's *adept* at binds, I grant him that, but he's unaccustomed to binding someone who fights back." Seeing my confusion, she explained, "Coileán is nearly Oberon's equal. Not quite his match, but close. When I transferred to him the gift I gave your mother, I amplified it to make up for his relative youth.

Do you follow?" I nodded, and she said, "An enchantment like a bind is always tied to its maker. For a bind like…well, for example, the one Coileán placed on Moyna, the maker seldom feels it—the object of the bind is too weak to fight it off. But Coileán is struggling with everything he has, and Oberon must fight to keep the bind intact. It requires a certain degree of concentration."

I thought of Ilunna, who had been unable to distract the old king with her charms. "So if he were forced to take his mind off Coileán…"

She nodded. "I have a proposal for you, Aiden. Will you hear it?"

"Anything."

I couldn't be sure, but I think she was pleased at that. "Some time ago, I made a compact with Oberon, Mab, and your mother," said Faerie. "I gave them power beyond their imagining with the understanding that they would abide by several conditions, one of them being that they would no longer seek to kill each other. Mab broke our covenant, and Titania met her fate, but Oberon, for all else that he has done, has kept the letter of our bargain. Not its spirit, evidently," she muttered, "but the letter. I will not break my word to him and withdraw my gift. But given his behavior, I would be willing to empower someone else to challenge him."

She looked up at me in silence, waiting, and I took a step backward. "Who, *me?*"

"If you're willing, child."

"But…but I can't," I said in a rush, "I'm a witch-blood, I can't do anything with magic, it…I mean, I see it, but I can't *do* anything…"

She let me babble for a moment, then held up one hand to stop the flow. "Your mother's and father's gifts war within you," she said gently. "What I can do—and what I am *willing* to do—is upset the balance. I can suppress your father's influence."

I stared at her, replaying what she had said. "You

mean…"

"From a functional perspective, you would be no different from the rest of the half fae," she finished. "With everything that entails. And until such time as Coileán is able to resume his duties, you would carry power equal to his. I can do this for you, child. But before you decide," she cautioned, "know that the process cannot be undone. If you make your choice"—she spread her hands—"you've made your choice. Is that clear?"

Somehow, I managed to nod.

"Very good. Are you willing, then?"

A million thoughts ran through my mind, but in the midst of the hurricane, I heard myself whisper, "Yes."

Faerie smiled. "This will hurt. Best if you close your eyes."

Hurt doesn't begin to describe what happened next. The blackness beneath me gave way, and I tumbled into the abyss. A split-second later, something broke my fall, but it felt like I'd been caught in a net made of barbed high-voltage wires, and then like every cell of my body decided to explode at once. I would have screamed, but I'd forgotten where my mouth was supposed to be. This wasn't pain, this wasn't agony—this was something red and sharp and nameless, and at that moment, I wanted nothing more than the mercy of death.

And then, as quickly as it had begun, the torment ended, and I felt hands on my shoulders.

"Aiden!" Joey whispered as he shook me. "*Aid*, come on, wake—"

He released me suddenly, and I opened my eyes to see the room around me suffused with white light. Squinting at the unexpected brightness, I eased myself into a sitting position and spotted Joey crouched halfway across the room, goggling at me. "Joey—"

"You're glowing," he said, wide-eyed and tense. "Why

the hell are you glowing?"

Dazed and unsure of what had just happened, I looked at my hand and realized the light was coming from *me*. "Realm made me an offer I couldn't refuse," I mumbled, flipping my hand over to see that, yes, the light came out the other side as well.

"What happened to—"

"We can't drag Coileán out of here," I interrupted, wiggling my fingers experimentally. "She said it'd kill us all. Got to distract Oberon. She gave me the power."

Joey scrambled upright and gripped his sword. "Mother of God," he whispered, "I've seen that light before." He pulled his sword out and flipped the hilt toward me. "Can you take it?"

Sure, I started to say, but as I reached for it, I felt a tingle race along my hand and arm, and I paused. Puzzled, I reached toward it with my other hand, but the tingle began there, too, and it strengthened to an unpleasant buzz as I got closer. "What—"

"Draw yours," he said, locking eyes with me.

I unsheathed my blade with no difficulty—even if I was still glowing—and stared at the bronze. "I don't under—" I began, but snapped my mouth closed as the realization hit.

Iron and silver, dangerous to the fae, lethal if used correctly.

Joey's hilt was wrapped with leather, but there was good steel hiding beneath.

"Holy shit," I whispered, looking back at him in shock, "I'm a *faerie*."

"I can see that," he muttered, putting his sword away. "And what do you mean, we can't take Colin out of here?"

"Door's warded, we'll all go boom," I mumbled, only half-listening to him. This wasn't right, I was the dud, this couldn't be happening...

Joey shook my shoulders, pulling me from my chaotic thoughts. "We've got to get out of here. Turn your highs off."

"Huh?"

"Stop glowing."

"I don't know how!" I protested.

He considered this for a second, then stepped back and lowered his hands in placation. "It's okay, Aiden, just focus. Breathe for me. Think about...you know, *not* glowing, yeah?"

I took a deep breath, then another, pushing down the rising fear...and suddenly, the light died away. "I...I did it..."

"Fireball," he said calmly, holding out his palm. "Come on, you can do this, just think about it."

Remembering what it had looked like when Coileán pulled off that trick, I tried to imagine a similar flame in my hand—and an instant later, there were green flames dancing all around me. "Joey!" I yelped in panic.

"*Breathe*," he ordered, and as I fought the surge of terror, the fire, like the corona, vanished. I stood there by Coileán's bed, trembling and blinded by the after-images, and Joey cocked his head toward the door. "Time to go. Let's get back to the woods, and we'll figure out our next step from there."

"But Coileán—"

"Aiden, listen to me," said Joey, stepping between the bed and me, "we can't help him like this. We've got to get out of here before they catch us."

"But...but all I have to do is distract Oberon—"

"You can't even control yourself! Pitting you against Oberon right now would be...I don't know, like giving a Cub Scout a rocket launcher and directing him toward a bear. *No.*" He pointed to the ground. "They're coming. Punch a hole in the floor."

"*What?*"

"Floor. Hole. Do it."

I started to protest that there was roughly no way in hell that I could punch a hole in anything, let alone a stone floor, but as I jabbed my finger toward the ground to drive the absurdity of Joey's suggestion home, the flagstones flew up around us in an explosion of gravel.

"Okay, maybe do it a little more quietly next time," said Joey as surprised voices rose in the hallway. Grabbing my wrist, he pulled me after him into the pit.

That turned out to be a rough landing, and I gasped after the floor knocked the wind from me. Joey had managed to release me and roll into the impact, and he was on his feet before I'd remembered why I was hurting. "Dungeon," he said, looking around at the torches on the walls, then pointed down the vaulted hall to the left. "Out that way. Come on, move." He pulled me off the floor and half-dragged me to the other end of the room, ignoring the shouts that echoed down from Coileán's room. "Hole there, do it."

I barely thought about it, and the stonework exploded again. Yanking my arm, Joey pulled me through, straight into the ornamental moat, and up the far bank. Dripping, we sprinted for the gardens and the distant tree line. My lungs burned, my heart pounded like a jackhammer, and with the night, I could barely see five feet in front of me, but Joey seemed to intuit the smoothest path through the flowerbeds and around the orchards, and he caught me each time I stumbled. Finally, as my battered body cried for mercy, we crested a hillock and dodged a thicket of brambles, and my exhausted legs gave way. I went down hard in the dirt, and I didn't care.

CHAPTER 12

We didn't make camp that night. I woke shortly before dawn with a raging headache and sore calves to find Joey resting with his back against a nearby tree, guarding our bags. He'd covered me with whatever camouflage he could find, and I smelled of decaying leaves and wet dirt. Carefully, going slowly as my stiff muscles protested, I pushed myself off the ground and brushed the foliage from my hair. I couldn't quite recall why we hadn't made a fire—we always made a fire for protection—but then my glance landed on Joey's scabbard, which peeked out from the side of his duster, and the night came rushing back.

The dungeon ceilings were *high*. I should have had at least a few broken bones with my ungainly landing, I realized, but a little test wiggling suggested that everything was intact. Even the bruises I found when I peeled off my shirt were brown and fading, not the violent purples and greens of fresh injuries.

"Colin heals quickly, even without adding enchantment to the mix," said Joey in an exhausted bass, interrupting my self-inspection. "So does Val. Are you all in one piece?"

"I...think so." I rubbed the grit from my eyes, then shook the dirt off my shirt and pulled it back on. "Joey...what just...last night, I..."

He sighed and climbed to his feet. "One minute, you were with me. The next, you were out cold on the floor. How's the head?"

"Sore." I patted the back of my skull and winced. "Bruised, I think."

"You went down like a pile of bricks. Lucky you didn't crack anything important open." He brushed off the back of his coat and popped his spine. "And as soon as you woke, the fireworks started. Remember?"

I nodded, wincing at the memory of the searing pain.

He crossed his arms and gave me a weary stare. "Want to tell me what happened?"

Leaning against a tree, I closed my eyes and rubbed my forehead. "Remember when I told you that I had a dream—"

"Woman warned you to run, might be this Lady that Lailu was talking about, yeah."

"She was. Is. She's the realm." I opened my eyes and found him still watching me. "And she said the only way to free Coileán is to distract Oberon long enough for Coileán to free himself. So she…well…gave me a boost."

"That's not a boost, that's a complete overhaul," Joey retorted. "Dude, you were *enchanting* last night."

"Yeah," I mumbled.

"How?"

I sighed and resumed my head massage. "She said she could suppress the wizard bits of me. Make me like a half faerie instead of a mongrel. And I guess she added some extra on top of that."

"Uh…yeah, there's no need to guess at that," he muttered. "Last time I saw someone glowing like that, Titania had just bit the dust, and Colin was dealing with the surge." He shook his head. "So what I'm hearing right now is that, more or less, you're currently packing the firepower of a faerie king."

I groaned and massaged harder. "Yeah, I think so. She didn't give me the full specs before she blasted me. And even if she had, I still don't know what to do with it."

"Yeah, that's a major problem. You're a danger to us both until you get yourself straightened out."

I dropped my hands again and glared at him in exasperation. "Well, if we walk in the woods long enough, maybe we'll run into someone who can give me a few lessons," I snapped. "Unless Oberon figures out what's going on and finds us first. I mean, I did just blow two holes in the fucking palace, but that's not really noticeable, right?"

"Aiden."

His voice was low and held a note of caution, and I realized I was glowing again. "Sorry," I muttered as the light died away.

"Try to stay calm, okay?"

"Right," I said, rubbing the back of my neck. "I'm sorry, I just...long night..."

"Rage." I looked at him in confusion, and he said, "When Colin flies off the handle...know what I mean?"

"Fireworks," I sighed, knowing exactly what Joey was talking about. Coileán had, with much embarrassed apology, explained it to me after he set a particularly aggravating petitioner's hair on fire. The half fae knew how to behave in polite society, but if they were pushed too far, someone was liable to end up fried or worse.

"Bingo," said Joey. He scowled at the ground, then looked back at me. "So, barring friendly hermit faeries in the woods, what do we do now?"

I don't know was on the tip of my tongue, but I froze when a familiar voice whispered in the back of my mind: *You are not safe here.*

I squeezed my eyes closed, finally understanding what Coileán had meant about the voice in his head. "Is he coming?" I muttered.

"Is who coming?" asked Joey.

Not yet. I showed him nothing to trouble him. A trick, he believes—a prank by one of his sons. You may have a few hours of safety, but I make no guarantees.

I looked at Joey and pointed to our bags. "Realm says we need to move. We could backtrack."

He bent and grabbed his pack. "You thinking what I'm thinking?"

"If it involves Lailu and a favor," I replied with a grunt,

swinging my bag into position, "then yes, I am."

I wasn't feeling social that long day. I wasn't feeling much of anything, really. Oh, I was feeling *something*, but it was too convoluted for me to put a label on it, so I tried to ignore it and concentrated on feeling numb.

The world around me hadn't changed. I don't know what I'd been expecting, but the sun rose as usual, the breeze blew, the woods thickened as we crossed the first of the ridges and valleys of the foothills, and something large, unseen, and quite probably predatory screeched at us from a tree as we hiked past. Nothing out of the ordinary there. We'd found water early in the morning, but I was still sore and growing hungrier with each passing hour. The feast of crumbs Astrid had given us only lasted so long, and my stomach restarted its old chorus of complaints. And the magic around us looked no different—it swirled in muted colors like a fog more perceived than seen, the usual kaleidoscope of potential.

We stopped on a hilltop in the early afternoon, maybe eight miles from the palace, and Joey left me with the gear while he stalked a flock of wild sheep upwind of us on the valley floor. Sitting was a relief, but I was bored, and without thinking, I started trying to move the nearby bits of magic around. As a kid, it had been something I did as a last resort, an almost meditative practice that helped me stay awake. That day, however, the magic did something new: rather than move where I nudged it, it burst into brilliant color...and then a line of fireballs shot out of my fingertip and straight through the nearest tree. I sat there, momentarily stunned by the sudden conflagration, then jumped up, grabbed my half-empty canteen, and tossed the contents onto the blaze.

But by then, the tree was a goner, and the little water I'd carried seemed to have no effect. I panicked and turned in circles to find a pond before the whole forest caught fire, but we'd stopped in a dry spot. Before I could run back down the hill and look for a place to refill my canteen, the voice spoke to me again: *Will it out.*

"How?" I yelled, looking around as if Faerie were going to show up with a fire extinguisher.

Focus. Fight your fear.

"Sure, great, no problem," I snapped. "I'll just sit here and find my center while I burn up a few acres. How about something *helpful?*"

I could have sworn the voice chuckled. *Consider the fire. You made it. You can unmake it. It's simple, just think—*

A pair of wooden buckets appeared at my feet, each filled to the brim with water, and I pushed the voice aside as I tossed their contents at the tree. The flame sputtered, and as I watched, the buckets refilled. By the time Joey ran up to see what all the smoke was about, I'd put out the fire and stood in the wet dirt, panting as my tired arms shook. He took one look at the scene, nodded, and murmured, "Accident?"

"Yeah."

"You all right?"

"Uh-huh."

"Okay. Take it easy," he cautioned, and started back down to retrieve his kill.

I sat down beside another tree and considered my buckets, which had again filled themselves of their own accord, then squeezed my hands into fists and imagined the buckets gone. They vanished without a sound, and I released the breath I'd been holding.

You know, the voice resumed, *you could have just willed the fire out. Simpler, more elegant...*

"It worked, didn't it?" I muttered to the air.

Well...yes, but the water was unnecessary.

I sighed and closed my eyes. "You do realize that I don't know how to handle magic, right? This isn't some revelation to you, is it?"

You're cranky when you're hungry.

"That shouldn't be news to you, either."

Eat something, the voice suggested.

"Joey's coming back with food," I said, hoping I could fall asleep for a few minutes and forget about the smoldering tree.

But she didn't let up. *You don't need to wait. Make yourself a sandwich. And you need to keep moving—I can't say whether Oberon will send a party after you.*

"Look," I muttered, resting my head on my knees, "if I try that right now, the odds are good that I'll either make myself some nice rat poison or burn the damn forest down. So I'm just going to sit here and wait for lamb, all right?"

You don't care for lamb, she pointed out.

"Better than rat poison."

Faerie had nothing to say to that, and so I waited in silence for Joey to return, hoping I could avoid inadvertently conjuring up, say, a swarm of killer bees.

Joey couldn't have been a better guide all day, since I was barely holding myself together. He hunted, made fires, found water, and cooked for us both, insisting that I sit and rest while he handled matters. Over leftover lamb that evening, as we nursed our fresh bruises and blisters, he kept the conversation light, pointedly avoiding topics that would circle back to Coileán or our current predicament. He talked about college and the crazier people he'd met in seminary, the one guy who had to pontificate in every class, the other who cracked halfway through the first year and ran off to Amsterdam. He brought up stories from the Ren Faire circuit—summers spent living in an RV parked in fields, subsisting on turkey legs and Pop Tarts, surreptitiously tapping a cask of cheap ale with his friends and drinking himself silly long after the last guests had gone home. He told me about the horse on which he'd learned to ride, a half-blind nag who'd answered to "Widowmaker." Finally, when the fire had burned low and the stars glittered above us through the trees and the blue smoke haze, he sent me to the tent for the first shift.

When I was alone in the stillness, the full impact of what I'd done hit me. I lay there in my sleeping bag, paralyzed as wave after wave of guilt and fear and horror crashed over me like a storm tide.

I'd run off to Faerie to escape my bedroom prison, but I'd done so partly in the hope that the experience would somehow make a wizard out of me. Not a great wizard, not even a good wizard, just a wizard strong enough to merit a wand of my own. Even a dragonscale wand, the crutch of low-talent witches. I didn't care—all I wanted was to show the Arcanum that I was more than the Carvers' dud.

So what had I done? In one moment, I hadn't just given up on my dream—I'd let the realm suppress the part of me, however weak, that could have been a wizard someday. I'd told Hel I wasn't turning my back on the Arcanum, but that was exactly what I'd done, wasn't it? I'd rejected them to become...

I couldn't bring myself to finish the thought.

The Arcanum may not have taught me much about magic, but I knew that faeries were dangerous, evil, and best destroyed. *Every* wizard knew that. And that was what the Arcanum stood for, wasn't it? Not only keeping the world's wizards in line, but also defending the realm against the horrors that lurked outside its borders? Plain and simple, the only good faerie was a dead one.

Well, I allowed, maybe not my brother. Maybe not Astrid or Rufus. And Toula...whatever she was, she was all right. I continued to hold out hope for Val, but I couldn't make a call on him yet.

But still, exceptions aside, I'd thrown my lot in with the enemy. I was a blood traitor after all. Dad was right about me, he was right about *everything*, and I was useless, worse than useless, undeniably evil. I wasn't his son—I was Titania's.

He should have left me where Val had dropped me.

And as for this—well, he would never forgive me. I'd never go home again, never be the wizard he had wanted, and Hel…

God, *Hel.*

How was Hel supposed to be the grand magus when her own brother was a damn faerie? When she found out…

No. Maybe she didn't have to find out. Maybe I could hide it, play it cool…just never, ever, touch silverware again. We could go out for sushi. Surely *someone* in Montana made sushi. Yeah. She didn't have to know what I'd done…

Oh, who the hell was I kidding? She was bound to find out, one way or another. I'd slip, or Joey would cave in and tell her…and then I'd never see her again. Hel would reject me, too. Even if she forgave me, she'd have to do it.

When I finally shifted in my bag, I felt the damp spot under my face and realized I'd been crying. I sniffed, rubbed my eyes dry, and crawled outside to join Joey by the fire.

He didn't seem surprised to see me. "It's just hot water," he said without preamble, passing me his mug, "but I found a Jolly Rancher in this pocket I'd forgotten, so it's got a little flavor. Nothing to write home about," he cautioned as I took a test sip, "but it gets the taste of mutton out of your mouth, right?"

Weak green apple was pretty pathetic as a palate cleanser, but I nodded and handed it back to him. "Decent."

"Liar." He turned to look at me more closely, then did a double take and frowned. "You okay, Aid?"

"Sure," I muttered.

"Your eyes are red…"

"Smoke."

Joey drank his weird concoction and looked away, giving me my privacy. After a long moment, he quietly said, "It's going to be okay, man. We're going to hide out here, and we're going to find someone who can help you, and then we're going to bust Colin out. Don't worry about that tree. It's just a tree—I think we've got a few to spare," he added, twirling one finger at the forest around us. "And if worst comes to worst, we'll find that lake again and figure out how to get the Tor gate open. Or maybe the piq know of one. We'll go back, call Rufus, regroup—"

"What am I going to tell Hel?" I mumbled.

He grunted. "You won't be telling *her* anything. The minute she sees us, she'll bless us out for pulling this stunt, and maybe we'll be able to get a word in over the next week or so. But really, it's going to be a monologue for a long time."

"You know what I mean."

He glanced back at me and sipped. "All right, tell her what? Tell her you were offered talent and immortality and accepted? She'll understand."

"No, she won't."

"Aiden," he sighed, "she's been hoping that Faerie would have an effect on you—"

"Not like this! Not like…" I saw that I was glowing again and paused, then concentrated until the light subsided. "Like that. Not like that."

Joey finished his drink and put the mug in the dirt beside him. "You know, I never had a sibling. Only child, heard all the jokes—you know what I mean. So I've obviously never been part of a sibling relationship, right, no rivalry, none of that. But I *do* know enough to know that Helen loves you," he said, looking me in the eye. "And it's pretty clear that you love her, too. So I wouldn't worry too much, if I were you."

I remained silent and unconvinced, and Joey lightly punched my arm. "Look, maybe I'm just the interloper here, but I know a bit about Helen by now," he said. "*And* you. Which is why I have hope that, you know, someday it won't be so weird for you that she's dating me," he added off-handedly.

"It's not—"

He shook his head, cutting my denial short. "She's your sister, and I'm the loser moving in on her. Believe me, I get it."

I realized that he was trying to change the topic, but I

went along with it. "You're not a loser."

"Right, I'm a twenty-six-year-old seminary dropout whose marketable skills include sword fighting and saddling dragons. I have zero savings because my boss bankrolled whatever it was I happened to be doing, at least until last month. And—here's the good part—I'm dating this incredibly talented wizard, and I can't even sense magic. No clue where it is."

"Joey—"

"Also, I live in a friggin' barn because my dragon gets lonely. I mean, there's a reason I sleep over at Helen's place more than she does at mine, you know? There's nothing sexy about barns."

"I thought her apartment was tiny."

"Still better than a barn. Don't get me wrong," he hastily added, "I love Georgie, but the place has a certain, shall we say, *funk*." He shifted on his backpack and looked up at the trees. "Helen's *something*, and for some reason, she lets me tag along. I don't get it," he said, shaking his head. "I don't know why I'm this lucky. But...Aiden," he continued, staring me down again, "I love your sister. Very much. I'll do just about anything to make her happy. And...you know," he said, rubbing his neck, "I like you, too, and I'd really like it if things weren't, uh...*awkward*...with you and me."

Neither of us said anything for a moment, but then a log split with a snapping crackle and a burst of orange sparks, and I cleared my throat. "Joey...I betrayed everything and everyone I've ever known in the silo, and you think *you're* the loser here?"

"Come on, you didn't—"

"I did. And I still don't know how I'm going to tell Hel that I've officially switched teams," I muttered. "I mean, what's this going to do to her career? The Council's never going to let her have the job as long as I'm in the picture..."

Joey shrugged. "What job? Last time I checked, she had a warrant hanging over her, remember?" He leaned against the tree behind him and shook his head. "Forget the Arcanum. If they don't want you, fine. Lord Aiden doesn't need their shit."

"Lord Aiden can't be trusted not to set random fires when his mind wanders."

"Then get some shut-eye, and we'll hope you can't enchant in your sleep. Deal?"

"What about—"

Joey cut me off with a raised finger. "We're safer if you're not asleep on your feet. I mean it, hit the hay. Listen to your elders."

I smirked but rose from the campfire. "Sir Percival, was it?"

"Don't start with that."

"Whatever you say." I ducked into the tent, but popped my head out a few seconds later. "Hey, Joey?"

"Yeah?"

"If we get out of this alive, you'd better damn well ask her."

He tucked his hands behind his head and grinned, and I returned to my sleeping bag, hoping for a miracle.

When I next rolled out of bed, the sun was climbing, and Joey had the last of the lamb reheating in his battered skillet over the fire. By then, the lack of regular washing had made the pan almost nonstick. "Well, looks like we've survived another night," he said, flipping the cutlets with a flick of his wrist. "Breakfast?"

"You realize we're going to have to stop for a nap at some point," I replied, but fished out my plate and headed toward the smell of meat.

"Oh, probably, but I've got at least another seven or eight miles in me before then." He portioned out the food and settled down beside me with his share, and I caught him absently rubbing his fresh crop of stubble as he waited for the lamb to cool. "Sleep well?"

"Like the dead." Physically, I felt fantastic—the muscle stiffness I'd anticipated was almost gone, and my fading bruises had vanished overnight—but I'd awoken with the world still on my mind. "Meant to ask you something."

"Shoot."

I hesitated briefly to formulate the question. "Are we...okay?"

He sawed off a fatty corner and popped it in his mouth. "Going to have to be more specific than that, man."

"I mean, aside from the random fires, are you, uh...all right with being out here with...you know—"

"*Aiden*," he interrupted, looking at me in disbelief, "are you seriously asking me that?"

I felt a fresh flush blooming up my neck. "If you're not, I understand, but—"

"I work for your brother," he said, putting his knife down. "The *vast* majority of my time is spent in Faerie. Honestly, if I had a problem being around people with fae leanings, do you think I'd have lasted here a week?"

My face burned. "Just...you know, checking."

He sighed and resumed his attack on breakfast. "I'm not Arcanum. All that baggage you're carrying around—I don't have it. We're cool."

"So you're not...I mean, with the fireballs..."

I left the thought unfinished, but he seemed to know where I was heading. "You're asking me if I'm a little scared of faeries?" he replied. I nodded, and he shrugged. "Of course I am. Only an idiot wouldn't be wary," he continued around a bite of meat. "But a healthy respect doesn't translate to hatred. I've known some *annoying* ones, now," he admitted. "A few days with the Puck in close quarters was about all I could handle of him, and his old man's no better. But come on, Aiden," he said, gesturing with his knife, "you and I have been roaming around together for more than a month, and we haven't killed each other yet, right? And anyway, I'm not one to let a few fireballs come between friends."

Though greasy, his blade flashed in the low fire, and I remembered something else I'd meant to do. "One other thing," I said as he ate. "You gave me a couple of knives back in Florida. If it's all the same to you, I'd like to give them back."

"Say no more. Still sheathed, or do I need to dig through your stuff?"

"I can handle them. And, uh…thank you," I mumbled, making the most of my hard plastic knife and spork. A few futile seconds later, I looked up from the overdone lamb when Joey gripped my shoulder.

"Forget the Arcanum," he said with a firm squeeze. "With all due respect to Helen, they're a bunch of inbred freaks in a missile silo. You know who else meets that description? Doomsday cults." I grinned, and Joey shook his head. "You expect me to base my self-worth on what a doomsday cult thinks of me? *Hell*, no. Same goes for you," he continued, locking his tired eyes on mine. "The last time I checked, you were a high lord. So why do you care if some wizards aren't happy about that? They can rot in their bunker."

I shrugged. "Family?"

"Family's the people who love you, not just the people related to you," he replied, settling back on his bag. "You know what your problem is, Aiden?"

"Which one?" I muttered, giving up on my utensils. The meat had cooled enough that I didn't burn my fingers when I went at it caveman-style.

"Exactly. You think there's something wrong with you."

I looked up from the chop in my hands and frowned. "Would you like a few examples?"

"No. I want you to do me a favor," said Joey, and put his plate aside. "I want you to stop thinking that you owe the universe an apology for existing. You don't. I firmly believe that on this count, there are no mistakes. So can you do that for me? Stop apologizing?"

As I stared back at Joey, a dozen voices echoed the

familiar litany in my head: *Dud. Mongrel. Loser. Dog. Reject. Worthless. Failure.* But as they rose to howling shouts, another voice cut through the cacophony: *He's right, you know. Listen to him.*

And just like that, the others were silenced.

"Yeah," I said, biting into my breakfast, "I think I can try."

Weeks on the run had put Joey in touch with his own limits, and his prediction about our next rest point couldn't have been far off. We made good time over the hills, but by midday, he was flagging, and we called a halt to let him catch up on the sleep he'd forfeited the night before. "Just an hour or two," he assured me, flashing the iPhone clone Rufus had given him. "I'll set the alarm."

The beauty of faerie-made electronics was that they never seemed to need charging. The phone was useless for communication—there was no signal to be found, and I had no idea how Coileán had made his usable between realms, even if I trusted myself to experiment on Joey's—but at least we had a sense of the world on the other side of the gate. Still set on Eastern Time, the phone no longer synched up with our days thanks to Faerie's inherent weirdness, but it gave us some idea of how long we'd been away.

Its calendar had insisted it was November 21—maybe a week to Thanksgiving, I mused as Joey slept. A month before, we'd been hiding out in the Keys with Georgie and Rufus, hoping for word from the merrow. A month before that, Coileán had taken me out for an afternoon at the British Museum, insisting that my buggy code would be waiting for me and that I needed a dose of sunlight. I'd protested that London was the last place I'd look for sun, but the weather had been glorious, cool with patchy clouds, and Coileán had stood behind me and quietly read aloud the Greek on the Rosetta Stone while I soaked it all in. It hadn't surprised me that my brother could translate from ancient

Greek—heck, it wouldn't have surprised me if he could read hieroglyphics—but I realized he wasn't doing it to impress me. He wanted me to understand. We'd moved on to the Elgin Marbles, and he took a spot beside me and folded his arms while I studied the line of sculptures. After a time, when the crowd around us thinned, he'd murmured, "This realm has its drawbacks, but there's so much here that's worth protecting."

"They're pretty neat," I said, nodding at the sculptures around us.

"Beyond those. People, I mean." We moved down the room, and he said, "I've found that no matter how trying things seem to become, there's always one or two good people around if you know where to look. Also," he added, pointing to the sculpture, "we've got a couple of those in the library. Seems like Elgin's people had some issues with accounting. Take your time, enjoy," he said, and stepped out of the room while I gawked at him.

But that was two months ago, another time and another place.

Two days ago, I'd found Coileán, only to leave him behind, helpless and trapped.

It was all up to me now. If I was going to get him back…

I held out my hand, and with a deep breath, I cleared my thoughts and stared at the hollow of my palm. "Come on," I whispered to the ether, "don't let me set the tent on fire."

There was nothing—and then, without warning, there was a ball of bright green flame burning in my hand.

Fighting my first urge to shake it off—or, that failing, to stop, drop, and roll—I studied it as it twisted and flickered. It had no fuel source, nothing to contain it, but it remained where it had appeared, bound by the enchantment governing it. I flexed my palm, and the fire moved with it, never burning my skin. If I looked away from the fire and focused on the magic around it, I could pick out the currents feeding the flame, dull patches of ambient magic that blazed as they moved into invisible channels around my hand, like a diverted river picking up speed as it's funneled through narrowing canals.

I breathed slowly and cradled the flame like a baby bird, scared to spook it. As I passed my empty hand over it, the fire compressed into a green sphere the size of a softball, but it showed no sign of going out. On impulse, I tossed the fireball into the air and caught it, marveling at its existence.

I made this. I did this.

I felt the power coursing around me, through me, *in* me, and as I cupped the tiny inferno in my hands, a sudden realization came to mind: Hel couldn't do this. Sure, she could do wonders with or without a wand, but I'd never seen a wizard conjure a fireball like the one I was holding. It was, Toula had explained, a faerie thing.

And it was *easy*.

The fire pulsed like a living creature, flickering and flush with magic.

Something inside of me insisted that I put it out, tell no one, pretend it had never happened. It was bad, it was *wrong*, it was dangerous—and who was I to ask questions? What business did a dud have with magic? Magic was beyond me—it would *always* be beyond me—and my job was to listen to my betters and stay out of the way.

But my betters couldn't make a little fire like this, a flame that glowed the neon green of the aurora. It was a beautiful thing, that fire. I couldn't see the evil in it—the magic, yes, but not the evil—and as I looked into its depths, another voice within me started to speak up. Not the realm's voice, not my father's, but a voice that I, with some surprise, recognized as my own.

You are not evil. You are not a monster. You are.

Slowly, I closed my hand into a fist, and the flame died away without so much as a puff of smoke. My palm tingled but wasn't singed, and I knew—I *knew*—that the fire would return at my call.

This…was me.

And if the Arcanum hated me—if they feared me—then

I could live with that. After all, they'd never liked me to begin with.

True to his word, Joey dragged himself out on schedule and forced us onward. The pickings were slim that night—we found berries on the way, and Joey managed to shoot a few squirrels with his nail gun—but we were both tired enough to sleep with half-empty stomachs. He gave me the second watch, and by the time he woke, I'd mashed up some of the tart berries and heated them for a change of pace. We ate quickly—then again, there wasn't much food to make us linger around the fire—and set off, looking for landmarks as we crossed the endless woods.

After a few missteps, an hour of backtracking, and, oddly enough, two very startled peacocks, we paused outside a familiar clearing as twilight descended on the forest. "Yeah?" Joey whispered.

I saw his eyes dart around and assumed that he, like I, was looking for evidence of lurking spiders. "Yeah," I replied, and pointed to a nearby bush. The yellow light flashed for only a few seconds, but it was enough to give away the piq's hiding place. "Let's hope she's feeling friendly, eh?"

With that, I adjusted my bag, took hold of the straps to keep my hands away from my sword, and marched into the clearing. In an instant, a swarm of lights surrounded me—a strand of Christmas lights come to life, albeit a prickly, well-armed strand—and I stopped but stood my ground. "I would speak with Lailu," I said slowly, hoping that at least some of the guards knew a word or two of Fae. "Tell her the daigul have returned."

One of the orange lights detached itself from the swarm and flew off toward the massive tree, and I motioned for Joey to join me. The cloud of guards reconfigured itself to trap him as well, and we waited, neither of us speaking, until the orange light flew back toward us with a larger purple light in its wake. The guards parted, and there she was, hovering in front of my face. Unsure of the protocol, I held out one hand, and she landed in my palm with a curt nod. The little queen's green toga had been exchanged for a flimsier golden drape, and her long black hair was gathered into a heavy braid, woven through with tiny flowers. "I was warned," she squeaked. "The Lady told me all. You may stay here, but I cannot offer you more than that."

She sounded distressed, and I slowly raised my hand to look her in the eye. "Any help is appreciated, Your Majesty," I replied, trying not to breathe directly on her as I recalled my uncomfortable day with Astrid. "And if the Lady has spoken to you, then you know—"

"That you are daig, yes. Untrained, but daig." She folded her bare arms and frowned in thought. "I know of no one who can assist you with that problem, but I can offer shelter and…"—she cocked her head and pursed her lips— "perhaps an opportunity to practice. Come, both of you," she said, pointing toward the tree. "You will be safer if hidden."

The guards dispersed, and the queen took a seat in my hand and folded her wings. The request was unspoken but clear, and I carried her back toward her hideout, stepping carefully through the grass in case of piq underfoot. But halfway to our destination, Joey slumped to the level of my hand and murmured, "Your Majesty…I don't mean to sound ungrateful, but we can't fit down that hole, and there's no way I'm letting Aiden experiment on me."

She glanced up at him and grinned. "Which is precisely why we're going through the opening in the ground *behind* the tree."

"Ah."

Pointing to a clump of bushes in the distance, she explained, "There is a large cave beneath this place. Dry, quite pleasant. There is room for you below ground." She paused and looked back at me over her shoulder. "I only ask that you not attempt anything…*untried*…where it might injure my people. Agreed?"

"Of course," I said. "And, uh…as for hunting—"

Lailu smiled. "A proposal. My hunters will accompany you and help you find game. In return, you split the spoils. Is this also agreeable?"

"Ma'am," said Joey, "for food, a roof, and a solid night's sleep, your folks can have first pick of the takings."

A short walk later, she directed us to part the bushes, revealing the opening to a cavern and a series of natural stone ledges that disappeared into the ground. With Lailu lighting the way, Joey and I climbed down and found ourselves in a deep limestone cave perhaps the size of a small stadium. When my eyes adjusted to the shadows, I found that the natural illumination of the piq was just enough to keep me from walking into the walls, but Joey, ever pragmatic, pulled out a glow stick for backup and followed Lailu to an empty expanse on one side of the cave. Looking up, I saw niches carved into the rock, some holding tiny occupants like jeweled lights, and then I noticed a few thick roots descending through the ceiling.

Lailu caught the direction of my gaze and landed on my shoulder. "We hollowed much of the tree and cut through the stone to connect it to this cave. This is a safe place," she assured me, and flitted to a ledge in the wall. "Will this suffice?"

"Perfectly," said Joey, and slung his pack to the floor. "Aiden, you set up our gear. I'm going hunting while we've got moonlight."

I felt him when he walked past me in the dark—well, not Joey so much as his sword—and got to work. The cave was pleasantly cool, and for the first time in weeks, we wouldn't be sleeping under the sky. There was no place to build a fire and no wood to make one, so I unrolled our sleeping bags, arranged our things against the wall, and stretched out to rest my aching feet. A stream of piq flew back and forth above me on unknown business, a light show in the darkness, and I let the flashing colors lull me to sleep.

CHAPTER 13

When I woke to twilight, my first thought was that I was back in my old bed in my parents' apartment, deep underground and sheltered from such inconveniences as sunlight. But then my eyes adjusted, I saw the flitting colors of passing piq overhead, and I remembered where I was and why.

Joey had returned and crawled into his bag during the night, and he still lay curled up with his head on his arm, sound asleep. He'd left out his skillet, however, and I found cooked, albeit cold, meat waiting for me, along with a note written on the white side of a piece of bark: *Didn't want to wake you. Don't wake me.*

Taking the hint, I slipped my shoes back on and picked up the skillet, planning to take it topside. I glanced around our campsite before I moved to be sure I wasn't about to trip into Joey's arsenal, and my eyes landed on his filthy motorcycle boots, now scuffed beyond repair. The left, which had fallen on its side when he shucked them off, had sprung a hole in the sole the size of a half-dollar. My sneakers weren't faring much better—the tread was getting a little too thin for proper gripping—but I put Joey's boots on my list of things to do.

That is, once I figured out how to do more than start fires. He wouldn't have thanked me if he woke to find his only shoes reduced to ash.

Climbing back to the surface was a cinch, especially with daylight overhead, and I squinted as I broke through the bushes. The sun was high—not quite noon, but surely close—and but for the birds I'd startled, I was alone in the woods. Realizing after the ascent that I was famished, I sat in the clearing by the giant tree and tore into my unidentified leftovers while a trio of deer grazed nearby. Joey's campfire cuisine wasn't going to win any awards, but having skipped at least dinner and breakfast, I was ready to eat almost anything.

As I wiped my greasy hands clean on the grass, I caught a flash of yellow out of the corner of my eye, creeping through the weeds. On closer inspection, it resolved into Kuni, who hobbled toward me on a pair of forked twigs. His crushed wing was heavily splinted and held straight back on a sort of scaffolding harness, but he still wore his thorn sword—and, as expected, nothing more than a loincloth. When he reached my knee, he shifted his weight and prodded me with the butt of one of his crutches, and I lowered my hand to retrieve him. He stepped aboard, wobbling a little as my flesh moved under his feet, and carefully settled down with a soft sigh. As he put his crutches aside, I lifted him to eye level, irrationally hoping he'd picked up Fae from his aunt overnight. "Kuni?" I asked.

The piq nodded and tapped his bronzed chest. "Kuni," he affirmed, then pointed to me and cocked his head.

"Aiden."

"Aiden," he repeated slowly, as if feeling it out. "T'ak nol."

I tried to puzzle this into coherence. "Tock...uh..."

"T'ak nol," said a voice above me, and I glanced up as Lailu glided down from the opening in the tree. She came to rest on my shoulder and gestured toward Kuni. "He thanks you. When you were last with us, he was too sedated to see you on your way. You understand, yes?"

Having her talk in my ear actually made our conversation much easier. "Too well," I muttered. "And sure, Kuni, any time. How's it, uh...healing?"

Lailu translated, and he grimaced back at me before

launching into a long reply. When he came up for air, she said, "It pains him greatly, but the leg will mend. The wing is…less certain."

"Delicate?"

"Exactly." She hesitated, then quietly said, "He may always be maimed. It's too soon to be sure, but with the damage…"

Kuni watched the queen silently, oblivious to her meaning, and I thought of the many times Mom had patched me back together: the strong grip holding my broken bones in place, the light strokes of the wand over the injury, the mumbled spell to focus her mind and intention, the odd expression she often wore, a blend of anger, frustration, and fear. I didn't suppose that Mom had any experience with piq injuries, but I imagined that she could have done something to help Kuni. But that was idle daydreaming; Mom would barely speak to me, let alone cross the border, and something told me that a piq in the silo would be as unwelcome as I was there.

"Tell him," I murmured, cutting my eyes to the woman on my shoulder, "that if I'm ever able to do more than start fires, I'll do what I can for him."

Lailu repeated this for Kuni, who smiled and patted my palm. "He is grateful," she told me, "and understands your present limitations. You saved his life—you certainly do not owe him a wing. But should you become more confident in your abilities…"

"If I can't, I know someone in the other realm who can. If we ever get back across, of course," I muttered.

"Daig?"

"Witch-blood. Half daig, half…other. Mab's daughter," I offered. "She's a friend."

The queen considered this as she cautiously sat, clinging to my T-shirt to steady herself. Her bare feet kicked into my collarbone as she made herself comfortable, and she held her wings slightly spread to counterbalance against my muscle twitches. "If you are interested," she began once situated, "I have a suggestion that might be of interest to you."

"Ma'am?"

"When our children come of age, they must learn to fly," she replied, flicking a piece of lint off my shirt. "Some of it is intuitive, but there is much that cannot be taught. Children learn by flying, not by speaking of flying. Do you follow?"

"I...think so," I said, suspecting where this was headed.

"I believe the same could be helpful in your case," she continued. "Learn through making the attempt. Jump from the tree and face the wind."

"What, uh...what, exactly, did you have in mind?"

Lailu looked up at me and smiled grimly. "Well, we seem to have a troll problem."

"**Y**ou agreed to do *what?*"

Joey's shout echoed around the cave, and I cringed as the reverberations died away. "Fight a troll," I repeated, feigning nonchalance as I strapped on my sword. "Lailu said they're nocturnal. If I can sneak up on it before sundown, I'll have a better shot."

"Hell, no. Sit your ass down," he ordered, shoving me against the wall with one arm. I struggled against his grip, but Joey had cultivated sinews of steel. "Now, let's think about this, okay?" he said, his voice low and warning. "Maybe it's just me, but I think a troll is *slightly* too much for your first go-around. Let's start with something smaller. Saner. Affected by iron."

I blinked first. "Trolls aren't?"

"Nope. Skin's tough as dragonhide, too. *Tanned* dragonhide. Double-thick, reinforced dragonhide."

"How do you—"

"If you ask nicely, Val tells war stories," he muttered. "Only way you're going to take out a troll is to blast a hole straight through it and wait for it to notice. Now, still feeling cocky, champ?"

He loosened his hold on me, and I pushed his arm away. "Got a better idea?" I snapped. "The sooner I figure this out, the sooner we get Coileán back."

"We only get Coileán back if you don't get yourself killed first," he countered, stepping in front of me before I could slip past him. "And I'm pretty sure I told Helen I'd look after you."

"This isn't her decision," I said, glaring at him from the shadows. "And it's not yours. Back off, Joey."

"No."

"Back *off.*"

He pinned me to the wall again, harder that time, and I grunted with the impact. "Don't be stupid," he said, leaning out of my kicking range. "I'm sorry that Lailu's got a rogue troll, but that's not our problem right now. You're not taking this on today." He waited until I stopped squirming, then said, "If I let go of you, will you stay put?" I said nothing, and with a sigh, Joey removed his arm and backed off a few steps. "All right, now, listen to me, I'm trying to help you—"

I feinted right, then left, and made a break for the ledges to the surface. Unfortunately, Joey had better reflexes and managed to snag me by the back of my shirt. "Damn it!" he yelled, and threw me against the wall so hard that I saw stars. When the lights cleared, he was still standing at a distance—but he'd drawn his sword and was holding it at my chest. "I'm really sorry, man," he panted, "but I can't let you do this. Sit down, and I'll put it away."

I sensed the blade's presence like a warning beacon. The logical part of my mind piped up to suggest that Joey was absolutely correct, he was trying to keep me from committing suicide by troll, and he probably felt awful about our current standoff. But another part—a sharper, louder part—saw only red.

"Back off," I heard myself growl. "Last warning."

He shook his head and held his ground. "For your own

good—"

The enchantment surged to life in an instant, and before he could finish his sentence, Joey was flying backward across the cave. As I watched in stunned horror, the parabola of his trajectory peaked and fell, and he slammed down and slid several yards across the stone before coming to a stop. Dazed, he groaned and struggled to rise, then gave up and slumped on the floor as the sword fell from his hand.

I stood where I was, paralyzed with the realization of what I'd done, then broke free and ran to his side. "Joey," I begged, patting his face in an effort to rouse him, "aw, shit, Joey, I'm sorry...come on, wake up, man, please...please wake up, I didn't mean to, Joey, come on, I'm sorry..."

He breathed but didn't open his eyes, and I knelt beside him in the cave, praying that I hadn't killed him.

I sat vigil all that afternoon and through the long night, occasionally touching Joey or saying his name in hopes of a response, but I didn't dare to do more. For all I knew, the landing had broken his back. His brain could have been swelling—it probably was, with my luck—and there was nothing I could do about it. I couldn't move him without risking further injury to him, and so we remained where he had fallen as the piq flew back and forth, avoiding us. Panic and hopelessness warred within me, and I struggled to keep my composure, fearing how much worse I could make the situation if I let myself go.

By sunrise, when Joey had yet to return to consciousness, Lailu landed on his chest and looked up at me as she bobbed with his steady breathing. "We cannot cure him," she said quietly, folding her arms. "I can set an arm, staunch a wound...but for him, I do not know how to treat his condition."

I nodded, saying nothing.

"Perhaps," she ventured, "he could be cured by magic."

"Magic," I said, my voice hoarse with my failed attempts

to wake him, "is what did this to him in the first place."

She shrugged. "You were pushed from the ledge, and you flew. We know that it works." I opened my mouth, but she held up her hands to dam the angry tide. "Your friend needs care that we cannot provide. You may be his only hope. How long will you hesitate, Aiden?" She pointed to the cave opening behind me and the soft glow filtering through the bushes above. "Daylight is upon us. Strike now and see what you can learn. Who knows?" she added, spreading her wings. "You might find a way to bring him back."

Lailu flew off, leaving me alone with Joey. I couldn't see much of him in the shadows, but his motionless face condemned me with its stillness.

I'd never felt anger like the rage that had bubbled up during those last days. Oh, I'd had plenty of excuses to be angry before—being the target of an acid spray will do terrible things to your mood—but I'd always been able to control my feelings, to suppress them and keep myself in check. There was no point in taking a swing at my bullies, after all. I might have gotten a punch or two in, but they'd have turned around and broken my hand.

This was something new, something raw and strong, and it welled to the surface at every opportunity. The Arcanum notes I'd read universally said that faeries were vindictive and cruel, quick to punish any perceived slight—was this the cause? Had this *always* been hiding inside me? And now that it was unleashed, was anyone safe from my anger? I'd knocked my friend into a coma, and he'd just been trying to protect me. Who else was I capable of hurting? Of killing?

I was terrified, then, of myself—of what I had become. My inner voice, which had only recently been so reassuring, had fallen silent with this proof of my monstrosity.

Had Dad known? Had he always known this was lurking in me, coiled and eager to strike? Had he suspected that I would someday lash out with a fury I couldn't check?

Hell, I'd have driven me away, too.

But as I sat there, wishing Joey would wake up, the realm spoke once more in my mind: *You can save him.*

"How?" I whispered.

First, you must learn control.

I stood, feeling my sword bump against my leg as I rose. "You promise he'll be all right while I'm gone?"

I make no promises.

I didn't want to leave Joey alone—not like that, laid out and helpless—but I knew I wasn't going to fix him with apologies. "Any tips?" I muttered, turning for the exit.

Faerie said nothing for a few seconds, then replied, *Joey was correct. Blasting a hole through it would be most effective.*

"I'll bear that in mind," I said, and pushed the voice to the back of my thoughts while I climbed to the surface.

I knew almost nothing about trolls when I set off to slay my first. Aside from Joey's warnings, Lailu had informed me only that the one nearby had been driving away their prey, ripping up trees, and generally making the piq's lives difficult. It was male, she offered, and lived a short distance to the west, in a cave set into the base of a cliff. Also, it was quite big. Just how big, she couldn't say—*big* to a piq was anything over about a foot tall—but she believed it was larger than me. She pointed me toward the path, whose broken trees evidenced the troll's passing, and wished me luck.

The short distance turned into half an hour's hike, and I sorely missed Joey's presence. In the last weeks, we'd rarely strayed far from each other's side, and now I was on my own, off in the woods with a dinky bronze sword and my new, virtually uncontrolled magical powers. Really, in hindsight, it was a recipe for disaster, but the queen had seemed positive about the idea, and I was too worried about Joey to give my other options much thought. Somehow, I'd gotten the idea that killing the troll would revive him, as if the two were locked in a zero-sum game, which was completely irrational but made perfect sense to me at the time. Killing the troll would make everything better. All I had to do was figure out how.

I came out of the woods down a steep slope into one of the many grassy valleys that pocked the hills around us. Even in the absence of fallen trees to show me the way, I could guess where the troll had hidden itself. Several trampled tracks converged on one point in the valley's wall, a dark discoloration in the green that had to be a cave. Stepping softly, I crept down the hillside and noticed an occasional footprint in the dirt path I followed. The troll had only four toes, a fact on which I focused in order to ignore the much more important fact that each footprint was nearly a yard long.

As I reached the valley floor, I started to smell the creature within, a musky stench like wet dog and old blood mixed with the mildewed dankness of an overgrown pond. And then I started to see the bones—not many, not that far from the cave, but enough to show me what had died along the way. I spotted a bleached leg bone longer than my whole leg and quickly averted my eyes, trying not to psych myself out. But the longer I walked, the more it hit me that I was completely alone—not just on my own, but *alone.* There had always been life in the valleys we'd crossed, at least birds if not sheep or deer or oversized monstrosities. There was always *something* that made each little meadow its home. Here, though, there were no birds, no passing deer, no half-glimpsed things lurking in the bushes.

I could guess why, but I tried not to dwell on it for fear that I'd turn around and sprint for cover.

As I trudged on, the cave swelled in my field of vision— now a dot, now a distinct opening, now a shaded tunnel two stories high—and the discarded bits of previous meals rose proportionally in number. Here, there were tufts of hair that had to be fur…and there, a bone that still had meat on it, all covered with buzzing flies. I passed a young buck's head and shuddered; what little I could see of its stump suggested it had been twisted off, not cut. The dirt below me took on a reddish cast, as did the grass, and I didn't have to wonder at the source.

And then, despite my foot-dragging, I was standing outside the cavern opening, trying not to choke on the combined stench of troll and decaying corpses. Most of the refuse had ended up here, scattered in the tall weeds to rot, and I hoped that what I was seeing was the buildup of months, not the work of a few days.

There was no way in hell that I was going in there. I was desperate, but not quite suicidal yet. The trick, I thought, was to drive the troll out to me—disorient him in the sunlight, pin him with his back to the cliff, and…well, figure out what I was supposed to be doing. Not the greatest plan I'd ever devised, but I didn't know how long Joey was going to linger. And so, steeling my nerve, I called up the green fireball I'd made once before, tried not to think too hard about how foolish this was, and hurled it into the cave.

It flickered as it sped into the darkness with a life of its own—I couldn't have thrown a ball half as far as the fire traveled—and then, with a hiss, it hit something solid.

Something that *roared*.

"Shit," I whispered, and looked around for cover. There was nowhere to hide in the valley—it was treeless, and the tallest weeds were only knee-high—but I waded through the gore beside the cave and crouched down in the troll's castoffs, hoping to go unnoticed while I thought about what I'd gotten myself into. Maybe it wouldn't be so bad, I reassured myself. Maybe he'd go back to sleep. And hey— weren't there stories about trolls turning to stone in daylight? Maybe this one would come out and be toast. Problem solved!

I can now state with authority that those stories about petrified trolls are nothing but filthy lies. The thing that barreled out of the cave like an overgrown, bipedal bull may have squinted a bit, but the light didn't slow him.

It was, I realized, a beginner's mistake to trust a piq for

any approximation as to size. I was a few inches shy of six feet that fall, and the troll was more than twice my height, and easily four times my width. He was gray and largely hairless but for a matted black mop on top of his somewhat pointed head and a long stripe down his back. The troll's arms were elongated like a gorilla's and thick with muscle. Overall, he looked knobby and lumpy, but when he stood still, raised his head, and sniffed the air, I saw that those bumps were signs of the rippling muscles just underneath his thick skin.

In short, I was staring down an oversized, body-building, apelike *thing* with reinforced armor—and, I realized as his piggy eyes locked on me in my impromptu hiding place, he had an excellent sense of smell. Distantly, I noted that the twin tusks jutting from his lower jaw were also somewhat porcine, but most of my brain gave up and shut down when the troll spotted me and bellowed. The bulk, the streaks of dried blood on his belly, the fists like sledgehammers—the whole package was enough to leave me frozen where I stood while the small part of me that was still keenly aware of the situation tried to reboot the rest of me and run.

The troll roared again, and I saw the blackened spot on his flank where my fireball had hit him. I could try that again, I reasoned with my paralyzed limbs. Maybe the next fireball would be more effective. Now, if I could just remember how my hands worked…

He dropped to all fours, snorted a challenge, and charged.

My bind broke a few seconds before he would have run me over, and I frantically threw a fireball at his face while I sprinted away from the cave. The troll howled, but a glance back showed me that all I'd done was scorch his hair—he was still charging, and he was *angry*.

I shifted left and right, trying to throw him off with a zigzag pattern, but the troll was too fast. As I vaulted over a pair of sheep skulls, I flung another pair of fireballs toward him, hitting him on the nose and left shoulder. The troll howled again and slowed to deal with the damage, buying me a few seconds to head up the trail.

I don't know what I would have done, had I made it to the woods. The troll obviously knew his way around, and as he'd picked me out of a pile of stinking offal, he could have tracked me through the trees with a head cold. But something irrationally insisted that I'd be safe if I could just get out of the valley.

And then I heard the troll closing behind me once again. I gasped for breath and willed my legs to stop burning, but he was too close, I could smell him all around me, feel his hot breath on the back of my neck...

Suddenly, the troll *screamed* and fell with a ground-shaking thud, and I wheeled around to see what had happened. Before I got a good look, the air beside me blurred, and something was shoving me backward, away from my pursuer.

An arm.

I landed on my back and scrambled to find my feet as the man who'd materialized beside me advanced on the wounded troll. He held his hands together above the creature's torso as if he were praying, then yanked them apart.

The troll's head and feet flew in opposite directions with a shower of blood, and the man turned to me. I froze again—I'd have known that face anywhere, even if the clothes were strangely ornamented—but before I knew what was happening, Val grabbed my arm and yanked me upright. "What were you *thinking?*" he shouted, ignoring the spatter on his white silk shirt. "Aiden...what are you doing here, you're supposed to be safe..." He gaped, too flabbergasted for words, then shook me by the shoulders and pointed to the troll's closer half. "Moon and stars, boy, that thing would have killed—"

Feeling the rage come over me, I pulled free of him and called up a fireball in each hand, and Val's harangue ended abruptly. "Did you betray my brother?" I asked, taking advantage of his shock.

Val stepped back, his dark eyes wide, and raised his hands in placation. "Of course not," he said calmly. "What happened to you?"

I looked at my arm and saw that I was glowing again. "Heard you were Oberon's right-hand man these days."

"I can explain—"

"*How?*"

Val maintained his composure, even as I shook with anger. "He offered me a court of my own."

"That's supposed to explain—"

"Let me finish. He wants me to take control of what's left of Mab's people, but he wants me indebted to him. If I didn't agree, he would have locked me away with the others. What was I supposed to do?"

"Coileán is trapped, and—"

"I know damn well what's happened to Coileán," he interrupted. "I check on him when I can." He paused, gauging my expression. "I'd heard it was you and Joey who'd broken in, but I couldn't believe it. The rumor from the dungeon was that the voices were yours, but…"

My arms tensed, readying themselves to throw. "Realm made me an offer, too."

"I see. Aiden," he murmured, lowering his hands, "look if you want. Go ahead, I've dropped my defenses. I've nothing to hide from you. But I swear, the only reason I've cooperated with Oberon is to protect your brother."

"And get a court."

"I don't *want* a court," he protested. "Especially not that one. Would you want to clean up the mess Mab made?"

We stood there in the meadow, staring each other down, and finally, I let my fire die and my corona extinguish itself. "I can't look at your thoughts," I mumbled. "Don't know how. Going after the troll was supposed to…I don't know, trigger something."

Val hesitated, then closed the distance between us. "Control takes time," he said, gripping my shoulder. "And practice. Believe me, I know—I didn't begin to come into my power until I was a man. But you're young, and your power is correspondingly slight—"

I shook my head, cutting him off. "Realm, uh…she gave me a boost."

His tanned face began to pale. "What sort of a boost?"

"Um…I'm not entirely sure, but I think she was aiming for Coileán."

He let that sink in for a moment as he continued to blanch. "You can't control it."

"Figured out fireballs. Joey's back that way," I muttered, pointing toward the woods. "I got pissed at him last night, and now he's in a coma. So no, I can't control it."

"A coma?"

"He won't wake up," I explained, and my words began to run together. "I could have killed him, I *may* have killed him, and this was…I was supposed to figure out how to fix him—"

"My lord."

I shut down the renewed glow before it could blossom and looked back at Val with pricking eyes. "Help me," I begged. "I don't know what to do, and I'm making everything worse."

If he noticed the tremor in my jaw, Val had the decency not to mention it. "Are you injured?"

"No."

"Then the first consideration is Joey," he said, releasing me. "Lead the way. Where did you leave him?"

"He's in a cave," I said, starting up the trail. "The piq are watching him, but—"

"The *what?*"

"Piq," I repeated, looking over my shoulder. "You didn't know about them, either?"

"What's a piq?"

"Basically, they're tiny, glowing people with butterfly wings."

Val considered that as he walked, then muttered, "If

Coileán learns of this—"

"I'd planned to have a video camera on hand," I said, then mumbled, "assuming we can wake him, of course."

"That's been my hope." The dirt path widened, and Val walked beside me through the forgotten bones. "What's your strategy? You can't carry him out of his room…"

"Yeah, the realm clued me in. She said I need to distract Oberon, buy Coileán some time." I frowned at him as another thought occurred to me. "She didn't mention that you were coming."

"I've been following your trail for days. Oberon wanted to be certain that the breakout was just a trick, so I said I'd investigate for him. The realm…it's been speaking to you?"

"Yeah."

"Well," he said, kicking a hoof out of his way, "bear in mind what you're dealing with. Come, now, would you expect Faerie to be anything less than capricious?"

CHAPTER 14

The piq swarmed when Val and I reached the clearing, but he threw a shield around us without so much as a twitch. The little things rebounded with a sound like bugs slamming into a window, and I paused as a few hit hard and fell to the ground in a stupor. "Uh...Val," I said, "they *are* hosting us."

"Then they can put their weapons away," he replied, unperturbed by the angrily buzzing guards. "Where is he?"

Climbing as quickly as I dared, I led him into the cave and down the ledges, and he tossed up a white orb to light the way. Another cloud of disturbed piq raced toward us when the orb brought daylight to the cave, but Val's shield held, and they shared the fate of their compatriots topside.

Lailu was waiting by the time we reached the bottom, hovering with a half-dozen guards at her side. "You've returned, I see," she said, cutting her eyes to the moaning, dazed piq on the cave floor. "And your...companion?"

"Daig," I replied. "Properly daig. And since he just fixed your troll problem, maybe you could call off the welcome committee."

"Yes...I suppose," she murmured, and turned to her guards with a series of rapid, unintelligible instructions.

I looked at Val, whose poker face barely betrayed his surprise at the encounter, then said, "Lailu is their queen, and from the looks of it, the only one fully fluent in Fae. I've picked up maybe ten words from them, so it would help if we all stayed on each other's good side."

He nodded, and when Lailu turned her attention back to us, he dropped the shield and showed his empty hands. "I mean no disrespect, my lady," he told her, "but under the circumstances"—his gaze drifted to Joey, who remained on the floor where I had left him—"I thought we might leave the negotiations for another time."

She gestured toward the patient and landed on my shoulder, grabbing my ear as a handhold. Ignoring the high-pitched cries of the agitated piq around us, Val knelt beside him and placed his hands on Joey's temples. He closed his eyes but said nothing, and in an instant, I saw the enchantment form around them both, a yellow-green net of working magic. It funneled through the backs of Val's hands into Joey, just as Mom's healing spells had channeled magic through her wand and into my broken limbs, and I waited, crossing my fingers and hoping for a miracle.

A moment later, Val released his hold and slid back, and the enchantment dissolved. "Is he—" I began, but Joey's gasp cut me off, and Val caught him before he could try to sit up.

As I exhaled the breath I hadn't realized I'd been holding and fought the sudden weakness of relief in my knees, Val tended to him. "Welcome back," he said, cradling Joey's head in the crook of his arm even as he pressed him to the floor. "Give it time. If you try to stand too quickly, you'll faint."

Joey looked around, taking in everything, then focused on the face above him. "Val—"

"I'm not your enemy," he said, cutting Joey off before he could panic. "And if I were going to kill you, I would have left you as you were. Understand?"

Joey's eyes shifted uncertainly, but he offered a slow nod.

"Good. Rest." He lowered Joey's head to the ground, then stood over him and glowered. "And were you *trying* to kill yourself?" he bellowed. His voice echoed around the cavern, and I winced as Joey flinched. "I expect foolishness from *him*," Val continued, jabbing his finger toward me, "but I thought you were beyond that!"

"Hey," I protested, "I'm not stupid…"

Val spared me an impatient glance before looking back at Joey. "Boys do foolish things. I thought you were a man by now."

Joey's eyes rolled in confusion. "I…I don't…"

"You don't remember? Aiden says you've been unconscious nearly a full day."

"Huh?" he mumbled, rubbing his forehead. "I…wait…where the hell did you come from?"

"You don't remember what happened?" I interrupted, stepping into Joey's line of vision. "I was going to go after a troll, and you tried to stop me, and—"

I shut up as realization dawned in Joey's face. "Dude, you *threw* me?" he yelped. "And you—"

"I'm so, *so* sorry," I rushed, stepping clear of his grasp. "I didn't mean to, I didn't know it was going to happen…"

Val raised his hand to silence me. "Joey," he said, glaring down at him, "you know he can't control himself. You provoked him. What did you *think* was going to happen?"

Joey cut his eyes to me but continued to massage his head. "Not that."

"You're lucky to be alive." Val stepped back and offered him a hand. "Come on, try to sit up. I want to check for bruising."

Though sullen, Joey took Val's hand and eased upright, and Val crouched behind him to prod at the back of his head. "Tell me if this hurts," he muttered, then paused as Joey hissed. "Yes…still a little swollen," he said, brushing Joey's hair back. "And blue. Have I yet told you how fortunate you are to be alive?"

"Joey," I said, squatting a safe distance from him, "I'm really sorry, please, I…I didn't mean to hurt you, I couldn't—"

Joey's voice was low, but it cut through my babbled apology. "I was trying to protect you."

"I know, you were right, I was stupid…"

Val snorted his agreement, and Joey flinched as his

fingers found yet another tender spot.

"…but I thought I'd killed you, and I wouldn't hurt you, Joey, you're my friend, I—"

"I know," Joey interrupted. "It's—damn it, that *hurts*!" he yelped, pulling his head away from Val. "Jeez, man, a little mercy!"

"You don't want to know what I just repaired," Val replied, resuming his exploration of Joey's scalp. "And if you'll be still, I may be able to fix the rest. Stop complaining."

Joey rolled his eyes but gritted his teeth while Val prodded his bruises. "So," he said to me, "after all that, you still went after the troll?"

"Eventually," Lailu piped up, and jumped off my shoulder. She drifted to a clean landing on Joey's knee and walked up his thigh while he watched and winced at the ongoing examination. "He would not have done so if he hadn't thought he might learn to heal your wounds in the process. He remained with you through the night, but when you did not improve…" She shrugged and glanced back at me. "You see, this solves two problems, does it not? The troll is dead, your friend will recover—"

"And *you* persuaded the boy to attack a troll in the first place," Val interrupted, glaring at her over Joey's shoulder. "Are you siding with Oberon?"

The queen seemed miffed. "Certainly not. We take no part in your wars. And as for the boy," she continued, folding her arms, "it was the Lady's suggestion, not my idea. I was merely the messenger."

"The lady?" said Val.

"She means the realm," I explained. "Faerie talks to her, too."

He sat back on his heels and rubbed his face. "So the realm somehow gives you power, lets you hide in the forest for days without telling you I'm on the way to assist, and tells *her* that the way to solve your problems is to send you on a suicide mission. Are you certain she's taking your part in this?"

I spread my hands helplessly. "She says she hasn't told Oberon that we're here."

"Well, he hasn't mentioned it," Val muttered. "When did you come across? And how? I thought I told you to stay safe," he added, and hit Joey's shoulder to drive the point home.

"Tor gate," said Joey, rubbing the struck spot. "Rufus opened it for us, and we made our way from there."

Val's face creased. "*Which* gate? And who?"

Joey sighed as the enchantment started again, a more delicate piece of work for the fine details. "The Tor gate," he repeated. "There's a hidden one at the top of the Glastonbury Tor."

"In England," I added, seeing Val's bemusement. "Uh…Britannia?"

"Yes, I know the place," he said brusquely, "but where did this gate—"

"A lake," Joey muttered. "It opens into a damn lake infested with a damn green hag in the middle of goddamn nowhere."

"To the northeast of here," I said.

"And there are giant damn spiders," Joey complained.

"Quite a ways to the northeast."

Val peered at me over Joey's shoulder. "How long have you two been out here?"

"Phone," Joey snapped, pointing to his bag, and I carried it to him while he healed. He rummaged in the pockets until he found his quasi-iPhone, then pulled up the calendar and grunted. "Today makes a month."

The enchantment broke, and Val stepped around Joey to look at his filthy, stained backpack and worn-through boots. "You've been living off the land for a *month*?" he said, visibly stunned.

"Surprised?" he replied with a smirk. "I'm not a complete imbecile, Val."

"I never said you were, but…" He took a second look at

the bloodstains on Joey's gear and nodded. "Well done. And who's the idiot who thought this was the safest place for you, then?"

"Vivi's brother," I said. "One of them."

"We left Georgie with him," Joey added before Val could ask. "Easier to hide without a dragon."

"And how were you hiding her in the other realm?" he pressed.

"Toula took care of it," said Joey. "She has a few choice words planned for you, by the way."

"I'm sure she does." Val looked at the two of us and Lailu, who had seated herself on Joey's jeans. "Well," he said to Joey, "you'll live for now, and as for you," he said, glancing my way, "training begins after lunch. Were you planning on cleaning out the larder here, or could I be of service?"

"I mean, I don't want to *impose* or anything," said Joey, "but seeing as Aiden ate the last of my kill…"

A gallon-sized ceramic bowl filled with goopy orange pasta appeared beside Joey, along with a fork. "Will that make you happier?" asked Val.

Joey shoveled in a few mouthfuls of macaroni, then nodded. "It's a start," he said, spraying bits of cheese sauce into his new beard with every word. "Food of the gods."

Val rolled his eyes. "I thought you only recognized one deity."

"Just an expression."

"Mm." He squinted at Joey's lunch and wrinkled his nose. "I trust that my gods could do better than that."

Val didn't hold a candle to Astrid in the food department, but that day, I'd have been grateful for a pack of bologna and a can of Easy Cheese. He managed a respectable pizza, to which he'd taken an immediate liking while traveling with Toula, and as Joey and I gorged ourselves on the carbohydrates we'd been craving, he told us what had happened in our absence.

"We did the best we could," he said, picking at his share of the pie, "but their numbers were overwhelming, and they caught us off guard. I've had security on the permanent gates for years—the practical gates, at least," he amended, "not your lake gate, but Oberon ripped open several new ones simultaneously, and we couldn't close them against him. He led his elite force straight into the palace, from what I've put together, and they took Coileán unawares."

Joey nodded. "That's what Astrid was saying."

"She was clever enough to stay out of the way until the first wave finished," he replied. "They killed eighty-four that night, and many more since..." He paused, suddenly uncertain. "Did Astrid tell you about—"

"My siblings?" I offered. "Yeah."

"I would offer my condolences, but honestly..."

"Got it. Go on," said Joey, picking dried cheese sauce out of his short mustache.

A damp hand towel appeared beside him, and Val shook his head as Joey tried to blindly find the leftovers clinging to his face. "There were simply too many of them," Val told me, "and we weren't prepared. It's my fault," he muttered. "Of all the threats I'd anticipated, an invasion by Oberon was low on the list. He could have returned whenever he'd liked, and he'd never have tried that with Titania—I suppose Coileán was a different matter."

"But he left Coileán alive," I said. "He *can't* kill him, or he *won't?*"

Val's face darkened. "He's biding his time. Keeping Coileán alive ensures that Moyna does as she's told."

"Yeah, about that," Joey interrupted. "When did those two team up?"

"I assume in the last months," said Val with a shrug. "My understanding is that after Nath threw the rest of Mab's people out of the Gray Lands, at least some of the exiles rallied around Moyna. The girl craves vengeance, and she's not stupid. They have no leader, but Moyna, at least, knows the right things to say."

The picture began to come into focus. "So she approaches Oberon," I said, "joins up with him, brings Mab's court with her as muscle, and helps him invade?"

"Not quite," Val replied with a bitter smirk. "Oberon approached *her*. As far as pure numbers go, Coileán's court and his were roughly equal before the attack. Adding Mab's refugees tipped the balance in Oberon's favor."

Joey's eyes widened, and he put the towel down. "Moyna helps Oberon, they take Coileán out, and the court's hers."

"Exactly. Or at least, that's their agreement." He picked up a slice and chewed slowly. "You must remember that Oberon never wanted to share power. The arrangement among the Three was a cessation of hostilities, not anyone's prearranged plan. He told me he'd had enough rest and thought the time was right to finish what he started."

"Shit," Joey grunted, "he's going to kill Moyna, isn't he?"

"And *that* would be the true plan," said Val, pointing his slice at Joey's chest. "Oberon's keeping Coileán alive for now while Moyna and her forces move on the Arcanum. When they've broken through and wiped out the silo— behead the organization and hope the survivors scatter, you know," he explained, "Moyna expects that he'll kill Coileán as her reward. He will, but only once he's killed her."

"He actually told you this?" I asked.

Val smirked again. "Well, as the old boy sees it, someone will need to take the reins with Mab's people. I'm of the blood, after all. Kill Moyna, leave them leaderless again, then prop me up as their new head. The position doesn't come with any extra power," he continued, "or so I'd assume, given Mab's state at the end, but if they follow me, then Oberon will have the third court under his control—I mean, I would be beholden to him, wouldn't I?"

"And what about Coileán's?"

He shrugged. "I'm sure Oberon will clean out the dungeons once he settles his affairs with Moyna. He's actually counting on me to help kill her," he added. "It's taking too much of his strength to keep Coileán subdued—more than Moyna realizes. He hides it well. But he's opened his thoughts to me, made it plain what he intends."

"You believe him?" asked Joey.

"I have no reason to doubt him," said Val. "You must understand his mind—he's *fae*. Wholly fae. The lust for power…it's not some idle desire. It drives him. Now, in his mind, he's offering me power, a title—all those things I've never had. He imagines that I crave what should have been mine through Mab. It's the only conclusion that makes sense to him." Val smiled and resumed his attack on the pizza. "So, logically, since one of the Three is making me this offer, how could I possibly do anything *but* play along? To do anything else would be acting against my self-interest."

Joey and I watched him as he ate, and after a moment, Val called a glass of red wine into existence and washed his meal down. "I don't want a court," he said, eyeing us carefully. "I have no desire to attempt to repair what Mab broke, nor do I want to fight to control a court that spent the last millennium in the Gray Lands. Mab's blood or not, I'm surely not among their favorite people at the moment. Not after that business with Geheret," he muttered. "Beyond that, Coileán has been good to me, and he is my king. But even more importantly," he continued as his eyes narrowed, "if Oberon wanted my cooperation, he made a tactical miscalculation in attacking the Arcanum."

"He didn't consider Toula at all?" I asked.

"Oh, he *considered* her—he just didn't imagine that I would value her over a court. And I've not seen fit to enlighten him," he murmured. "If some harm should befall my sister as a result of Oberon's idiocy…"

He didn't need to finish that thought—the flash in his eyes said it all.

"So yes," said Val, "I've played my role. It's reassuring to hear that Astrid thinks me a traitor—I suppose I've been more convincing than I realized. But I swear to you," he said, turning to me, "if you fight Oberon, I'll be at your side." He paused, giving me quick consideration, then added, "Just not today. Let's make this plan slightly less suicidal first, shall we?" He stood, brushed the crumbs off his hands, and nodded toward the cave opening. "Meet you in the clearing shortly. Try to make sure there are no piq underfoot before we begin. I'd rather not explain any unnecessary casualties."

Though Joey was eager to help, Val forbade it. "If Aiden is as strong as he thinks he is," Val explained, "then *I* am taking a risk. For your own safety, stay underground. Let your head rest," he added, lightly rapping his knuckles against Joey's temple. "Take a nap. Just stay away from any place that could be within Aiden's line of fire."

Word circulated among the piq as well, and so when I met Val in the assigned location, I found the clearing empty but for a pair of cautious doves in the trees. "So," I said, trying not to sound nervous, "what first? Warm-up exercises?"

Val sat cross-legged in the grass—which, I noticed, was strangely damp for that late in the day—and motioned for me to sit facing him. "You still can't block your thoughts?" he asked.

"No…"

"Good."

I barely felt it when Val started poking around inside my mind. The sensation was odd, like the fluttering of a microscopic moth against my brain, but almost unnoticeable. He retreated after about ten seconds, smiled to himself, then looked over my left shoulder into the distance. "What was that about?" I asked, absently rubbing my head.

Val continued to stare at nothing, and, puzzled, I turned around and froze.

Not ten yards away stood Russell Mulligan, messy

ponytail and all.

It couldn't be Russell, my rational mind insisted—the last time I'd seen him was in the silo, crying as one of the wizards whose breakfast we'd interrupted led him and his burned hand off to be treated. There was no conceivable way that Russell had found his way into Faerie and stumbled onto my hiding place. It was an illusion, I told myself, nothing more than glamour. Val had pulled something out of my memories to mess with me, that was all.

But even as I talked to myself, I felt my arms tighten and my fists clench—and as I looked down, having realized that I'd gone to my feet, I saw the glow begin to flicker around me.

"Hey, Dudley," said Russell, smirking as he pulled his wand from behind his back. "I thought I told you I didn't like your face. Let's see what we can do to make it prettier, huh?"

I knew he wasn't real—I *knew* it—but my racing heart had yet to get the memo. "Back off," I told the illusion. "I'm not afraid of you."

Russell chuckled as he raised his wand. "You should be, you little mongrel shit."

The rage washed over me then, white-hot and sparking, and without quite knowing what I was doing, I threw a stream of fireballs at Russell's head. In an instant, the illusion dissolved, the grass smoldered, and I shook as the adrenaline rush ran its course.

I jumped and shrieked when Val came up behind me and squeezed my shoulder. "Congratulations," he said quietly. "You just killed the boy."

My response came out as a jumbled rush. "I…I mean, he…I didn't, he was—"

"He got the best of you, you lost control, and now he's dead." Val released me and pointed to the grass. "As I'd expected. I took the liberty of soaking the area in advance," he added as the smoke curled above the scorched patches. "Ready to try again? Breathe, calm down."

I closed my eyes and focused on my exhalations until I felt my pulse slow to a reasonable speed. "All right, I'm ready," I muttered. "What's next?"

Something hit me in the gut, and my eyes shot open, only to see Milo Brown's other fist flying toward my face with his impeccable form. The blow connected with my chin, and I reeled, tasting blood.

Within seconds, the clearing had acquired a new set of burned pockmarks, and I was prodding my sore jaw and split lip as the glow subsided. "The *hell*?" I shouted, spotting Val a few yards behind me. "That hurt, man!"

He folded his arms and shrugged, unbothered by my complaints. "And the boy is dead. Do you see a pattern emerging?"

Milo and Russell flickered back into existence, but that time, they had been reduced to blackened bodies in the grass, distinguishable only by the little tufts of blond still visible on the ruins of Milo's head. "Yeah," I mumbled.

"Good. You know what's going to happen," he said, waving the illusions away again. "Now figure out how to control it."

"But I don't know—"

He held up one finger, silencing my protest. "You're telling me you've never been angry in the past? Not once?"

"Of course I've been angry."

I felt Val prod into my thoughts once again, and suddenly, my mother was standing beside me with her hands on her hips. "MIT?" she exclaimed. "Are you out of your *mind*, Aiden? You're fifteen—I'm not sending you across the country to do God-knows-what in Boston!" She shook her head and pursed her lips, an expression I knew all too well. "Come on, sweetie, you're smarter than that. You didn't really think we would just go, 'Okay, have a good four years,' did you?"

It was like watching a video I'd replayed a dozen times before. I knew my lines—mumbled promises that I wouldn't get in trouble, that I could get a scholarship, that no school in Montana offered anything close—but Mom inevitably shot me down. In the live performance, I'd stormed off and slammed my bedroom door, defeated and furious. But hearing her again in that meadow, seeing her mixed look of annoyance and pity…

"Careful," said Val.

I was glowing, and I hadn't even noticed. "What do I do?" I asked through clenched teeth.

"Acknowledge what you're feeling. You're angry—even the memory stirs it in you." He stepped beside the illusion of my mother, whose expression was frozen as it had been at the moment when she crushed my hopes of escape. "What do you want to do?"

My stomach knotted with the memory, and I felt my muscles tightening in anticipation. "Something."

The corner of his mouth twitched. "Just something? Come now, surely you have stronger feelings than that. What do you want to do to her?"

"Nothing," I muttered.

"I didn't ask what you *should* do. I asked what you *wanted* to do. Admit the truth and face it, boy, or I can't help you."

I closed my eyes against Mom's unblinking stare, and in the darkness, I took stock of my feelings. No matter what she had done the last time I saw her, I loved her—she was my *mom*, for crying out loud—but anger overwhelmed the rest of my thoughts. I could lash out. Strike back. I was stronger than she was, stronger than she would ever be, and I didn't have to take no for an answer. How dare she—

Damn it, that was Mom. No matter how angry I was, fireballs couldn't be the answer.

I blinked and turned to Val. "I want to strike her down. Maybe set her on fire. It's kind of nebulous, but those are the main options right now."

He nodded, apparently unconcerned with my expressed desire. "Are you going to do so?"

My arms were still tense, ready to attack or defend, but I breathed deeply and forced them to relax. "No."

"Sure about that? You seem uncertain."

I glared at him and felt the anger swell again, and Val cocked an eyebrow. "You're cheating," I snapped.

"Fight it."

So I did. I wrestled with the overwhelming rage until I could look at the illusion of my mother and feel only peeved instead of homicidal, and when Val was satisfied with my mental state, the vision disappeared. "How was that?" I asked, wincing at the headache on the horizon.

He shrugged. "A beginning. Too slow. Try again."

The surprise bolt threw me off my feet, and I jumped up and turned around to find Morgan Kramer and Leo Rossi, the shortest of the pack but the best with their wands, standing at the ready. "Hiya, Dudley," said Leo, casually brushing his straw-like bangs out of his dark eyes. Morgan said nothing, but that wasn't unusual—he'd been reading Dr. Seuss in the third grade, long after the rest of us had discovered chapter books. As his ample baby fat had solidified to muscle, I'd always thought that Morgan resembled a troll. Having finally *seen* a troll, I had to reconsider my assessment, but that did nothing to change the fact that Morgan had no neck and biceps as big around as my thighs.

"Two? Really?" I yelled at Val.

He stood back and grinned. "You need the challenge."

"You're an asshole," I said under my breath, but turned my attention back to the illusionary wizards. "Okay, I'm not killing—"

A shot from Leo's wand threw me halfway across the clearing, and I held my aching head as I struggled back to my feet. "How do I—"

"Figure it out," said Val. "And you might want to hurry."

Morgan struck that time, hard and fast, and I screamed as my left leg shattered. My eyes watered, and I cried, "Val, I can't—"

"Fight it."

Leo raised his wand, and my fear and pain overwhelmed

my defenses. When the red haze cleared, I saw more smoldering fires in the grass and groaned. "I lost it, didn't I?"

"Yes." Val squatted beside me and rested his hand on my broken leg, and the healing enchantment commenced. "It's all about control," he said, concentrating on his work. "There's a wide ground between doing nothing and blasting your opponent to dust, but you must learn for yourself how hard you can hit. I can't teach you that—no one can. So we practice until you figure it out." He focused on my leg for another moment, then stood and nodded. "Better?"

I tested my weight and found only a twinge of pain remaining, though the bones were still soft. "Better."

"Then I suggest you focus on creating a shield," he said, and pointed to the far side of the clearing, where Terrance Anders and Dan Solomon were coming into focus. "And do it quickly."

CHAPTER 15

Val was nothing if not a patient teacher. For five days straight, dawn to dusk, he conjured up my darkest memories, ignored my mental trigger warnings, and systematically broke every bone in my body. He never seemed to get angry—even when I screamed and cursed, he wouldn't speak above a conversationally moderate tone—but he was ruthless in his attacks. Sure, he was quick to patch me up between bouts, and I was actually getting to eat my fill at every meal, a real treat after weeks in the woods, but I spent most of that week in pain, and I woke every morning with the ghosts of healed injuries on my mind.

"It's Val's method," Joey whispered after I collapsed into my sleeping bag after my fifth full day of training. "It's hell while you're doing it, but you'll be stronger for it later."

"He's going to kill me first," I mumbled into my pillow between shallow breaths. My lungs hadn't yet accepted that my repaired ribs weren't about to puncture them.

"He knows your limits. He pushes you right up to the edge, that's all. You saw how long he left me black and blue last year."

"I don't know, man."

"Come on," said Joey, nudging me in the shoulder, "you're not giving up, are you?"

I rolled over and glared at him. "No, I'm not giving up. But the last time I checked, he wasn't teaching *you* to fight by cracking your legs in half."

Joey grimaced. "Ouch."

"Yeah. *Ouch*."

I flopped back onto my stomach and closed my eyes, willing myself to be calm and go to sleep—and that was when it hit me.

I'd been annoyed with Joey, I'd been thinking about the day's injuries...and I hadn't blown up at him. Instantly, subconsciously, I'd suppressed the instinct to turn his sleeping bag into a flaming crater. Yeah, I'd flared a bit, but Joey wasn't a threat, and I'd avoided maiming him.

As little as I liked to admit it, Val's methods were working.

I told him as much the next morning after breakfast, when Joey had disappeared with a piq hunting party for something to do and Val and I were alone again in the clearing. "Excellent news!" he said, beaming. "Your control is improving. As soon as we're comfortable with it, we can transition to your offensive work."

My heart sank. "You're not satisfied yet?"

"Not quite, but prove me wrong," he said, and cut his eyes to the open space behind me, a gesture that by then made me flinch on cue.

"Hey!" I heard Russell yell. "Going to cry today, Dudley? Huh? Going to run like a little baby?"

"You know," I said, calling up the basic shield that I'd learned to make with a stroke of luck and seven broken limbs, "this would all be more convincing if he were speaking English."

Val snorted and grinned smugly. "I'll learn the barbarian tongue once you learn to defend yourself. On your guard, now," he cautioned, just as the first bolt shot through my shield and shattered my knee.

I dropped and grabbed at the wound, forgetting Russell with the pain. "Son of a *bitch*!" I shouted, and followed it with a long string of multilingual profanity.

My tutor crouched beside me and began the healing enchantment. "See?" he said. "You teach me even now. We're learning together."

I recognized the rising urge to lash out at him and forced

it down. "Jerk," I muttered in Fae.

"Now, that's not fair. If I were a jerk, I would let you keep fighting with one leg and see how much more damage we could do." I glared at him, and he shrugged. "Combat doesn't stop after a single hit. You'll need to learn how to handle yourself injured eventually."

I glanced at the illusion of Russell, which was frozen mid-step, wand raised and ready. "Or I could just kill him."

"Well, obviously," he allowed. "But unless the realm makes up its mind and empowers you more than it has, you won't be able to kill Oberon. Not alone. And believe me," he said, patting my sore knee, "Oberon won't stop if he hurts you. He won't stop until you're ashes."

"If we work together—"

"Perhaps. But Aiden, you must understand that I'm neither his equal nor yours. Not with the realm behind you." I started to protest, but Val shook his head. "I know what I'm doing, and I've been around long enough to build my strength—but next to him, I'm still a boy. Bear that in mind while you plan," he said, then looked up from his ministrations and met my eyes. "And let that also show you exactly how much power you wield beyond your years. Do you see why I'm putting you through this?"

I nodded and gave my knee a testing flex, then mumbled, "I'm a danger to you."

Val broke the enchantment and stood. "Why do you think I've been directing your focus elsewhere these last days? Shield up, now, and try to hold it together, hmm?"

Even with a belly full of fresh venison, courtesy of Joey and his team of piq, I couldn't sleep that night. Stiff from the day's training, I limped up to the surface and climbed through the bushes, intending to stretch out in the clearing and stargaze until I dozed off. But before I could get comfortable in the grass, I heard footsteps behind me and turned to see Val on my tail. "Pleasant evening, isn't it?" he said, taking a seat beside me. "Good weather. And if you don't sleep, you'll be useless in the morning."

"Just not feeling it yet." I winced as I bent my thrice-broken knee. After considering my state for a moment, trying to deduce what would make it better, I hesitantly stretched out my hand and focused. A plastic bag half-full of ice cubes appeared from thin air, and, grateful that I hadn't accidentally set something on fire again, I held it against my jeans and tried to numb the pain.

Val kept his face still, but when I called up a flame in my empty hand, I read the approval in his eyes. "Not yet prepared to address the problem directly?" he asked.

"Since there's a fifty-fifty chance that letting me work on my own knee would end in an amputation, I'll stick with icing it down," I replied. "Besides, healing takes practice."

"No time like the present."

"Val," I groaned, "I'm exhausted, and I'm in pain. Now's not a great time to try to teach me anything."

"On the contrary," he said, producing for himself a gallon jug of wine and a glass. "The true test isn't whether you can enchant while you're calm and happy and focused—it's whether you can do so when conditions are less than ideal. Which is why we're going to see how well you can fight injured tomorrow," he added as he poured.

I sighed and shifted my ice pack. "You're having entirely too much fun, Captain."

He swirled his wine, watching it sparkle in the light of my fire, then took a long sip. "I know this is difficult for you," he said quietly. "Training should be a matter of years, not days. Of course," he muttered, "the trainee shouldn't be half as strong as you are, but there's nothing we can do about that. The situation is what it is, and we don't have long." He leaned back on his elbow and drank again. "When I was trained, I had my share of broken bones and burns and such, but my injuries were spread out over years of work. Practical lessons, a bit of theory, continued weapons training—a proper education, you understand. But we don't have that luxury now, and I'm sorry. I'd train you another way if I knew of one half as effective, but I don't."

I snuffed out my flame, and after a moment's thought, I managed to produce a glass of my own. Val didn't protest when I helped myself to the wine. "So, who trained you?"

He was quiet for a long moment as he drank and watched the sky. "Her name was Citca," he finally said. "Third in command of the queen's guard when I arrived. The captain and second had neither the time nor the inclination to work with me, but she had a knack for instruction."

I didn't think Val could see my grin in the darkness, but he sensed it nonetheless. "Yes, most of my practical training was at the hands of a woman," he said, reaching for a refill. "I protested at first, but I was twenty-three and stupid. Citca was five hundred or so, born and raised in the realm, and I was her favorite target for the next ten years." He sounded almost wistful in his reminiscing.

"Just magic, or swords, too?"

"Everything." He drank slowly, listening to the night around us. "She'd been a guard for centuries. Trained with some of the best. I wasn't a complete novice with a blade or spear, mind you—I'd seen combat by then, and I thought I was more than competent. Cocky, really. So at our first session together, I made some idiotic jab about the weakness of women, and she broke me in nine places. That's when I started to learn." He paused, savoring his wine. "She was half fae, and she was built like a man—tall, broad, hairier than the women I'd known. Her father was from one of the far northern tribes, I believe, or so the rumor went. Citca never spoke of him, if she'd ever known him, but she was pale and fair enough for the story to be plausible. She looked like a Northman, at least."

I hesitated as I tried to assess his mood, then asked, "You two, uh…were you—"

"Never," he interrupted, and chuckled. "She was a warrior, and I was a boy. I was her project, eventually her comrade, but never her lover. Besides," he added, "she was in a long-term relationship with our captain, and I knew better than to meddle." Catching me fiddling with my ice pack, Val passed me the wine jug. "The first lesson of training was to never antagonize anyone who could blast a hole through my chest before I learned to reliably shield, and believe me, that took time. At least you came here with some general conception of magic—I knew less than nothing."

"What do you mean?" I asked, pausing with the cork half-out of the jug's neck.

Val laughed again, softly and deep in his throat. "I never met a wizard until I killed one who'd sneaked across the border. My family left matters of magic and miracles up to the gods. Well," he amended, "my father bought a few amulets and such for me—the poor man tried to cure me for years—but of course, that never worked." He shifted in the grass and shook his head. "I'm sorry, you don't want to know—"

"No, go on," I said, pushing the jug back to him. "You've never told me about your family."

He answered me with a grunt. "I seldom see the need to bring it up."

"Okay, fair enough. But you had *no* idea what you were?" I pressed.

Val drank and waited while a multicolored cluster of piq passed overhead. "I had no reason to doubt that I was mortal," he replied after a moment. "You, now, you're Arcanum-reared, you knew there was another option. But for me..." He shrugged. "Outside of stories and legends, there was no one who wasn't purely human. My father teased," he continued, staring into the woods. "He knew nothing about Mab aside from her sex and her willingness. But he used to say that he'd have known it, had he bedded a goddess—she'd have struck him dead for passing out on top of her."

"Seriously?"

"So he said. I wasn't there to witness the deed, of course, but that's what I can report." Val leaned back and groaned as he stretched his legs. "You really want to know this, Aiden?"

"Hey," I countered, "you've got all the dirt on me, man. Fair's fair, and this wine's not bad."

"It's a decent vintage, I grant you that, and remind me to fix your hangover before you sleep," he replied. "You don't yet have your brother's...*constitution*."

"That's the polite term for it, yeah?"

He chuckled, and I heard him pull the cork free again. "All right, you want the details?" he said as he poured. "For many years, my father had only two sons, Publius and Gaius. After Gaius was born, my mother—I mean the woman I consider my mother, you understand."

I nodded.

"She lost five children in as many years—three were never born, and two never drew breath. She was, as it happened, newly pregnant for the sixth time when my father had business in Capua—his father's brother had died, and there was some dispute among his heirs about a farm he'd acquired outside the city. While he was away, he chanced upon a woman sitting on the side of the road one evening, one thing led to another, and he brought her back to the house where he was staying for the night. Apparently, they drank for a few hours, and then they did what they'd come together to do." Val snorted and sipped his wine. "His story was that he fell asleep atop her and was so drunk that he never heard her slip away, but before she left, she took his ring. A large emerald in heavy gold—he assumed she'd sell it, and he asked a few merchants to alert him if it surfaced, but there was no sign of the ring or the woman before he returned to his wife.

"Naturally, he didn't mention any of this to her," he continued. "She had a difficult enough pregnancy without his indiscretions to consider—they forced her to bed for several months, I believe. In any case, the child—another boy—lived for only three weeks."

"I'm sorry."

Val lifted his glass. "Thank you, but I never knew him. They called him Marcus." He drank for a long moment, staring into the trees as he sipped. "My mother was inconsolable for several days, half-mad with the loss…and then one of the slaves found me abandoned by the gate at dawn, wearing my father's missing ring on a chain around my neck. My father thought he'd have to confess, but my mother announced that I was Marcus returned to her by the grace of the gods, and she refused to be convinced otherwise. If she ever changed her mind, she never said anything about it to me."

Setting his glass aside, Val reclined on his elbows and looked at the heavens. "My father told me the truth when I was about your age—there were few whispers, but still, he thought I should know. Of course, there was no way to tell whether I was actually his son—the ring meant nothing but a possibility if the woman he'd bedded was a prostitute, and he had been too eager to bed her to press her for details about herself. I like to think that I was his," he murmured, turning to me. "I look very much like him and his sons, and he claimed me. And my mother, who was all kindness, never treated me differently."

He fell quiet, and I thought of Mom, who had chosen me, protected me…and now could barely meet my eyes. Pushing that image aside, I said, "But didn't they notice the metal allergy?"

"What of it?" he replied with a shrug. "One of my brothers couldn't eat shellfish without risking his life, the other almost died from a bee, and I couldn't abide iron or silver. My father assumed he'd done something to displease the gods, but in light of my brothers' conditions, it was almost expected that I'd discover some weakness. Everyone knew that we were touched in some way—I was merely the most extreme of the lot."

I drained my glass, realized that my head was beginning

to feel fuzzy, and resisted the temptation to refill. "So when did you change your name?"

"What do you mean?"

"I thought you said they called you Marcus."

"They did. Marcus Valerius Maximus, son of Publius Valerius Maximus. But there was already a man called Marcus in the queen's guard when I arrived, and Citca called me whatever she liked. It stuck."

I stared at him, trying in vain to see the details of his face in the dark. "Two thousand years, and nobody's bothered to call you by your real name?"

"It *is* my real name. As long as I've been here, the custom has been to use only one. Praenomen, nomen gentilicium, cognomen—one serves as well as another here." He paused, considering my reaction. "Why is this distressing to you?"

"Well…I mean, I feel bad…"

"Don't. The true Marcus Valerius barely lived. If I'd been insistent, I probably could have reclaimed it, but why bother? It's only a name." He sat up and pushed himself to his feet, and I followed suit. "But enough of that," he said, brushing off the dirt. The wine and his glass vanished, and he steered me back toward the cave opening. "Sleep. And before I forget…" His fingertips landed on my temples, and an instant later, the alcohol haze faded into plain exhaustion. "There, now. I don't want to hear any excuses about overindulgence in the morning."

I followed him into the trees, but I couldn't quite let it go. "Would you *rather* be called Marcus?"

Val stopped and looked back at me, his expression enigmatic under the strobing lights of passing piq. "I haven't been Marcus to anyone since I was twenty-three," he said. "I'd surely forget to respond to it if someone tried to bring it back. But…" He paused, and I saw the corner of his mouth twitch. "Thank you."

"Yeah, no problem," I said, turning to start the climb down. "I mean, speaking as someone who's learned to answer to Dudley…"

"I was meaning to ask why that bothered you," he replied, waiting until I'd dropped a couple of steps before beginning the descent.

I resisted the instinctive urge to swat at a piq who passed me, heading toward the surface. "If wizards have a kid without magical talent, the kid's called a *dud*," I said, using the English term. "Russell thought that one up once he realized there was something wrong with me, and it spread."

"Ah. And that explains your reaction—there's nothing else I can call you that makes you quite so angry." He jumped the last few feet and landed in a smooth crouch, and I stepped off the bottom ledge onto the cave floor. "Aiden, uh...you know I only do that to test you, yes?" he asked, suddenly unsure. "I don't mean any offense, but—"

"I'm not offended. You're helping me." I started toward the corner of the cave we'd staked out, then stopped and waited for Val, remembering what I'd meant to ask him in the clearing. "You said you didn't know anything about magic when you got here, right? How did you go that long without figuring it out?"

He called up a fireball in his hand and lit his way across the room to the cot he'd made for himself. "No wizards around, no faeries, no reason to experiment," he replied, settling onto his bed. "A friend of mine was almost run through with a spear. I panicked and somehow threw up a shield around him—that was my first time."

"Bet your friend was grateful."

"Terrified." He grimaced, then stretched out and folded his arms behind his head. "As were the rest of the men. They ran me off, I wandered for a few months, and I stumbled onto Titania. Never went home again."

We lay there in the darkness, listening as Joey snored in his bag beside me.

"So," I finally ventured, "your father—"

"Had I returned to Rome," said Val, "I would have put my family at risk. Better for them to think that Marcus died abroad." He paused briefly. "I suppose that Marcus did, in a way."

"Yeah," I muttered, wincing as my dad's voice echoed in my head. "Probably better that they never found out."

"Oh, I don't know about that. The whole 'half-human immortal with untold power' situation might have been *surprising*, but…" He rolled onto his side and glanced down at me. "My father was a religious man, even if not always the most devout in his observances. In all likelihood, he'd have thought me touched by the gods, if not semi-divine. *That* would have been awkward," he said with a sigh, flopping onto his back. "I considered making my way home at first, before I crossed into Faerie, but you know…one man's demigod is another man's monster. Sometimes you're the hero, sometimes you're the creature to be slain. Depends on who's telling the story, I suppose."

"Guess you're lucky, then," I mumbled, zipping up my bag. "Assuming I get out of here alive, if Dad finds out what I've done, he won't stop at disowning me."

I closed my eyes, but I heard Val's cot creak as he stirred again. "Listen to me carefully," he murmured, bending close to my ear. "By the time I finish with you, your father won't be able to harm a hair on your head. This I swear, Aiden. Let go of your fear."

I felt him staring at me. "It's not that I'm afraid," I began, but Val cut me off before I could try to explain.

"You *are* afraid. I've seen the fear in you—and there is so much of it, boy. But as for your father, you fear that you will never make him proud."

I mulled that over and willed my throat to unclench. "Never will now, will I?"

"Then the worst has come to pass, and you're still standing. Metaphorically, I mean," he amended. "Are you sure you don't want something more substantial to sleep on?"

"I'm fine. Thanks, though."

"You're a terrible liar," he replied. "But try to remember that in the end, he doesn't determine your worth. Yes?"

"Sure."

Val snorted. "Glad we had this talk, Aiden."

"Me, too."

"Good. I'm still going to make you fight injured tomorrow."

I groaned and pulled the bag over my head, hoping to delay the dawn.

Having recuperated for a week and exhausted his options for entertaining himself, Joey came along to training the next morning. "I'm assuming the risk," he announced on arrival before Val could throw him out. "It's either this or watch the stalactites drip, and geology has never been my passion. So, what can I do to help speed this along?" he asked, leaning against the nearest tree with his arms folded.

Val sighed and rubbed his head. "You can stay out of the way."

"Come on," he cajoled, "give me *something* to do. Anything. Shoot, I'll play water boy if need be."

In reply, Val swung his finger around the clearing, pointing to the dozens of blackened pockmarks in the grass. "See those?"

"Yeah…"

"That's what happens when Aiden loses focus. I repeat: stay out of the way."

Fortunately, self-preservation won out over Joey's quest for entertainment, and he stood well behind Val for most of the day. As for me, I spent much of the morning down a limb or two, struggling to juggle my pain, my shield, and the ever-present urge to reduce my opponent to ash. By the time Val called lunch, I'd managed to keep copies of Leo and Milo at bay for half an hour, even with a dead arm, and Val seemed content as he patched me up. "That was better than I'd anticipated," he said, working on my shattered elbow. "You're learning more quickly now. A good sign."

"Pain's a good teacher?" I muttered as the bones knit.

"Well, yes, but it also means that you're beginning to internalize all of this—you're anticipating the necessary enchantment, even if you aren't consciously aware of doing so. In fact…"

The bright colors of the active magic around my arm muted, and Val stepped away with a little smile. I gave my arm a test flex and winced at the scrape of bone against bone. "It's not—"

"Finish the job."

I opened my mouth to protest, but Val's smile was firm, and I knew better than to waste my breath. Hoping I wasn't about to blow my arm off, I eased it straight, gritted my teeth, and clamped my other hand over the worst of the fractures. "If there's some trick to this that you're not telling me," I said, glaring at Val, "and I end up requiring a hospital, I'm going to forget all of my training and come after you in the night. With a claymore."

"You'd need both hands for one of those," Joey offered. "And decent gloves, don't forget."

Before I could reply, Val stepped between us and turned around. I don't know what sort of look he gave Joey, but from the way Joey's eyes widened and he slinked into the trees with his hands raised in surrender, I can make a good guess.

"The only trick," said Val, pivoting back to me as Joey retreated, "is to envision what you want and make it happen. That's enchantment at its most elementary. Leave the technical games to the wizards—what you need to do is focus on effecting a change. If the will is there, the power will follow."

He crossed his arms and waited, and I closed my eyes. I could imagine what the break looked like inside—I'd had enough compound fractures to picture the jagged edge of a bone—and the radiating pain from the impact bruises helped me zero in on the deep injury. Keeping that thought in mind, I imagined the bones rejoining…and as I did, I felt a familiar tingle spread over my arm. My eyes shot open to see the enchantment I'd created, and while it wasn't as neat or bright as Val's had been, it was *working*.

I looked at Val in surprise, and he nodded. "When you've finished, you may eat," he said, and a trio of pizzas appeared on the wooden table that had sprung from the ether. "Joey, if you've decided not to be stupid, you may have a head start." Val shrugged and grinned. "He has an appetite, you know. I'd work quickly, were I you."

Somehow, despite being left with only half a pizza by the time I reassembled my arm, I managed not to kill anyone. That afternoon, Val decided to try a different track and produced a full-length mirror, which hovered motionless in the middle of the clearing. "Glamour," he said, positioning me in front of the glass, "is innate. If you can do this—if you can *understand* this—then everything that comes after will fall into place." He rested his hand on my shoulder, and I realized with a start that sometime in the last few months, I'd managed to catch him in height. Val wasn't a large man, a few inches short of six feet, but he'd always had at least a hair on me. Standing beside him, I saw that I'd finally shot up a bit, even if I was still scrawny in comparison to his lean-muscled physique.

"How does this work?" I asked, watching his face in the mirror.

"Again, it's all a matter of putting your will into action," he replied, releasing me. "And this is far simpler than repairing a bone because you're not actually changing anything—you're creating an illusion. Give it a try."

Suddenly self-conscious, I considered my face and tried to think of what to change. My hair, always straight, had darkened to the color of dirty honey and grown unruly, perfect for a punk rocker but odd for me. A smattering of pimples of varying stages dotted my face, the product of stress and our general lack of bathing opportunities. I still had a fading black eye, earned the previous day when my shield collapsed, and a pair of fresh, healing scratches down my cheek from the morning's lessons.

"Eye color," Val suggested, seeing my hesitation. "Start small."

I stood there like an idiot, trying to figure out exactly how I was supposed to do this, and then I felt Val at the back of my mind. He gently brushed through my thoughts before smiling to himself. "You're overthinking it, Aiden. Feel it. Let it happen."

I began to ask him how, then stopped.

There.

It was waiting there, that potential. All I had to do was give it life, give it purpose, give it power from the magic flowing around me. Give it direction and *nudge* it…

My eyes, which had always been dark brown like Titania's, flickered green.

"Good," Val murmured. "Very good. Try something else."

I looked around and squinted, testing the limits of the illusion, but my reflection insisted that my eyes were green—Coileán's eyes, I recognized, having wondered why they seemed simultaneously foreign and familiar. Our eyes were the same shape, then. I hadn't managed to capture his look—my eyes still seemed sixteen, and maybe a little scared—but I'd definitely copied them from him.

Well, as long as I was going that route…

My hair darkened and shortened, then kinked into messy waves. My eyebrows darkened to match, and my cheeks shifted, the apples dropping as the zits smoothed away. The chin was still close, and the nose could maybe be a little broader at the tip, but his lips were definitely thinner than mine, and I molded them to match.

"Taller," said Val, momentarily breaking my concentration. "He's slightly taller than me. Broaden your shoulders, thicken your chest and arms."

I followed his instructions, watching in fascination as my reflection shifted toward my brother's. When I finished, the man staring back at me wasn't Coileán, not quite, but he could have fooled a careless observer. I blinked and moved, and the stranger's reflection moved in time with me, as if this had always been the face I'd seen in the mirror and my memory was playing tricks on me. "Did I do it right?" I asked Val, looking away from the mirror while my eyes tried to process what I'd been seeing.

He began to nod, then paused. "Voice. Drop it a bit—you're still using yours."

I concentrated, pretending puberty was just a bad memory. "Better?"

"Much. Joey," he said, beckoning for him to join us, "any thoughts?"

Joey ambled over, looked me up and down, and nodded. "Not exactly the boss, but not bad for a first try. Are you keeping it together?"

"Actually, yeah. It's…I don't know, it just *holds*," I said, then pulled him in front of the mirror with me. "Okay, stand there, let me concentrate."

Joey was a little taller than Coileán—six feet, he'd once said—and I stretched and filled out to match what I was seeing beside me. His arms and legs were proportionally longer, too, his hands broader and callused, his nails short and dirty from the woods. I lightened my hair to sandy blond and lengthened it to my shoulders, then darkened my eyes back to brown, twisted my features, and pulled together a copy of Joey's full beard. "Yeah?" I asked, trying to inflect a touch of his light Virginia drawl into my voice.

He goggled for a moment, then began to laugh. "That's creepy as hell, Aid."

"But is it close?"

"*Yeah.* And that's why it's creepy." He elbowed me in the arm, but my glamour held. "Okay, seriously," he muttered, "can I have my face back now, please? That's weirding me out."

Val stepped up behind us, threw his arms over our shoulders, and grinned as his reflection instantly morphed into another copy of Joey's. "Ready for the next lesson?" he asked, letting the glamour fall just as quickly.

"Sure," I said, "just let me—"

"No, keep it together," Val interrupted, releasing us as Russell and Dan appeared across the clearing. "Glamour, shield…and try for an offensive this time, hmm? Nothing fatal, just painful." The mirror vanished, and Val pulled Joey out of the way. "Go ahead, make it work."

And to my surprise, I did.

After dinner that evening, with Val supervising and Lailu standing by as our translator, I plopped cross-legged on the cave floor, and Kuni hobbled into my hand and sat with his back against my curled fingers. He stretched out his splinted leg and looked up at me, waiting. Due to their size, it usually wasn't easy for me to read piq expressions, but there was no disguising the tension in his face.

Carefully, I rested my fingertip on Kuni's well-splinted leg and concentrated. After a few silent minutes, when I broke the clumsy enchantment, he removed his splint and let me help him to the ground and back to his feet. He tested his weight on the leg, bending his knee and even jumping, then tossed his crutches aside and beamed.

"He says the pain is almost gone," Lailu reported over Kuni's rapid babbling. "And his leg feels strong again. He thanks you…profusely," she added, chuckling as Kuni continued to talk and slap my thumb. "Honestly, I do not know if he can be still long enough for the wing, but if you're willing to try…"

"Hey, Kuni," I said, raising my voice over his, and he paused in his speech, thrown by the interruption. I pointed to the empty space over my left shoulder and raised my eyebrows, and he nodded vehemently, spun around, and braced himself against my leg. I looked to Val, who waved me on, and then I barely touched Kuni's crumpled wing and tried to will it back into being the twin of its mate. Kuni whimpered as the enchantment began to work, but the wing started to unkink under my fingertips, straightening and re-growing as needed. About ten minutes and a gallon of nervous sweat later, it looked much like the whole one on the right. The color of the new bits was too faint for a perfect match, I thought, comparing them in the light of the white orb Val had tossed overhead, but structurally, the wing seemed sound. I broke the enchantment, wiped my damp palms against my jeans, and said to Lailu, "Ask him if that did the trick. It's going to be a little soft for now—the leg, too—but is it close?"

She relayed my message, and Kuni slowly twitched his left wing back and forth. When that didn't result in agony, he sped up the tempo, then took a risk and leapt.

I wasn't expecting him to dart up and plant kisses all over my face, but I managed to hold still and not re-injure him with a swat. Lailu laughed in earnest, and Val patted my shoulder.

"Enough for tonight," he said, gently shooing Kuni back toward his waiting aunt. "That will do."

CHAPTER 16

Val awarded me only light praise over the next three days, but I could tell he was pleased. I had my temper better in hand, I'd successfully patched myself up a dozen times, and my shielding had improved—quite literally overnight. Like so many other techniques, shielding seemed to snap into place one morning, as if Val had finally found the right switch inside my head. The hardest part from that point on wasn't forming a shield, but rather keeping a constant power flow running through it while executing offensive maneuvers. Successful combat was a juggling act, and if I let any of the balls drop...well, at least I got more practice repairing compound fractures.

I was feeling better about my performance when I crawled into my sleeping bag on the third evening. I'd even made myself a proper mat to pad it after dinner, and once Val saw that I was showing a bit of confidence, he'd demonstrated how to spontaneously clean things—including, he insisted, myself. Days of fleeing, hiding, and training had undone all of Astrid's cleansing work, and it was a relief to get the grime out of my skin and the bloodstains out of my clothing. That night, my bag smelled faintly of lavender and was finally free from its patina of dirt, and I stretched my mending muscles out to rest.

But my sleep was light and troubled, and I woke in the darkness with a feeling of foreboding. Lying on my side, I glanced around our corner of the cave for the source of my disquietude for a moment before I heard the realm in my mind and knew what was bothering me.

Time grows short, Faerie insisted.

Before I could press her for details, I spotted Lailu's soft purple glow as she descended toward us and landed on the edge of Val's cot. To my surprise, he was already awake and sitting up. "You, too, my lady?" he murmured, taking her in his hand.

If I strained, I could just make out Lailu's words. "She says the time has come. You cannot stay any longer."

"Did she say why?"

"He waits for you. You have been gone for days and days," she said, balancing even as Val's hand twitched.

"Only fifteen," he protested. "I told him I would be thorough in my search—"

"The Lady says he grows fearful. Paranoid. You must return."

Val sighed through his teeth. "The boy's not ready. I can't leave him, not like this. He's only begun his training."

"I understand," she said quietly, "but if Oberon seeks you out…"

She left the rest unspoken, and Val's cot creaked as he stood. "Did she give any sense of the time remaining?"

"She did not, but she fears he may begin the search in the morning. He is weakened, she tells me. Afraid."

"Then Coileán is still fighting."

I closed my eyes, but I felt it when Val padded past Joey's bag on bare feet and stood over me. "He's not ready," he repeated. "Eager and improving quickly, but he's not ready for Oberon."

"And how many days would it take to make him ready?" Lailu replied. "Days and days? Days and days and *days*?"

"Honestly?" Val muttered. "Lifetimes. But I suppose we're out of options." He stepped away, crossing back toward his bed. "I need a little rest, my lady. If you would, send a messenger well before dawn. I'll take my leave of you at daybreak."

When I was sure that Val was asleep again, I turned over and stared at the ceiling, watching the piq come and go overhead. He was right—there was no question about that. Certainly, I'd improved, but two weeks of experimentation, even with the extra power the realm had bequeathed, could hardly prepare me to take on the last of the Three.

But I wouldn't be alone, would I? Val was weaker but skilled, and Joey had plenty of nails left in his ammo kit.

If Val was going back already, though, how were we going to get to Oberon? Fight our way in? Surely his guards knew what they were doing, so Joey and I would have to mow through them just to get to the target.

Unless...

I reached around in my mind until I felt the presence of the realm. "Will you do something for me?" I whispered.

She hesitated. *Perhaps. What would you have me do?*

"Do you know Astrid? Coileán's cook?"

I do.

"Would you ask her to meet me in the orchard tomorrow after sundown?"

If you like. How do you plan to cross the distance, child?

"Don't you think it's about time I figured out how these gates work?"

There was a smile in her reply. *I'm sure there's no reason for Oberon to know of this.*

As could have been predicted, Joey was less than psyched about the new wrinkle when Val woke us in the wee hours of the morning. "So what are we going to do?" he asked, pacing in his newly laundered boxers. "I can't train Aiden. Are you going to send us back to Toula or something?"

"No," I interrupted, cutting Val off as his mouth opened. "We're not leaving again. Go back to Oberon," I told Val. "The realm and I have an understanding. I won't be long behind you."

His eyebrow arched. "Aiden, you'll forgive me for saying this, but—"

"But I'm not ready. I know." I shrugged. "Coileán is."

"And Coileán is still bound. Unless the realm has yet to share something…"

"Oh no, he's still bound." I cocked my head and grinned. "So what would happen if he just waltzed into the palace?"

Val's eyes widened at the shared thought. "If you held the glamour together and were quick…you don't have his precision, but—"

"But you've got the raw juice," Joey cut in, seeing where this was going. "Make it fast and messy. And if I start shooting, it would give you cover."

Val drummed his fingers against his bare arm. "We haven't practiced shielding others," he said. "Conceivably, you could protect yourself and Joey, but with glamour added in, *plus* an attack…" He grimaced. "Risky at best. You're almost certainly going to overextend yourself."

"True," I said. "So I thought I'd bring in some reinforcements."

"*What* reinforcements?" He looked around the cave and spread his hands. "Unless you want to drag our sisters into this, I don't have people to offer you."

I glanced at Joey's questioning eyes, then nodded to Val. "Leave it to me. The less you know, the better."

"Aiden…"

"Captain?"

His mouth tightened, but after a moment, Val huffed his exasperation. "As you like, my lord," he murmured. "Try not to get killed."

Just as he'd promised Lailu, Val stepped into the forest at sunrise and opened a gate to the palace's gardens, taking care to angle it so as not to reveal any trace of the piq settlement. Joey and I stood behind the gate, and after a brief hesitation, Val slipped through and closed the rip behind him.

Once we were alone, Joey asked, "And the plan would be?"

"We wait for nightfall," I replied, heading back toward the cave. "And we go armed. Let's sleep today," I said, parting the bushes for what I hoped was the last time. "One way or another, this ends tonight."

I stepped onto the first ledge, and Joey turned to climb down after me. "So who were you planning on asking to be our backup?"

When he reached the floor, I lowered my voice and smiled. "Astrid was willing to sneak us into the palace. Surely she's not the only person in there who's still loyal to Coileán."

He mulled that over. "You think they'll fall in line once we're on the scene?"

"I think Oberon's got a palace with dissenters in the ranks, and he's got a dungeon full of pissed-off faeries. See where I'm going?"

"Yeah," he said, stroking his beard, "I can see the potential there. But if they leave us hanging?"

I shrugged and headed for my sleeping bag. "Then let's hope I've learned something and you don't run out of ammo."

As twilight stretched the trees' long shadows into the spreading night, Lailu, Kuni, and a few of her guards gathered with Joey and me in the clearing to see if I could improvise. We'd left our gear safely underground—all, that is, but our weapons—and while I wore only a semi-useful sword at my hip, Joey looked like he was ready for a melee. Though Joey's good armor was still in the barn, Val had made him a custom holster for his nail gun, which he wore at his right side for quick access. He'd slung the arming sword on his back, also in reach of his right hand. Around his waist and down his left leg, he'd strapped on every small blade the two of us had carried into Faerie, and an oversized fanny pack held the rest of his ammunition. I didn't know the weight of the gear he was sporting, but suffice it to say that Joey wasn't getting past a metal detector.

I sincerely hoped I wasn't about to embarrass myself. Otherwise, we had another forty-mile hike ahead of us, and I was going to miss my appointment—and if I couldn't reach Astrid, the plan would fall apart.

As the nearby frogs struck up their nightly chorus, I wished Lailu and her retinue would leave me to my work. They had only come out to give us a proper send-off, I knew, but having an audience wasn't doing anything to help my self-confidence.

"Breathe, bud," Joey muttered beside me, and I flashed him a brief smile before turning to the task I'd set for myself.

I wasn't trying to go between realms—just within Faerie. I could do this.

Surely the realm would have mentioned something if I couldn't, right?

Raising my hand, I spread my fingers and imagined a door pressing against them. When I could almost feel the wood grain beneath my fingertips, I visualized the door morphing into a painted paper screen, and then into gauzy curtains. The skin of the world began to yield as I built the necessary enchantment, and I pictured the orchard on the other side of the curtains, no farther away than the back side of a thin wall. Suddenly, I felt the enchantment click into place, and with a surge of magic, a gate ripped open in the middle of the clearing.

The gate wasn't particularly large or stable. It was kind of jagged, really, and the edges flickered with raw magic as my enchantment tried to keep up with the changing situation. But it was *my* gate, and that evening, I wasn't going for style points.

"Thank you, Your Majesty," I said, glancing at Lailu.

She smiled and motioned to the gate as if pushing us on, and without another thought, I stepped into the orchard. Joey followed a few seconds later, and I broke the enchantment behind us, sealing the rift and our escape route.

"Now what?" he whispered.

Tensing in the presence of so much steel, I slid a step away from him and hoped he didn't notice. "Pick a tree, any tree. We wait."

He grimaced, then slowly climbed the nearest gnarled apple tree, taking his time as he worked against the added weight he was carrying. I took the one beside him, though I caught my sword in the branches three times on the way up and had to stop and disentangle myself even as Joey made his slow upward progression. He chuckled as I swore and yanked at the cumbersome blade, and I considered telling him off, but before I could, I heard footsteps crunching over the gravel path and froze where I'd landed. Joey also fell silent, and we waited in the darkness as the footsteps neared—slowly, hesitantly, the scurry-and-pause pattern of someone who knows he's not supposed to be poking around.

It was too dark to see the person approaching—I could barely see my hand in front of my face—but the realm's voice echoed in my head: *As promised.*

Hoping that Faerie lacked a sick sense of humor, I jumped out of the tree and whispered, "Astrid?"

The footsteps paused. "My lord?"

"It's Aiden, I'm—"

I'd meant to say something reassuring, but I never got the chance. Astrid threw her arms around me and squeezed, and I saw stars flicker in the corners of my eyes before she finally let me breathe. "What happened?" she hissed, gripping my arms to hold me in place. "You never returned, and they said there was a *hole* in the floor of the king's room, and—"

I pulled my left arm free of her grasp and held out my hand, and Astrid gasped as the green fireball in my palm flickered to life. "The realm and I had a little chat," I whispered, extinguishing the fire before we could be spotted. The orchard was a fair distance from the palace, but there was no sense in taking stupid risks. "She's letting me borrow Coileán's power for now."

"You mean—"

Joey hit the ground beside us with a jangling thud. "There's a reason why I'm carrying most of the gear," he whispered.

Astrid stepped away from his armory, but she continued to squeeze my arm. "My lord, you...you don't mean to confront—"

"I do," I replied, extricating myself. "And I'm asking for your help again. We need a diversion."

"Turns out we can't just carry the boss out of that room," said Joey. "Booby-trap enchantment or some such. But if we can give Oberon a fight, make him divert his attention to protect himself instead of concentrate on Colin..."

"I'm not asking you to go near Oberon," I added. "But if there's anyone left in the palace who might be willing to distract his guards...you know, give us a better chance of reaching him..."

"I could give you ten names without thinking," said Astrid in a low murmur, "and it might be possible to break into the dungeon, should the distraction be sufficient. But if this fails, Oberon will kill us all. You understand this, yes?"

"Of course. Wish I had a better idea."

Her dress rustled as she folded her arms. "My lord, I mean no disrespect, but are you certain that you're...uh...*capable* of fighting—"

"I am," I interrupted, praying that Joey went along with the lie. "Val's been working with me, and he says I'm ready."

"*Valerius*? But he—"

"Is as much a traitor as you, Astrid."

She stood there silently for a long moment, mulling this over, then blew out a long breath. "The last time I saw him," she said softly, "he was at Oberon's side."

"So he's already in position, isn't he?" said Joey.

My eyes had begun to adjust, and so I caught the flicker

of motion when Astrid instinctively reached for Joey, then remembered what he was packing and recoiled. "You think you have strength enough?" she asked him. "You and your toys, you think you can stand against Oberon?"

"I had less than this when I went up against Titania and Mab," he replied.

He neglected to mention the fact that he'd also had Coileán, Robin, and Toula with him on that occasion, but if Astrid realized this, she let it pass. "My lord," she said, turning back to me, "if you think this is the best plan, then tell me what you would have me do."

She jumped in surprise when I hugged her, but I didn't care about propriety that night. "When does the palace sleep?" I asked when I released her.

"Never fully, but in the small hours, it drowses. All but the essential staff."

I nodded to myself. "Then that's when we'll kick this off. Go back," I told her. "Find the people you trust, and tell them to distract as many guards as they can. If they can open the dungeons, so much the better. And tell them…" I paused, hastily throwing my planned glamour back together, then held up a fireball to reveal my borrowed face. "Tell them to look for me," I said in a voice almost like my brother's.

Astrid grinned in the greenish glow. "Quite passable, my lord."

"It's not too obvious?"

She cocked her head and squinted. "I can barely see the enchantment around the edges—it's *there*, but it's subtle enough for tonight. With a little more practice…"

"I can live with subtle," I muttered, letting the glamour fall. "Let's synchronize watches and let you get to work."

"What watches?" Astrid asked, holding up her bare wrists. "Any timepiece you make is useless after a few days—the realm can't stick to a schedule, you know."

I held out my free hand and focused, and a trio of thin, clear wristbands appeared. "Countdown timer," I explained as Joey and Astrid took theirs and slipped them on. "Assuming we launch this around, say, two or three..." I tapped my band, and *07:00* appeared in bright red where a watch face should have been. The numbers flickered, and I waited until the first minute had clicked down before tapping the band again and hiding the readout. The others copied me, and Astrid pulled her cuff over the band, hiding it from view.

"Will that give you enough time?" I asked her.

She smiled grimly and nodded. "Until the morning, my lord," she said, then stepped away from my fire and melted into the trees.

When we were alone again, Joey sighed, and his hand crept to the nail gun at his hip. "There's a decent chance that we're going to die, isn't there?" he muttered.

"Yeah."

"I mean, it's even elevated by 'roaming the wilds of Faerie' standards."

"Uh-huh." I cut my eyes to him and found him standing with his hand resting on the holster. "Look, Joey, I can try to open a gate out of here if you—"

"Don't start with that." He stared into the darkness after Astrid for a minute, then sighed again and adjusted his sword. "If you'll excuse me, I need to be alone for a bit."

I sank to the dirt under an apple tree and extinguished my fire, then watched the sky through the leafy canopy to keep my eyes from drifting to the timer on my wrist. Fighting the urge to simultaneously crawl into a hole and throw up, I wrestled with myself to maintain at least the façade of serenity.

I wanted Joey beside me. I wanted Val there to talk me down and tell me it was going to be okay. I wanted my sister and her protective wand. I wanted my mother to hug me again and tell me I was just fine the way I was. I wanted to hide behind my brother, who could seemingly do *anything*.

But Coileán was enchanted, Mom wasn't speaking to me, Hel was probably still avoiding the Arcanum's thugs,

Val was keeping up appearances with Oberon, and Joey was making his peace with God. This one was on me.

The future of the court was riding on how well Aiden Theodore Carver, Dudley to his enemies, remembered his two weeks of magical training—and *that* thought alone was almost enough to let my queasy stomach triumph. But then I heard the little voice from deep within me speak up once again:

Dudley is dead. Dudley is gone.

Which left…what? Beneath the rage, the power, the veneer of confidence, *something* was still hiding inside me, shaking with fear and *this* close to working out a gate back to Montana, where if things were bad, at least they were predictable. That part of me certainly hadn't gone anywhere—if anything, it had grown louder that night. This was a terrible idea, it insisted, my worst yet, and I was going to get Joey and Astrid and all the court killed…

Child, said the realm, interrupting my runaway train of thought, *do you believe you are the only one who knows fear? Who doubts himself?*

"Well, uh…" I whispered, but she cut me off again.

The boy hiding in the bunker will always live in you, she continued, but there was no chastisement in her pronouncement. *There are boys rather like him living inside Coileán and Valerius and Joey. Girls like him inside Toula and Helen and Astrid, in Mab and Titania. You cannot kill the boy, child—but you can learn to close the door on him. Lock him in his room, where he's safe. He'll come out from time to time, often when he's least wanted, and you will have to lock him away again because you are braver than he could ever be, and you have work to do.* She paused, letting that sink in. *He is what you fear you truly are. And in some way, that is the case—the boy is part of you. But Aiden, you are so much more than the boy*, she insisted, *and you can silence him. Do you understand?*

In my mind's eye, I saw myself as I'd been little more than a year before, pasty in the fluorescent lights and the glow of my monitor's screen, hiding in my bedroom and fearing any unexpected knock at the door. I'd hoped to study robotics. I'd yearned to be a wizard. And I'd never imagined the awful, wonderful truth.

Hang in there, I thought, and closed the door on my younger self. With that accomplished, I took stock of my emotions, then frowned at the orchard. "Still terrified," I told the realm.

Of course you are. You're not stupid.

"You're saying this plan is a bad one?"

Not the wisest course of action.

I leaned against the tree and sighed. "Got a better one you'd like to share, then?"

She said nothing for a time. I thought she'd left me until I heard her murmur, *Remember that there is a boy much like yours inside of Oberon, child.* With that, Faerie went quiet, and I kept my lonely vigil, waiting for Joey to return and the clock to tick the night away.

There was too much on the line to risk making a gate into the palace, and so Joey and I approached on foot through the dark gardens. Marine crawling was out of the question—our gear clanked enough when we were walking, let alone sliding over the terrain—but I was relieved to see that the palace didn't appear to have been affected by a case of mass insomnia. When we were within shooting distance of the walls, we hid behind a hedge and considered our options. Our timing had been spot-on—the readout on my wrist flicked over to *00:01* when I checked the clock—and I considered our options as I called up the glamour once again that would disguise me as an imperfect copy of my brother. "Preference as to door?" I asked Joey. "There's a chance that he hasn't patched the hole in the dungeon yet."

"Mess up your hair," he replied, and I tousled it to get the desired effect. "Better. And I'm pretty sure that Coileán would go in the front."

I gave him a hard look. "That's fine and dandy, but

appearances aside, I'm not—"

A blue-flamed explosion ripped through the still night, propelling a wave of stone and glass shrapnel over our heads and through the bushes around us. Joey dropped into a crouch, and I raised a shield over us both, waiting until the larger chunks thudded into the grass. "The hell," he muttered, peering through the hedge, then stood and pointed toward the palace, wide-eyed. "Shit, man," he whispered, "there's a hole in the back wall the size of a semi!"

I split the holly for a look and saw shadows running around the massive wound in the stone, jumping inside and out like ants defending a disturbed mound. My wristband informed me that the appointed hour had arrived, and I grunted as I dropped the shield. "Right on schedule. She's good."

"And that's our cue," said Joey, pulling his nail gun from its holster. "Who's on point?"

I pushed him back and marched toward the palace's front doors, trying to channel my brother. "Cover me," I said as my hands began to spark.

"Do we give quarter?"

"That's up to you."

"Fair enough," he muttered, and followed me up the wide stone staircase toward the bronze-banded oaken doors.

At the top of the steps, I paused for the space of a breath and considered for the last time what we were about to attempt. But instead of the expected fear, which had dogged me all night, I felt an upwelling of the now-familiar anger. The palace had been my safe place, damn it all. Oberon and his invaders were in *my* home. And the things he had done to Coileán…

"Aid?" Joey murmured beside me. "Got it under control, bud?"

I was glowing again, but for once, I welcomed it. "Close enough," I replied, then glared at the doors, extended my hand, and punched them open with a blast of force. The wave knocked one door from its hinges, but the other was shredded into a cloud of splinters, catching the two guards on the far side unawares. As they ducked behind their shields, I stepped through the opening I'd made, looked at both of the ashen-faced strangers, and called up a fireball in either hand. "Anything to say for yourselves?" I asked, smirking as they cowered.

Before I could incinerate them, Joey stepped up and let fly a rapid series of shots. The iron nails easily drove through the young guards' shields and into their flesh, and both howled as their wounds began to smoke and blacken. "I'm going with no quarter," Joey told me, raising his voice above their wails. "Want to do the honors, or are you sitting this one out?"

Twenty seconds later, the guards were blackened husks, and the room stank of overdone pork. I threw a shield around Joey and muttered, "Stay close," then hurried down the long stone-walled hallway, looking for signs of life.

Mercifully, Astrid's demolition team seemed to have their act together. I gathered from the cacophony of shouting and running feet that something nasty was going on at the back of the palace—I mean, it had to be bad, as at least half of the people we encountered completely overlooked us in their rush to get to the action. As for the rest, Joey and I didn't give them time to raise the alarm. I wasn't accustomed to killing, and I hadn't been sure how I would handle it, but that night, I could just as well have been swatting flies. Val's training, even as brief as it had been, had made my defenses automatic, and I was able to keep my attacks effective under pressure, riding the wave of anger that carried me on. As I played with fire, Joey practiced his marksmanship, and I caught the dark look of satisfaction that crossed his face when his projectiles hit home.

And then, as we pushed into the largest of Coileán's formal parlors, I got sloppy.

Three guards were still in the room—lieutenants, I

assumed, judging by the hologram of the palace that floated in the middle of their huddle. The bright dots within the structure must have corresponded to people, given the luminous rear wall, but I didn't have time to study their security system before the guards noticed us and jumped into action. Two ran, and I shot them in the back before they reached the far door. But while I was focused on them, I neglected the shield around Joey, and the third guard aimed a bolt at him.

Joey survived that attack only because the guard's aim was less than perfect. It struck him in the right arm, and he screamed as his bones shattered and the nail gun fell. I killed the guard without much trouble, then dragged Joey out of the room and into the smaller salon next door to assess the damage. Two doors were easier to defend than four, after all, and my backup had been neutralized.

His arm was a mess, and I suspected that the wrist and elbow had sustained damage as well. Joey had managed to retrieve his gun with his left hand, but he couldn't quite fit it into the holster on the other side of his body—not with his right arm in that state, at least. I looked around the room for suitable tools, then grabbed a decorative pillow off the overdone pink loveseat and shoved the corner into Joey's mouth. "Bite," I muttered. "This is probably going to hurt."

Tears leaked from Joey's eyes as I moved his broken bones into position, but he didn't scream. I quickly pulled together the healing enchantment that had worked so well on me and waited for him to mend. After a few minutes, however, once it had become clear that Joey's arm was still useless, he pulled the pillow out of his mouth and said, "I don't heal like you do, remember? It's going to take at least another half-hour at this rate, and the bones will still be soft."

The footsteps in the hall outside the salon were growing louder. "Damn it," I grunted, leaving the enchantment in place, then yanked a lacy tablecloth off a little side table and twisted it into a sling. "We've got to keep moving," I told

Joey as I slipped it over his head. "I can't make it work any faster."

He eased his arm into the improvised sling and winced as the bones ground together. "I know, man."

"Can you shoot left-handed?"

Joey tested the gun in his working hand, then nodded. "But I'm still pretty weak with a sword. It's right hand or nothing."

"You know what?" I said as the door slammed open and a pair of guards appeared. "We'll manage. *Die!*" I shouted at them in my brother's voice, and the two tried to beat a retreat. Unfortunately for them, the door was only large enough to let one through at a time, and I fried them both when they struggled to fit through simultaneously.

Joey followed me out, stepping gingerly over the smoking corpses sprawled on the floor. "Not bad. You've almost got his intonation down."

"Working on it."

"Arm doesn't hurt so much now."

"Enchantment numbs the pain," I replied, throwing a line of fireballs at the unlucky guard who appeared from around the corner.

"And you couldn't have done that *before* you set it?"

I gave him a long-suffering look over my shoulder, an expression Coileán favored whenever Joey or I said something stupid. "It's part of the enchantment I've been using. Creating a new one just to numb the pain would have taken longer."

"Ahead," he said, then rested his left wrist on my shoulder and fired twice, sending the next guard to the floor.

"Shit, be careful with that!" I yelped, pulling away from the gun as the side of my head tingled in warning. I dispatched the guard, then pointed to the lowered gun. "Do you have *any* idea how unpleasant that feels?"

"Yeah," he said, giving me a one-shouldered shrug, "but I shoot straighter when I can steady my wrist."

Another guard ran past, and I incinerated him before he

could round the next corner. "How about warning me the next time you use me as a tripod, okay?"

"If I've got time." He nodded to the empty hallway and pressed onward, holding his gun like a steel extension of his hand.

When we reached another parlor, I nudged Joey inside and closed the door. "Watch for me," I said, then closed my eyes and tried to feel the realm in my mind. "Any chance of a status update?" I asked Faerie.

What would you know?

"Oberon's location would be a good start."

She chuckled. *That I will not tell you. But here*, she offered, and the guards' model appeared in my head, rotating at my direction. *The yellow dots are Oberon's people. The orange ones are your allies. See what you can learn.*

I studied the model for a moment, then flipped it around and glanced at the dungeon. "Cells are empty."

Your allies have been busy.

"Mm. And the hole in the wall?"

A distraction while they opened the cells. The true fighting is here, she explained, illuminating the long hallway that connected to the spiral staircase leading to the dungeon. I could see pockets of pure yellow and orange, but most of the dots were mixed together and jostling each other.

As my gaze drifted around the model, however, I noticed a room in the east wing of the palace—a large bedroom, from the looks of it—holding six dots. Five were yellow, but one inside shone orange. "That's not Coileán's room," I muttered.

It is not.

"Can you show me the fastest way up?"

A red ribbon wound from our position up and around to the protected suite, and I dismissed the vision and opened my eyes. "Found him," I told Joey. "Ready?"

Joey snorted. "As ready as I'm going to be without my good arm. Lead on."

Oberon's personal bodyguards were good, the best of his fighters, old and seasoned and wise to the ways of combat. I was young and largely untested, and Joey was wounded. In a fair fight, we would have been toast.

But ours wasn't a fair fight. I shot at the two who held the suite's door with everything the realm had given me, and when that weakened them, I tried to simply reach across the space between us and stop their hearts. To my surprise, the guards dropped dead at my feet, as did their pair of fellows, who ran out to replace them when the screaming stopped. Joey had switched from chest shots to face shots by then, and he killed one guard before I realized he'd begun firing. When all four were dead on the rug, we stepped over the mess we'd made and marched into Oberon's room, and I stopped cold.

To be kind, the old king looked like shit.

The Oberon I remembered was a redheaded beach bum with board shorts and a constant tan, a cocky bastard with the face of a recent college dropout and the eyes of an ancient. He was muscular in the way of a surfer, a couple of inches shorter than Coileán but larger through the chest and biceps. He always smelled a little like sea salt and beer, and his laughter, while frequent, was seldom kind.

The man I found crouching in the corner of the bedroom looked enough like Oberon to assure me that I'd located my target, but there was little of the Floridian bartender left in him. He'd lost weight to the point of emaciation, and his clothes—a floor-length blue robe over a matching tunic and pants, not his familiar swimwear— hung off his shoulders when he stood. His face was gaunt, his green eyes sunken and seemingly bruised from exhaustion, and his hair bore striking streaks of white. The brocaded coverlet on the large four-poster bed that dominated the room was barely rumpled, and I could tell that if Oberon had stretched out to rest that night, he hadn't been sleeping.

For once, Oberon wasn't laughing. He looked at Joey

with alarm, but when he saw me, his pointing finger began to tremble. "You...you can't be here," he rasped, "the bind—"

I didn't give him time to finish before flinging a string of fireballs at his face. Oberon shielded reflexively, and the fires died on the stone floor.

"*The bind is still intact!*" he yelled across the room, watching me from behind the haze of his shield. "You're not...you can't have...*how...*"

By then, Joey had dropped to one knee and was shooting. Most of the nails bounced off, but two penetrated the shield and embedded themselves in Oberon's thigh, and he screamed in shock and pain. Furious, he took his attention off me for a second and turned to my friend.

That bolt wouldn't have merely killed Joey. Had it hit him, it would have reduced him to a wet, pink haze and a gory puddle. But the shield that materialized around Joey an instant before the impact was strong and thick, and definitely not of my making. I looked across the bedroom and spotted Val standing by the window, one arm outstretched and shaking with the effort of holding the shield together. The bolt dissipated, but Joey, who continued to shoot through both Val's shield and Oberon's, seemed either unaware of how close he had come to death or unfazed by the brush.

At that moment, realization crossed Oberon's haggard face, and he aimed a blast at Val—a blast that Val had anticipated and easily deflected. "What's the matter, old boy?" I taunted, seeing Oberon's expression shift back and forth between anger and fear. "Feeling a little weak today?"

His shield strengthened against Joey's continued barrage and Val's onslaught of lightning. "The bind is still intact," he repeated, yanking a nail out of his smoking leg. "And Coileán is bound. I feel him. So who"—he shrieked as he pulled another nail free—"the hell are you?"

I smiled as he limped toward me, then let the glamour fall away. Oberon's watering eyes went wide. "The mongrel?" he muttered, momentarily frozen in his tracks. "That's impossible, you—"

"Maybe no one ever told you," I interrupted, calling up a basketball-sized sphere of green flame, "but mongrels have *teeth*."

My shot broke against his shield, but the impact was enough to distract Oberon from the attack on his flank, and one of Val's bolts slipped through. He screamed and fell to his knees, then growled with rage and turned on Val. Before he could shoot, however, another of Joey's nails hit him in the back, and Oberon again switched his focus.

I saw his shield strengthen anew, first matching mine, then surpassing it, until the air around him was nearly opaque with activated magic, an iridescent shell that blocked Val's shots. A handful of Joey's were still getting through, however, and the more that Val and I forced Oberon to block, the better the chance that a nail would strike.

For ten long minutes, the four of us danced around the bedroom, jumping over and ducking behind furniture to avoid each other's fire. As sweat ran into my eyes, I realized that we probably weren't going to get a kill shot in—I was strong, Val was doing his best to make up for my inexperience, and Joey had entered a sort of Zen state of focus in which he could shoot left-handed and still dodge the worst of Oberon's attacks, but Oberon had thrown his weight into his shield, and very little that we tossed at him was getting past the barrier. I was beginning to wonder how much more he could pour into the shield before his attacks started to weaken when I tripped over the corner of the thick rug. Catching my balance, I let down my guard for a split-second.

Oberon seized his chance, and my world exploded in pain.

I flew backward and slammed into the stone wall. The impact knocked the breath from my lungs, and I saw stars as my head cracked against rock and rang from the blow. Before I could gather my wits, I felt something clamp around my neck and tighten, and I saw Oberon squeezing his hand into a fist.

Looking down at him as the world began to swim, all I could think was, *Huh. He's a Sith.*

And then, as my brain registered that I was rapidly losing oxygen, I started to struggle against the vise around my throat. Oberon clenched his teeth and redoubled his efforts, and he and I fought for control, the one crouched behind a shield, the other pinned to the wall and beginning to suffocate. As the black specks of impending unconsciousness crept into the corners of my field of vision, I noticed distantly that Oberon's shield wasn't solid all the way around—sure, he was blocking Joey and Val, but he extended little of the shield between the two of us, and almost none in the direction of the open door. It was an idle observation, seeing as I was pouring everything I had into getting the invisible hand off my windpipe, but I hoped one of the others would notice and take advantage of the opening.

They didn't. But as it so happened, they didn't need to.

I was seconds away from losing my fight when Coileán dragged himself through the door. Before Oberon had time to register that the newcomer was the real deal, my brother had flung a fast volley of fireballs at the gap in his shield, and Oberon rushed to block them before they burned him alive. With his attention elsewhere, his grip on me weakened, and I fell to the floor, coughing and gasping.

There were no words exchanged between the two kings, no taunts, no pleas for mercy. They simply threw together the best shields they could and began slinging fire at each other.

Of the two, Coileán looked to be in better physical shape, but he was slower than usual, his attacks weaker, his shield thinner. Breaking through the bind had obviously taken its toll on him, on top of which he'd been continually fighting Oberon for nearly two months. But he was enraged, and that gave him the strength to go on.

Val and I helped where we could, but Oberon managed to hold his own, desperately shielding and striking with every bit of his power. As he and Coileán began to flicker into and out of existence, chasing each other around the room, I looked to the door and saw that the mass fight had made its way toward us—the smoke and screams were a dead giveaway. "Val!" I yelled, pointing to the fray, and he moved to the doorway to guard against incursions.

Just as he got into position, Oberon and Coileán reappeared across the room, barely visible through the shields around them. Coileán's back was to the wall, but Oberon, focused on the opponent at hand, had left himself vulnerable from behind.

I didn't give myself time to think. "Down," I said to Joey, who dropped to one knee without hesitation. Praying that the leather around his sword's hilt was thick and intact, I yanked it free from the scabbard on his back, told my hands to stop complaining, and wound the sword back like a baseball bat as I ran toward Oberon.

He never saw me coming. I didn't completely behead him, but the cut was deep enough to do the trick.

When Oberon fell and didn't rise, Coileán dropped his shield, and we stared at each other over the body for a few silent seconds while the fight continued to rage in the corridor. Finally, he mumbled, "Aiden?"

"Hey," I panted, then remembered what I was still holding and tossed Joey's sword away. My left hand, which had partly covered the naked pommel, felt like it was on fire, and when I opened my fingers, I saw that a good portion of the skin on my palm had gone with the sword. "*Shit*," I hissed, wrapping the edge of my T-shirt around the weeping wound as the pain began to register. "Oh, damn it, that hurts…"

"You…"

"Realm fixed me up," I muttered, gritting my teeth to keep from crying out, then stripped off my shirt and started winding it around the wound. "If you could cover for me for just a few minutes, I need to fix this—"

"Won't heal. Not...for a while. Iron burns...difficult." He staggered backward until his shoulders hit the wall, and he sank to the ground. "Aiden...need rest."

"I can't. Joey's already down an arm, and Val—"

"*I* need rest," he clarified, and I saw the exhaustion in his eyes when I looked up from my injury. "You..."

"I'll hold them back," I promised, checking to be sure that Val was still secure at the door. "Take it easy, you've done enough."

But Coileán shook his head, then collapsed and sprawled on the stone beside Oberon with his eyes closed. "You...regent."

I crouched beside him and shook his shoulder, trying to keep him conscious. "Come on, stay with me," I said, jostling him until he flopped onto his back. "*Come on*, Coileán, you've got to stay awake!"

Despite my efforts, his breathing was already slowing. "Need rest," he whispered. "Aiden..."

He struggled to raise his hand, and I clasped it with my uninjured one. "I'm here," I murmured, leaning close to hear him over the noise.

Hold the fort, he mouthed, and his hand went limp in mine.

My brother wasn't dead, I realized after an initial moment of panic, but nothing I could do roused him from the deep sleep into which he had tumbled before my eyes. When I was sure that the cause was hopeless, I let his hand go, then rose and found Val and Joey watching me. "So, it looks like I'm in charge until he wakes," I muttered. "What the hell am I going to do?"

Val pointed to the open door. "Just a thought, my lord, but why don't you start by ending this mess?"

I looked down at my sleeping brother and the dead king. *Hold the fort.*

Like it or not, this was my show now, and I had to act the part. With a last look at Coileán, I started the healing enchantment over my burned hand, tried to push the pain away, and nodded to Val. "Yeah, let's go break up the fight. I think I owe Astrid that much," I said, hoping I sounded more confident than I felt.

CHAPTER 17

We didn't have to go far to find the fighting. The front lines had reached Oberon's room by the time I poked my head into the hallway, and from what I could see, fortune was with our side. Oberon really should have killed the ones who wouldn't kneel, I mused, watching a bolt of lightning incinerate one of his guards. A pissed-off faerie is a dangerous faerie, and many of the ones who'd been locked in the dungeon were full-blooded and *angry*.

Even working with Val and Joey, it took me nearly half an hour to end the free-for-all and explain what had happened. The newly released members of Coileán's court—*my* court, for the moment—were only too willing to escort the surviving members of Oberon's down to their vacated cells. I told myself that Coileán could deal with them, or if he was asleep for more than a day or two, that I could make the call, but I had bigger issues to consider at the moment than the defeated invaders.

Among the captives were eleven of Oberon's children, ranging in age from one hundred or so to six hundred and change. None of them was the successor, however—the realm made that clear to me—which meant that someone out there, probably in the mortal realm, had just inherited a ton of power. I expected that he or she would come forth in the next few days, but my more immediate concern was the Arcanum and Moyna's siege. Having had no word from the other side for weeks, I wanted reassurance that Hel was okay—and I wanted to nab Moyna for Coileán.

But there were certain formalities that needed to be

addressed first, and at Val's insistence, I donned a replacement shirt, gathered the available members of the court in my brother's throne room, and perched uneasily on his seat. "Coileán is alive," I said once the room had quieted. "And freed from Oberon's bind. But he's recuperating for now, and he's, uh…he's left me in charge. The realm doesn't seem opposed to this." I waited while a wave of muttering swept around the room, then raised my unburned hand. "I'm serving as regent at his request. If you have a problem with that, you can take it up with him when he wakes."

One of the lower ladies stepped out from the pack. "My lord," she began, a sneer in her voice, "do correct me if I'm mistaken, but surely a *mongrel* cannot—"

Her mouth snapped shut as I called a fireball into existence in my palm. "As I said," I murmured, "the realm is on board with this arrangement. *This* hand," I continued, lifting my wrapped left, "is a wreck right now because I took Oberon's head two-thirds of the way off with Joey's sword"—he raised the blade as an exhibit—"and I ran out of covered hilt. Now, if you want a demonstration…"

She held up her empty hands in surrender, shook her head, and melted into the crowd.

"All right, then." I sighed, slumping back onto Coileán's throne. "Moyna is still at large, and I understand that she has an army of some size. If you have concrete knowledge for me, stick around. Everyone else, stay close—as soon as I find her, I'm going after her." I looked down at the room from the dais and smiled tightly. "Am I correct in assuming that a few of you would like a word with her?"

The court, particularly the ones who'd just come from the dungeon, clapped and cheered until I stood and raised my hand to restore order. "Good to know. Captain?" Val stepped out of the throng, and I pointed him out to the others. "You're in charge of attack preparations. Astrid, please take Coileán to his room and make him secure. As for Oberon…" I cut my eyes back to Val. "I don't know how many of your team are left, but get someone you trust to take a blood sample from him, at least a few pints. We might need it. When he's finished with that, he can burn the body."

He nodded. "Yes, my lord. As for the other bodies? And the ones we've yet to capture?"

"How many of each?" I asked.

Val glanced around the room, then beckoned to a man and a woman I recognized as guards. "Between the three of us and the diversionary force, we have fifty-six dead in the palace, not counting Oberon. Ten of those are our own. And there are many others of his in the realm besides the ones in custody—his lords and ladies have helped themselves to the land and built what they liked." He looked to his guards, who nodded in confirmation.

The room began to rumble again, and I spoke over the noise. "The bodies can be disposed of once their identities are confirmed. But as for the rest of his court, I want them found," I told him. "Go house to house if you need to. This is your area of expertise, Val, not mine—do what you think best."

He took three steps up the dais to give him height enough to see over the crowd, then pointed to a few other faces in the throng. "Give us an hour or two," he told me. "If we go with a sufficient force before dawn, we should be able to avoid significant casualties."

"Thank you," I said, and looked back at Joey. "If you're feeling strong enough, you're coming with me."

"Uh…where, exactly?" Joey asked from the foot of the dais.

I grinned, ignoring the pain in my hand. "Thought we'd start in Rigby. How do you feel about breaking and entering?"

I needed to find my sister, which meant I had three options: pop by the silo and move around as the leads suggested, call her once we were back in the mortal realm with cell service and hope I wasn't blowing her cover, or get the information I wanted from the Fringe. Given that my most recent trip back to the silo had resulted in house arrest and I had no idea where Hel might have been hiding, I chose the third option, but this was complicated by the fact that the last I'd seen of my Fringe contacts was when they were packed off to Alaska for safekeeping. I didn't know how to find the Stowes' house...but then again, maybe I didn't have to go looking.

To my relief, my first trans-realm gate went off without a hitch, and Joey and I stepped through into the alley beside Slim's, Rick Matherson's grungy bar, shortly before sunrise. The realm voiced her displeasure that I was leaving, but I muttered to her that I would be back and ignored her thrum of disapproval as I looked around the quiet, snowy streets.

"Saturday morning," Joey murmured, rubbing his solidifying arm through his coat. "And looks like winter's getting serious about it early this year."

I stepped around a refrozen pile of gray slush, leaving a trail of footprints through the dusting on the sidewalk as we walked around the building. "You okay?"

"Yeah," he replied with a white puff of breath, "fine, but if we could go inside, I wouldn't complain."

"See, that's the issue." I rested my hand on the brick beside the bar's front door and felt the wards humming. If I concentrated, I could see them running just beneath the surface of the wall, a tight network of spellcraft. The wizard who had constructed them had done a brilliant job—when the wards were depowered during business hours, they blended seamlessly into the usual background magic, giving Rick a bit of anonymity and protection from magically gifted strangers—but Rick had locked the place up before leaving town, and the wards were most definitely armed and ready that morning. "We're going to have to break in," I told Joey.

"Maybe he hid a key," Joey suggested, but I shook my head.

"There's a security network on the building. I can

probably break through it, but I don't know what'll happen if I trip the wards."

His face tightened. "Bar go boom?"

"Maybe. Want to risk it?"

"We're here, aren't we?" he replied with a shrug, then stepped back a few paces. "Hit it, Aid."

I concentrated, feeling for a weak point in the wards, then focused on a joint near the doors and shot a tight bolt of force into the network. The wards flashed, absorbing what they could, but I kept feeding the enchantment until the system, almost disappointingly, fried and went dark. It was harder work to break the steel lock—the metal would barely cooperate, and I was soaked with sweat by the time I broke in—and I slid to the side and crossed my fingers against explosions while Joey opened the door for us.

It was anticlimactic, to say the least. Nothing blew up. There was no fire, no smoke, just a plaque on the wall that blinked red. When I touched it, the blob of color resolved into the crossed-wand star of Arcanum security, and I nodded in relief. "Under ordinary circumstances, I'd say we didn't have long," I told Joey, "but if the Arcanum's under siege right now, I kind of doubt that a break-in here is their top priority. Where do you think he keeps his computer?"

Joey pointed to the staircase leading to the second floor. "If this is like Colin's building, the apartment's up there. Unless he took it with him, of course…"

"Don't jinx this, man," I muttered, and headed up the creaking stairs to Rick's place.

The bartender had left his apartment unlocked—why bother with keys when you have a ward system, right?—and so Joey and I let ourselves in without difficulty. What we found on the other side of the door was unexpected, considering the bar below, which was decorated with paneling the color of tobacco juice and cracking vinyl. Rick's apartment could have doubled as a Scandinavian designer's showroom but for the six weeks' worth of dust coating every horizontal surface. Joey flipped a switch, and the recessed lighting in the ceiling cast a soft, cool glow over Rick's immaculate white leather sofas and the neatly stacked collection of *Architectural Digest* back issues on the tray atop the ottoman.

"O…*kay*," I said, wondering if I should take off my shoes. I suspected that Rick wouldn't appreciate bloodstains on his white carpet.

Joey looked around, taking it in, then pointed to a pine desk in the corner of the den. "Computer's over there. And you know, we all need our places of serenity."

"I guess." Sloughing off my sneakers, I tiptoed across the room and took a seat at the desk.

Rick's computer was a laptop, a clunky desktop replacement model of mid-2000s vintage, complete with peripheral mouse and a pair of oversized external speakers. He'd left the laptop plugged in, which told me that either he didn't think he'd need it on the run—unlikely, considering how prepared Rick usually was—or that the battery was too old to hold a charge for long, which seemed more probable to me. Making a mental note to build Rick a better computer as an apology for messing up his wards, I carefully started rummaging through the desk's drawers.

"What are you looking for?" asked Joey, who had also pulled off his dirty boots before walking on the pristine carpet.

"Passwords," I muttered, pawing through a pile of open envelopes. "Rick's old enough that he's probably written his down for safekeeping, so maybe there's some around here—*ouch!*" I yelped, accidentally brushing my fingertips against the steel three-hole punch lurking in the bottom of the drawer.

While I sucked on my burned fingers, Joey lifted the laptop and glanced underneath. "Found 'em," he said, pulling a faded Post-It off the underside of the computer.

I took it from him, a little miffed to have neglected the obvious hiding place, and raised the screen. "Right. Might want to get comfortable," I said, logging in to Rick's computer. "This could take a while."

I'd helped myself to the Arcanum Archives as a kid, but that system was laughably easy to crack. The Fringe, which couldn't rely on magic as a safeguard, had actual security protocols in place, and one wrong keystroke aborted the entire convoluted login process. Rick might have listed his passwords, but he hadn't put them in the correct *order*. At least he'd left an icon on the desktop for the software.

It took me nearly twenty minutes to access the Fringe's network, during which time Joey went below to help himself to Rick's top shelf and dropped a flat ginger ale on a coaster beside the mouse for me. "Seriously?" I muttered after the first sip. "You couldn't have at least grabbed a beer?"

Joey flopped onto one of Rick's couches and tilted his tumbler toward me. "That's a bar, and you're a minor."

"I just killed two dozen faeries," I griped. "Come on, man."

"You're still a minor."

With a little concentration, the ginger ale morphed into a passable impression of hard lemonade, and I smirked at Joey as I raised the glass.

"Remember the chestnut about great power and great responsibility," he replied, then pointed to the computer behind me. "Window just opened, if you're interested."

I swiveled around to find that a video chat was asking for me to join. After accepting, I waited for the feed to start, and my screen filled with a grainy picture of a middle-aged woman in a fluffy peach sweater. She looked at me over her thick-rimmed glasses in surprise, and her dark brows rose. "*You're* not Slim," she said in a voice that would have been right at home in a British period drama. "Who the devil—"

"I'm Aiden Carver," I interrupted. "Looking for Vivian Stowe. Can you help me?"

Her over-rouged lips pursed, and she ducked out of the shot for a moment to lift an obese dachshund in a matching sweater onto her lap. "Carver, you say?"

"Helen's brother."

The woman's eyebrows rose again. "Oh, *you're* the Carver boy..."

"Uh, yeah, I—"

"We know all about you."

"Great," I muttered. "And you are..."

She settled back in her chair and rubbed her dog's head. "Call me Butterfly. And I'd heard you'd run off to Faerie."

"Yeah."

"And you...made it back?"

"*Yes*," I snapped, fighting my fraying temper. "Just now. So would you *kindly* tell me how to get in touch with Vivi?"

"How?"

"How *what*?"

"How on earth did you get back?" she asked, leaning toward the camera. "The gates are guarded, which tells me that you had help. And if you had help, then you're probably working with Oberon," she continued, staring at me over her lenses. "Now, in light of the current siege, I'm sure he would love to know where your sister and Ms. Pavli are hiding, and you're working off the assumption that Vivian would know their whereabouts. Is that accurate, my lord?" she said with a smirk.

Before I could do something stupid, Joey jumped off the couch, pushed my chair out of the way, and squatted in front of the computer. "Count to ten," he told me, then said to the screen, "If you think for one minute that he'd do something to hurt his sister, or that I would let him, you're out of your damn mind."

She remained unperturbed. "And you are?"

"Joey Bolin. And we got back with a lot of help from Toula's brother, if it matters so much to you."

Technically, I reasoned, that wasn't a lie.

"Have you any proof of this story?" she asked, cocking her head. "It seems rather far-fetched that you two would just reappear after all this time..."

The computer *dinged*, and another window opened to reveal Vivi, who was sporting a pair of fat headphones over her ears. "Easy, Butterfly," she said, but didn't smile. "Where are you two, and how did you get on here?"

"Rick's apartment. He kept a list of his passwords out," said Joey.

Vivi rolled her eyes and groaned. "Damn it," she muttered, "I've *told* him…okay, whatever, you're in. And how do we know you're not Oberon's spies all glamoured up?"

Joey stood and tilted the screen back. "Send Rufus over. He'll vouch for us."

She seemed unconvinced, but she pulled off her headphones and nodded. "Don't go anywhere. He'll be there soon."

Both video windows closed, and Joey shrugged at me. "Well, it sounds like they've been having a party in our absence, doesn't it?"

"The paranoia is fun enough." I pushed myself out of the chair and looked through the window at the quiet, dawn-lit street. "Guess we're going to have to be honest," I mumbled, waiting for a gate to appear.

"Why? I covered well enough, didn't I?"

"Val could have gotten us back, but that doesn't explain how we broke through the wards around the bar."

"Oh," he muttered. "Well, crap. Sorry, Aiden, I thought that would do it…"

I brushed it aside. "Hel was going to figure it out eventually, but…" I blew out a long breath. "This is going to be one of those days, isn't it?"

"Not to split hairs, but I think it's been one of those days all night." He downed the rest of his drink in a long gulp and tapped on the windowpane as the gate materialized. "Okay, there's Rufus, and…I don't know that guy."

The other man was a little shorter than Rufus, with lighter hair and, as I saw when he looked up at the window, eyes that squinted in thought. "No clue," I replied. "Should we go down to meet them?"

"No reason to spook them," said Joey, stepping away from their line of sight. "Play it cool."

We waited for a few minutes while the newcomers walked around the building, then took a seat on the couch as Rick's apartment door opened. The other man entered first, a fireball at the ready, and studied us both. "Secure," he said in Fae, his accent noticeable but vague, and stepped aside as Rufus walked in.

"Hey, Rufus," said Joey, keeping his hands in his lap. "Who's your muscle?"

"This would be Ned," he replied, cocking his head toward the other man. "My brother. So, Vivi's not convinced that you are who you say you are. I don't see any signs of glamour, but if you wanted to prove it to us, I wouldn't stand in your way…"

Moving slowly, Joey pushed his coat aside to reveal the knives strapped all around his left leg. "I'm going to pull one of these out, okay?" he said, looking at both Stowes. "No sudden moves." Rufus nodded, and Joey eased a hunting knife from its holster, then pressed the flat of the blade against his palm. "That's steel," he said, extending the handle toward Rufus. "Go on and try for yourself if you don't believe me."

Rufus held up his hands, rejecting the offer, and Joey started to put the knife away when Rufus said, "Wait. Aiden, too. Let's see it."

I met Joey's worried eyes, then looked at our interrogators. "Slight problem there," I told them. "Take a look, Rufus," I offered, tapping the side of my head. "I'm not great at blocking yet. Val could only do so much in the time we had."

He traded uneasy glances with Ned, and then I felt him in my mind—not like Val's delicate, almost unnoticeable fluttering, but more like a jackhammer on concrete. "The hell!" I yelled as he retreated, and massaged my throbbing temples. "Jeez, how about a little finesse next time?"

Rufus stared at me for a moment with his mouth slightly agape, then remembered his brother. "Ned," he said softly, "Oberon is dead."

Ned recoiled. "*Dead*? How?"

He pointed to me, then to the handle peeking over Joey's shoulder. "It seems that Lord Aiden finally...figured himself out, shall we say," he said with a little smirk in my direction. "I told you that you'd be amazing someday, didn't I?" he added, smiling in earnest.

"Wouldn't go as far as 'amazing,'" I replied, "but can we get off the couch now?" Ned stepped back and beckoned, and Joey and I stood. "So," I said, looking at the other three as I picked up my abandoned drink, "I've got a restless, eager crew back across the border that would love to come over and wreak a little havoc. Where should I deploy it?"

Ned's smooth brow furrowed. "*You* are in charge of deployments?"

"I'm in charge of the court until Coileán wakes. Got a problem with that?"

He stiffened and briskly shook his head. "My lord."

"Great." I downed the rest of my lemonade, grimaced at the sour finish, and tossed the glass into the air, intending to send it back into the ether as my brother usually did. Instead, it crashed to the carpet and rolled into the ottoman, and I sighed. "Okay, I'm new to this. Can we all just pretend no one saw that?"

Rufus snorted, and the glass vanished. "Saw what? And while your offer is generous, it's not going to do the Arcanum much good at the moment."

"What do you mean?" Joey asked, frowning. "Last time I checked, a gang of angry faeries was a force to be reckoned with."

"Oh, most certainly," he replied, "if one has sufficient magic to make them more than an angry gang with a severe metal allergy. Make yourselves comfortable, kids," he said, taking a seat on the far couch. A topographic map materialized on the ottoman between us, and he dropped

Rick's stack of magazines onto the floor. "Here's what you missed while you were away."

The nearest town to the Arcanum silo—well, the nearest town to speak of—was Glasgow, which at least had an airport and a McDonald's to recommend it. Beyond that stretched grasslands and hills to the horizon, dotted with the occasional farmhouse or bit of woods, and if you veered far enough to the east, a reservation. Most of the silo dwellers did their occasional shopping in Glasgow, but their children went to school in Wright's Mill, a wide patch of county road that consisted mostly of the school complex, a gas station, and a trio of abandoned houses used primarily by the high schoolers for making out, drinking, and selling pot. Whatever mill there may once have been was long gone by the time I started school there.

Once Moyna appeared with her forces, the Fringe and its allies had set up camp in the least decrepit of the abandoned houses, installed a good ward system, and camouflaged the building as a construction site. "The sign promises a Dairy Queen," said Rufus. "Helen says we're going to disappoint a lot of children, but at least no one's tried to sabotage the 'construction,'" he continued, punctuating his explanation with air quotes. "And by the way, she almost killed me when she found out what you two did, so be prepared for *that* reunion."

"Flowers and body armor," Joey muttered. "And Georgie?"

"Anxious. She's been suggesting for a month that all of our problems would be solved if only Toula would take the spell off her," he replied, and pressed on.

Our team—Toula, Hel, Rick, Vivi, Hal, and Stuart—only hid out with the Stowes until the last week of October. By the time Rufus slunk home with Georgie to face my sister's wrath, the Fringe tech specialists had finally broken through the last of the Arcanum's security protocols and accessed the cameras around the silo. What they found was, to be mild, worrisome. "We estimate between one hundred and two hundred of them," said Rufus, sketching out a campsite on his map. "There's no way of knowing if that's really all that remains of Mab's court, but it's enough to stop the Arcanum. Here's the silo entrance," he said, tapping one of the Xs on the map, "and here's the back entrance, per Toula and Helen. Now, they're within a relatively small distance of each other...and here's Moyna's perimeter." Rufus made a dotted circle around the two entrances and grimaced. "She's not stupid enough to attack directly—the entrances are narrow, and a solid Arcanum defense could hold them at bay. The communiqués we've intercepted suggest that she's trying to break their wards instead."

He didn't need to spell it out for me. The silo's defensive wards kept nosy neighbors, census takers, and the occasional Jehovah's Witness away, but they also protected the silo against, for instance, tunneling. Anyone who tried to break in from the surface would quickly encounter concrete and steel, but with enough experienced faeries working in tandem, even steel would fail eventually.

"Why don't they evacuate?" I asked.

Ned pointed to the dotted line. "Moyna's people have two major enchantments working at the moment. The first is to break through the defenses, as Rufus said, but the other placed a barrier around the complex. It interferes with gates—one cannot get in or out by magical means."

"So it's the door or nothing," Rufus added. "And here," he said, producing a photograph from memory. "See for yourself."

The shot was black and white and grainy—I could expect no better from the Arcanum's tech—but I saw a line of tents and pavilions a short distance beyond the decoy trailer park's fence.

Joey looked over my shoulder and grunted. "Got a Ren Faire vibe going on, don't they?"

Ned's eyebrow rose as he regarded Joey. "Ah, yes. I was

told about you."

"Me?"

"The quasi-knight. Helen says you're relatively skilled with a blade."

Joey gave Ned a once-over and sniffed. "Relatively. You?"

"Relatively," he echoed, "but something tells me we're not using the same standard of measurement."

At that, Joey began to bristle. "I ride, I joust, and I fight. *Without* enchantment. I won my first tournament at twenty."

"But what was the field like?" asked Ned. "Amateurs fighting amateurs—not the stiffest competition, I'd wager."

"Want a demo?"

My shoulders clenched as the two of them postured. All of the painful work I'd done with Val had only taught me to leash my newfound temper—it had done nothing to dull it. "Guys," I muttered, not looking up from the security photo, "cool it."

Joey had sense enough to shut up, but Ned had to get the last word in, and he snorted his derision. "Saved by the babe. How convenient for you."

Under other circumstances, I might have been more tactful, but the little booze in my system was doing nothing to smooth over the jagged edges of my psyche. I'd killed a dozen faeries. I'd beheaded fucking *Oberon*. I was supposed to run the court, but Ned was looking at me like I was a useless child…

"*Shut up*," I snapped, then created a decent fireball and began tossing it up and down as I stared him in the face. He blinked first, but I held his gaze, wrestling with the internal impulse to incinerate the annoyance. "I like your brother and sister," I finally said. "And I'd hate to upset them. But I swear, if you don't sit down and stop provoking Joey, I will toss your sorry ass out the window and see if you bounce. Got it?"

Maybe it was because I'd started glowing a little by then, but Ned took the hint, held up his hands in placation, and let Rufus continue filling us in.

"And that's the front line," said Rufus, returning to the map as if nothing had happened. "Now, here's the interesting part: the other Arcanum installations sent reinforcements, who have set up like so." He drew another dotted line about a quarter-mile from the first, forming concentric rings. "What this means is that Moyna's forces are fractured—a third of them on each major enchantment, and the last third defending against the wizards at their backs. She's locked them into a stalemate."

"What about you?" Joey asked.

Rufus smirked. "You know, crises are such interesting things. Here, you've got the vast majority of the most powerful wizards in the world stuck inside the bunker—grand magus, councilors, et cetera. You've got a bunch of lesser wizards on the outside, unable to communicate with the mother ship and, quite frankly, outclassed by the fae horde. And then, who should show up but Helen?"

"And that minor matter of the warrant?" I pressed.

"They seem to have forgotten all about it. Toula's, too. Once the Fringe offered to share their connections and run messages, the Arcanum crowd reconsidered. Oh, *we* don't have much to do with them," he clarified, thumbing his hand at his brother, "but the powers that be on the field are well aware that we're around."

"The two of us and Harry," said Ned. "The rest of our kin are in Alaska."

"The fewer of us there are that run around here," said Rufus, "the smaller the chance that Oberon will get wind of it. *Would* get wind of it, I suppose," he amended. "Who's the new king?"

I could only shrug. "As far as I can tell, it's no one in Faerie right now. But Oberon had enough kids…"

"He could be anywhere," Ned concluded. "Well, he'll show himself eventually. For the moment—"

"We go to Montana," I interrupted. "We have a chat with the Arcanum heads. And then we end this." I stood again and waited while Rufus rolled up his map. "Are you with me?"

"I am," said Rufus, "but you didn't let me finish. There's one *minor* complication you're overlooking, Aiden—remember your history?"

He waited, watching me expectantly, and I imagined I was getting a taste of what his poor students went through. "Can you be more specific?"

Rufus steepled his fingers, falling easily into professorial mode. "The Great War. The big wizard tiff. You've heard of it, I trust?"

"Sure, but what does…oh, *shit*," I groaned as the missing piece fell into place.

Having grown up in the silo, of course I'd learned about the Great War—well, half of it was self-taught, but I had the basics down. The Arcanum had won in the end only because Simon Magus or one of his underlings had figured out how to store and transport magic. On the battlefield, when the big spells were flying and the magic supply was being depleted faster than it could flow in from Faerie, the Arcanum had their backup batteries to draw upon, allowing them to cast spells once their opponents were out of ammo.

"How bad is it on the scene?" I muttered.

Ned grimaced. "Everything is weak. Equally weak, but weak. And the deficit is being worsened by the glamour Toula threw around the area. She's hidden the tents from view, but the added construction is taxing the reserves." He drummed his fingers on the arm of the couch. "This is an estimate, naturally, but I'd say we don't have more than another three or four days' worth of magic in the area. Not unless someone opens extra gates and strengthens the local flow."

"And no one's done that yet because Oberon held the other side," said Joey. "Okay, so we get over there and someone punches a few gates open…how long would it take to get you up and running?"

"Too long," I said, considering the experiments I'd done

the year before. "The flow's strong, but dispersal takes time. Anyone right in front of the gate could tap the magic, but get more than a few feet away…"

"And we're back in the Gray Lands again," Joey finished, glowering at the map. "Damn. But…wait a sec," he said, perking up as he looked at me, "you can pump it, right? Like you did last time? You can move it, spread it out—"

"Not anymore," I mumbled. "I tried pushing it around like before, and it just activated. If we've depleted our resources…" I sighed and rubbed my face. "Okay. So what I'm hearing right now is that my merry band of faeries is going to be useless unless we open a hundred gates or they opt for more conventional weaponry. Assume magic's out. That leaves us with—"

"Dark magic."

The three of us stared at Joey. "Well, *yes*," said Ned, "but unless you're hiding something from us, no one involved in this debacle can use dark magic."

Joey's grin revealed more than a hint of smugness. "Maybe you chumps can't, but Georgie can."

Five minutes and a few thrown-back drinks later, we were standing under a sputtering streetlight in the icy predawn wind and a foot of hard-packed snow outside of the Fringe's appropriated house in Wright's Mill, which was now masquerading as a pit and a pile of rebar. "I like what you've done with the place," I muttered, picking out the telltale lines of enchantment around the site. "Couldn't have gotten much worse, at any rate."

Rufus gestured toward the lot. "Shall we—"

Before he could finish, Georgie sprinted out from behind the enchantment, barefoot and coatless. "*Joey!*" she shouted, racing across the empty street. "Joey, Joey, *Joey!*"

He braced himself for impact, but the force of Georgie's embrace almost sent him flying. "Told you I'd be back," he wheezed. "And when did you learn to speak?"

She loosened her grip just enough to allow him to breathe and grinned. "Three weeks. Rufus help. Not so hard. Not easy, but not *hard* hard. It…" She paused, looking for the word, then finished, "It is slower. But it makes them happy, so—"

"Joey! Aiden!"

I looked up in time to see Hel appear on the sidewalk, properly dressed for the weather but running as quickly as Georgie had. Joey, who was standing closer to her than I was, took the initial brunt of her greeting, and Georgie wisely slipped out from between them before Hel grabbed him and again tried to squeeze the air from his lungs. "Oh, my God, you're alive!" she cried, standing on tiptoe to cling to his neck. "You're *alive*! You stupid, idiotic, dumbass…"

Toula stepped out from the site and waved at us before stuffing her bare hands into her coat pockets. "This has been building for a while," she said when she got close, nodding to Hel, who was still in the middle of her harangue. "Let her get it out of her system, eh? And what the hell happened to you, Aiden?"

I remembered too late my bandage and the enchantment working around my hand to slowly heal the burn. "Sword," I muttered, trying to casually ease my injured hand into my pocket, but Toula grabbed my wrist and inspected the setup.

"Enchantment's sloppy," she said after a moment's study. "This is beginner's work—fine for Faerie, but once you get over here, there's not enough ambient magic to keep it at full power. See these connections?" she said, pointing to half a dozen lines of light that crossed my palm. "Redundant and power-sucking. May I?"

I nodded and waited while she tweaked the enchantment until it brightened. "Whose work was that?" she asked. "I'm going to guess it wasn't Val. Rufus?"

"Not mine," he muttered.

I said nothing, and a flicker of understanding crossed Toula's face. "Sword, you said?" she murmured, then carefully unwrapped my hand until the burn was tingling in the cold wind. She tossed a little orb into the air between us for better light, then inspected the wound and nodded to herself. "How?"

"Realm took care of it," I said quietly, leaning closer to her to be heard over Hel's impassioned rant.

"All the perks?"

"And then some. I've pretty much got Coileán's power for now," I replied, then hesitated. "And I'm heading up the court while he recuperates."

"So he's alive?"

"Yeah. And Val's fine."

Toula sighed with relief. "Oberon?"

"Dead."

"Yeah?"

I nodded. "Got the burn when I used Joey's sword on his neck."

She made a face, then patted the uninjured back of my hand and stepped away. "Hey, Carver? Come up for air."

Hel paused, red-faced in the orb's light. "*What?* Tell Aid to wait his turn. I've got plenty to say to him when I'm finished with—"

"Aiden," she interrupted, "is now functionally a faerie king, and he and Joey are alive. Can we take this inside, please? I'm freezing my ass off out here."

That caught my sister off guard, and she released Joey as she stared at me in confusion. "What are you—"

"Please don't hate me," I said in a rush, cringing as the words tumbled out. "I did it to save Coileán, and it's just a temporary gig, no one in the Arcanum has to know, I'm not going to screw up your job…"

Hel shook her head and blinked rapidly, then held up her gloved hands to stop my spewing apology. "Wait. Hold it," she ordered. "You did *what*, exactly?"

I took a deep breath to slow down. "The realm…she told me that she could, uh…suppress the wizard bits. I mean, I'm still a witch-blood, technically, but for practical purposes—"

"You're fae?"

I nodded miserably. "I'm so sorry, Hel, I—"

That was as far as I got before she had transferred her boa constrictor squeeze to me. "I don't care what you are," she mumbled into my jacket. "You're my baby brother, Aid. You will *always* be my baby brother. Got it?"

"Thanks," I managed to gasp.

She stepped back and glared up at me. "And what were you *thinking*, imbecile? Sneaking off without me? You know that place is dangerous! What the hell kind of stupid plan was *that*, you dummy?" she demanded, reaching up to smack me in the head. "Come on, Aid, I thought you were smarter than that!"

I tucked my burned hand into my pocket to shield it from my sister's blows. "I've got an army waiting to come over and help!" I protested.

"You're still an idiot! Shit, do you have any idea how *worried* I've been? Honest to God, why don't you ever listen?"

"Come on, Carver," Toula interrupted, pulling me toward the house, "you can chew him out inside. Georgie, honey," she said, beckoning to the dragon, "let go of Joey so he can walk, okay? Just until we get indoors."

Having grown up around Wright's Mill, I expected to see the familiar shack once we were past the glamour. What greeted me instead inside the bubble of illusion was a sleek, windowless marble building, three stories tall and topped with a copper roof, an almost monolithic white vault rising from the prairie.

I stopped in my tracks and gaped. "What…"

"The old one leaked," said Ned. "And smelled like marijuana and cheap beer. And there were vermin."

"It was a little lacking in terms of basic amenities," Rufus added with a note of apology in his voice. "Ned, uh…he had some ideas."

"You'd prefer the condemned ruin?" Ned asked me, cocking an eyebrow.

"No," I said, "but this is, uh…well…uh…"

"Completely out of keeping with the architectural aesthetic of the area, but no one listens to me," said Stuart, who was waiting for us just inside the ten-foot-tall copper doors with his arms folded across the front of a knit sweater festooned with leaping reindeer. "Welcome back. Helen decided to let you live?"

"For now," Hel muttered, pulling Joey past Stuart as Georgie raced behind them, trying to breathlessly fill him in on everything he'd missed.

I watched them go and sighed. "He's in for it."

"He's the one dating her—he assumed *that* risk," said Toula, leading me inside. "Now, while they're making up, come with me. You'll like this bit."

She steered us through candlelit marble corridors, over rugs plush enough to cover the tops of my shoes. "Neddy's been kind of a prima donna," she whispered when we were alone, "but he does good work, and he's the oldest faerie we've got on hand. This place is a little grandiose for me, but whatever, he's happy. Here, this way," she said, pushing another door open. "And be quiet."

I stepped past her into a well-lit room, another marble-walled, heavily carpeted chamber. This one was dominated by a heavy wooden table covered with computer components and notepads, however, around which a scattering of matching chairs formed a broken ring. There was no sound but the whirring of fans, both the tiny ones cooling the machines from the inside and the larger pair that pivoted in the corners of the room, and the soft clacking of fingers on a keyboard. Across the table and behind a bank of monitors sat Vivi, earphones on and eyes focused on the screen in front of her as her fingers danced. Rick waved when he saw us but said nothing until he walked around the table, and even then, he whispered. "She just went on shift, but she said to tell you hello if it was really you," he relayed.

"I trust you didn't trash my place. And we'll get word to Harrison momentarily."

"Good," said Toula. Seeing my bemusement, she whispered, "Hacking into the Arcanum's network allowed us to open communication lines with the silo. We use Morse," she explained, "hence the earphones. Vivi's getting a morning report."

"You think Moyna's intercepting?" I asked. "And…wait, *Harrison*? I thought the grand magus had been dismissed."

"Funny thing about that. Seems no one on the Council wanted to take the reins when Moyna showed up. There was a minor populist uprising, you might say—he's back in office for now, whether the Council likes it or not. As for Moyna"—she shrugged—"hard to tell. But in case she's eavesdropping, we figured that most of her people predate Morse code and never had a need to learn it…and to be safe, we keep changing languages." She pointed to a pin-up calendar on the table, a giveaway from the gas station down the road featuring pictures of vintage cars. "Random number generator selected the roster, and we have a different one than the silo. They've got enough bilingual folks underground, and we've got the entire Fringe network to do the translating for us. It's not Enigma, but it's the best we came up with in this particular pinch." She turned to Rick and whispered, "What's the outgoing today?"

"Russian," he replied with a grimace. "Incoming is English, thank heavens, but I'm going to have to run everything through the Bear."

"Skip it," she said, taking a notepad from the table. "Just send it as-is—no sense in delaying."

I looked over her shoulder as she scrawled out a message for Vivi: *Boys came back. C alive, O dead, A in charge for now. Awaiting backup.*

Toula caught me watching her and handed the notepad to Rick. "The tech team's been invaluable," she whispered, leading me out of the room and quietly shutting the door. "They have a rotation of four-hour shifts lined up—we've got a dozen Fringers lurking around here to handle communications and equipment issues."

"You couldn't just call the silo?" I asked.

"Believe me, we tried, but with all of the activated magic in the area, we barely got more than static. The Fringe setup is extraordinary, really," she continued, heading back toward the front of the building. "The hacker nerds did their bit up top, and the few in the group who had any magical abilities actually put a repulsive net around the silo's underground cables. The mesh is bits of enchantment and spellcraft working in parallel—and I've been patching it, of course," she added, opening a door into what appeared to be a conference room. "Rufus, Harry, and Ned have had their hands full, and your sister has been playing substitute grand magus for weeks."

I pulled up a chair to the polished mahogany table and rested my head on my good hand, realizing for the first time that day just how exhausted I was. "They're actually following Hel?" I mumbled.

A mug of something that smelled like strong Kona appeared in front of me, and Toula grinned as my fingers found the handle. "Everyone knows she's Greg's choice. They're just taking the training wheels off early, since he can't do much from inside the silo. Girl knows the players," she said, sliding into the chair beside me. "She's on speaking terms with the top brass at each of the installations, which is a hell of a lot more than any of the brass can say. And the Fringe is willing to work with her. She's young, sure, but all things considered, there wasn't a better choice." Toula plucked a cup of lemon tea from the air and sipped. "Council's going to have a lot of explaining to do when all's said and done—I mean, you don't just put warrants out like that. Not on someone like her."

"And you?"

She smirked. "I can take care of myself. But if things get a little hairy, you wouldn't mind if I crashed at your place for a while, eh?"

"The realm would get over it."

"You've got the voice in your head now, too?"

I nodded, fighting the urge to fall asleep on the table. "She can be helpful."

"I'm sure. Want a nap, bud?"

"Maybe."

Toula snorted and stood. "Come on," she said, grabbing me under the arms, "there's a bed with your name on it upstairs. I'm sure we can last another hour without you."

CHAPTER 18

I don't remember actually leaving the conference room or falling asleep, but the next time I opened my eyes, I was horizontal and warm, burrowed under the blankets in a dark bedroom, and the linens smelled like an artificial mountain meadow. My hand still ached—and I was beginning to suspect that it would hurt for some time—but the rest of me seemed to be intact on first inspection, and I risked sitting up in bed to find out how long I'd been unconscious.

"Rest," said my sister, pushing me back toward the pillows. "Don't make me break out the sleeping spell on you, too."

She materialized from the shadows as my eyes remembered how to focus in the dark. "Wha—"

"*Rest*, Aid," she insisted.

I gave in and flopped backward, and she pulled a chair close to the bed. "Both of you are cut and banged up to pieces," said Hel. "Joey's arm is still mending—it's almost there, but it's kind of soft—and I have no idea what to do with you, so do us all a favor and don't move for a little while, okay?"

I sighed and looked up at her. "Hel, I'm really sorry."

"Yeah, well," she muttered, "the next time you sneak off and give me a heart attack, maybe drop me some warning in advance, huh? I'd tell you what I told Joey," she continued, folding her arms, "but shouting in the sleeping wing is frowned upon."

"You know what I mean."

I could just make out her shrug in the low light. "And

you heard what I said. You're my brother—I don't care what else you might be."

"Your job—"

"Aid," she said, smoothing my dirty hair out of my eyes, "I've been holding this operation together since October. That alone should qualify me to be grand magus, and you have nothing to do with it. Besides," she added, settling back in her chair, "the magi have known about you all along. This shouldn't come as a shock."

"He left me in charge of the *court*."

"And he and I going to have a nice, long, possibly even civil chat about that once he's feeling himself again, but in the meantime, do what you need to do. Try not to kill anyone unnecessarily." Hel crossed her legs and grunted. "I can't exactly blame you. I mean, if someone offered me loads of power and eternal youth, I'd be tempted."

"But you wouldn't take it," I mumbled.

"Hypothetically? Tough call."

"*Huh*?"

"You sound surprised," she said dryly, and her chair creaked as she shifted position. "Think about it. Someone offers you massive power and virtual immortality, and the only condition is dumping your silver jewelry? I mean, that's a pretty sweet deal."

I was momentarily lost for words, but managed, "You're going to be the grand magus—"

"And I still think it's objectively sweet. Aside from the whole thing about court allegiance and having to put up with sociopaths every day, but still. Most folks could make it work, I imagine." She leaned toward me and lowered her voice to a soft murmur. "I think we both know that deep down, there's a little jealousy involved where the Arcanum is concerned. Well, that, plus millennia of putting up with the mess that leaks out of Faerie, but you see what I'm saying. Look, the bottom line is that I...you know, I think you made the right choice, Aid."

I found her hand in the dark, and she squeezed back.

"Seeing as Dad has already disowned me," I said, "maybe this won't be such a big deal to him if it doesn't get you fired."

Hel snorted her disdain. "He can disown you all he wants, but at the end of the day, every magus in the Arcanum knows that his son's a high lord—or what is it now? Substitute king?"

"Lord regent, I think. That's what the realm was suggesting, anyway."

"Whatever." She stood and ground her knuckles against my head until I swatted her away. "Take it easy. Toula popped over to tell Val what's going on, and she says he's waiting on the signal. There's no need to rush," she added, heading for the door. "It's Saturday, after all. We don't really get weekends around here, but since it's just now getting light outside, I won't hold it against you if you sleep in for a few minutes."

The next thing I knew, Rufus was shaking my shoulder and promising breakfast. "I know you're hungry," he said as I tried to roll away. "Up you go, Rick made pancakes, and there's plenty left over. Or steaks, if you're of that mind. Come on, now," he said over my groans, "we're wasting daylight."

"Hel said I could sleep," I grumbled into the pillow.

"That was four hours ago. The natives are restless." He slipped back as I bolted upright, startled and disoriented, then pointed to the door. "Shower's out there, food's on the first floor. Rise and shine, kid."

I ran my good hand through the squirrel's nest that had developed on top of my head and blearily watched as Rufus waited for me to give in and get up. "Joey—"

"Is still sleeping, but he's not the one with a waiting army. Now march," he said, clearing a path to the door. "Go wash, clear the cobwebs—"

"Disinfect the hand," I mumbled, swinging my legs out

of my warm cocoon.

"Why bother? We're immune. Just try not to get it too wet—I imagine that would sting," he cautioned, following me into the hall. "Never had one that nasty before—Toula gave me the details," he explained when I glanced his way in befuddlement. "Well, live and learn, eh?"

"Sure," I said through a yawn as I pushed my way into the bathroom.

Rufus parked himself outside and continued to talk through the closed door. "They do call your brother the Ironhand, you know. Maybe it's genetic."

I abandoned further conversation in favor of a hot shower, the first real one I'd had in days. After five minutes under the pounding water, I woke enough to take note of my surroundings. The fixtures were all brass, I realized as I peered through the steam, as were the towel racks, the sinks, and the door handle. My burned hand had stopped complaining quite so badly after the first shock of water, but the sharp twinges of pain and the constant flashes from the enchantment working around it served as a reminder of the night before.

So this was life now. Metal substitutions and conferences with wizards and waiting armies and so many enchantments to make the world a more bearable or terrible place. I'd walked into this mess with open arms.

I slowly flexed my hand, letting the water soften the blisters.

I'd chosen this, and I could damn well make it work.

I shut the water off, forgoing a shampoo, and willed myself clean as I toweled dry. "Rufus?" I called through the door. "Still there?"

"Well, I wasn't going to leave you to wander around on your own," he replied. "That was quick."

"Things to do." I imagined boxers, a pair of jeans, and a decently thick sweater into existence and rubbed the water out of my hair, which had progressed far beyond shaggy in recent weeks and was well on its way to "eighties rocker."

After tying it back, I slid on a new pair of hiking boots, cleaned my teeth, and rejoined Rufus. "You mentioned food?"

"I thought that might motivate you," he said with a grin, and turned for the wide marble staircase. "Have you figured out how to make your own yet?"

"It's mediocre," I admitted, trailing two steps behind him. "Either bland or off, you know?" I cut my eyes to an open door as we passed and spotted a Joey-sized lump on the bed, beside which Georgie had curled up and was snoring.

"That's a matter of practice," Rufus replied, "and in the meanwhile, Rick is a respectable short-order cook. When he's not helping Vivi, he's usually near the kitchen." We rounded the bend in the stairs, and I saw the warm lights of the foyer's wall sconces below us. "Hal and Stuart help out," he added, "but if you have the choice, go with Rick."

"They wouldn't stay in Alaska, huh?"

He looked over his shoulder and smirked. "I knew Hal was a lost cause. If Vivi sets up camp in a volcano, I expect Hal will be right behind her, lugging her gear up the mountain. And Stuart..."

"Still Wizard Stu?"

"He does his best. Toula's sent him home a few times to deal with Eunice's affairs and look after his cats, but he keeps coming back. Rather like herpes. Oh," he hastened, "he's not *that* bad—he's actually been useful on occasion— but he knows he's outclassed."

We reached the floor, and Rufus turned toward the smell of bacon. "Useful *how*, exactly?" I pressed. "Don't tell me he's really a wizard. I've seen some weird stuff of late, but I've got my limits, man."

"Of course he isn't," said Rufus as he sidestepped an abandoned tea cart. "But he sees things the rest of us miss. We're wrapped up in the larger issue—he notices the mundane bits. The school, for instance." He pushed the door open and swept his arm toward the covered dishes on the counter. "Eat up, don't be shy. But the school—no one thought twice about it until Stuart asked what would happen when all the Arcanum kiddies suddenly stopped showing up for class."

I paused with my hand over the pile of cooling bacon. "Ooh, good point. What happened?"

"Well, lucky for us, we caught the last days of fall break, so we had time to get our act together." Rufus poured himself a cup of coffee and perched on a barstool beside the leftovers while I grazed. "Harrison was able to give us the specs on their students—names, ages, pictures, identifying details, you get the point. That was before we switched to Morse code, so he sent us batches of files. Spreadsheets. Wizards and their beloved data," he muttered into his mug. "So Ned and Harry and I worked with Toula and Hel to make glamour constructs—illusory kids, if you will—and sent just enough to school each day to ward off suspicion. Suffice it to say that no one in the silo will be receiving a perfect attendance award this year."

"Wait," I said through a mouthful of dry pancake, "you did *what*?"

"Think of solid holograms, each with its own voice, memories, and personality," he explained. "And the three of us sat at the controls of all of them. Some were easy— the shy kids, the sleepers—but the Arcanum has its share of social butterflies. One of the kids Ned was running was on the football team. I had to teach the old boy the rules," he said, smiling to himself.

"So you—"

"Sneaked around the school invisibly until we had the basics down, then ran the constructs from here. It's not fun," he said. "*Raging* headaches. It's like being in one of those security rooms, you know, the ones with a monitor for each of twenty cameras, only you have to concentrate on all twenty at once. We had a few close calls," he admitted as I devoured my short stack. "But between that and the enchantments around our respective campsites, we haven't had any casualties from concerned teachers and truant officers wandering around. A small victory, but I'll take it. And there's syrup in the cabinet, you know."

"Don't care," I mumbled. My stomach, having remembered that I was ravenous, couldn't fill quickly enough.

"As you like." He sipped his coffee while I stuffed my face. "So, lord regent, was it?"

"Mm-hmm," I grunted as I chewed.

"How's it feel?"

I looked around for something to cut the grease and dough, pulled a pitcher of orange juice out of the fridge, and drank at least a pint. "Weird," I managed once I came up for air. "Kind of terrifying, actually, the more I think about it, so I'm not going there right now, okay?"

Rufus chuckled, and the pitcher refilled as I put it away. "You're what, sixteen?" he asked.

"Yeah," I said, resuming my attack on the carbohydrates.

"You haven't even come of age, kid." Pushing his mug aside, Rufus rested his elbows on the counter and watched me eat. "So who's the regent for the regent, then?"

I swallowed hard to clear the pancake and frowned. "Come again?"

"I'm not suggesting that there needs to be a formal arrangement," he continued, "but what did Coileán leave you in terms of a support network? Who's left to guide you? No offense, I know you're bright, but at least your sister has had some training in this area."

I thought over the familiar faces back in Faerie and shrugged. "Val, I guess. He's the captain of Coileán's guard—he's not going to let me start a war."

"Toula's brother, right? Half fae, older than dirt?" Rufus considered this for a moment, then nodded. "That could suffice."

I eyed him closely. "Why do you care, anyway? Not your court, not your problem."

"And that's where you're wrong," he replied, cocking his

mug at me. "Someone's going to claim Oberon's throne eventually. In case he's insane, I"—he paused, choosing his words carefully—"I might want a backup plan. We all might."

"Allegiance shift?"

He nodded. "And if, say, I were to swear fealty, would you offer protection? Or, more importantly, would Coileán?"

"I don't see why not."

"Good to know." He listened as a door in the distance slammed open, then pointed to the hallway from which we'd come. "Sounds like the Arcanum posse has arrived. Want to go say hello?"

I wrinkled my nose and grabbed another handful of bacon. "Do I *have* to?"

"Nah," he replied with a shrug, "but then again, a unified front is a stronger front…"

"Fine, I'm going," I sighed, but I carried the bacon on a plate with me. If the magi weren't impressed, I decided I wouldn't really care.

I found them in the foyer, a half-dozen senior wizards in robes and sweatpants and hunting gear, crowded around Hel and talking softly. "Hey," I said when my boots rang on the bare marble, "Hel, did you eat? This is good stuff."

"And now your grubby paws are all over it," said Hel. "Good morning, Sleeping Beauty. Ready to get to work?"

The assembled knot of magi stared at me, and an older woman with the crisp articulation of a Shakespearean actor peered up at me over her half-moon glasses. "My word," she murmured, "Magus Carver, is that—"

"*Magus* Carver?" I echoed, cutting my eyes to Hel. "When did that happen?"

"Eh, courtesy title," she said, brushing it off. "Magus Jenner, honored magi, this is my brother."

"Hi," I said. "I'd shake your hands, but you know…" I bit into another piece of bacon. "Messy. Where to, Hel?"

"Conference one," she replied, but she lingered while

the wizards headed off toward the conference room I'd seen that morning. When we were alone, she murmured, "Aid."

"Hel?" I said, all innocence and bacon grease.

"Be *nice.*"

"Why bother?" asked Rufus, who appeared from behind us with a fresh cup of coffee. "They already look at us like dog shit on a satin shoe—that's not going to change. And here, at least take a napkin," he chided, handing me a folded stack of paper towels. "You may have grown up Arcanum, kid, but surely they teach table manners down in the bunker."

Hel watched with mild disapproval while I tidied myself up. "You remember that saying about flies, honey, and vinegar, right?"

"Sure," I told her, tossing the napkins into the ether. "And I also know that look they all just gave me. Not quite as bad as Dad's, but it was in the neighborhood."

She turned to Rufus, but he shook his head. "I know it hurts," she told me quietly. "And you have every right to be sensitive about it, Aid. But for my sake, and for the sake of everyone camped out around the silo, could we all please be adults about this?"

"I will if they will," I replied, going back to the bacon. Rufus rolled his eyes and handed me another napkin.

"Fair enough," she said with a sigh, then led the way toward the waiting wizards.

I'd long been accustomed to being on the receiving end of odd looks from Arcanum members. Duds merit a certain amount of pity, after all, and those wizards that didn't know better smiled too brightly when they spoke to me, as if I were not only magically inept, but also slow. The magi who *did* know about my dirty little secret preferred the tight-lipped smile, an expression that conveyed their overall displeasure with my presence and their simultaneous recognition of societal niceties.

I was getting a lot of tight lips from the installation heads, but few smiles. Instead, they watched me with unease, either fidgeting or sitting perfectly still but for a telltale tapping foot or clenching fist. These were some of the top wizards in the world, the territorial governors whose portraits hung around the silo's halls, and I realized as I watched them watching me that they were afraid.

The Arcanum's best and brightest—save Hel, who silently pleaded with me from the head of the table to not be a jackass—feared *me*.

Honestly, it was intoxicating, but I did my best not to embarrass my sister.

"There's a force waiting back in Faerie. I don't have an exact figure, but it's substantial," I told them, punctuating my words with jabs of the broken bacon in my hand. "And they've had a few hours to rest up, so they should be ready to go. Bring them over, point them in the right direction, and see if they can't find Moyna. Assuming, that is, that we can get a sufficient quantity of magic flowing into the area."

One of the more talkative magi, whose lined face was tanned a deep chestnut under a shock of white hair, sounded like he'd strolled out of the Outback and could only have come from Arcanum 7. He pushed up his sleeves and gave me a hard look. "You aren't even going to try to talk her down first? Girl's your blood."

I ignored the overtone of disgust in his declaration. "I'll give it a shot. But have *you* spent any quality time with her, Magus…"

"Bartow."

"Magus Bartow. Ever had any dealings with Moyna before this? Because I've seen what she can do. She's closed to negotiation when she's pissed, and she's been pissed for months. I'm not holding out a lot of hope."

The corner of his mouth twitched into a little smirk. "And here I'd heard that the half fae were reasonable."

"There's really no telling what percentage she is," I replied, catching the look Hel was shooting me. "Coileán's half, Meggy was half, but that half was one of the Three on both sides. She could be almost fully fae, for all I know. Whatever she is, she's strong."

"And you think you can beat her?" Magus Jenner interjected as she polished her glasses on her robe's dangling sleeve.

"Yes. But if I'm sending my forces in, you're going with us," I told her, then cut my eyes to Hel. "And we're going to need Georgie."

"Of course," said the old man I recognized as Magus Aminu, the long-serving head of Arcanum 5 and the first magus ever chosen out of Nigeria, "this solution would leave us with an army of faeries outside Arcanum 1. Surely we should wait until the grand magus decides."

"Which will take how long?" I asked. "I mean, my Morse isn't up to snuff, but I'm betting someone in here could shoot him a message. Who's manning the communications room right now?"

"Justine Lin," Hel offered, "and I gave her a message for the grand magus before this meeting began." The other wizards stiffened and turned to her, and Hel smiled. "I didn't call you here to ask your permission for this attack," she told them. "I called you here to explain what was going to happen. And Justine is telling Greg what to expect. We're tired, *they're* tired, and I don't know about you, but I'd like to break the siege by morning if at all possible. Aid's in control," she continued, meeting my eyes, "and he has assured me that his forces won't turn on ours."

Her look dared me to call her out on the lie, and I held my tongue.

"So go back and ready your people," said Hel. "This ends today."

"Let's shoot for high noon," I added, waiting as the room swiveled back to face me, and chomped into my cold bacon. "Seems appropriate, doesn't it?"

A few minutes and some halfhearted protests later, the wizards filed out as a muttering herd. Once the door slammed behind them and their footsteps ceased to echo outside the conference room, Hel leaned against the wall and slowly exhaled. "Please tell me I'm not off base," she mumbled, glancing at me and my bacon crumbs. "You do have this in hand, yes?"

"I think so."

"You *think* so?" she echoed. Her voice cracked, revealing a flash of the stress she was holding in beneath the surface. "That's not good enough. I need some reassurances—"

"I'm flying blind," I interrupted, pushing my plate away, "and I'm going to do the best I can, but Hel…they've been locked up for weeks, and they're out for blood. You should see some of the corpses," I added, rubbing my forehead to dispel the images that had popped up uninvited. "*Abused* doesn't begin to describe it. Know what I mean?"

"Psychos on a rampage? Yeah." She perched on the table beside me and shook her head. "You think *you're* flying blind?" she murmured. "At least you can strong-arm them into listening, right?"

The pictures weren't going away, and I rubbed harder. "Theoretically."

"Well, I can't. I've got magi old enough to be my grandparents second-guessing every decision I make, and I'm *barely* holding on to control, but only because they have enough respect for Greg to follow me. But that's fraying, and this may have been the final straw." She leaned back and stared at the ceiling. "If this goes to hell and we somehow still live through it, then I can kiss the grand magus spot goodbye. That's if the Council doesn't reissue the warrant, of course. I mean, helping you run off was bad enough, but to stand back and let a pack of faeries get within spitting distance of the silo…to *invite* them…" She turned to me again, and I saw desperation in her eyes. "Even if there's not enough magic left for them to power up, if that's not treason, Aid, it's damn close."

The look on my sister's face scared me more than I wanted to admit, but I tried not to show it. "I'll talk to Val," I said. "Make sure we've got a game plan that includes a clean exit. And if things go awry...well," I muttered, "then I guess the court will get that demonstration of my power after all."

The tightness lingered in Hel's shoulders as she watched me. I was about to try to come up with something more reassuring when she softly asked, "How strong are you, really? Be honest with me. If I'm trusting you as my safety net, I need to know the truth."

I thought for a moment, looking for the right words. "The realm loaned me Coileán's power, or something close, but I...you know, actually *wielding* it properly..."

"In other words, you have no idea what you're doing?"

"More now than I did before Val started working with me, but I've got a long way to go."

She ran one hand over her face, up and down. "Rufus said you killed Oberon."

"Yeah," I muttered.

"And a bunch of others." I said nothing, but Hel didn't blink. "Look, I'm not trying to make you feel bad, but I need to know that you have this thing under control, that you're not going to get out there and go full berserker. I..." She hesitated, reading my face. "I've got a lot of lives on the line, Aid, and I know you wouldn't do anything intentionally, but do you—"

"That part's solid," I told her. "Ask Joey if you don't believe me."

"I do," she said gently. "No need to drag Joey into this."

"You're sure? He can vouch for me."

She slid off the table and straightened her shirt. "I trust my brother. And if Joey were to sleep through the next few hours, I wouldn't be too upset."

I stood and joined her as she headed for the door. "We *need* Georgie, Hel. She's the only one of us who can use dark magic."

My sister's face twisted. "I don't know, she's still so *young…*"

"She's done it before!"

"Okay, granted," she mumbled, "but that doesn't mean Joey has to go with her."

I couldn't quite read the subtext in my sister's expression, and having been on the wrong end of an amateur's mental exploration, I wasn't about to pry into her thoughts. But there was enough in the way she hugged herself to confirm what I suspected.

"He really loves you," I told her. "And I know you're worried about him, but Joey's tougher than you think. Let him help you."

When she replied, her voice barely broke a whisper. "If something happens to him…"

She let the thought hang, and I shrugged. "Wake him up. You know it's what he'd want. If you sent Georgie without him, he'd never forgive you."

She glanced off down the hallway, visibly torn, then shot me an exasperated glare before heading toward the staircase. "When did you get so bossy, anyway?"

"Oh, excuse me, *Magus*," I retorted, "did I not kowtow quickly enough for you that time?"

"Dork."

"That's 'Lord Dork' to you, jerk."

Hel shoved me in the shoulder and kept walking, shaking her head and muttering about the incorrigibility of the males in her life. And finding nothing further there to let me stall against facing my army, I opened a wobbly gate and struck out to locate Val.

To my surprise, the throne room was halfway full but calm when I returned. People milled about—a few had set up tables and chairs, and a little crowd was gathered around a chessboard—but the chaos I had feared was nowhere to be seen. I looked around and quickly spotted Val, who had placed a long desk at the foot of the dais and was sitting behind it with several of the guards, making notes on sheaves of paper as one person after another approached with questions or information. I knew most of the guards by face, not dress—Coileán never insisted on uniforms, and their attire ran the gamut, from the senior lieutenant at Val's left in his formal robes to the younger man at the end of the table who favored, of all things, jorts and sandals.

There were also guards on the doors, I noticed, and suddenly understood the subdued mood.

No one seemed to notice my arrival but the realm, who jubilantly welcomed me back, so I walked over to the table for an update. "Is anything burning?" I asked as I neared.

Val's head shot up from his ledgers, and he smiled wearily as he and the other guards stood. "Not anymore, my lord. The fires have been extinguished. And I'd begun to fear that they would let you sleep all day."

"Not quite. I heard that Toula stopped by."

"We had a few issues to discuss," he replied. One of my eyebrows rose, and Val snorted. "More of a speech, really. I assume Helen gave you a similar reception."

"Joey got the worst of it. And, uh…" Val sat, and the others followed suit. "Thanks," I muttered, leaning against the stone pillar beside the table, and cradled my sore hand. "Did you flush out the others?"

Val cut his eyes to the brunette to his right, whose freckled face broke into a grim smile. "Hence the fires, my lord," she said.

"How many dead?" I asked her, trying and failing to place her among the guards I'd met.

She consulted her notes. "Most came quietly. Another fifty-three dead since this morning, three hundred twenty-seven more in custody. Have you decided what's to be done with them?" she asked, putting her pen aside. "The dungeons are overflowing. We could expand them, but at the moment"—she paused to look at the throng around the throne room—"no one's really of a mind to worry about their comfort."

"Understandable. And you are…"

"Lady Mina," Val cut in. "My second, recently back from sea."

She sighed and rolled her eyes. "Must you remind me, Captain? Two years on a boat with those idiots, and I come home to *this* nonsense. Honestly, you should have summoned me sooner." Mina rested her chin in her hand and looked up at me. "Five of my imbecile cousins had the bright idea of mapping the western sea. I told them it's been attempted. I showed them the books, but were they deterred? Of course not. So Grandmother sent me along to keep them from…from I don't know, trying to swim back or some such," she said, shaking her chestnut ringlets, "and out of nowhere, I had this vision of a woman who warned me away from shore. We all did."

"Short, blonde, likes her clothing see-through?" I asked.

Mina nodded. "Oh good, I'm not crazy. Anyway, she returned at dawn today and told us to get back here with all speed, so here I am. And I come ashore to find Grandmother gone, Oberon on a pyre, my little uncle sleeping it off, and…I take it you're Lord Aiden, then?"

I thought briefly, putting her rapid story together. "You…you're Titania's—"

"Granddaughter," she offered. "One of Oberon's brats killed my mother some years ago. You wouldn't have known her."

"About twelve hundred years ago, more or less," Val added. "Lady Autel. Mina is—"

"A half-breed mess who grows bored easily," she interrupted with a grin. "And Valerius continues to tolerate me, for some reason. I can't imagine why." She brushed her hair from her shoulder and sobered. "Captain thinks you might be in need of some crowd control, my lord. Accepting volunteers?"

Distantly, I registered the fact that I was talking to my

niece, who was considerably older than Coileán. "Uh...*yeah*, sure. Can you keep them from turning on the Arcanum troops?"

"Quite possibly. I often find that deploying a few well-placed threats of violence works wonders. And if the Ironhand is really on the throne," she muttered, "then I think we all know what could happen if he should wake up cranky. So Moyna's his, then? I missed that."

"Apparently..."

Mina smiled. "Well, I suppose there's no one to fight with you for the title of Grandmother's youngest, is there? And it's just you and Coileán..." She grimaced. "I never had any strong attachment to my younger aunts and uncles, but still, family. What are you going to do about it?"

I glanced out at the waiting crowd, then back at Mina, Val, and the other listening guards. "I'd thought about trying to capture Moyna and kill anyone else who didn't surrender, but if you've got a better plan, I'm listening."

Mina drummed her fingers on the tabletop. "Oh, I think I'm going to like *you*. And did I understand correctly that you're kin to the grand magus?"

Val subtly nodded reassurance, and I made a face. "Close. My sister's next in line. She's also heading up the Arcanum's assault force, and I told her there wouldn't be friendly fire."

She considered this briefly, then nodded. "It's doable, but why don't you leave the pre-attack remarks to the captain and me? I appreciate that you're keeping the throne warm," she added with a friendly smirk, "but I'm going to assume that you've not done this before."

I folded my arms. "That obvious, huh?"

"A good guess, my lord," said Mina, smiling in earnest.

"And did anyone mention to you the fact that there's almost no magic left around the silo?"

"That's what swords are for, dear." She went to her feet again and patted the bronze hilt at her left hip. "Now, shall we begin?"

CHAPTER 19

I didn't know at the time what Val and Mina told our forces by way of a pep talk. Later, I'd hear it in snatches when the conversation returned to that morning: warnings to follow orders, followed by a thrice-repeated list of targets that were explicitly off-limits, and finishing with a graphic depiction of what would happen to anyone who disregarded the earlier parts of the speech. Val painted me as *just* this side of stable, liable to lose my temper and control if provoked, and reminded the assembled that despite earlier indications to the contrary, I most certainly was Titania's son—with all that entailed.

And for my army, who knew too well what my mother had been capable of, that seemed to do the trick. The faeries who marched by twos and threes into Wright's Mill were an orderly lot, dressed for comfort and protection, most wearing blades, a few with crossbows. They bunched up as they stood in the snow—many produced coats and cloaks after a few minutes of turning their backs to the wind—and simply waited for instructions.

When I finally figured out how those two had cowed the court into unquestioning compliance, I was somewhat peeved. I'd never been a loose cannon, and if at all possible, I wanted to avoid hurting my own fighters. But Val had been around long enough to read the writing on the wall, and he was making preparations for the months ahead. Overly empowered high lord or not, Coileán's designee or not, I was still a teenage mongrel in the eyes of many, and Val put his propaganda campaign into action without bothering to run it past me.

He knew then what I wouldn't for weeks: my brother wasn't going to be waking any time soon.

From his place at Oberon's side, Val had seen what an incredible effort Oberon had been forced to make to keep the bind in place on Coileán. The old king had barely dared to sleep for fear of losing his control on the enchantment, he'd almost entirely stopped eating, and by the end, he'd hardly been doing more than sitting in bed, staring into space. With the power Oberon had been expending, it had taken a gargantuan effort for Coileán to cast off the enchantment and an even larger effort to climb upstairs and fight him. Even if Coileán had looked to be the healthier of the two, he'd still been scraping the bottom of the barrel of his last reserves. Sleep was his body's final defense, a last-ditch effort to keep him alive and allow him time to heal.

Val had seen it happen plenty of times in the days before Mab and Oberon left the realm, and he'd lost guards for a week or a month or a season while the wounded recuperated. But given the circumstances, he knew that my brother's was an extreme case, and Val couldn't predict the duration of his absence. And so, whether because he knew it needed to be done or because he didn't want to add one more worry to my mind while I was preoccupied with thoughts of faeries overrunning the silo, Val started laying the groundwork for a long regency without bothering to warn me up front of what could be ahead.

In retrospect, he made the right call. Even with the army on its best behavior, I was a nervous wreck, and Hel looked no happier as we watched from the steps of the Fringe's fortress. As the last filed through the gate—a large, stable gate of Val's creation, I noticed with a twinge of envy—Mina strolled through the camouflaging glamour to join us. She'd opted for a long-sleeved tunic belted over soft leather leggings and tall boots, but a thick fur mantle materialized around her even as she walked. "My lord. Magus Carver, I trust?" she asked in Fae, nodding at Hel.

My sister smiled tightly. "Lady Mina?"

She spread her gloved hands. "And I see that word travels. I'll be heading the van, and Valerius will take the rear. Are your people in position?"

"As much as possible," she replied, folding her arms against the chill. "We've got a skeleton crew at the front to keep up appearances, but anyone nonessential has been pulled back to give you room."

"Excellent," said Mina, then looked over Hel's shoulder as the heavy doors opened and Vivi stepped out, sporting a black headset. "Your, uh...lieutenant?"

"Tech liaison," said Vivi, inserting herself between Hel and me as she began passing around a short stack of papers. "These are the latest aerials," she explained as I looked at the pictures she thrust into my hands. "Red circle is Moyna's probable location—still on the southern side of the ring, same as yesterday. If you want to grab her quickly, strike from that angle."

Mina frowned as she flipped through the grainy pictures. "How did you—"

"Drones," Vivi interrupted. "Homemade drones with cameras. We used the quietest motors we could make, and then Toula cloaked the heck out of them. Lost a few," she admitted, "but we've had eyes in the sky almost every day for the last month."

"That...is impressive. Most impressive," Mina murmured. "Have you any clearer images?"

"Sorry, no. Best we could do with what we had."

"Hey, *you* try running sensitive electronics in a high-magic environment," said Toula as she slipped out the front. "We had to make compromises between our toys and the amount of cloaking I could put on them."

Mina nodded to her in acquiescence. "Only an enquiry, Toula. I'm in the habit of seeking information."

"Understood," said Toula, "but recognize that the Fringe has done wonders."

"Undoubtedly." She handed the pictures back to Vivi

and stuffed her hands into her fur. "Toula told me of your organization," she said, watching as Vivi shuffled the pictures back into order. "You're a neutral party?"

"We fight for the greater good," said Vivi. "Whatever that might be. The definition is a little hazy, you know, but for the moment, we're here."

"Mm. And your, uh…allegiance?"

"It's to the Fringe," she said, and smirked. "I *have* no other allegiance."

"Ah," said Mina, "a witch. Understood."

Vivi bristled, and Toula slipped between them. "Actually," she told Mina, "Vivi's parents are of Oberon's court—technically, that is, and I suppose it's not his court any longer, but you get what I'm saying."

Mina seemed momentarily confused, but her face softened as she noticed Vivi's steel wristwatch. "Oh. *Oh.* I meant no offense, child, but when you said—"

"Yeah, whatever," Vivi muttered, waving the apology off. "I've been called worse. So, I see the gang's all here," she continued, pointing to the massed troops—who, while my attention was diverted, had built themselves fire pits in the street. "What are we working with?"

"Three hundred and fourteen volunteers," said Mina, looking at me. "The captain thought you would prefer volunteers to conscripts, my lord."

I nodded. "As long as they accept the game plan."

"They do." She turned then to Hel and asked, "And the Arcanum? We may be able to rout them with the van alone, but if you're taking the main, can you fill it?"

"I've got about six hundred in fighting condition," my sister told her. "But that's counting everyone from magi down to twenty-somethings with dragonscale wands."

Mina's brow wrinkled, and Toula explained, "Weaklings. Arcanum's got the cannon fodder covered."

"Let's *not* use that term, all right?" Hel snapped. "So you're splitting the court pack?" she asked, cutting her eyes between Mina and me.

I wasn't sure of the right answer, but Mina stepped into the breach. "We thought half and half. Let the well-seasoned lead, but hold a good number in reserve. And...um..."

I turned around, following the direction of her sudden stare, and found Joey standing in the doorway, clad entirely in black body armor. His motorcycle boots seemed to have been polished, and he carried a helmet with a smoked visor under his arm. "Ladies," he said, rubbing his beard with his gloved hand. "Sorry I'm late. Rufus and Harry couldn't decide on the best places to pad."

Georgie followed him out of the building, looking wide-eyed at the five of us on the stairs. "You fix me now?" she asked hopefully.

Hel turned to Toula and nodded, and Toula gave her shoulder a little squeeze in passing. "Come on, kid, let's do this," she said, beckoning to Georgie, who scampered after her, barefoot in the snow.

Mina looked at Joey, then at the retreating pair. "What—"

"Just watch," Hel muttered, avoiding Joey's eyes.

Toula led Georgie out from the glamour and down the street, past the milling crowd of faeries, then stopped in the middle of the road, far away from any buildings. She positioned Georgie in a safe spot, stepped well clear of her, and flicked her wrist.

The blue explosion of the breaking spell made me squint, even with the sun high and bright overhead, but when the spots cleared, the Georgie I knew was back.

Mina's jaw dropped. "That...that's a...how did you *hide*..."

Joey! Georgie interrupted, stretching her wings with what passed for a look of bliss on her scaly face. *Come on, let's go! Why are you waiting?*

Before Joey could join her, Rufus jogged around the building. "Ah," he said, pointing to Joey, "*there* you are. Thought I'd missed you. I was going to ask—do you need some sort of saddle?"

"Actually, that would be fantastic," he replied, slipping past us, and waved to Georgie as she snorted smoke above the nervous faeries. "Coming, sweetie!" he called, cupping his hands around his mouth. "Just a few more minutes, okay?"

Someone grunted softly behind me, and I turned to find Ned leaning against the door where Joey had been. "And *that*," I told him, gesturing to the one hundred fifty feet of dragon down the road, "is Joey's preferred mount. What were you saying about his martial skill, again?"

"Let's just hope she remembers what she's doing," said Hel, and glanced at her watch. "I've got five minutes to noon. Vivi, tell them we're on schedule, eh?"

Vivi stepped away, then touched her earpiece and mumbled into the microphone in her headset. As she relayed the message, Ned approached Hel and stuck out his hand. "Good luck, Carver."

She hesitated only long enough to push her watch out of the way before meeting his grip. "Thanks. And if this goes belly-up—"

"Mother is standing by." He released her and stepped back. "Do send Rufus along once he's finished playing at saddlery, won't you?"

"You've got it. Be *safe*," said Hel, and led the way down the stairs toward the street.

Ned nodded at me before ducking back into the house, and I followed my sister, with Mina and Toula at our heels. "My lord," Mina began, "you'll have to pardon my ignorance, but who was—"

"Vivi's brother. One of them," I replied, scanning the crowd for Val.

"The Stowe boys are watching out for the Fringers," Toula explained. "If the worst happens and Moyna's people find them…"

"I see." Her boots clipped on the cold concrete, a walkway that I was almost positive had been shoveled by magical means. "And the, uh…dragon?"

"Georgie and Joey are with us," said Toula, patting Hel's shoulder, "whether Carver here likes it or not."

"Not to start an argument, Magus Carver," said Mina, "but you're opposed to using a *dragon*? Why? I've killed a few—they're tough to take down. If that one is willing to fight with us—"

"It's not about Georgie," I muttered, glancing at Mina. "Joey is Hel's boyfriend."

"Fiancé."

I whipped back around and caught Hel looking at me. "He's my fiancé," she repeated.

"Since when?"

"You'd already sneaked out this morning." She glanced at Georgie, who was impatiently waiting while Rufus and Joey tested and tightened the new harness. "But seeing as neither of them listens to reason at times like this, yes, we're using a dragon."

We passed through the bubble of glamour, and the waiting faeries scrambled back to their ranks. "Congrats, Hel," I murmured, catching the sleeve of her coat to slow her. "That's…that's really fantastic."

She looked up at me, and I saw fear hiding in her smile. "Assuming we make it through this. Come on," she said as Mina headed for the troops. "Let's take a walk."

I'd made the two-mile trek from Wright's Mill to the silo thousands of times, but never with an army at my back. At least there was no one around on the weekend, I mused as we marched down the two-lane highway. Something told me that no one in the ranks would see anything to be gained by stepping aside for vehicular traffic.

As Vivi had suggested, we made our approach from the south of the silo, hoping to cut the head off our opponents before they quite knew what was upon them. Still, I doubted that we'd have much in the way of surprise on our side, given that the Arcanum forces were massing to meet us, we were processing in a three-hundred-strong pack, and walking at the head of the column was Georgie, who kept turning to shoot us impatient glances as she slowed again and again to keep pace. Joey, who was tucked in at his normal position on her long neck, kept patting her and offering reassurance that we'd be there soon enough, but Georgie was clearly itching to fly again after weeks on the ground. If she was at all saddened to lose the vocal skills she'd gained in our absence, she didn't show it. Georgie kept up a telepathic conversation with Joey and Hel all the way to the silo, and she thought so loudly that I couldn't help but overhear.

So, what difference does this make? she asked. *You...mate more frequently? Try for a clutch? Help me out.*

I couldn't hear my sister's explanation of her and Joey's change in relationship status, nor was I at all confident that they could convey to the dragon the significance of taking that step, but Toula chuckled beside me and grinned when she met my eyes. "Seems like Georgie forgot her volume control. You want to tell her this isn't a private conversation?"

"And risk making Hel drop dead from embarrassment before we actually get to the fight? Nah."

She smirked. "At least it's giving them something else to think about for the next couple of miles. You ready?"

I thought for a moment, listening to the familiar competing voices in my head, then nodded as the one I recognized as my own drowned them out. "Yeah. I think so."

"Good." Toula nudged my shoulder and smiled. "You've got this, bud," she murmured. "Forget the rest. You've got this."

"You seem awfully confident," I muttered, glancing down at her.

Toula flipped the fur-rimmed hood of her parka over her head as the wind gusted again. "Val believes in you," she replied, keeping her voice low. "I think I can trust his judgment this time."

I snorted. "Do you have any idea how many times he's kicked my ass in the last two weeks?"

"And somehow, you're still standing," she countered, then pointed to the horizon. "Home sweet silo, dead ahead."

The snow drifts masked the land, but I could still make out the familiar silhouettes of the old trailers that hid the entrance to the silo. But as I watched the active magic swirling in my field of vision, I realized I was seeing an illusion. "Nice glamour," I said.

"Thanks. Easier than asking the magi to do it—you know how twitchy they get," she replied smugly. "The defensive wards are still running, but I didn't want curious drivers stopping to have a look at the tents. The fewer mundanes running around here, the better."

"Good call." Something seemed off about the glamour, and as I was wondering if what I was seeing was just the end result of Toula's hybridized magic, it hit me what was wrong: the colors were muted, far fainter than active magic usually was. While the construction seemed solid, there was barely enough magic flowing through the glamour to hold it intact. "Since we're getting close, how about dropping it?"

The glamour fell like a lightbulb going out, and I stopped in the middle of the road to take in the scene before me.

The silo had been built in the middle of a wide plain of pastureland, and though mountains rose around it in the distance, you could easily see the trailer park from a couple of miles off on a clear day. Even in winter, when snow piled up against everything and created a new landscape of frozen hillocks, I'd always been able to pick the trailers out, a sort of beacon in the tundra. I'd learned to run in that stretch between school and home, pushing myself in an effort to outpace the boys who used me for target practice. I knew every inch of the road, every ankle-twisting dip in its shoulders, every turn of the creek bed to the east and the shallowest places to cross it in a pinch. This was *my* turf, and for better or worse, this land had always signaled that home was at hand.

I couldn't see the silo.

Blocking the view, first and foremost, was the approaching mob of wizards, who seemed to have divided themselves into companies along installation lines. The magi and their senior assistants walked in the front, but these were far from the images of magi that usually came to mind. All were bundled against the cold except the middle-aged blonde I'd pegged as Irina Durov, the Russian-born head of Arcanum 4—a few years in Mongolia had presumably done for her what Alaska had done for the Stowes. The procession moved slowly, almost haltingly, as people fell back and were replaced in the crowd, and I saw how weary the Arcanum's forces were. They'd been camping in the middle of nothing and struggling against large-scale enchantments for weeks, and the effort had almost broken them. A few older wizards walked along only with the assistance of their children and grandchildren, leaning on them as they navigated the frozen ground.

Behind the pack of weary wizards rose a line of tents, which stretched far into the cow pastures before curving toward the horizon. I could make out the faint haze of magic rising behind the tents—the front line, I assumed—and through the gaps in the Arcanum's camp, I could see more tents, elaborate constructions with colorful flashes of pennants and banners. Smoke hung over everything, the bluish fog of a dozen fires. I saw no trace of the cattle and presumed them dead, easy meals for the Arcanum army that was putting all of its magical resources into the fight.

I couldn't say what condition Moyna's siege army was in, but the Arcanum's looked to be on the brink of giving up. Hel's refusal to wait for the Council's permission suddenly made more sense.

My sister crossed her arms and stared at her approaching troops. "You know, I think I liked it better with the glamour. Cleaner."

"They're *wizards*," I said. "Surely someone's emptied the port-a-lets—"

"You'd be surprised. With the number of casualties we've sustained thus far, you would think that sanitation would be a higher priority, but some people just can't be bothered. I've done what I can, but you see how critical the magic deficit is becoming." She wrinkled her nose as the wind carried to us the acrid smell of smoke and the stench of unwashed bodies.

Hel seemed older than I'd ever seen her, tired and worn but still defiant. "Did you warn them that we'd have a dragon?" I asked.

"Of course. They wouldn't still be walking this way otherwise." With a deep breath, she stepped out from our ranks to meet the approaching columns and raised her hand in greeting. The magi responded in kind, and Georgie, at Joey's prodding, sank to her belly in the snow.

Behind me, I heard Val and Mina start shouting orders, and our forces began to split, the rear retreating and the van spreading to give the wizards passage. As Hel led the first of the newcomers toward us, I could see the tension on their faces—proximity to faeries was bad enough, but walking straight through a gauntlet of them was beyond a stupid idea for most wizards. Then again, we all knew the silo's situation was desperate, and Magus Ehrler from Arcanum 3 gave me a curt nod as he led his people through our ranks.

I counted them off, one by one. Heinrich Ehrler I knew from his official portrait, a little man with close-cropped white curls and a gray-streaked Van Dyke. Behind his group came Gabriela Montes of Arcanum 6, who walked with a silver-tipped rosewood cane and wore her gray hair in long braids. Her hazel eyes, pale with age, peered at me distrustfully from behind her glasses. Next through were Stephen Bartow, who had thrown a well-worn slouch hat on as his concession to the weather, and Gowon Aminu, whose dark face was barely visible in the layers of scarves and hoods protecting him from the cold. Irina Durov spared a glare for Hel, tossed her hair, and refused to look at me. Last to fill out the hole in my forces was Margaret Jenner, who had selected a thick white Aran sweater and an incongruous pair of track pants for the occasion. She paused to give me a quick once-over, then murmured, "I sincerely hope that Helen's trust hasn't been misplaced," before shepherding her people into the gap.

When the last of the Arcanum stragglers had joined us, our ranks closed again, sandwiching their masses between two smaller groups of faeries. "Well," Hel muttered, looking back over the crowd, "everyone looks happy and not at all homicidal, but just in case, let's get a move on." She turned back toward the silo, shielded her eyes from the sun, and scowled. "They're massing."

"Good," I said, then found Mina in the front line. "Hold back," I told her, and flipped up my collar against the wind. "I'm going to see if she'll come quietly."

Mina's dark eyes widened in incredulity. "You're not going alone. We'll pull a delegation from—"

"I need to do this solo."

"My lord—"

"*Please.*"

Mina frowned, but she turned to look at the crowd behind us and seemed to realize what I was doing. Her shoulders tensed in frustration, but I could see that she was conflicted when she looked again at me. "It's not weak to take backup," she murmured. "In fact, under the circumstances—"

"They're not going to follow me if they don't think I can stand on my own," I muttered. "I'm going. Just…do me a favor and have Georgie on standby, yeah?"

"Valerius isn't going to like this," she said, but she reluctantly stepped aside.

I walked back to Hel, who was waiting for a cue. "I'm going to try to end this before it gets messy," I told her. "If things don't work out, be ready."

She began to protest, then tightened her lips and sighed. "I'll go with you."

"Not this time."

"Aid…"

"She might talk to me," I said. "She won't do anything if she thinks it's an ambush. Come on, you remember what happened the last time you and Moyna got into it."

"I should have let her drown," Hel muttered, then surprised me with a hug. I hugged her back, conscious of the eyes on us, and heard her whisper, "Damn it, don't get killed."

"Ditto," I said, and we released each other. "Worst comes to worst, head to Alaska."

But my sister shook her head. "The grand magus doesn't run when the Arcanum's on the line. Go, if you're going," she said, shooing me off. "It's too cold for sentiment. I can't feel my fingertips."

I smirked and rubbed my gloves together. "Love you, too, Hel."

And with that, I marched off to find Moyna.

I've never felt as alone as I did at that moment, walking away from our combined armies and straight for Moyna's line. The road, at least, was relatively clear, meaning that the odds of slipping and making a spectacle of myself were low, but my stomach flopped, and I began to reconsider the amount of bacon I'd put down that morning. I could see Moyna's people forming up ahead of me, tightening into a line with a thick bulge in the center, and I paused a quarter-mile away. Willing my voice to amplify, I drew upon the draining magic and yelled, "Moyna! Let's talk about this!"

There was no response for a moment, and I was beginning to wonder if my enchantment hadn't worked when I heard her yell back at me: "You dare, mongrel?"

"Nice to see you again, too. Come out here."

I heard her laugh across the distance. "Or what? Your

little Arcanum friends are going to attack?"

I paused, letting her stew, then said, "It's over. Oberon's dead. Coileán's court is waiting behind me, and they're not happy with you. Surrender now, and I can protect you. That's my offer."

"Liar!" she yelled, but I caught a note of hesitation in her voice.

I swept my arm back toward our ranks. "Look at them! Do those look like wizards to you?"

Moyna stepped free of the pack, and I saw a flash of gold as her hair flew around her face. "You expect me to believe that you've bested *Oberon*, dog?"

"The name's Aiden," I snapped, "and it's amazing what steel can do." I didn't give her time to counter that before calling up the white corona, though I hoped she wouldn't comment on how faint it was. "The realm backs our cause, Moyna. It's over. Oberon was never going to give you a court, anyway. He was going to kill you as soon as it was convenient. Work with me, and we can avoid more death today. Come on," I added, "how would I be here, with that court, if I wasn't telling the truth?"

"*That court* is mine by right!" she shouted.

"Not while Coileán lives. And who are these idiots following you?" I continued. "Mab's people? What claim do you have on them?"

"They found a new leader," she retorted. "Since Coileán killed their queen—"

"The realm didn't even recognize Mab!" I exclaimed. "Did no one tell them that? She had no claim on Faerie at the end! And even if she had, you're not her blood—"

"Oh, yes," Moyna snapped, "they should all follow Mab's witch-blood daughter, shouldn't they? You'd like that, wouldn't you? Mongrels stick together, I suppose."

"No, they shouldn't follow Toula," I said quietly, but my amplified voice still rang across the field. "She isn't Mab's eldest. There's another with a much better claim than yours."

"Then let her step forward!" she yelled, but the uncertainty in her voice was evident—as was the susurrus in the line behind her.

"Not at this time," I said, then spread my hands. "If you won't listen, then maybe your followers will." I looked past her at her waiting army and raised my voice. "Surrender now. If you don't, we're going to kill you. Moyna's no queen, and she can't protect you. I'm no king," I said as I fought to amp up my glow, "but right now, I'm a halfway decent substitute. Come forward, surrender, and you may live."

No one took me up on the offer, but I could tell from the movement in the line that there was discussion in the ranks. After a moment, Moyna called out again. "And how do you think you'll even wound us, dog? Look around you—what magic were you going to call on? Are you carrying steel enough to make your little wizards brave?"

I shrugged. "What magic? Well, as you seem to be exhausting our regular supply, I thought we might try dark."

"*Dark?*" she scoffed. "You've recruited Nath as well?"

I turned and headed back toward our line, but not without a parting shot. "You never learned much about dragons, did you?" I said, then took the enchantment off my voice and pointed to Georgie. She immediately rose from the snow, screeching her joy at being airborne, and Joey raised his nail gun into position.

"Fire at will!" I yelled.

I could have sworn that Georgie smiled before she opened her maw to spit forth a blast of flame. In an instant, the tents were on fire, as were some of Moyna's troops, who screamed and dove for the snow. Georgie circled for a second pass, and Joey shot into the scattering crowd as she banked, peppering the line with nails even as the luckless faeries burned. With their major enchantments still sucking up the available magic, they barely had enough to shield themselves, let alone attack the dragon. A few managed to toss off fireballs, but Georgie was grace incarnate on the wing, and Joey rode like a champion.

Beside me, Toula folded her arms and whistled softly. "Go, Godzilla."

I looked at her, then at Hel and Mina as the smell of roasting flesh began to waft our way. "Someone want to open a gate or ten?" I asked. "Mine are still kind of sub-par."

"Got it," said Toula, ripping open a new hole between the worlds. The influx of magic made my corona brighten, and Hel rolled her eyes.

"What?" I said.

"Show off," my sister muttered. "Are we going in, or were you planning on wasting magic all day?"

I cut my brights, called up a fireball in each hand, and grinned. "Race you home. Toula, keep the gates coming."

Hel broke into a sprint, and I followed at her heels with the van screaming behind us as we ran toward the inferno.

Moyna's people might not have been as weary as the wizards that ran after us, but they were far from fresh when they joined us in battle, and they had precious little magic to call upon. We were able to draw from the river flowing behind us, plus the weapons our soldiers carried—not to mention Georgie, who continued to barbeque the heart of Moyna's line.

Toula told me later that it took less than an hour to break them. I'll have to trust her clock, because time had little meaning for me once I opened fire. I remember seeing Hel ahead of me with sparks dancing from her fingertips, and then I was throwing green fire in all directions, letting my anger at the last two months flow through me, and it felt so *good*.

I killed at least seven in that field. I can't be sure of the actual total—to say I saw red and started shooting would be a gross understatement—but I'm positive that at least seven deaths were on my head. Mina claimed three, as did Hel, and Toula mostly busied herself with checking the charred for signs of life. Georgie was the true hero of the day, though, and after counting the corpses, Joey and I stood back and let her eat her fill. The wizards muttered, but they managed to pull their dead out before Georgie started eating, so as far as I was concerned, they had no reason to complain. They lost nine, mostly young men who had ventured too close to the fire and got caught in the conflagration. We lost five in total, but compared to the fatalities on the other side, we were the clear victors.

But though the siege was broken, we had no true cause for celebration. We inspected every corpse on the field, but no one was able to account for Moyna—or, Hel pointed out, for a few dozen of her followers.

"They must have run," Mina fumed, glaring at the dead. "When the dragon attack began, they must have run like rats."

"The gate-blocking enchantment didn't extend this far," Toula pointed out. "So, what next? She's on the lam again—do we wait for her to surface, or do I do a little bloodwork now and track her down?"

I thought of Coileán, asleep back in Faerie. Getting a blood sample from him would be simple, and Toula could put it to work easily enough. If Moyna was still hiding in the mortal realm, we could find her, corner her…try not to get her killed…

And then what? If I took her alive and threw her in a cell until Coileán woke—and I took care to be sure that no one came after her for revenge—then he could deal with her as he liked…

But how long could he possibly sleep? Surely Coileán would wake soon, and when he did, he could hunt Moyna as he chose. I had enough blood on my hands that day—and besides, the far more important missing person was Oberon's heir.

"Maybe later," I told Toula. "I've got another blood sample for you to work on first."

She looked at me askance but shrugged her assent, and I sighed as I considered the muddy field. I almost jumped when Val's hand landed on my shoulder, but when I turned, expecting chastisement, he gave me a little smile instead. "You're probably saving her life," he murmured.

"I thought so," I mumbled. "If Coileán wants her dead...I don't want to be the one, you know? She..."

When I couldn't find the words, he offered, "She has a point?" I gave him no reply, and he cocked his head. "Trying to have her revenge against her mother's killers. She's not entirely wrong."

"You said it, not me."

His smile widened for an instant before he sobered. "Titania did some terrible things in her time. All three of them did. So has Coileán. So may you," he added, pointing to the nearest clump of bodies. He paused, studying me closely, then said, "You're not wrong to try to understand her, Aiden. You're not wrong to give her a chance. Coileán...I can't say what he would do now, were he here, but I can't imagine that he would be angry with your choice. He could have sought her out months ago," Val continued, lowering his voice. "Do you think he wants to destroy his own child?"

"Which is why I'm going after the heir to Oberon's court. Someone got the blood sample I asked for, right?" I asked, feeling a momentary flash of panic.

"As requested." Val squeezed my shoulder and released me. "And thank you."

"For what?"

He smiled again. "As I told you, I don't want a court. Certainly not *that* one." He looked aside at a flash of movement, then pointed to the trailer park. "Ah. Company. I was wondering when they might crawl out of their hole."

I followed his finger and saw not *they*, but only one man: the grand magus, walking alone through the churned snow and muck. He hesitated at the entrance of the trailer park, leaning on the rusted mailbox as he surveyed the scene before him. After a moment of silent contemplation, he began to trudge across the field toward us, limping along on arthritic knees as his overcoat flapped around his boots.

"Hold back," Val called to our army, who stopped where they were and waited as the order was passed through the lines.

I noticed a few fires begin to spark in the crowd, but I kept my attention on the grand magus as he made his slow march through the dead. Finally, when he was close enough for his face to resolve into more than a dark blur, he paused and cleared his throat. "You know," he said, speaking to no one in particular, "I've had this nightmare a few times. But heretofore, I've always managed to wake up and find that there isn't, in fact, an army of faeries outside my front door. This time's going to be different, isn't it?" He craned his neck to look up at Georgie, who still had a leg dangling out of her mouth like a toothpick, then shook his head and shuddered. "Quite a bit different."

Hel and I looked at each other, and she stepped forward to meet him. "Grand Magus. Is everyone all right?"

"Well, that all depends on the next few minutes, I suppose." He surveyed the silent throng gathered in the field, then turned to me and nodded. "I take it these folks are with you, son."

I heard Toula muttering to my left and realized she was translating for Val and Mina. "They are."

"Found your brother, I trust?"

"He's recovering. Oberon isn't."

"Ah," the grand magus murmured. "That's…not the worst possible outcome, I suppose."

"And that's rather non-committal," Toula interjected.

He gave her a look, then pointedly cut his eyes to the mass of wizards standing to the side. She smirked, and he said, "I'll have a fuller statement at a later time, assuming the Council doesn't fire me again."

"They won't."

We turned as Magus Montes pushed through the crowd,

using her cane to knock legs aside as required. "The rest of the Council has come," she continued. "There will not be another dismissal without a full vote, and I assure you, Greg, that we have been listening to the messages from the silo."

The grand magus bowed stiffly to her. "Gabriela."

"You tell the upstarts in that hole that we are also Council," she said as the rest of the magi joined her, "and our voices will be heard."

The others nodded, and the grand magus looked momentarily relieved before he turned his attention back to me. "So…Lord Aiden."

"Actually," said Toula, "it's 'Lord Regent' for the time being. Just so you know. I'm translating as well as I can," she added, pointing to her waiting listeners, "and if there's any perceived slight, you know what could happen."

To his credit, the grand magus's poker face didn't crack. "Of course. What are your terms…my lord?"

"Terms?" I asked, suddenly cognizant of the weight of the eyes on me. "Terms for—"

"Leaving in peace," he prompted.

"*Right.* That. Uh…" I glanced at Val, whose eyes were focused on Toula, then back at the grand magus. "Our fight isn't with you," I told him. "But before I go, I want some guarantees."

"Such as?"

"Like, I'm not going to walk away and find out tomorrow that there are warrants on Hel and Toula again."

"Aid," my sister muttered, "I can handle this."

"I know," I said, keeping my eyes on the grand magus. "But you've fought an awful lot of my battles for me. It's about time I returned the favor, yeah?"

"That was different," she protested.

"Tally up the number of broken bones you prevented, and you'll see that I owe you a *lot* more than this. So, Grand Magus," I continued as Hel huffed her displeasure, "about those warrants."

"If I may interrupt," said Magus Jenner, "I can assure

you, young man, that there will be no further proceedings against Magus Carver." She pushed her glasses down her nose and stared at the grand magus, who backed away with his palms raised in placation.

"Have you administered the oaths?" he asked her.

"No. We thought it only proper that you be the one to make it official."

"Tonight," he replied, then looked at me and cocked his eyebrow. "Satisfactory?"

"You're forgetting Toula," I told him. "I can walk away, I can take those folks with me," I continued, pointing to the army at my back, "but my captain's not going anywhere without a guarantee."

I cut my eyes to Val as Toula translated, and he nodded emphatically.

The grand magus considered our silent communication, then studied Toula and Val, who stood side by side in the snow. Toula had their mother's blue eyes, and Val's hair was lighter than his sister's, but the resemblance was undeniable, and the grand magus wasn't blind. "I guarantee her safety," he said, looking back and forth between them and me as Toula muttered in Fae. "No more warrants. And should that prove untrue…" He spread his hands. "You know where to find me."

Toula rolled her eyes and snorted. "Okay, people, enough with the formalities and the theatrics. Carver and I have it from here, boys."

"What?" I protested. "I've got an army, man. Let me do *something* with it!"

"Believe me, you've done enough. Now scoot."

"Seriously, Toula?"

"*Scoot.*"

"Don't translate that," I muttered, then pointed to the open gates. "Val, Mina…"

In a matter of minutes, all of my court had disappeared but for Joey, Georgie, and me. "Want me to take care of her?" I asked Joey as he slid off Georgie's neck. "The barn was still intact, and I'm pretty sure she's not going to be hungry for a while…"

Georgie belched a thin stream of fire. *Nope.*

"So if you want to stay with Hel for a while, I mean…it's under control."

Before Joey could respond, Hel wrapped her arm around his waist and shook her head. "I'm going to be doing nothing but Council clean-up for at least the next week," she said. "And if I tried to tell Georgie that you wouldn't be in the barn tonight…look, she's full now, but girl's got a metabolism."

The dragon lowered her head to the snow and fixed her enormous red eyes on Hel. *I wouldn't eat you.*

"Just making a point, sweetie," she replied, standing on tiptoe to pat Georgie's snout.

But I wouldn't, she insisted, sounding confused. *You're his mate.*

"Mate?" the grand magus murmured. "I thought you two were just dating."

Joey and Hel looked at each other uncertainly, and then Hel grabbed him again. "He proposed," she said, grinning at her boss. "I accepted. Georgie's not so good with relationship nuances."

The grand magus's white eyebrows bunched. "You…Helen, I—"

"This is not up for discussion," she interrupted. "Joey, honey…"

Joey kissed her and let her go. "Let me know when things calm down."

"I'll be over as soon as I can," she promised, and stepped back while he climbed into the saddle again. "Georgie, you take care of him!"

Always do, she thought, and the two of them lumbered off toward the last gate.

I looked around, saw that I was vastly outnumbered, and nodded to the grand magus. "All right, then. Is someone going to let the Fringe know they can pack up?"

"I'll take care of it," said Toula. "Go on, rest. Take care of that hand."

I studied the trailer park one last time, then sighed and felt my throat clench. "Right. Hel, uh—"

She hugged me in front of the magi and the weary wizards and the Arcanum's terrible security cameras. "Love you," she whispered, then stepped away and watched until I closed the gate behind me.

CHAPTER 20

Two days later, Toula popped in, but only long enough to tell me that Hel was still alive and our father was loudly disowning me to anyone who had heard the truth, and to pick up the promised blood sample. "This could take some time," she cautioned before she went back to Montana, but I didn't care. I had enough fires to put out in Faerie without worrying about Oberon's missing eldest.

The realm complained quietly even after Toula departed—and again, a few days later, when Hel sneaked over to retrieve Joey for the night. I listened, then told her that Hel and Toula were welcome, and I didn't want to hear anything else about it. Maybe the realm realized how stressed I was that week, as she backed off on the complaints.

I knew what Coileán did, but I didn't know until I started filling in just how much work his position entailed. Val kept me on schedule, Astrid and the other aides held the palace together, and I took pleasure in every single item I checked off my swollen to-do list. Once I was sure that my prisoners were at least eating, I pushed them to the back burner, hoping Coileán would wake in the next few days, and set about dealing with the more practical considerations of running the court. Rebuilding didn't take long—not with so much magic at our disposal—but I suddenly found myself with a host of territorial squabbles and audience requests from minor lords and ladies, all of them hoping to curry favor while my brother was out of the picture.

And then there were the sheep.

Oberon's crew had left the palace largely untouched, but they'd failed to do anything about Georgie's food supply, which doubled several times per day when left unchecked. Eventually, the flock had grown so rapidly that the sheer pressure of the sheep on the wooden rails broke the pen, and the magical mutants had wandered off to the meadows and lawns south of the palace, quite literally in search of greener pastures. By the time I arrived, the sheep were everywhere, breeding out of control and eating every ornamental plant in sight.

I gave a kill order on them, and then I sent Joey and Georgie out to round up the stragglers. For Joey, it was a way to get his mind off Hel's problems, but for Georgie, the exercise was a massive game. *They taste so much better when you eat them fresh*, she explained one evening as she stretched out in the barn with a full belly. *You should try it. Bacon is all right, but fresh sheep...* Her forked tongue flicked in and out of her mouth, working at a chunk of wool stuck between her teeth. *Delicious.*

Having caught a small flock budding on her own manor, Mina offered her services in sheep eradication since Val had the guard rotation well in hand. She even dragged in my nieces and nephews, her former sailing charges—all of them half fae, but none younger than three hundred—to introduce them and offer their assistance, whether they liked it or not. Once they understood the problem, however, they proved willing to pitch in, especially if their participation carried with it the potential of a ride on Georgie. "Biologists, botanists, geographers," Mina told me as they circled around Joey to meet the dragon. "Amateurs, certainly, but they have their little hobbies."

I watched as one of them pulled a battered notebook from his long coat and a pencil from thin air. "You know, Joey was telling me that he wanted to do a proper field guide to the realm. Do you think—"

"Oh, I think they'd be interested," she said, nodding slowly. "But may I ask a favor?"

"Sure."

"Don't make me chaperone, my lord. *Please*. I don't know what I did to Grandmother to make her send me with them last time, but if I have to spend another year with those fools, chasing after every damn fish…"

I patted her shoulder. "No chance of that. I'd like you around here, if that's agreeable."

Mina seemed taken aback at that. "Well…yes, certainly, but…"

"But?" I asked, bemused.

She frowned and studied my expression. "I've been a guard for a long time," she finally replied. "No one's ever asked if I found an assignment *agreeable*."

I rubbed my elbow and shrugged. "You know the rest of the family, right? Coileán sheltered me. I'd like to know who and what I'm dealing with."

She mulled that over. "I believe I could be of assistance, my lord."

"Thanks. And, uh…" I hesitated, then mumbled, "Look, I never knew Titania, but I know what Coileán and Toula did. If you were close to her, I'm sorry—"

Mina chuckled and shook her head. "She tolerated me, but that was all. And don't be too upset, little uncle," she said with the ghost of a smirk. "If I recall, the captain was supposed to have eliminated you."

"Yeah," I muttered, "I heard."

She nodded. "And that's why he's the captain."

It was ten days into the new year before Toula came by with her findings.

"Here's what we've got," she said, dropping a stack of atlases and road maps onto Coileán's desk. I'd moved into his office for the sake of convenience, but I couldn't bring myself to touch the décor, even as I'd begun to fear that my brother's nap was going to be longer than I'd expected. Toula opened the top book, an old Rand McNally, and flipped through page after page of maps, each pocked with colored dots. "This family tree is obscenely large," she explained, "and I thought you'd prefer Sharpie to bloodstains, so I color-coded it. Red is for Oberon's presumptive children, orange for grands, yellow for great-grands, et cetera."

I continued paging through, noting a plethora of blues and purples among the warmer colors. "How many?"

"Thousands. I wouldn't have paid any attention to the lesser bloods, but the Fringe wants the data. You know, in case someone out there has a little power and doesn't understand why or what to do with it. They're going to be making their own searches—I didn't think you'd mind sharing the sample," she added, warning me with her eyes not to object, "but I've got solid geographical leads on all of Oberon's children for you to explore."

The stack of maps was daunting. "Dare I ask?"

"About two hundred or so, and they're everywhere. These are your copies," she said, patting the books. "Officially, I can't do much more to help you—Greg wants us to stay out of court issues for now—but I'll run more refined searches if you can narrow your geographic scope."

"Thanks, Toula," I mumbled, wondering when I was going to find time to start hunting for faeries hiding in the mortal realm. Whoever Oberon's heir was, he had yet to make a peep.

"No sweat. Oh, and here." She pulled an envelope out of her messenger bag and slapped it on the desk, and I recognized the grand magus's seal over the flap. "They're having a big shindig for Carver next Friday night. You're invited."

I frowned and opened the envelope. "Her magus swear-in?"

"No, they took care of that before the semester started. She's been back in Nashville for the last couple of weeks," Toula explained. "Got her 'medical leave' squared away, sorted out her classes, all that mess. But Greg's bringing back this old tradition—the outgoing grand magus makes his intended successor a sort of junior grand magus for a few months. Carver will only have a magus's power on the Council, but this'll put her firmly in the public eye."

"And *I'm* invited?" I asked in disbelief, holding up the calligraphed card. "Why?"

Toula adjusted her bag's shoulder strap and opened a gate behind her. "Because she wants her little brother there, that's why. You in?"

I reread the invitation, then nodded slowly. "Yeah. Tell her I'll clear my calendar."

As it so happened, Hel wanted her fiancé there for her big night as well, and Joey and I managed to come up with halfway presentable suits by the time we stepped through into the grand magus's office for my sister's ceremony. "Wizard formal is like any other formal," I'd explained to Joey, "except that the magi will look like they're off to a costume party or the world's weirdest graduation." The grand magus didn't disappoint that night: he'd selected crimson robes with gold trim and his heavy chain of office for the occasion, though he'd forgone the floppy hats that so many of the magi seemed to favor.

Joey gave him a quick look, straightened his tie, and whistled. "And here I thought I'd gone fancy with French cuffs."

The grand magus cocked his head to inspect Joey's cufflinks, a pair of tiny onyx dragons with ruby eyes. "Classy. Welcome, gentlemen," he said as I closed the gate. "We're about fifteen minutes out. I thought I'd get you into the hall in ten minutes or so—no point in making you deal with small talk, is there?"

Neither of us needed clarification. Toula had been by that week to fill us in on the situation in the silo and on the cover stories we'd be using.

The Council knew about me, of course, and some of the

wizards from outside the silo had seen Hel and me together and suspected that we had a history, but by and large, news of my new position hadn't made it through the silo. To the average wizard, I was still the Carvers' dud, the new magus's unfortunate kid brother who had been sent off to boarding school to prepare me for a life outside the bosom of the Arcanum. Joey, according to his new cover story, was a witch who just so happened to have met Hel in college, a friend she'd taken under her wing and invited to the silo to see a glimpse of a world of which he'd never be a part. "The Council's still not cool with their engagement," Toula told me, "but Carver keeps shutting the discussion down." To keep up appearances, however, Joey agreed to play his part, and I saw nothing to be gained by provoking the Council.

"I'm afraid I'm going to have to put you two near the back of the hall," the grand magus continued. "I tried to bring up the issue of seating you with your parents," he told me, "but…well. I'm sure Toula's kept you apprised of current sentiment."

"You mean that bit about how Dad wishes I'd die in a fiery explosion? Yeah, I've heard."

"Aiden," he tried after a moment's pause, "you know, Howard…with enough time…"

"Save it, sir." I called a mirror into existence, checked my tie again, and winced inwardly at the fingerless glove on my left hand. Val had designed it to match my skin tone and cushion only the burn, but it was still noticeable in the light of the grand magus's office. I didn't want to risk using glamour on it—with so many wizards around, all it would take would be one eagle-eyed neighbor to ask what was up with my hand—and at least with the protective glove, I could explain it away as a lab accident. The burn had scabbed over, and skin was continuing to regrow, but the new tissue puckered, hinting at the nasty scar to come. I dismissed the mirror with a wave, then took a deep breath and tried to smile. "For Hel."

"Very nice," said the grand magus. "We'll head down in

a—"

The sudden pounding on his door cut him off, and he scowled as he crossed the room. "Just a minute," he muttered, then threw the door open and took a step back. "Howard, Rachel," he said, sounding perplexed. "She's with the Council now, not here—"

But Dad had already seen me, and he brushed past the grand magus without a word. Joey tensed, but I stood my ground and waited until he'd stormed across the office— the better, apparently, to glower at me. "You came," he said, clenching his fists. "You son of a bitch, you're actually showing your face."

"Hi, Dad. Nice suit," I replied. "Good to see you again. Sorry about all the mess left topside—the dragon got full before she could finish the cleanup. But hey, fresh air must be a nice change for you, right?"

As if realizing that he had lost most of his height advantage on me, Dad settled for grabbing my lapels and glared. "If you ruin this for her, you little shit—"

"Howard, please," Mom murmured, "not tonight, you don't want to do this tonight, your blood pressure…"

"Shut up," he snapped, and yanked me closer. "One toe out of line, boy, and so help me, I'll—"

"Apologize," I ordered.

His dark eyes blazed. "What did you say?"

"Apologize," I repeated slowly. "To Mom."

I could see her face working even as Dad's reddened, and I wondered again what he had done to her after I left. Dad had a temper, but I'd never seen him turn it on Mom…but then again, she was the reason that I'd been thrust into his life to begin with. I saw the loathing in his eyes as he stared at me, and I saw the fear in hers every time he raised his voice.

"Who are you," he sputtered, "to tell me to do *anything*?"

I paused long enough to wipe the fleck of his spittle off my cheek. "Like it or not," I said calmly, "your son."

He never had time to defend himself before I ripped his

hands off my jacket and threw him into the far wall with a blast of pure force. Dad grunted as the air was slammed out of him, and I took my time in straightening myself up as he squirmed three feet off the ground against my hold. "Now, you listen to me," I said as I strolled toward him. "And you listen carefully, you bastard: if I ever hear of you talking to Mom like that again, I will make you regret it. And then I'll tell Hel, and *she* will make you regret it. Understood?"

I dropped him, and as he landed in a heap at my feet, I turned to Mom, who wrung her hands at a safe distance. "Has he hurt you?" I asked her. She shook her head, and I sighed, seeing the lie written all over her face. "All right, then. I'll be on my best behavior tonight, but it's for Hel's sake. And for you," I said, then cut my eyes to my father and resisted the urge to kick him while he was still on the carpet. "*You* can rot."

He wheezed as he pushed himself to his feet, but the grand magus managed to usher my parents out of the office without further incident. When the door latched behind them, he opened a gate into a little-used corridor near the hall and muttered, "Maybe we should take the back route tonight."

Joey and I sat in a dark corner of the very last row, peeking through a sea of wizards as my sister, resplendent in indigo robes, made her formal oaths and sat demurely as one magus after another made glowing remarks. The speakers were all installation heads, I noticed—Magus Ehrler, Magus Aminu, and Magus Jenner, whose spectacles twinkled in the candlelight—but if the local Council magi had other thoughts, they kept silent. I whispered tidbits of information to Joey as the ceremony progressed, filling him in on the people seated across the stage. He clapped in all the right places, then beamed as Hel received a small chain of office from the grand magus.

Soon enough, the ceremony ended, and I slipped off

down a quiet dead-end corridor while the audience emptied out of the room. There was a reception, the grand magus had told us. He'd said we were both welcome, but I urged Joey to go ahead, telling him I'd stay back until the crowd thinned. The fewer people who saw me, the lower the chance of awkward questions.

Ten minutes later, as I leaned against the cracked plaster and absently flexed the fingers of my burned hand, I heard a familiar voice at the other end of the hallway: "So *that's* where you're hiding, Dudley."

I looked up, startled, and saw Russell standing in the middle of the hall, blocking my exit. "What do you want?" I asked, resisting the impulse to call up a fireball.

A pair of shadows filled the space behind him, then moved into the light to reveal Morgan and Dan, respectively Russell's widest and tallest lieutenants. All three had lost their jackets and ties, though they still wore the thin gold necklaces that marked them as direct kin to magi. As I watched, the rest of the gang crowded the hallway: Milo with his bone-breaking fists, Terrance, a distant cousin of the grand magus's wife, and Leo, whose wand was ready and glowing.

Russell tightened his ponytail and grinned. "We've got some unfinished business, don't we, Dudley? You burned my hand. That's going to cost you."

I raised my injured palm to show him the glove. "Beat you to it. Back off, Russell."

He laughed, and the rest of his pack chimed in. "Or *what?* Big sis is going to be pressing the flesh all night—there's no one here to save you now."

Russell took a step toward me, and I retreated, keeping my distance. "Come on," I begged, "this is Hel's big night, don't do this—"

"Not doing anything to her," said Terrance. "Just going to settle a few things with you. We've missed you, Dud."

"Don't," I pleaded, feeling my adrenaline surge, but in a matter of seconds, the pack was on me.

I tried. Really, I tried. I went limp as usual, hoping they'd get bored and walk off, but all the while, I struggled against my own anger, the force inside that was building and needed an outlet.

I might even have been able to control it, had someone not broken my nose.

The fact that the pain was familiar made it no less pleasant, and I screamed as blood gushed over my face and shirt. The hands that had been holding me in place dropped me, and as I staggered toward the wall, I heard Russell's mocking voice behind me: "Oh no, Dudley, we're not finished yet. You're not leaving that quickly."

I cupped my hands around my busted nose, willing the healing enchantment into action, and then, shaking and infuriated, I let myself go.

I flung the pack away from me with a wave of force, denting the plaster and knocking Dan unconscious immediately. "My name is not *Dudley*," I growled as the other five picked themselves up. "You want a fight? Okay. Here's one."

The bodies that were still moving flew into the air again, then bashed against the walls, over and over, until I heard ribs break and all five were crying in fear. "Still want a fight?" I yelled as a green fireball appeared in either hand. "I'll give you a fight! I'll give you *every damn fight!*"

And then, just before I burned them alive, I heard my sister's voice at the other end of the hall, calling my name.

Hel. I was there for Hel, and no one was supposed to…

The fireballs fizzled, and I dropped my opponents. "Shit, Hel, I'm sorry," I said, turning to her, only to find that the corridor behind her was packed with wide-eyed wizards. In the heat of the moment, I hadn't realized how loud our brawl had been. "I…they broke my nose, and—"

"Oh, *Aid*," she murmured, leaving the wizards behind as she ran to meet me. "Here, let me see." She started gently prodding my nose, then muttered until a wet washcloth appeared in her hand. "You've got blood all over you," she said, wiping off my face. "And I think it's still leaking. Here, take this, go stand over there, and pinch it off until the bleeding stops, okay?"

"Hel—"

"No buts. And as for you," she said, turning to the groaning guys on the floor, "I don't think you're ready for this level of responsibility." With that, she pulled each one's wand free, snapped it in half, and left the pieces on the carpet. "What have I told you idiots about beating up my brother?" she demanded, and when that got no response, she gave the nearest a swift kick in the groin. "*Don't do it!*" How hard is that to remember?"

By then, Russell had recovered enough to climb to his knees and point a shaking finger at me. "That...*that*..."

Hel looked at me and my bloody washcloth, then turned back to Russell and folded her arms. "That would be the lord regent for the reigning king of Faerie," she said quietly. "And you have no idea how lucky you are that I got here when I did." With that, she marched back to me, inspected the progress of my nosebleed, and frowned. "You know," she began, "power is great, but it's even better when you know when to use it."

I discarded her washcloth in favor of a fresh one. "And what would you have had me do differently?" I protested. "They jumped *me*—I didn't start this."

"I'm not complaining," she soothed, "just offering a word of advice for down the line. Let's go," she said, waving Joey over as he pushed his way through the muttering throng. "I think there's still plenty of cake."

Hel led us on as the crowd parted, ignoring the voices that rose and fell around us, but paused before we reached the reception. "Here," she said, then mumbled again until my suit was clean and whole once more. "Sorry, Aid, I can't fix the nose that quickly."

I took the cloth away, sniffed, and tossed the rag back into the ether. "I've had worse. But really, you don't have to do this."

She smiled, then looped her arm around mine. "Come on, little brother. The night is young."

There were magi all around the reception hall. Wizards. Kids I'd known. People who had pitied me, who had mocked me when they thought I couldn't hear them. All of them were whispering, murmuring, gasping as the news began to spread.

Their eyes were on me, with my new suit and my swollen nose. I had a moment's flash of panic, and then the grand magus walked out of the press with a glass in his hand. "Lord Regent," he said, "I'm terribly sorry about that. May I offer you a drink?"

It was a lousy apology, but I felt the warmth of my sister's arm against mine and let it slide. "Kind of you," I said as a bottle of beer appeared in my hand. "But I think I'll start with one of my own."

I sipped. It wasn't going down in history as the world's greatest beer, but at that moment, surrounded by the stunned Arcanum, I couldn't have imagined anything tasting better.

ACKNOWLEDGEMENTS

Thank you, *thank you*, to those of you who've come along with me on this strange trip.

As always, my gratitude goes to the Novel Chicks for their advice and friendship. A special thank-you is due to Adam Domby, beta reader extraordinaire.

And of course, here's to you, Mom and Dad.

ABOUT THE AUTHOR

When not writing fiction, Ash Fitzsimmons is an appellate attorney and an unrepentant car singer.

Find her online:
www.ashfitzsimmons.com